DEVOURED BY DARKNESS

Perhaps sensing she was too impatient for a marathon seduction, Tane lifted himself off Laylah long enough to shed his shorts before returning to cover her.

He groaned in approval as her hands scraped down his back, digging into his hips with her nails.

"Tane . . ." she choked. "I need you."

As if her words snapped the last thread of his composure, Tane gave a low growl. "Mine," he rasped, burying his face in the curve of her neck. "My mate."

She quivered as his tongue ran a wet path down the line of her jugular, arching her head back to offer what he desired. Tane didn't hesitate. With a harsh groan, he plunged his fangs through her skin . . .

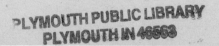

Books by Alexandra Ivy

WHEN DARKNESS COMES

EMBRACE THE DARKNESS

DARKNESS EVERLASTING

DARKNESS REVEALED

DARKNESS UNLEASHED

BEYOND THE DARKNESS

DEVOURED BY DARKNESS

And don't miss this Guardians of Eternity novella

TAKEN BY DARKNESS in YOURS FOR ETERNITY

Published by Kensington Publishing Corporation

Devoured by Darkness

ALEXANDRA IVY

ZEBRA BOOKS
KENSINGTON PUBLISHING CORP.
http://www.kensingtonbooks.com

ZEBRA BOOKS are published by

Kensington Publishing Corp.
119 West 40th Street
New York, NY 10018

All Kensington titles, imprints, and distributed lines are available at special quantity discounts for bulk purchases for sales
promotion, premiums, fund-raising, educational, or institu-
tional use.

Special book excerpts or customized printings can also be
created to fit specific needs. For details, write or phone the
office of the Kensington Special Sales Manager: Attn. Special
Sales Department. Kensington Publishing Corp., 119 West
40th Street, New York, NY 10018. Phone: 1-800-221-2647.

Zebra and the Z logo Reg. U.S. Pat. & TM Off.

ISBN-13: 978-1-4201-1135-4
ISBN-10: 1-4201-1135-3

First Printing: December 2010
10 9 8 7 6 5 4 3 2 1

Printed in the United States of America

Chapter 1

Laylah was tired.

She was tired of the dark, cramped tunnels sprawling beneath the northeast corner of Missouri that she'd been running through for the past two days. She was tired of being chased by an enemy she couldn't see. She was tired of her stomach cramping with hunger and her limbs screaming in protest at her relentless pace.

Reaching a small cavern, she came to an abrupt halt, shoving her fingers through the short, spiky strands of her brilliant red hair, her black eyes searching the shadows for her pursuer.

Not that she expected to actually catch sight of the frigid pain in her ass.

Vampires not only possessed supernatural speed and strength, but they could shroud themselves in shadows, making them impossible to sense, even to most demons. It was only because she had the power of Jinn blood running through her veins that she could detect the relentless leech following her mad dash through the tunnels.

What she didn't know was . . .

Why.

She shivered, her mouth dry. Christ. She'd thought she

was being so clever when she'd initially allowed the vamp to catch her scent. She'd hoped to lure him, along with the other intruders, away from Caine's private lair.

Not that she gave a damn about the cur, but she'd hidden her most precious treasure at his estate, and she couldn't afford to allow any creature with the superior senses of a vampire, or even a full-blooded Were, near her secret. She'd thought the demons would give chase for a few hours and then grow tired of the game, hopefully returning to Hannibal or even St. Louis.

But her hasty plan had fallen apart right from the start.

The Were had continued on his path to Caine's lair, and the vampire had refused to give up, no matter how far or how fast she'd run.

Now she was too weak to call upon her shadow walking powers, and too far from Caine to call for his help.

"Oh, screw it," she muttered, planting her hands on her hips and tilting her chin in unspoken defiance. "I know you're following me, vampire. Why don't you just show yourself?"

A warning chill thickened the air, prickling painfully over her skin.

"You think you can give me orders, half-breed?" A dark, sinfully beautiful voice filled the cavern.

Laylah's heart missed a beat. Even with her demon blood she wasn't immune to the ruthless sensuality that was as much a part of a vampire as his lethal fangs.

"What I think is that I'm done running," she gritted. "So either kill me or go chase someone else."

"Ah. Then you're confident you've managed to lead me far enough away?"

"Away?" Laylah stiffened, licking her suddenly dry lips. He couldn't know. *No one* knew. "Away from what?"

"That's what I'm wondering," the dark voice drawled. "It must be of great importance."

Laylah forced herself to suck in a deep breath, refusing to panic. The stupid vamp was simply trying to press her buttons. Everyone knew that they loved to toy with their prey.

"I don't know what the hell you're talking about."

"Hmmm. Have you ever watched a quail?"

She felt unseen fingers brush her nape, the cold touch ironically sending a bolt of heat straight to the pit of her stomach. She whirled around, not surprised that the predator had disappeared.

"The bird?" she rasped, belatedly wishing she was wearing more than a pair of cutoff jeans and a muscle shirt. Having so much skin exposed was making her feel oddly vulnerable.

Not that clothing would halt a determined vampire.

It wouldn't matter if she were dipped in cement and wrapped with barbed wire.

"When a predator approaches the nest, the mother quail will feign a broken wing and dash away to lure the danger from her chicks," her tormentor murmured, his voice seeming to speak directly into her ear.

She instinctively stumbled backward, her mouth dry with a sudden fear.

"The only quail I care about are baked and served on a bed of rice."

"What are you trying to protect?" There was a deliberate pause. "Or is it who?"

"I don't know what the hell you're talking about."

"Is it a lover? A sibling? A child?" His soft chuckle grazed her cheek as the sharp leap of her pulse gave her away. "Ah, that's it. Your child?"

Laylah bunched her hands into fists of frustration. He was getting too close. She had to distract the bastard.

"I thought vampires were known for their courage," she deliberately taunted, willing to risk a battle she couldn't win if it would keep her secrets. "Are you such a coward you have to hide in the shadows?"

The chill thickened, the danger a tangible force in the air. Then, the shadows directly before her stirred, and the vampire slowly became visible.

Laylah reeled, feeling as if she'd just been punched in the gut.

All vampires were beautiful. And sexy.

Wickedly, indecently sexy.

But this one . . .

Reminding herself to breathe, Laylah allowed her gaze to skim over the elegant features that revealed his Polynesian ancestors, lingering on the slanted eyes that were a brilliant shade of honey and the inky black hair that had been shaved on the sides, leaving the top to form a mohawk that fell past his broad shoulders.

Her gaze lowered, that vicious awareness twisting her gut at the sight of his half naked body barely covered by a pair of khaki shorts.

Damn the annoying leech.

Had he deliberately left his body on full, wondrous display? After all, he had to know it would make her fingers twitch with the desire to investigate the smooth muscles of his chest. Or wait . . . maybe she would go down the flat plane of his stomach . . .

Lost in her helpless response to his sensual beauty, she was jerked back to the danger of her situation as the demon stepped far too close, his fingers casually stroking along the curve of her neck.

"Have you never been told the dangers of provoking a vampire?" he murmured.

A chill inched down her spine, but she forced herself to meet his hypnotic gaze.

"Do you intend to drain me?"

His lips twitched. "Tell me about the child."

"No."

"It's yours?" He paused, his fingers drifting to the pulse that hammered at the base of her throat, an intense concentration etched on his beautiful face. "No. Not yours. You are as pure as an angel."

Genuine fear speared through her heart. Damn the interfering leech.

"Leave me alone," she breathed.

The honey eyes darkened with a dangerous hunger. Laylah wasn't sure if it was for blood or sex.

Probably both.

"A beautiful angel," he husked, his arms wrapping around her to yank her hard against the strength of his body. "And I have waited too long to have a taste."

Unable to halt her panic any longer, Laylah's unpredictable powers lashed out, the electrical charge that filled the air enough to make the vampire leap back in wary surprise.

"I said, leave me alone," she hissed, wrapping her arms around her waist.

A dark brow arched. "Well, well. You like to play rough?"

"I don't like to play at all," she snapped. "What do you want from me?"

"My first intent was to capture you so you could be brought before the Commission."

She jerked at the threat, her powers abruptly faltering. She'd been hiding from the official leaders of the demon world for two centuries. To be taken to the Oracles that made up the Commission was nothing less than a death-sentence.

"I've done nothing to earn such a punishment," she attempted to bluff.

"Your very existence is worthy of punishment." The vampire smoothly countered. "Half-breed Jinns have been forbidden."

Laylah squashed the familiar anger at the sheer injustice. Now was not the time to debate whether or not she should be exterminated for the sins of her parents.

"You said that was your first intent," she said, her voice thick. "Have you changed your mind?"

A dangerous smile curved the vampire's lips as he reached to trace the plunging neckline of her shirt, his touch searing a path of pure pleasure.

"Let us say I'm willing to postpone our journey with the proper incentive."

"Incentive?"

"Do you need me to demonstrate?" he murmured, his lips softly brushing over her mouth.

"No . . ." she choked, attempting to deny the piercing need that lashed through her.

Gods. She had been alone for so long.

So very long.

"Tell me your name," he whispered against her lips. "Tell me."

"Laylah."

"Laylah." He said her name slowly, as if testing it on his tongue. Pulling back he studied her pale features, his hands skimming down her sides to grasp her hips and boldly press her against the hard evidence of his arousal. "Exquisite."

Laylah clenched her teeth, ignoring the sizzle of excitement racing through her blood.

"I assume you have a name as well?"

There was a brief pause. Not surprising. A name in the hands of a magic user could give them power over a person. Then he shrugged.

"Tane."

It suited him. Ruthless. Powerful. Stunningly male.

"Great." Placing her hands against the steely hardness of his chest, she arched back to meet the honey heat of his gaze. "Let me make this perfectly clear, Tane. I don't use sex as a bargaining chip. Not. Ever."

Expecting him to be angered by her blunt rejection, Laylah was unnerved when his lips curled in a smile of pure anticipation. Hauling her tightly against him, he spoke directly into her ear.

"Now let me make this perfectly clear, Laylah," he whispered. "When we have sex it will only be after you have begged me to take you."

It was the explosion of awareness that jolted through her lower stomach as much as his arrogance that pissed her off. After all, vamps were flaming narcissists. He would naturally assume she was frantic to jump his bones.

No, it was the fact he was right that made her want to punch him.

"Never going to happen, bloodsucker."

He smiled with wicked promise. "Want to bet, mongrel?"

She shoved him away, wrapping arms around her waist in a protective motion.

"If it isn't sex, then what do you want from me?"

"The truth."

Damn. Were they back to that already? He was supposed to be distracted.

Well, she could easily correct that.

No matter what the sacrifice.

"Could you be a little more vague?" she deliberately taunted.

"Most lesser demons have the sense to show respect when in the presence of a vampire."

"You've already let the cat out of the bag that you intend to haul me to the Commission to be put down like a rabid dog, so what the hell?" She shrugged. "I might as well have a bit of fun before I go out."

His slender fingers stroked the hilt of his knife. His big-enough-to-slice-off-her-head knife.

"I can promise you that trying to provoke me is not the sort of fun you want."

She curled her lips in what she hoped was a sneer, but might very well have been a grimace of terror.

"True, the sort of fun I want involves a piece of wood with a very pointy end decorating the center of your chest, but for the moment I'll take what I can get."

Braced for his punishment, Laylah swore when he did precisely what she didn't want.

Instead of striking out in fury, he stilled, his expression intent. Just like a predator about to pounce.

"Intriguing," he murmured.

"What?"

"Your desperation to keep me from discovering your secret." He reached to trace a finger down the line of her stubborn jaw. "I should warn you that your games only make me more determined to find out what you're hiding."

Laylah spun away from his piercing gaze. What the hell did she have to do to get this vampire off her back?

"There's nothing."

There was an icy chill as he moved to stand directly behind her.

"Let's start at the beginning. Why did you kill Duncan?"

"I . . ." She licked her lips, her hands pressing to her stomach at the familiar sickness that rolled through her. She didn't want to remember Caine leading her through the secret tunnel and into the small cabin next to the Mississippi River. They'd expected to find Duncan hidden there. The cur, after all, was intending to save his own hide by selling out Caine to the King of Weres. But neither had expected the less dominant cur to try and attack. Or for Laylah's powers to strike out with such force. It was yet another regret, in a very long line of regrets, that Laylah would have to live with. "That was an accident."

"You fried a cur," Tane pointed out dryly, "which doesn't make my heart bleed, but those little accidents are exactly why mongrel Jinn have been banned."

She shuddered. Did he think that she didn't try and control her powers? That she wouldn't give anything to stop another senseless death staining her conscience?

"Shut up."

"What happened?"

She sucked in the cool, damp air that filled the cave. She had been running blindly the past few days, backtracking and taking side tunnels until she had no idea where they were, but there was no missing the unmistakable scent of a nearby river, which meant they still must be near the Mississippi.

"Caine learned where Duncan was to meet with Salvatore. When we startled him the cur went nuts and attacked." Her jaw clenched. She had done her best to stay out of Caine's crazy ass scheme to change curs into purebloods. Why not decide to sprout wings and become a dew fairy? But, Caine had been adamant that he'd been given a vision that revealed he was to become an immortal Were. Personally she'd thought the vision was more likely an overdose of the pharmaceuticals he mass-produced. "I merely protected myself. Or are mongrels supposed to let themselves be mauled to death? Would that make everyone happy? The disgusting half-breed ripped to shreds?"

"A touch bitter?" Tane murmured, but his hands were oddly tender as he stroked a path over her shoulders and down her arms.

Tender, but capable of sending a rash of fire over her bare skin.

"Go to hell."

"I've already visited, sweet Laylah, and I have no intention of returning anytime soon." He leaned down to press his lips to the curve of her neck. "I'll accept that the death of the cur was an accident."

If she hadn't been near the point of collapse she might have gone completely mental and thrown herself on the beautiful brute. Her body felt as if it were on fire.

Damned vamp pheromones.

Instead she forced herself to step away from his destructive touch, turning to glare into his too-handsome face.

"Patronizing ass."

"Why didn't you return to Caine's lair instead of taking off on your own?"

She unconsciously rubbed her arms that still tingled from his touch.

"I knew we were being tracked and I assumed that you would follow Caine. I took off to save my own skin."

"No, you took off to try and lead us away from Caine's estate." He deliberately paused. "And the child you are protecting."

"If you already have it all figured out then why are you pestering me with your questions?" she gritted.

"Because I want to know why you would be willing to sacrifice your life for a child that isn't yours."

Tane watched the emotions ripple over the Jinn's expressive face, annoyed by his unfamiliar fascination.

Granted Laylah was a beautiful creature.

Stunningly beautiful.

And she stirred his lust to a fever pitch he hadn't enjoyed for centuries.

But, he had one purpose in following this female.

When he'd first entered the tunnels, he'd been chasing after Salvatore, King of Weres, and the aggravating gargoyle, Levet. They'd gone missing from a cabin in Hannibal and while he would be pleased-as-fucking-punch to let both of them die a miserable death, Styx had been clear he wanted a better relationship between Weres and vampires. And what the Anasso (leader of all vampires) wanted, he got.

So Tane had led Salvatore's servants in pursuit of Caine and the mysterious demon who had kidnapped them, not surprised when the cur had abandoned his hostages and fled in the futile hope of avoiding his impending death. What had been surprising was the gargoyle's insistence that the demon he had sensed was a Jinn half-breed.

Suddenly his simple rescue mission had turned into a hunt for the renegade demon. The Commission had a strict policy. Jinn mongrels were to be captured and turned over the moment they were found.

He had been designated to snag and tag the abomination.

Unfortunately, things had gone to hell from the moment he had charged in pursuit.

For two days he'd trailed behind her, ignoring the realization he could put an end to the chase any time he wanted. He told himself it was mere curiosity. Why was the female so determined to lead him away from Caine's estate? It had to be something worth risking her life for.

But, curiosity couldn't explain why he had been plagued with fantasies of having the female locked in his lair, sprawled across his bed with her dark eyes glowing with pleasure. Or why even now the thought of hauling her before the mighty Oracles who made up the Commission seemed a sin against nature.

His brooding glance swept over her delicate features. They were frighteningly familiar. As if they'd been seared into his mind.

It made it easy to notice that there was a growing pallor beneath her perfect skin and shadows beneath the midnight beauty of her eyes.

"I don't have to tell you anything," she was muttering, as stubborn as ever despite her growing weakness.

"What's wrong with you?" he abruptly demanded.

"Nothing."

"Don't be an idiot," he snapped, swiftly scooping her into his arms when her knees buckled. He choked back a groan as he was slammed by the delectable feminine heat and the scent of spring rain. Dammit. The female was going to be the death of him. "It's obvious you're unwell."

She trembled, a thin sheen of sweat glistening on her brow. "I haven't eaten in days."

Barely aware he was moving, he carried her to the back of the cavern, gently settling her on the dirt floor before kneeling at her side.

Just like a regular Mary Poppins, he thought wryly.

Except he was a cold-hearted Charon. A vampire so ruthless he was feared by his own brothers.

"I thought Jinn absorbed their energy from their surroundings?"

Her eyes fluttered shut, her breathing shallow.

"As you've monotonously pointed out I'm a mongrel," she husked. "I need food and rest."

Against his will, Tane brushed his fingers over the smooth porcelain of her cheek, savoring the feel of her satin skin.

"Tell me about your parents."

"No."

"Laylah."

She huffed a sigh at the edge of warning in his soft tone. "I can't tell you what I don't know. My foster mother found me abandoned in the sewers of London."

"So you don't know anything about who they were?"

"It's obvious one of my parents was a Jinn. The other . . ." With an effort she opened her eyes, pretending that his probing questions didn't bother her. "I don't have a clue."

"Do you have powers beyond those of a Jinn?"

"Yeah right. As if I'd tell you." Her eyes closed again, her expression fretful. "Please just go away and let me rest in peace."

He gazed down at her delicate beauty, his brows drawn together in a scowl.

Why was he hesitating?

All he had to do was toss her over his shoulders and head for the caves the Commission had taken over south of Chicago. It would take him less than a few hours to be done with the task.

Best of all, he could stop by Santiago's club on his way back to his lair and relieve his stress with a willing imp. Or ten.

The more the merrier.

Besides, he'd learned a brutal lesson in protecting a dangerous, unstable female.

A lesson that had led to his entire clan being slaughtered like helpless cattle.

Walking among their mangled bodies, he had sworn he would never again put his emotions ahead of his duty.

His fingers tightened on her cheek, then he muttered a curse and straightened.

"Do you eat human food?" he demanded.

"Yes."

"Remain here."

Without allowing himself the opportunity to consider the depths of his stupidity, Tane flowed through the darkness of the tunnels, swiftly finding an opening that led to the countryside above.

A swift glance revealed the recently planted fields and farmhouses that slumbered beneath the silver moonlight. In the distance he could catch a glimpse of the Mississippi River and even farther the pinpricks of street lights that revealed a small town.

The typical, sleepy landscape of the Midwest.

Too sleepy for most vampires, but Tane preferred the peace. A bitter smile twisted his lips. And most vampires preferred him to remain in his self-imposed isolation.

Few were comfortable in the presence of a Charon.

Not that Tane allowed their prejudice to bother him. He'd become an executioner of rogue vampires for a reason. And that reason hadn't changed.

Would *never* change.

Almost as if to mock his assurance he was alone in the darkness, Tane stiffened and tested the late spring air. What the hell? There were vamps in the area.

Not that he was afraid. He possessed a greater power than most clan chiefs, although he refused to endure the trials necessary to claim the title. And there were few of his brothers stupid enough to annoy their Anasso. Styx would be severely pissed off to discover one of his precious Charons had been killed.

But he'd left Laylah alone and helpless in the tunnels.

He'd be damned if any other vampire was going to get his fangs, or anything else, in her.

With a blinding speed he was entering the nearest farmhouse, a two-story white home with a wraparound porch and gingham curtains.

He paused long enough to determine there was nothing more terrifying than the humans sleeping upstairs and an aging hound who had knocked over the trash and was happily chewing on a bone, before entering the house and pillaging the refrigerator, tossing a number of leftovers into a bag he found underneath the sink. He added in milk and several bottles of water, before turning and leaving as silently as he had arrived.

Like the Grinch.

Only with fangs.

With equal speed he returned to the tunnels and to the cave where he had left Laylah.

Empty.

Of course.

Dropping his bag he followed her trail, easily finding her in the adjoining cave. For a minute he watched in disbelief as she crawled toward the entrance to the tunnels on her hands and knees, her entire body drenched in sweat.

"Dammit." Striding forward, he leaned down and snatched her into his arms, cradling her against his chest as he retraced his steps. "What are you doing?"

She managed a glare, but she couldn't disguise her growing weakness.

"Looking for a portal to Narnia." She futilely attempted to wriggle from his arms. "Where are they when you need one?"

"Stop it," he snapped, his eyes narrowing as they rested on the sluggishly healing cut on her forehead. She obviously had smacked it on the ground in her ridiculous bid for freedom. "You hurt yourself."

"It's your fault," she muttered.

"Typical female logic."

She narrowed her gaze as he gently lowered her back onto the ground and moved to retrieve the bag. Tane drew in the musty air of the cavern, hoping to dilute the potent scent of her fresh blood.

His entire body was clenched with a clawing hunger. As if it had been centuries and not mere days since he'd had sex.

What was it about this female?

Everything about her turned him on. From the ridiculous spiky hair to the tips of her dust-covered toes. And all those tasty spots in between.

"I suppose you think you know all about women?"

He returned to her, crouching at her side with a smile that revealed his extended fangs.

"Enough to make them scream for more."

"Just kill me," she muttered, but she could not disguise the rapid flutter of her pulse. He wasn't alone in the powerful awareness. A damned good thing since he intended to have her naked and beneath him before everything was said and done. "A swift decapitation would be preferable to listening to your gloating."

His lips twitched. Trapped and weary and obviously terrified she still was spitting like a cornered kitten.

Plucking one of the containers from the bag, he opened

it to discover what smelled like chicken and rice and a handful of other human ingredients.

"Eat," he commanded.

She snatched the container from his grasp, using her fingers to scoop the casserole into her mouth. Tane remained silent as he emptied the bag conveniently near her, not wanting to distract her from regaining her strength.

Draining the milk and then the water, she cleaned out two more containers of food before she at last lifted her head to regard him with suspicion.

"Where did it come from?"

He swallowed a growl as she unconsciously licked her fingers clean.

"Does it matter?"

Her breath hitched as she easily sensed his savage pang of need. "Stop looking at me like that."

His fangs throbbed in tempo with the pounding of her heart. "Like what?"

"Like you're wondering if I'm B positive or A negative."

"I did go to considerable trouble to bring you dinner," he husked, his gaze lingering on the vulnerable curve of her neck. "Fair is fair."

With a sudden shove she was on her feet, danger sparkling in her magnificent eyes.

"If you want my blood you'll have to fight me for it."

Tane lifted a brow. She recovered quickly. Already he could detect a color returning to her cheeks and her trembling had ceased.

Still, he knew it would take little effort to knock her flat on her back. A position that he wanted her in with a desperation that was making him hard and aching, but not until she was fully recovered.

"Sit down and finish your food." He shrugged. "I fed before I left Hannibal."

She grudgingly sat back down and reached for the chocolate cake.

"I hope they gave you indigestion."

"Actually she was a tasty morsel." He leaned forward, allowing the scent of spring rain to wrap around him. "A pity I couldn't linger. She was eager to offer more than dinner."

"Feel free to rush back and finish your meal and whatever else you want. Take your time." She took a large bite of cake, a dab of icing clinging to her lower lip. "In fact, take an eternity."

Unable to resist temptation, Tane swooped forward, licking the icing off her lip before returning to snare a kiss of pure, unrestrained desire.

He swore as hunger slammed into him with a shocking force. He hadn't lied when he said he'd fed before entering the cabin in Hannibal, but just having this female near was enough to stir a dangerous craving.

For blood and so much more.

"I could release you, Laylah," he whispered against her lips.

With enough force to crack a rib she shoved him away, rising to her feet with an expression of panic.

Not that he entirely blamed her.

He wasn't sure that he shouldn't be doing his own share of panicking.

He never let his cock rule his head. Not anymore.

But he was beginning to suspect that with the proper incentive this woman could make him sacrifice his own sanity to complete what he just started.

"Great, then I'll be on my way. Don't bother to write . . ."

He flowed to his feet, wrapping his arms around her slender body to prevent her escape.

"And where would you go?"

"Anywhere that's not here."

He cupped her chin, forcing her face up to meet his searching gaze. "Caine's lair is now in the hands of Salvatore."

She bit her lip, attempting to pretend that she wasn't shaken by his words.

"You don't know that for sure."

He didn't, of course. But, when he'd left Salvatore in the tunnel with his curs and the aggravating gargoyle, the King of Weres was foaming at the mouth to get his claws into Caine so he could rip out his heart.

And when a furious Were decided to rip out a heart, there were few things that could stop him.

"A cur is no match for a full-blooded Were. Especially when that Were happens to be the King. By now Caine is dead and the rest of the curs are being punished for their treachery." His hands instinctively skimmed down her back, lingering on the tantalizing curve of her hips. "The moment you try to get near the lair you'll be captured."

Distracted by his acute pleasure in having her pressed so tightly against him, Tane was unprepared when she sucked in a sharp breath, her eyes darkening with horror.

Shoving out of his arms, she dropped to her knees, her hands pressed together in the universal sign of pleading.

"Please, I beg of you," she whispered. "Let me go."

Chapter 2

It wasn't the first time that Laylah had been on her knees. She had turned begging into an art form during her time in Sergei Krakov's brutal care.

What the hell did pride matter when the safety of a helpless child was at stake?

"Tane . . ."

He brought an abrupt end to her plea as he grabbed her arms and jerked her upright, pressing her tight against his body as he whispered directly in her ear.

"Ssh, my sweet. We are no longer alone."

Laylah stiffened. She'd been so distracted by Tane she'd failed to notice the unmistakable scent that filled the air.

"Vampires." Her eyes narrowed. "Friends of yours?"

His impossibly beautiful face tightened, a cruel smile curving his lips.

"I don't have friends."

"Jeez," she muttered, pretending that a pang of sympathy didn't slice through her heart. She was painfully familiar how it felt to go through the world without a soul to care if she was alive or dead. It sucked. "I can't imagine why not."

"Stay here." Releasing her, Tane stepped back to stab

her with a warning glare. "And Laylah, when I say stay here I mean stay here. Most of my brethren aren't interested in your pedigree or turning you over to the Commission." The honey gaze slid down her slender body exposed by her shorts and tiny, tiny top. "They'll see you as a beautiful female who can sate more than one of their hungers."

With fluid grace he had the large dagger in his hand and was gliding silently into the tunnel.

Left alone, Laylah scrubbed her hand through her hair and tried to concentrate.

The food helped her to regain a portion of her strength, but she was still weary. Which meant her powers would be unpredictable.

A very bad thing since they weren't exactly stable under the best of circumstances.

Did she dare shadow walk?

The talent of moving between dimensions had been a gift from her Jinn ancestors, although she'd discovered the ability quite by accident. She would never forget her terror of suddenly being surrounded in the mists that hovered between worlds. And her even greater terror when she'd managed to free herself from the strange fog to discover she'd traveled halfway around the world.

Over the years she'd trained herself to use her rare skill, but she avoided using it unless absolutely necessary.

Not only was there danger of accidentally slipping into another dimension, many of which were the worse hells imaginable. But she had nightmares of being trapped in the misty corridors.

Still debating, Laylah abruptly darted behind a stalagmite as the scent of vampire filled the air.

"Here, kitty, kitty, kitty," a low voice called.

Laylah shifted to catch a glimpse of the approaching

vampire, her nose wrinkling at the sight of his filthy jeans and bare chest. His long blond hair hung in tangled clumps, and his gaunt face was twisted with an expression of malevolent anticipation.

Most vampires used their unearthly beauty to lure their victims. But this one . . . yow. He'd obviously let himself go downhill.

Really, could an occasional dip in a hot bath be that hard?

She swore as he continued forward, clearly aware she was cowering behind the stalagmite.

She didn't want to hurt anyone. Hell, she would give anything to find a place where she could hide away with her child in absolute peace.

Yeah, as if such a place actually existed.

Grimly she stepped toward the center of the cavern, her hands held out in warning.

"Stay back or I'll hurt you."

The vamp flashed his fangs, his nasty gaze taking an intimate survey of her body.

"Do you promise?"

Reluctantly, Laylah began to gather her sorely depleted power, wishing she could instead absorb the energy of her surroundings. As a Jinn she was a creature of nature. She should be able to manipulate the powers of the earth. Unfortunately she'd never been able to tap into anything other than her own inner powers.

Still, it was a potent force.

She shuddered, her blood heating and bubbling as the spiritual essence flowed through her.

Gods. It was so beautiful. Beautiful and terrifying and oh, so seductively addictive.

A pity she never knew what the hell was going to happen when she loosened her restraints.

"I mean it," she gritted.

Ignoring her warning, the vampire slowly circled her trembling form, his hand cupping his crotch.

"What are you? You smell tasty."

"I won't warn you again."

The vamp leaped forward, his fangs bared. Laylah didn't hesitate. Lifting her hand she released a burst of power, her eyes narrowing as a blinding jolt of lightning streaked through the air, barely missing the shocked vampire.

"You bitch," the demon hissed, reaching behind his back to pull a handgun from the waistband of his jeans. "You're gonna pay for that."

She prepared to strike again, only to be halted when Tane abruptly returned to the cave, moving with shocking speed to put himself between Laylah and the infuriated vamp.

"Why don't you play with someone your own size?"

"Charon." The unknown vamp smiled, forgetting Laylah as he eyed Tane with a weird triumph. Just as if he'd won the lottery.

Could vampires go crazy?

A chilling thought.

"Have we met?" Tane drawled.

"You killed my clan brother."

An insulting smile touched Tane's lips. "And you decided to track me down so I can kill you too? How thoughtful."

The demon growled, his gun pointed at Tane's head. "I came across your scent when I went out for my evening hunt. It's been almost a hundred years but I'll never forget your stench." He shuddered, his pale eyes shimmering with a fanatical fire. "It's haunted me."

"I'm afraid I can't return the creepy obsession." With

slow steps Tane moved to the side, deliberately leading the vampire away from Laylah. "I don't know who you are and I don't give a shit."

Laylah frowned. Why was Tane risking himself to protect a Jinn mongrel who he intended to see exterminated? And why had the other vampire called him Charon?

"I suppose being a mercenary lapdog for Styx means one kill is just like another for you?" the vamp gritted.

"There are some I anticipate more than others." Tane wagged his dagger in invitation. "Are we going to fight or do you intend to bore me to death?"

"Oh, we're going to fight," the vamp rasped, squeezing the trigger of his gun.

Laylah swallowed a scream as at least one bullet lodged in Tane's arm before he had crashed into the smaller vamp and wrenched the gun from his grasp. The pistol went sailing toward the back of the cave and Tane's dagger sliced deep into his opponent's chest.

Blood flowed freely as the demons used their fangs and claws to cause the maximum damage.

Laylah hovered at the edge of the carnage, mesmerized by the battle between the two lethal predators.

Tane was obviously the superior fighter. Not only did he have the size advantage, but his frigid power spilled through the air with enough force to make her grit her teeth in pain. She could only imagine the agony if he were directing it at her.

But the smaller vamp had an utter lack of sanity in his favor.

With a horrifying disregard for the brutal injuries that Tane was inflicting, the intruder slammed his fangs into Tane, ripping through flesh and muscle like a rabid dog. In return, Tane sliced through the vamp's back with his dagger, spraying blood throughout the cave.

Instinctively Laylah backed away, pressing a hand to her heaving stomach. It was time to go. Tane was suitably distracted and the food she'd consumed was easing her exhaustion.

At least enough that she could run for a few more hours.

She wouldn't have a better opportunity to escape.

So why wasn't she going?

It couldn't be because she was reluctant to leave Tane alone to battle the crazy-ass vampire or his band of lunatics that she could sense heading in their direction. Or even the approaching . . .

She frowned at the musty scent of granite. It was familiar, but why?

"Tane," she muttered.

With a grunt, Tane ripped his arm from his opponent's fangs. "Now is not the best time, Laylah."

"There is someone else in the tunnels."

With a ferocious motion, Tane wrapped his arms around the vamp and heaved him against the distant wall. The vamp fell limply to the ground, briefly knocked unconscious.

Tane stood in the middle of the cave, covered in blood and looking like some magnificent conqueror. Just for a moment, Laylah had the opportunity to appreciate the fierce elegance of his profile, the chiseled perfection of his muscular body, and the bronzed satin of his skin.

Then, shoving a hand through his mohawk, he turned to reveal his eyes glowing with a honey fire and his fangs extended in fury.

She shivered. Holy shit. She'd met dangerous predators before, but nothing like Tane.

"I sense the other vampires," he rasped.

"Not vampires."

He frowned. "What is it?"

Realization hit at the same moment the stunted gargoyle waddled into the cave.

Laylah grimaced, easily recognizing the tiny demon.

Of course. Who could forget a gargoyle who stood barely three foot tall with large gossamer wings in brilliant shades of crimson and blue with veins of gold that were more suitable for a fairy than a fearsome beast? Not that he was entirely a un-gargoylish. He did have the usual grotesque features of his ancestors, as well as the long tail that was lovingly polished and horns atop his head.

He had been a companion of Salvatore when she and Caine had kidnapped the Were, and it had been her duty to carry him back to Caine's lair.

It hadn't been her fault that Tane and his gang of curs had been in such quick pursuit and she'd been forced to literally drop the gargoyle on his head and shadow walk to escape.

Or that in her haste she had released a small surge of power.

"Oh," she breathed, her gaze remaining on the approaching gargoyle even as two new vampires burst into the room and launched themselves at Tane.

"Damn," Tane muttered, his dagger slicing into the dark-haired vampire who looked like an extra out of a Tim Burton movie. "Like I don't have enough troubles."

Laylah frowned. "I thought he was on your side?"

"Can we save the discussion for later?" Tane grunted as the second vampire slammed into him from behind. "I could use some help here."

She clenched her hands, ignoring the ridiculous urge to wade into the battle.

"Why should I help the man who intends to turn me over to the Oracles? I don't care if you get killed." She tilted her chin. She didn't care. She didn't. Dammit. "In fact it'll save me from having to do it myself."

Slipping past the smack down Tane was delivering, the tiny gargoyle halted next to Laylah, his gray eyes sparkling with amusement.

"Ah, a *belle femme* after my own heart," he murmured with a thick French accent, sinking into a small bow. "Allow me to introduce myself. Levet, Defender of Damsels in Distress, Prince Charming, and overall Knight in Shining Armor, at your service."

Laylah blinked. She'd knocked out the gargoyle with a bolt of lightning during their first encounter. She had no idea he was so . . . hmmm. Flamboyant?

"Good God," she breathed.

He waved a dismissive hand. "*Non, non.* It is a common mistake, but I am not a deity. Well, not unless you consider being a sex god as . . ." His eyes abruptly narrowed, his head tilted back as he sniffed the air. "*Sacrebleu.* You are the Jinn."

Tane swore, pinning one vamp to the ground with his knee while he tried to dislodge the other that was latched onto his back.

"Levet, either make yourself useful or get the hell out of here."

The gargoyle ignored Tane's command, turning about to reveal the imprint of her hand that she had scorched onto his ass just before she'd dropped him in the tunnels.

"Look what you have done."

"It was an accident."

"An accident?" Levet turned back, his wings twitching. "You have marred perfection. It is like desecrating the Mona Lisa."

In spite of herself, Laylah found her lips twitching. Levet was unlike any creature she'd ever met before.

"I truly didn't mean to hurt you," she said with genuine sincerity. "Please forgive me."

He pursed his lips. "Well, I suppose I could consider a measure of forgiveness. I am, after all, renowned for the generosity of my heart." He sent a raspberry toward Tane as the vampire muttered his opinion of worthless gargoyles. "And our introduction was not under the best of circumstances."

"No." She cleared her throat. "I suppose that Caine's been captured and his lair overrun with Weres?"

The tiny demon snorted. "The last I saw of Salvatore he had rescued Harley and they were fleeing from Caine while his mangy minions were in pursuit."

Laylah sucked in a sharp breath, her heart slamming against her ribs. So Caine was away from his lair and obviously distracted.

She would never have a better opportunity.

"Can we save the reminiscing?" Tane abruptly intruded into their conversation. "Levet, get over here."

They turned to watch as Tane decapitated one of the vampires just as the one he had knocked out earlier came to his senses and rose to his feet to barrel across the cave.

"Surely the mighty Charon does not need assistance to deal with three scrawny vampires?" Levet demanded.

Tane managed to yank the vampire clinging to his back over his head, stabbing his dagger deep into the attacker's chest.

"Not if they're busy draining a mouthy gargoyle," he muttered.

"As if I would allow such nasty creatures to touch me." Levet wrinkled his snout. "*Mon Dieu,* they smell like they just crawled from their graves."

Tane flashed his fangs at the tiny gargoyle. "Then do something to help put them back in."

"Well, I do have a magnificent fireball spell," Levet offered. "Although there was the teeniest trouble the last time I used it."

"What trouble?"

"There might have been a minor cave-in."

Tane yanked the dagger from the vampire's chest and pointed it toward Levet.

"No fireballs."

"There is no need to bellow." Levet sniffed in offense. "Either you want my help or you do not, please make up your mind."

Laylah forced her attention away from Tane as he cut out the heart of the nearest vamp. Although he was injured from dozens of wounds, it was obvious he would soon be done with his attackers.

"Thank you, Levet." She patted him between the horns. "I really am sorry for your . . . injury. Now, I really must run."

Tane growled low in his throat, grasping the remaining vampire by the throat and lifting him off the ground as he turned his attention to Laylah.

"What do you think you're doing?"

"Leaving."

"Now?"

"Yes."

"You intend to abandon me in the middle of a battle?"

She glanced toward the two disintegrating vampires on the ground and the third who was all but dead, again, struggling to escape Tane's crushing grip.

"Do you think I'm stupid enough to wait around so you can force me to the Commission?"

Something that perilously close to amusement shimmered in the honey eyes.

"I brought you chocolate cake." His black brows lifted. "It was homemade."

It *had* been delicious. German chocolate with fresh coconut and pecans . . .

She shook her head, moving toward the entrance to the tunnel. "I don't care if the cake was orgasmic, it's not worth being exterminated."

A wicked smile curved his lips. "If it's orgasmic you want, my sweet . . ."

"Goodbye, Tane." She gave him a finger wave, pretending she didn't notice the sizzle of heat that raced through her blood. Stupid vampire smiles. "I can't say it's been a pleasure."

"Laylah."

Ignoring Tane's bellow and Levet's flurry of French protests, Laylah charged through the darkness, knowing she was wasting her energy unless she came up with a plan for escape.

She had to get out of the tunnel.

And she had to do it before Tane finished off the last of the boneheads who'd been stupid enough to attack him.

Rounding a curve, she skidded to an abrupt halt. What was that? A breeze? Her hand lifted to her cheek. Yes, definitely a breeze. And the air was fresh. Which meant there had to be an opening nearby.

Her heart was pounding so loudly she wouldn't have been able to hear a train approaching as she scrambled up the side of the wall, using her strength to crack open the small fissures in the ceiling.

It would all be a hell of a lot easier if she could just shadow walk, but it was difficult enough to crack open the stone of the tunnel until she rested, let alone rip a hole through space.

That was something you really wanted to be on top of your game to try.

She choked on the clouds of dust that filled the air, her eyes watering as a shower of rocks pelted her on the top of her head. The mini cave-in, however, had the intended result and, hoping the yummy chocolate cake hadn't widened her ass, she wriggled through the narrow opening.

For a heart-stopping moment, her jean shorts were caught on a jagged rock, but grasping a nearby clump of grass she pulled herself out of the tunnel.

Panting and covered in dust, Laylah crawled away from the hole she'd created, impatiently brushing away the blood that dripped from a wound on her forehead. She wanted to flop on the damp grass and catch her breath, but she forced herself to her feet and jogged over the rolling field.

For the moment she might have outmaneuvered pain-in-the-ass-Tane, since no vampire, regardless of how arrogant, would dare the sun that threatened to rise at any minute. But he wasn't stupid, and he already suspected she'd deliberately led him away from Caine's lair.

He would use the tunnels to return there.

Thankfully she had a straight shot back to Caine's, while the tunnels twisted and turned, forcing Tane to travel almost twice the distance.

With any luck at all she could retrieve her baby and disappear before anyone could follow.

Her lips thinned to a hard line as she found a dirt road that wound its way through empty countryside and picked up her speed. For the past fifty years her luck had been nothing but shitty.

Why should it change now?

Chapter 3

The sun was setting by the time that Laylah arrived at Caine's lair, but as Levet had promised, Caine was long gone. And so were most of his guards.

Thank the gods.

She wasted no time in silently slipping into the private outbuilding that was wrapped in layers of thick illusion that kept her presence hidden from the world. Or at least it had until Caine had insisted she travel with him to Hannibal.

Inside there were few comforts. A ratty couch and chair that she'd found in an abandoned house along with a television was the sum total of furniture in her living room. While the attached room held a narrow cot and a crib. She didn't collect possessions.

She'd learned since the death of her foster mother not to become attached. Whether it was to people or places.

Both could be snatched away.

Well . . . she *rarely* became attached, she had to qualify as she scooped the sleeping baby from the crib and headed away from the lair.

From the moment she'd caught sight of the golden-haired child that appeared to be no more than a few months of age she'd tumbled head over heels in love. A perfect angel. Not that she knew if he possessed a claim to heaven or not. Actually, she didn't know anything about the baby.

Nothing beyond the fact she'd taken it from the mists. And that it was held in a stasis spell so he remained locked in a web of protection, impervious to the world around him.

For nearly fifty years, she'd kept him hidden. Not a particularly difficult task since there was no need to offer the usual care that an infant would demand.

The child was . . . inanimate. Or at least that was the only description that came to her mind. As if he was a beautiful doll awaiting the spark of life to be breathed into him.

And, as far as she knew, she was the only creature in the world who could touch the spell that surrounded him.

Which made it all the more imperative that she keep him safe.

Fleeing from Caine's lair, Laylah made a brief stop among the local wood sprites. Despite their flighty natures the tribe owed her a favor after she'd saved the life of the queen. The time had come to call in her marker.

Then, with a brief prayer her luck would hold, she headed across the recently planted fields and cow-filled meadows, aimlessly headed in a northwest direction.

She didn't know where she was going.

Just . . . away.

Far, far away.

By midday her lurking exhaustion crashed over her with a compulsion that could no longer be denied.

She either found someplace to rest or she collapsed in the middle of a corn field.

Searching out the nearest house, she helped herself to a

few of their groceries, then made herself as comfortable as possible in the hayloft of the nearby barn. Hardly the Waldorf Astoria, but it would keep off the drizzling rain that had started to fall. And best of all it was vampire-free.

Biting into an apple, she glared at the barn filled with the usual machinery needed for a small farm as well as a pile of old bikes and forgotten toys that were tossed in a corner. A rusting museum dedicated to the passing years of a typical human family.

She pretended she didn't notice the treacherous pang of envy in the center of her chest.

She was ecstatic, wasn't she?

She'd managed to escape certain death.

And if she was alone in a stupid barn with mushy apples instead of decadent chocolate cake and wicked vampire kisses, it was a small price to pay.

Grumbling beneath her breath, Laylah snuggled between the stacks of hay and closed her eyes.

The past few days had been one disaster after another.

Once she was rested she would go out and steal a box of Ding Dongs. A chocolate fix was all she needed to drag herself out of her weird mood.

She barely closed her eyes when she tumbled into a deep sleep that was long overdue. Which no doubt explained why she didn't pick up the approaching danger until too late.

Far, far too late she realized as she awoke to discover her body already on fire with a sizzling excitement that wrenched a moan from her throat. Her eyes snapped open, not entirely surprised to find Tane stretched out beside her, his slender fingers running a path of destruction along the plunging neckline of her muscle shirt.

He might be a cold-hearted brute, but for reasons

that defied explanation, she responded to him like a harpy in heat.

Okay, there were plenty of reasons to become hot and bothered by the vampire.

The soul-stealing beauty of his lean face. The broad chest left bare to reveal the smooth bronzed skin and rippling muscles. The flat stomach and long thrust of his legs half covered by the loose khaki shorts.

And above all the raw, potent sexuality he wielded like a lethal weapon.

For a mindless moment, she became lost in the wicked honey temptation of his eyes, her body instinctively arching toward his teasing touch.

Then, as his lips parted to reveal his fully extended fangs, she was jerked to her senses.

"You son of a bitch." With a hiss of outrage she slammed her hands against his chest. "Get away from me."

With infuriating ease, he shrugged off her blow and rolled to pin her to the wooden planks of the hayloft, a mocking smile tugging at his lips.

"You didn't really think you could outrun me, did you, sweet Laylah?"

She silently cursed the scalding pleasure as he pressed against her, the intimate position revealing he wasn't indifferent to her proximity.

Gods. Her mouth went dry at the feel of his large and fully aroused cock pressed against her inner thigh. If he became any less indifferent she might faint.

"Why won't you leave me alone?" she muttered.

His head lowered to scrape his fangs along the curve of her neck.

"Why do you think?" he demanded, his tongue brushing the frantic pulse that beat at the base of her throat.

Her eyes flashed with fury even as a violent shudder of awareness wracked her body.

"Dammit, I've been polluting the world for the past two hundred years without the sky falling or the gates of hell opening." Her fingernails bit into his chest as his seeking lips skimmed over her collarbone, her toes curling at the tiny jolts of lust. "Is it really that important to turn me over to the Commission?"

He chuckled, his hands skimming up the curve of her waist, heading ever higher.

"You underestimate your charms if you believe the only reason a man would chase you is to turn you over to someone else."

"Tane." She sucked in a sharp breath as his hands cupped the mounds of her breasts. Oh . . . yum. His thumb brushed the tip of her nipple, teasing it to a pleading peak. She wanted to yank down his head and devour his sexy lips. She wanted to reach between their bodies and take command of that hard length of him and stroke him until he was begging for release. She wanted to guide him into her body and ease the aching need that had plagued her since the damned vampire had cornered her in the cave. Instead she grit her teeth, and reminded herself that this demon was not only a threat to her, but the child she had sworn to protect. "You'd better watch where you put those hands if you want to keep them."

He lifted his head to regard her with a brooding gaze. "Would you rather I put them here?" His dark voice slid over her skin like cool satin, his fingers lingering on her nipples before gliding down her stomach. "Or here?" he husked, the honey eyes shimmering with sinful intent as he tugged at the button fly of her jean shorts. "Or maybe here?"

Exactly there. Her hips were already lifting in silent invitation when Laylah came to her senses.

"Keep that up and I'll zap you," she snapped.

"Do you promise?"

She reached down to slap his hand from her shorts. If he managed to get her naked there would be no halting the inevitable.

It might embarrass the hell out of her, but Tane managed to stir needs she didn't even know she possessed.

"Don't think I won't fry your ass," she warned. "You saw what I did to Duncan."

"You said that was an accident."

"Accident or not, bad things happen when people piss me off."

"Which must mean that good things happen when people please you." He lowered his head to lick her beaded nipple through the thin fabric of her T-shirt. "And I promise I can please you. Over and over and over."

"Gods." She squeezed her eyes shut as the sense of an impending lightning strike gathered in the pit of her gut. Her powers had never been stimulated during sex. But then again, she'd never been so aroused. Not even during the actual act. A flare of panic squeezed her heart and grasping his mohawk, she yanked his head up to meet her frantic gaze. "Stop it."

His eyes smoldered with heat, his fangs shimmering in the faint moonlight that slanted through a hole in the tin roof.

"Spring rain."

"What?"

"You smell of spring rain."

"Why are you doing this?"

He shifted so his erection pressed directly against her

most tender spot. She choked back a groan as she nearly
came from the mere contact.

"I'm trying to demonstrate," he murmured.

"I'm a Jinn mongrel."

His gaze swept over her half naked body, deliberately
allowing his lust to blast through the air.

"You're exquisite."

"Tane."

He lowered his head to whisper directly in her ear.
"You should know better than to run from a predator."

It was the shiver of longing, as much as his patronizing
tone, that made her release a trickle of her pent-up powers,
causing Tane to jerk back with satisfying swiftness.

"Don't ever make the mistake of thinking I'm some
sort of helpless prey," she snapped.

He sprawled on the loose hay, a taunting smile curving
his lips as she scrambled to her feet.

"Helpless? Never. But prey . . ." He ran a slow, thor-
ough appraisal down her tense body, his tongue stroking
his massive fang. "Shall I discover if you taste as sweet
as you smell?"

She lifted a warning hand. She should just zap his ass
as she had promised. Unfortunately when she tried to do
more than release the smallest trickle of energy, she never
knew if she was going to create a bolt of lightning or a
tornado or an earthquake or some other wholesale destruction that could wipe out an entire town.

"No."

With the liquid grace only a master vampire could
claim, Tane was on his feet, prowling toward her.

"You're sure?"

"Back off, He-man," she warned, her outstretched hand
clenching as he continued forward. "I'm not kidding.
Come near me and I'll hurt you."

He halted, but before she could be stupid enough to think he was frightened by her threat, he folded his arms over his muscular chest.

"Where's the child?"

She flinched at the abrupt question, a stab of self-disgust slicing through her heart.

Was that the reason for the sexy vampire routine?

Did he suspect the child she was hiding was another Jinn mongrel who he needed to drag from his hiding place and turn over to the Oracles? Or was it just his attempt to satisfy his twisted curiosity before he was at last rid of her?

Whatever the reason, the thought of her ready response to his touch made her want to split open the earth and stuff him in the bowels of hell.

"You have a creepy obsession with this mythical child." She forced a mocking smile. "Do you eat babies for breakfast or something?"

He tilted back his head, testing the air with his superior senses.

"I can't believe that you left it behind. Not after your panic to rescue it from Caine's lair."

"It? A baby, mythical or not, is not an *it*."

He ignored the dangerous edge in her voice. "But, it's not here. Unless you've hidden it with a spell." Without warning he'd stepped forward and grabbed her upper arms. "Are you a witch?"

She glared into the too-handsome face. "If I were a witch you'd already be turned into a newt and stuck in a jar."

"Be careful, Laylah. A vampire has no tolerance for magic."

"And I have no tolerance for interfering vampires." She jerked away from his hands. "We're done."

He allowed her to back away, but that didn't ease her sudden jitters as he stood in the center of the loft, the moonlight sliding with sinuous beauty over his grim features and broad chest.

He didn't need the large dagger stuck in the waistband of his khaki shorts or the pearly white fangs to make him dangerous.

It oozed from every pore.

"Are you a witch?"

She instinctively backed away, not halting until she hit a stack of hay bales.

"No."

He moved until he was crowding her, his eyes narrowed as he sensed her lie.

"You have no magical abilities?"

"The charm of my personality."

His slender fingers stroked down her throat. A subtle threat.

"Tell me."

"I . . ." She halted. Gods, she'd gone as cowardly as a snallus demon. Reclaiming her spine, she shot him a furious glare. "I have a few skills, but I'm not a witch."

"Explain."

"Bossy. Arrogant. Ass."

"Laylah."

Her hands curled into fists. Dammit. The vampire wasn't going to let this go until he had an answer. Of course, there wasn't a chance in hell she was going to give him the truth.

He might just decide she was worth more on the black market than he could get from the Commission.

"My foster mother was a witch, but she claimed the magic she could sense in me was dormant," she bit out.

"It didn't matter how often I tried to conjure spells, I was hopeless."

"So what is your magic?" he pressed, obviously convinced she was hiding some major magical mojo.

If only.

"You've seen." She shrugged. "I can manipulate nature . . ."

"No, those are the powers of a Jinn," he ruthlessly overrode her. "What magic do you possess?"

Like a gift from heaven (or more likely hell) the doors to the barn were abruptly shoved open and a tiny gargoyle stepped into view, a frown on his ugly features as he glanced toward the hayloft.

"There you are." His wings twitched, his tone petulant. "Really, *ma cherie*, I shall begin to suspect that you are attempting to avoid me."

Ignoring Tane's muttered opinion of interfering gargoyles and the pleasure of chopping them into tiny bits of stone, Laylah moved to jump from the hayloft, landing lightly in front of her savior.

"I promise, Levet, you're not the one I've been trying to avoid." She deliberately glanced toward Tane as he landed beside her, his expression grim.

The gargoyle grimaced. "Ah well, that is perfectly understandable."

Sublimely indifferent to the insults, Tane circled behind the demon, peering out the door as if expecting to discover Levet had brought along a horde of ravaging zombies.

"Why are you here?" he demanded.

"Your fearless leader is concerned that he has not heard from his pet Charon."

Seemingly convinced Levet had come alone, Tane turned to study the gargoyle with a disbelieving scowl.

"Styx sent you?"

Levet gave an airy wave of his hand. "In a manner of speaking."

The honey eyes narrowed. "Did he send you or not?"

Levet took a sudden interest in polishing the end of his tail. "Well, it is difficult to say precisely what he desired considering I was speaking through a portal and our connection was not exactly 3G. There was some yadda yadda about this and some yadda yadda about that . . ."

"Levet."

Sensing death in the air, Laylah hurriedly searched for a distraction.

"What the hell is a Charon anyway?"

It was Levet who answered. "A vampire executioner."

"Nice." She turned to meet Tane's guarded gaze, belatedly realizing why the vampires had been so anxious to kill him in the cave. She'd bet he was the least popular guy at the family reunions. "No wonder you're so eager to hand me over to the lynch squad."

His dark brows lifted. "Lynch squad?"

"Tell me, is there some sort of Executioner Code of Honor?" she demanded. "Do you share bounties?"

"I do my duty."

"You deal in death."

He stiffened, almost as if her harsh words had wounded him. Which was beyond ridiculous.

"Deal in death." Levet chuckled, blithely unconcerned by the lethal vampire that hovered mere feet away. "Death Dealer . . . get it?" His gray eyes widened. "Helloooo, did no one watch *Underworld*?"

Tane shot him a furious glare. "Go away, gargoyle."

"And leave poor Laylah alone with a cold-hearted Charon? Do not be absurd."

With a slow deliberate motion, Tane removed the dagger from his waistband.

"That wasn't a request."

"No." Laylah stepped between the two bristling males. "I want him to stay."

Levet peeked around her knee to spray a raspberry at the towering demon.

"What can I say? I am irresistible to women."

Tane ran a finger along the sharpened blade. "I doubt she would find you so irresistible if she'd heard your earlier opinion of Jinns and their offspring. As I recall you were foaming at the mouth to have Laylah hauled to the Commission."

"*Non, non, ma cherie.* Never foaming," the tiny gargoyle protested, moving to regard her with a pleading gaze. "It was merely that I had a most unpleasant encounter with a Jinn some years ago. Can you believe he mutilated one of my beautiful wings? It took me years to grow it back."

Laylah shrugged aside the familiar sting of rejection. What did it matter? Levet was merely another to add to the very long list of those who judged her a monster without even knowing anything about her.

Instead she concentrated on his shocking revelation as she fell to her knees and grasped his shoulders.

"A Jinn?" she breathed. "Are you certain?"

"I assure you that it was an encounter that has been barbecued into my mind."

"Barbecued?" She frowned before giving a dismissive shake of her head. "Never mind. Was the Jinn in this dimension?"

"Just barely." Levet shuddered.

"Where?"

Another shudder. "London."

"Gods." Laylah struggled to breathe, her heart squeezed in a tight fist of disbelief. Since the day she'd been old enough to discover she was a mongrel she'd desperately sought to discover another with Jinn blood. She had finally accepted that she was completely alone in this world. "When?"

Levet blinked in surprise. "Really, *ma belle*, a gargoyle does not reveal his age."

"Please, Levet. It's important."

"Two hundred years ago." He shrugged. "Give or take a decade."

Tane stepped forward, his expression suspicious as he easily sensed her trembling excitement.

"Laylah, we need to talk . . ."

"I don't think so." She licked her dry lips. "Levet and I have business to attend to."

"Ah, now that is the kind of business I am always eager to conduct." He waggled his heavy brow. "I do hope it involves the removal of clothing and the rubbing of wings."

"Actually it involves a trip to London."

"London." Levet shook his head. "*Non,* such a damp and gray place. I far prefer Paris. Now that is a city created for lovers."

She slowly straightened, keeping her hand on Levet's shoulder. She had never tried to carry someone into the mists, but now seemed like the perfect moment to give it a whirl.

"I need to find the Jinn."

Levet cleared his throat. "Ummm, Laylah . . ."

Tane instinctively moved to block the door to the barn, his expression unreadable.

"I can't let you leave, Laylah."

Arrogant ass.

Her smile was taunting. "I don't need your permission, vampire."

His muscles coiled as he prepared to pounce, belatedly realizing that a Jinn had more than one means of travelling.

"*Adios,* He-Man."

Closing her eyes, Laylah called on the faint echoes that were forever whispering in the back of her mind. At the same time she ignored the infuriated Tane as he rushed toward her, his icy power filling the barn, as well as the gargoyle at her side who was frantically tugging at the frayed hem of her denim shorts.

"Laylah, there's something I need to tell you . . ."

Did they not realize just how dangerous it was to distract her at this delicate point?

Conjuring the image of a shimmering curtain, she mentally squared her shoulders and stepped forward, dragging a reluctant Levet with her.

She unconsciously grimaced, as always unnerved by the sensation that she was stepping through a nasty shroud of cobwebs. It felt so tangible that it was always a shock when she tried to brush them away and found nothing.

And then there was the pain. Tiny pinpricks that bit into her as if trying to flay the flesh from her bones.

One thing was certain, she acknowledged grimly, shadow walking would never replace airplanes and cruise ships.

Hell, riding a donkey had to be preferable.

The inane thought barely crossed her mind when the pinpricks abruptly became a deluge of agony.

She grabbed Levet close, screaming as they were roughly jerked through the barrier. Gods, she felt as if someone was attempting to jerk her inside out.

After a hellacious journey that ended with a jarring landing that left her splayed across a hard ground hidden by the thick, silvery mist, Laylah took a much needed moment to catch her breath.

WTF?

Not even her first fumbling forage through the barrier that separated dimensions had been so harrowing. Or brutal. A good thing. She'd never have tried it again.

Grimacing as her body struggled to heal her crushed ribs and several internal injuries that she didn't even want to think about, she battled to push herself into a sitting position, her eyes widening with furious disbelief at the sight of the vampire crouched at her feet.

The bastard.

No wonder she'd nearly been ripped into a thousand pieces.

It was bad enough she'd brought Levet through the barrier, but to add a huge, freaking vampire who had been clinging like a barnacle to her ass . . .

She shuddered.

Wasn't that how black holes were created?

As if sensing her feral glare, Tane struggled to lift his head, obviously as battered by the trip as she was.

Good. He deserved to suffer.

"Damn you," he rasped, his gaze darting about the silver mists that swirled around them. "What have you done?"

"Me?" Her mouth dropped in sheer disbelief. "You nearly killed me you oversized, troll-brained brute." She slowly pushed herself to her feet, unwilling to remain in the corridor any longer than necessary. Not only did she fear that the doorways to other dimensions might open and suck her from the mist, but time tended to move oddly. When she emerged it could be a few minutes had passed, or it could be days. Once she'd even come out to discover that it was two days before she'd ever entered. Talk about screwing with the whole space/time continuum. She turned her attention to the tiny gray bundle that was nearly hidden in the fog. Her heart gave a tiny leap of alarm. "Is Levet hurt?"

With a loud hiss, Tane rose to his feet, absently brushing the dried blood from his chest as he moved to stand beside her.

"Just unconscious."

"Thank God." She lifted a hand to rub her aching neck as the relief poured through her.

He frowned. "What's wrong?"

"I feel like I was hit by a semi."

He brushed aside her hand and replaced it with his own, his touch firm, but insanely talented as he worked the knots from her muscles.

Mmmm. Her muscles slowly uncoiled as he moved down her spine, a delectable warmth easing the persistent ache in her joints.

Whatever his faults, and they were numerous, this vampire did have talented hands.

Clever, wicked, powerful hands.

Hands that could send a woman to heaven or condemn her to hell, a voice whispered in the back of her mind.

It was the whole hell part that had her spinning away from his mesmerizing massage before she could melt into a puddle at his feet.

"Don't touch me."

His lips twisted, revealing he was all too aware of her rampant awareness.

"You didn't answer my question."

"Don't try to bully me, He-Man," she muttered. "This is my domain."

"Your domain?" He lifted a brow. "And that would make you Skeletor?"

"Ha, ha. Hysterical."

He stepped closer, his expression hardening with an unmistakable warning.

"Tell me where we are."

"I don't know if it has a name or not." She shrugged. "I stumbled into it by accident."

He glanced around, an odd fire burning in the honey eyes. "It's another dimension?"

"No, it's more a corridor that runs between them. I use it when I need to travel in a hurry." She flicked a deliberate glance down his half naked body. "Or when I'm trying to escape from a demented vampire."

He turned a complete circle, his hand clutching his dagger as he studied the seemingly solid mist that surrounded them.

"How do we get out?"

Laylah frowned. Tane was acting . . . peculiar. Which in itself was peculiar.

Vamps were nothing if not predictable.

Arrogant, dangerous, and sickeningly aware of their superiority.

Could it be that the mighty Tane was actually anxious to find himself in the mists?

Swift to take advantage, Laylah headed toward the unconscious gargoyle.

"The same way we got in," she said.

"Then do it."

"No."

"Laylah."

She scooped Levet into her arms, swallowing a groan. Gods. What did the creature eat? Lead?

"I'm taking the gargoyle to London and you can't stop me," she grunted, headed through the mists.

Swearing, Tane followed in her wake. "Why is it so important that you go to London?"

"I have to find the Jinn."

"Is it a relative of yours?" he snapped.

"That's what I intend to discover. I never . . ." she bit off her revealing words.

Naturally he couldn't let well enough alone.

"What?"

She flashed him an annoyed frown. "I thought I was the only one. Okay?"

He abruptly stiffened, as if bothered by her stark honesty. Then with a curse, he glanced toward the fog, his expression shuttered.

"Get us out of here and I will see that you get to London."

Did she have stupid tattooed on her forehead?

"Liar."

"What did you call me?" he snapped.

"I called you a liar." She turned her head to meet the smoldering honey gaze. "We both know if I was idiotic enough to return us to the barn there's no way in hell you would let me go to London."

Chapter 4

The eighteenth century terrace house near Green Park in London was considered a fine example of Robert Adam's architecture. It was, in fact, a great pride of the historical society, although the neighbors weren't nearly so enthused.

Certainly there was a classical beauty in the aging bricks and simple portico. The windows were tall with carved stone swags set above them. And it was rumored the interior was even more stunning. Carved marble staircases and grand rooms with painted ceilings, Chippendale furniture, and priceless works of art.

But the museum-quality perfection couldn't erase the chill of evil that shrouded the building or make the beautiful Lady Havassy any less unnerving when she made her rare appearance.

It was said that the exquisitely beautiful woman with long dark curls and flashing black eyes that contrasted so sharply with her pale, pale skin was some sort of Hungarian nobility. The locals didn't care where she came from, only that there had been a rash of disappearances since her arrival some ten years before.

More amused than concerned by the suspicions of the

humans, Marika ran a hand through her glossy curls as she absently descended into the cellars deep beneath the city streets. She was wearing a thin, gauzy gown that emphasized her lush curves, but did nothing to battle the damp chill in the air. Not that it mattered. A vampire was as impervious to the weather as she was to nosy neighbors.

As she reached the cement floor, the torches flared to life and a tall man with silver hair that spilled halfway down his back approached from the shadows.

Most women would consider Sergei Krakov handsome. He had a narrow face with high Slavic cheekbones and icy blue eyes that held a cunning intelligence. His body was lean and muscular and at the moment covered in a fine Gucci suit in a pale shade of gray.

Marika, however, didn't keep the mage around for his male beauty or for his taste in expensive clothing.

Allowing him to take her hand and lead her across the open room, she glanced through the window at the attached cell. She grimaced at the pretty young blonde who was chained to the wall.

The female's head was slumped forward, her long curtain of hair covering her face. Her naked body was boneless, straining against the manacles that held her upright.

"Is she to your taste?" Sergei urged.

Marika tapped a crimson nail against the window, not particularly surprised when the woman remained in her comatose state. The bruises blooming on her pale skin revealed that Sergei had already taken his own pleasure.

"Did you break her?"

Sergei chuckled, no hint of apology on his lean face. "She might be a trifle damaged around the edges, but she still has some fight left in her."

With a sound of disgust, Marika turned away, a hand pressed to her aching forehead.

"Perhaps later."

Sergei hurried to her side, his arm wrapping around her shoulders.

"You must eat, Marika. You are too important to allow yourself to become weakened." He made a shallow effort at concern. "Do you prefer a fey? Or maybe you're in the mood for a harpy? They always scream so sweetly."

"Enough, Sergei." With a casual twist of her hand she had Sergei by the neck and was slamming him against the wall. "I'm not a child. If you want to fuss over someone return to your plaything."

Sergei passively dangled from the fingers wrapped around his throat. He hadn't survived several centuries as her favorite pet by being stupid.

Waiting until she'd regained control of her swift, gypsy temper and at last released him, Sergei smoothed his black satin tie and summoned an expression of concern that was almost convincing.

"Please, tell me what's troubling you."

With a hiss, she paced to the center of the floor, her hand again pressed to her temple.

"It's her. She's restless."

Sergei didn't need any further explanation.

There was only one *her*.

His brows snapped together. "Impossible."

She narrowed her dark eyes. "Be careful how you speak to me. In my current mood I might just manage to forget I have need of you."

He raised his hands in a gesture of peace. "I only meant that she is wrapped in layers of protective spells. A nuclear explosion couldn't disturb her."

"Maybe your spells are losing their . . ." She deliberately paused, her gaze lowering to his impressive package tucked into the Gucci slacks. "Potency. Do they have Viagra for magic? You're growing old, after all."

His lips curled with a pure male confidence. "There's nothing wrong with my potency."

"Then why is she whispering in my head?"

His cockiness faded as Marika allowed her power to sear into his skin with a brief, icy warning. It was ironic really. Her gift had once been to heal others. Since being turned, that same gift allowed her to torture with exquisite precision.

He nervously cleared his throat. "What is she saying?"

Marika's pleasure in causing another pain was forgotten as she clenched her hands. She wasn't sure when the provoking whispers had started. At first they had been so faint that she'd dismissed them. It wasn't that unusual for her to sense Kata despite the numerous barriers that separated them.

Their connection was too intimate to be completely muted.

But over the past nights the distant buzz had become a desperate chant that refused to leave her in peace.

"Laylah," she revealed. "Over and over again."

"Laylah. A name?"

"How would I know?" she snapped.

"The two of you have always been close," Sergei attempted to soothe. "You're certain it has no meaning for you?"

She sank onto the divan, the heavy gold bangles that encircled her wrists shimmering in the torchlight.

"The bitch is obviously trying to drive me insane."

Sergei paced the room, his brow furrowed. "Or offer a warning."

Marika reached for the goblet of fresh blood that had been left on the lacquer table beside the divan. She preferred her dinner straight from the source, but at the moment she was too distracted to make the effort.

"Bloody twit," she growled. "In case you've forgotten the last few times we roused Kata she tried to curse me. Why the hell would she try to warn me now?"

"I didn't mean she was trying to warn you on purpose," Sergei protested, grimacing at the reminder of Kata's insane fury when they'd attempted to question her. "Obviously something is disturbing her enough that she's managed to battle through the spells I laid on her. I doubt she's even aware you're picking up her thoughts."

"What the hell could be bothering her? She's buried beneath six feet of earth, surrounded by rune stones and guarded by the Sylvermyst." She took another deep drink of the blood, pausing to deliberately lick the thick sweetness from her lips, enjoying the sight of Sergei's twitch of unease. He should be nervous, she thought with savage pleasure. She was in the mood to hurt someone. Of course, she was always in the mood to hurt someone. "Unless there's something you need to tell me?" she continued in icy tones. "You surely couldn't be stupid enough to try and speak with Kata without me, would you?"

His throat convulsed as he struggled to swallow. "I've learned my lesson."

"Are you certain?" she purred. "I could give you a small reminder of what happens to those creatures who attempt to betray me."

The handsome face paled. As well it should. Although it had been nearly fifty years ago, a man did not forget being slowly skinned alive during the long hours of the night, only to be healed the next morning so the torture could begin again. Especially when the punishment lasted for several years.

A cruel smile twisted her lips. He should have known

the minute he'd managed to trick Kata into revealing the location of her half-breed daughter he should have come to her. No, he should have run like a bat out of hell to her to reveal what he'd discovered.

Instead he'd turned traitor and nearly ruined everything.

Stupid bastard.

"I did it for us."

Her laugh sliced through the cellar. "Oh Sergei, you're a vain, grasping son of a bitch who would happily put his own mother on the sacrificial altar to gain the power you so desperately crave."

He flinched, but a mage didn't remain in the employ of a temperamental vampire without a set of titanium balls. He pasted a smile on his lips as he smoothly moved to kneel in front of her, his hands running an intimate path from her knees to her upper thighs.

"I may have my faults, but you need me."

She polished off the last of the blood and set aside the goblet.

"Unfortunately," she conceded in disgust. She deeply resented having to rely on the treacherous rat. But while Kata had some magical talents she was a mere human and Marika had no powers to keep her alive. Not unless she made her into a vampire. A tempting thought, but one she couldn't afford to indulge. Not when she'd lose her one last connection to the missing child. "It would be so much easier if she were immortal."

Sergei chuckled, sliding his hands between her thighs to caress her with a skill that took centuries to perfect.

"Perhaps easier, but you would miss me if I were gone," he husked.

"So sure of yourself?"

The pale eyes shimmered with ready heat. "I fulfill more than one purpose."

With a blur of motion she planted her foot in the center of his chest and sent him flying into the far wall.

"Later," she growled, rising from the divan. "I want to know what is bothering Kata. Let me see her."

"See her?"

Marika narrowed her gaze. "Are you deaf as well as stupid? I said let me see her."

"Yes. Of course."

Straightening, Sergei dusted off his expensive suit and stiffly moved to the heavy wooden door across the room. Marika followed behind, waiting as the mage fumbled with the lock and at last led her into the barren room carved from stone.

She curled her lips at the stench of mold and nasty things rotting beneath the stone. Unlike her innate powers that called upon nature, Sergei was forced to use blood and death to create his spells.

Magical hack.

Bypassing the stone altar stained with blood that was set in the center of the floor, he halted beside a small depression filled with stagnant water. Then squatting at the edge, he waved his hands over the surface, muttering words beneath his breath.

Marika impatiently waited at his side, alert to any hint that Sergei was attempting to deceive her. The fool would learn that a nightly skinning was nothing compared to what would come next.

The water began to swirl, as if being stirred from beneath, and Sergei's chants deepened, echoing eerily through the cavern.

At last he reached beneath his jacket to withdraw a slender stiletto and sliced a small wound at the tip of his finger. One, then two drops of blood hit the water, spreading over the surface with a strange shimmer.

Marika bent downward as an image began to form, slowly revealing a woman who was stretched on a narrow cot in a dark, iron-lined cell.

A woman who bore a striking resemblance to Marika.

The same black curls and pale, perfect features. And if her eyes had not been shut they would have flashed as dark as midnight.

Even her lush curves were the same beneath the shroud that covered them.

Perfect twins.

Or at least they had been before Marika had been turned.

Once she'd awoken as a vampire her ties to her previous life, including her family, had been severed. Or at least they should have been.

Any memories of her past life were forgotten, but there had been a persistent voice whispering in her head that refused to be ignored. For weeks she'd struggled to rid herself of the annoying buzz. Then she'd spent the next weeks hunting down the source of the aggravation.

It'd been a nasty surprise to discover an exact replica of herself living among a caravan of gypsies.

Her first impulse had been to kill the bitch.

That would put an end to her intrusion into Marika's mind, not to mention the creepy knowledge there was an identical copy of herself walking around.

But some mysterious impulse had halted her bloodlust.

Almost as if she'd glimpsed into the future to sense she would have need of her dear, sweet sister.

"You see," Sergei said. "Sleeping Beauty safely tucked in her bed."

Marika frowned, infuriated by the stab of fear that pierced her heart.

Kata might be a mere human, but she had gypsy blood

flowing through her veins. Which meant she possessed a unique ability to injure a vampire. Something her tender heart had been reluctant to do in the early days. Back then she still thought of Marika as her beloved sister.

Stupid female.

But over the last decades each time Sergei had released her from his spells Kata had been crazed, striking out so swiftly that it had been a miracle that Marika hadn't been harmed.

She wasn't about to put herself at risk again.

"She's stirring," she hissed.

Sergei frowned as the woman in the watery vision turned her head, almost as if aware she was being watched.

"Yes." He shook his head. "That shouldn't be possible."

"It shouldn't be, but obviously it is. Find out why."

"I could wake her and . . ."

His words were squeezed to a halt as Marika grabbed him by the throat and shoved him against the roughly hewed wall.

"No."

He smiled through his pain. "You're still worried about the curse?"

Her fingers tightened. She was not pleased that Kata had outmaneuvered her.

Again.

She dare not allow the little bitch to awaken, and yet she could not simply allow her to die.

Not when there was still the possibility that Marika could rule the world.

"Careful, Sergei, you're not the only mage in London," she said in a frigid warning.

"You can't mean Lord Hawthorne?" Sergei's expression twisted with a jealous hatred of the rival mage. "The man's a third rate magician who hasn't been worth a damn since he lost his imp apprentice."

"He would serve my purpose."

The pale eyes flashed with annoyance at her mocking taunt.

"Yes, but could he serve you?" he hit back, his insolent gaze running a path down her curves exposed by the thin material of her gown. "You're a demanding mistress, Marika."

It was a valid point. Few men survived a night in her arms. Not that they complained. Most of them died with a smile on their face.

But she had reached the end of her short patience. Her fingers squeezed until they were a breath from crushing his larynx.

"Find out what's bothering my twin and find out quickly."

He hissed in pain. "Without delay."

Tane was a vampire feared throughout the demon world.

Rooms emptied when he entered. Clan chiefs barricaded themselves in their lairs when he approached their territories. His name was used to terrify foundlings.

He was the vampire that even vampires feared.

With good reason.

Which put him at the very top of the food chain.

A pity all his power and props were worth jack shit in the cold, clinging mists.

Silently cursing the strange surroundings, he followed Laylah through the thick fog, her arms still filled with the unconscious gargoyle.

He'd devoted grim centuries to ensuring he would

never again feel like an impotent bystander, no matter what the situation. He was a take charge kind of vamp and his ruthless power made certain no one questioned his authority.

Now a pint-sized mongrel had managed to drag him into this damned maze of endless fog, stirring ancient sensations he'd buried along with his massacred clan.

"How do you know where you're going?" he demanded.

She tossed a mocking glance over her shoulder. "I just fumble around until I find the place I want."

He growled low in his throat. "Laylah."

With a sigh she returned her attention to the dense mist spread before them, walking with a confidence that set Tane's teeth on edge.

It was bad enough to be stuck in the bizarro place without being able to see if there were any dangers lurking nearby.

"What do you want me to say?" she rasped. "It's not something I can explain. I think of the location I want to go and start walking. Eventually I sense that I'm there."

He grimaced. It wasn't exactly an explanation that offered comfort.

But then again, would anything offer comfort at this point?

What the hell had he been thinking when he'd tried to stop Laylah from disappearing?

He always allowed his warrior's instinct to guide him. It was the only way to survive for nearly a thousand years. So why hadn't his instinct warned him to allow Laylah to escape with a wave of his hand and a pat on his back for being rid of the nagging, ill-tempered female?

Because when she was near it wasn't his warrior's instinct that was driving him, but an instinct far more primitive.

Why not admit it?

He had gone far beyond his duty to track down a stray Jinn mongrel. Not even Styx would have blamed him if he'd chosen to return to his lair and report that the female had managed to slip away while he was battling for his life.

As Charon he was expected to hunt down those rare vampires who drank blood tainted with drugs or alcohol. Few creatures knew that a vampire could become addicted, or that it would eventually drive them to madness.

And it was up to him to keep it that way, not to chase after Laylah like a hound in heat.

So why had he?

His gaze lowered to her slender body barely covered by the shorts that snugly cupped her perfect booty and the muscle shirt that did nothing to disguise the soft mound of her breasts.

The mere thought of having her pressed beneath him, her lips crushed beneath his kiss, and those slender legs wrapped around his waist . . .

His gut twisted with a ravaging need he hadn't felt in centuries.

Shit.

He didn't know why this particular woman stirred his darkest passions, or how she managed to bewitch him to the point of reckless stupidity.

All he truly knew was that he'd let his cock do the thinking instead of his brain and it had led him straight to disaster.

Angered more with himself than the woman who had slowed, as if they were nearing their destination, Tane moved to her side, his fingers clutching his dagger as if it could stem his rising dread.

"And how do you get out?"

Laylah halted, turning to meet his wary gaze with a lift of her brows.

"Obviously, the same way I got in."

"We barely survived the entry," he gritted. "Are you certain the exit won't be worse?"

"We barely survived because I had an unwelcomed passenger," she tartly reminded him. "A passenger I don't intend to have on my way out."

He stilled, his eyes narrowing to dangerous slits. "You can't abandon me here."

"Why not?" she challenged, her chin tilted to a defiant angle. As if she weren't facing down one of the most lethal demons in the entire world. "I certainly didn't invite you to come along for the trip. You can find your own way home."

"That's not amusing."

The chin went up another inch. "It wasn't meant to be."

He reached to grasp that stubborn chin, ignoring the gargoyle sleeping in her arms.

"I would be trapped."

"So what?" The dark eyes smoldered with a direct challenge. "You intend to have me executed. Why the hell shouldn't I leave you here to rot?"

His brooding gaze swept over her fragile features and the weariness she couldn't entirely disguise. He wasn't about to confess that he'd followed her for far more personal reasons than turning her over to the Oracles.

She had enough weapons to wield against him.

Dangerous, potent weapons, he grimly conceded, a fiery awareness sizzling through his body.

"The Commission has commanded that Jinn mongrels be brought to them," he said with a shrug. "There's nothing to say that they won't decide you're not a danger and release you."

"Yeah right." Her sharp laugh was oddly muffled by the surrounding fog. "I suppose you also have some Bernie Madoff stock you want me to buy?"

His brows drew together. "What?"

"I'm not stupid," she clarified. "As soon as they get their nasty hands on me I'll be sacrificed for the greater good."

"Very dramatic, but I can promise you that the Commission has far more important matters to concentrate on than a stray half-breed."

His thumb absently stroked over the lush fullness of her lower lip, his body throbbing in tempo with her rapid heartbeat.

"What matters?"

He grimaced. He left demon politics to Styx. Why stab someone in the back when it was far more satisfying to stab them in the heart? But not even a complete hermit could have ignored the gathering tension.

Something big was coming and the Commission was bracing to head it off.

"The private discussions are above my pay grade, but there's no secret that the Oracles have been gathered in Styx's former lair south of Chicago for weeks," he said.

"And what does that prove?" She jerked away from his touch, as if he'd scalded her. "That they're a bunch of freeloaders who overstay their welcome?"

Tane shook his head, caught between the urge to wrap her into his arms and drink deeply of her passionate nature or to shake some sense into her thick skull.

As fascinating as he might find her fire and brimstone the Commission wouldn't be even a little amused by her lack of respect.

"They're not a fraternity who like to hang out and play Wii together," he said, saving his lecture on treating the

Commission with the proper reverence for later. Did he really want to point out just how dangerous the temperamental demons could be when he needed Laylah to get out of the damned fog? "Each of the Oracles are powerful demons of different species, some of them mortal enemies who are forced to play nice when they must meet to resolve conflicts or offer rulings. But they never linger a second longer than necessary."

"Which only means that they are conveniently gathered for a lynching."

Unable to deny her accusation, he smoothly slid into diversion mode.

Any warrior knew that a timely distraction was as effective as a full out attack.

"If they didn't lynch Cezar then you should be safe enough," he said with a shrug.

She awkwardly shifted the sleeping gargoyle still clutched in her arms.

"Who is Cezar?"

"A brother of mine who was reckless enough to mate the newest Oracle."

"There's another one? Perfect." She glared at him as if it were entirely his fault that Anna had been revealed as the latest Oracle a few weeks before. "You're just overflowing with good news."

"A new Oracle is always a sign of coming trouble."

"Like a mule-headed Charon?"

"Like a bad omen." He grimaced. He wasn't an adrenaline junkie who liked playing hero, nor did he subscribe to the theory it was thrilling to "live in interesting times." He did his duty and returned to the privacy of his lair where he could indulge his various hungers and forget his past. The sense of looming danger was something that he had done his best to ignore, preferring the ostrich approach. But now . . . now he couldn't entirely shake the disturbing premonition that this Jinn was somehow involved in the big bad future. And that an unseen hunter was stalking her. A thought that sent a shocking bolt of fury through him. "Believe me, if they didn't consider the pleasure of continuing their torment of Cezar worthy of their attention, then you're nothing more than a blip on the radar."

She regarded him with blatant suspicion. "If I'm so unimportant, then why were you bothering to chase me at all?"

Wicked heat curled through his gut as he slid a lingering glance down her slender body.

"Do I need to remind you?" he husked. "Because I'm ready, willing, and eager to do so."

The pulse at the base of her throat fluttered in response.

"I don't doubt you're always eager."

He smiled, his gaze deliberately lingering on that revealing pulse.

"There are times when I'm more eager than others."

She stepped back, the mists swirling around her slender body.

"You must think I'm a moron," she accused.

"I think you're feeling cornered and making hasty decisions that might get us all killed," he soothed, his voice laced with enough compulsion to send a grown Ungmas demon to its knees. "Let me help you."

Predictably she shrugged off his coercion. The woman was too damned obstinate to be compelled, no matter how powerful he might be.

"I don't need your help." Her jaw tightened, a bleak darkness flashing through her eyes. "I don't need anyone's help."

Tane fought back the fierce urge to crush her in his

arms and banish her shadows. The same shadows that haunted him.

Alone.

Always and forever alone.

"Think, Laylah," he urged. "You're no longer protected by whatever spell Caine used to keep you hidden. As soon as you arrive in London you will be vulnerable." He folded his arms over his chest. "And trust me, a bounty hunter won't care if they capture you dead or alive."

"Yeah, like you do?"

"We both know you would be dead if that's what I wanted."

Her lips thinned at his blunt honesty. "If you're trying to barter with me I have to tell you that you suck at it."

"It's never been one of my finer talents."

"Then just spit it out."

His brows lifted at her imperious tone, even as he hid a smile. Why the hell would he be amused by a creature half his size trying to boss him around?

"If you hope to survive, you'll need my help."

She bit her bottom lip, smart enough to know she was going to be a sitting duck, or rather a sitting Jinn, the moment she arrived in London.

"And what would your help consist of?"

He held her wary gaze. "I would do my best to protect you."

"I could hire bodyguards."

Was she deliberately trying to offend him?

"You keep reminding me that you're not an idiot," he drawled. "There's no bodyguard you could hire for any amount of money who could match my strength or skill in battle."

"And so modest."

"I'm the best. No amount of modesty can change that."

She paused, continuing to gnaw on her lip. "Do you promise not to try and force me to the Commission?"

"Don't be ridiculous. You know I can't make that promise."

"Then stay here," she snapped.

"Damn you, Laylah." With a blinding speed, he reached out to grasp her arm, sensing she was a breath from disappearing and leaving him stranded. "You want my promise? You have it."

"You'd say anything to get out of here." She held his gaze, refusing to back down. Dammit. That insane courage was going to put her in her grave. "You're going to have to do better than a promise that isn't worth jack squat."

"What do you want?"

There was the briefest hesitation. "I want you to make a wish."

Chapter 5

Laylah was prepared for Tane's foul curse.

Jinn were universally disliked for their cunning guile, their unpredictable natures, and merciless power that few demons could match. And of course, there was always their charming lust for violence.

But while most creatures wouldn't admit the truth, it was the Jinn's ability to enslave others that truly made them itchy.

It wasn't the pansy ass version the water sprites could conjure.

The fey magic could capture humans, and only if the mortals were foolish enough to accept three wishes.

There was nothing pansy ass about the Jinn.

They only needed a victim to willingly fall into their debt, no matter how slight an IOU, to make a claim on their soul. And it didn't matter if they were mortals or dew fairies or vampires. They all fell beneath the Jinn's spell of enchantment.

When Laylah was barely more than a child she had accidentally enslaved an imp she'd found caught in an iron trap used by a poacher. It was her nature to heal those in need and she hadn't realized the danger until the imp refused to leave her foster mother's farm, his desperate attempts to please her causing complete chaos until she'd finally figured out how to release him.

She'd done her best over the years to keep the talent locked deep inside her. It seemed immoral to claim another's soul. Even worse than killing them.

And it was only when the mage had taken her captive that she'd deliberately tried to bind another to her will. Unfortunately the bastard had kept her so weak she hadn't been able to use any of her powers.

Now she was left flying with a wing and a prayer.

Her usual state of affairs.

Tane narrowed his eyes, looking at her as if she'd sprouted horns.

"You have the power to bind a vampire?"

Well, that was the question wasn't it?

She had no way to calculate how much strength it would take to enslave a vampire, but she was fairly certain it was waaaay more than she could claim. Her only hope was being able to . . . prompt him to do her bidding.

"I can't turn you into my private puppet, if that's what you're worried about, but it does give me the upper hand in our negotiations," she smoothly said, pretending she wasn't completely clueless.

His hand lifted to cup her cheek as he easily sensed her shaky confidence.

"You're lying."

"Whatever." She shrugged. "Are you coming with me or not?"

"Maybe I want to wish for something beyond . . ."

"I'm counting to three, you can come or stay, I don't give a crap," she hastily interrupted.

"Oh, I intend to come," he assured her with a sinful smile. "In more ways than you can imagine."

"One," she gritted.

"And you're coming with me."

"Two."

He brushed his lips softly over her mouth. "You got it, sweet Laylah?"

"Three."

As the word tumbled from her lips the fog began to swirl, twirling ever faster as she thinned the veil between worlds. Dammit. She'd made her decision and no arrogant bloodsucker was going to stand in her way.

"I wish to remain at your side," he muttered, grabbing her arm just as she began to step through the veil.

There was the sensation of clinging spider webs and the prickles of electricity that became stabs of lightning as she pressed through the veil. And pain. Enough pain to send her to her knees as they tumbled through the fog and into a chilled darkness.

The combination of pain from the entry and the shock at being wrenched from the ephemeral mists to the very real world of hard stone and damp air briefly disoriented her. She sucked in a shaky breath.

This was the very last time she was taking passengers along for the ride.

Slowly working through the pain, Laylah became aware of her surroundings.

The dark tunnels that ran beneath the outskirts of London. The faint scent of rain from overhead. The sound of Tane's curses as he struggled to his feet. And . . .

Awareness.

Awareness of Tane that tingled deep inside her.

Holy crap, had it actually worked?

Had she actually leashed a powerful vampire?

And if she had, was it a good thing or the worst mistake in the history of the world?

Fairly certain it was the mistake thing, Laylah was distracted by the sight of Levet lying like a frozen statue on the smoothly worn floor of the tunnel.

"Shit." She scrambled forward, touching the tiny demon who was now as hard as granite. "Levet?"

"It's daylight," Tane said, his dagger clutched in his hands as he tested the air for danger. "He won't awaken until dusk."

Thank God. With her current streak of piss-poor luck, she'd feared she managed to kill the poor thing.

Scooping the gargoyle into her arms, she straightened with a groan. The creature weighed a ton. Then, deciding there was no time like the present to test her hold on Tane, she nervously cleared her throat.

"You need to find us someplace safe to rest."

There was a brief, dangerous hesitation, and Laylah tensed, her mouth dry with fear. She was too weakened by the shadow walk to battle Tane if he remained unrestrained.

In fact, until she rested and fed she was entirely at his mercy.

Not the most comforting thought.

Braced for the worst, Laylah nearly fell to her knees in relief as Tane offered a mocking bow.

"Your wish is my command, mistress. This way."

He turned to flow through a side tunnel, not bothering to see if she were following or not. She hoped it was a sign his powers were at least muted.

In silence they moved through the cramped passageways. Laylah knew she was taking a desperate risk. If she hadn't gone skitzo with the need to track down information of the Jinn she might already be back under the protection of Caine with the child safely in her care.

Instead she was risking all for what?

Information?

Affirmation?

Lost in her broodings, Laylah allowed herself to be led through the maze of tunnels, only vaguely aware they were headed away from London.

Nearly half an hour later, however, she was jerked out of her dangerous distraction. She came to a sharp halt, her eyes narrowed with suspicion.

"Stop," she commanded.

With a low growl, Tane spun around to stab her with an impatient frown.

"Laylah, we don't have long until your scent begins to stir unwanted attention."

She matched him glare for glare. If she'd managed to bind him, he was already proving to be the worst slave ever.

"I'm more interested in the scent that's already here," she snarled. "You've brought me to a vampire lair."

He shrugged, completely unrepentant. "What place could offer you more protection?"

"Yeah, and when they learn your companion is a half Jinn they'll serve me up for dinner."

Without warning he was standing directly before her, his eyes glowing with a frightening intensity.

"There's not a chance in hell another vampire is going to sink his fangs into you," he swore, his voice harsh with male possession. "Not as long as I'm alive."

She ignored the strange excitement that arrowed in the direction of her pelvis. She wasn't going to be distracted again.

"I'm not walking into a trap."

"Trust me, my sweet, if I decide to lead you into a trap you'll never see it coming."

She ground her teeth. "Not helping."

He made a resigned bid for patience. "Victor is clan chief of London. We will need his permission if you intend to remain more than a few hours."

She grimaced. The last thing she wanted was more vampires. One was enough, thank you very much.

"What we need is a witch who is willing to sell us an amulet to hide our scents," she countered.

Expecting an argument, she was caught off guard when he shrugged.

"Yet another reason to approach Victor."

"He has a witch on the payroll?"

"Actually he mated one."

"Seriously?" She gave a disbelieving shake of her head. Magic was the one power a vampire had no defense against. They couldn't even sense a spell until too late. As a result they possessed a pathological hatred for both witches and mages. "A witch and a vampire? Isn't that illegal or something?"

"Or something," he said dryly, his own thoughts of a vampire taking a witch as a mate carefully hidden. No doubt a wise precaution. "Actually, Juliet is half witch and half imp, with a rare talent that allows her to sense magical artifacts. If anyone has a spare disguise amulet lying around it will be her."

"And that's the only reason you brought me here?" she demanded, concentrating on her tenuous awareness of Tane in an attempt to impose her will. "The truth."

"I've heard rumors that Victor had a brief encounter with a Jinn."

His brooding expression made it impossible to know if he was being coerced to speak the truth or merely playing along.

"Recently?"

"I suppose that's a matter of perspective."

Her brows snapped together. "Tane."

"A few hundred years ago."

"What happened?"

He folded his arms over his bare chest, making his muscles ripple beneath his golden skin.

"That's his story to tell."

She turned away from his compelling beauty as she considered her options.

Or lack of options.

If Victor had the information she desired, what choice did she have but to approach him? Even if it meant bearding the lion in his den, so to speak.

Besides, Tane was right, may his aggravating soul rot in hell.

Without protection she would soon be at the mercy of every demon in London who wanted to make brownie points with the Commission by turning over a rogue mongrel.

"And you swear you aren't using the vampires to break my binding?" she demanded.

"I swear." He pressed a hand to that gorgeous chest. Laylah swallowed a groan. She was terrified and weary and covered in filth, but a liquid heat raced through her at the thought of kissing and nibbling and licking her way down the smooth golden skin until she reached the waistband of his khakis and the . . . "Laylah."

Tane's rough growl jerked her head up to meet his smoldering gaze, a blush staining her cheeks at the sight of his extended fangs and rigid expression as he battled his savage reaction to her arousal.

"Fine, let's go," she muttered.

His jaw clenched, his urge to go caveman a tangible force in the air. Then, with grim effort he whirled around and led her through the darkness.

Laylah followed in silence, pissed off by her lingering

awareness. Not that her panting eagerness was a shocker. She'd spent the majority of her life on a small farm in the remote outback of Australia before being captured by the mage and hidden in Siberia. After Caine had rescued her, she had the baby to consider, which meant she remained all but a hermit, no matter where they traveled.

Male demons had been few and far between. And those of the tall, dark, and orgasmic sort had been all but nonexistent.

Was it any wonder her hormones were charged into hyperdrive?

They had traveled only a few miles when Tane slowed to a mere crawl, glancing over his shoulder.

"Wait here," he commanded.

"No . . ."

Without giving her the opportunity to command that he explain what was going on, Tane disappeared down a side tunnel, leaving Laylah alone to stew in frustration.

He really truly was the worst slave ever.

Tane's instincts were on full alert as he came to a halt and waited for the lurking vampire to make his appearance.

He was taking a risk.

Not only by entering another vampire's territory unannounced, but by bringing Laylah among his brothers.

Victor's clan had no reason to protect a mongrel Jinn and every reason to turn her over to the Oracles with all possible speed. No one wanted to be on the wrong side of an argument when it came to the Commission.

But he didn't have much choice. Already Laylah's scent was spreading through the tunnels. He needed to get her into the protection of Victor's lair. The sooner, the better.

Why?

His lips twisted with a rueful smile.

He wanted to claim it was because she'd bound him with her magic. After all, it was far less disturbing to believe the constant awareness that was nagging at him was a spell rather than something far more dangerous.

Instead he blamed his refusal to do his duty on the growing suspicion that there were forces swirling around Laylah and her mysterious baby that might directly impact the future.

There was a frigid breeze as a vampire of considerable strength neared and with a deliberate motion he tucked the dagger into the waistband of his khakis and held up his hands in a gesture of peace.

"Uriel?" he called softly, having met Victor's second in command nearly three centuries before.

On cue a tall vampire with a halo of brown curls and large brown eyes stepped into view.

A cynical smile curved Tane's lips at the air of guileless youth that shrouded about Uriel in his faded jeans and casual T-shirt. His deceptively angelic appearance had been the downfall of many an enemy. And one that Tane had never been stupid enough to make.

Although . . .

He frowned, realizing that the younger vampire's power had increased significantly since their last encounter.

Strange. Usually a vampire developed to their full potential mere years after their turning. He'd never heard of one acquiring more power centuries after maturing from their foundling stage.

A mystery, but not one he had time to dwell upon.

Not when Uriel was fondling a sword that could cut the head off a troll.

"We had no warning the Charon was traveling to

London," Uriel said, his bland tone not disguising his aversion to Tane's presence.

Tane shrugged, inured to the less than warm greeting.

His brothers either feared him or loathed him.

None of them wanted to be BFFs.

"I'm not here in my official capacity."

Uriel didn't look comforted. "You're here on vacation?"

"Not exactly. I must speak with Victor." Tane reached out with his senses, his brows pulling together as he belatedly realized that he should have been able to sense Victor's power signature by now. Unlike Viper, the Chicago clan chief, the big cheese of London was never subtle. His presence was like a sledgehammer. "He's not in London," he absently murmured. "He's traveled north."

Uriel's fingers twitched on the hilt of his sword at Tane's unconscious display of his talent.

He was a Charon who could find his prey with unerring skill.

"Victor was forced to travel to Dublin to meet with Lansbury, the current Prince of Fairies," he grudgingly confessed.

"Trouble?"

"There are whispers among the fey that there have been sightings of Sylvermyst."

"Impossible." Tane instinctively denied the nasty possibilities. The Sylvermyst were the distant cousins of the fey with a taste for evil that made vampires seem like boy scouts. "They were banished centuries ago along with the Dark Lord."

"So were any number of creatures who've managed to make unwelcomed appearances over the past year," Uriel said dryly.

Tane grimaced. "True enough."

With a sudden motion, Uriel whirled the sword over

his head and shoved it into a leather sheath strapped to his back.

"Why are you here, Tane?"

More amused than offended by his companion's blunt approach, Tane smiled.

"Obviously Victor didn't hire you for your diplomatic skills."

"He hired me to keep peace." Uriel's jaw tightened. "Something that's been difficult enough lately without tossing a Charon into the mix."

Tane flicked a brow upward. He sympathized with Uriel's predicament. The growing unrest throughout the demon world was a bitch for everyone. But he was here with a purpose and no one was standing in his path.

"Are you trying to imply I'm unwelcomed?"

"Having you here is like throwing gasoline on a smoldering fire."

"It's not my fault you can't control your peeps," Tane mocked.

"Peeps?"

"Minions? Flunkies? Sycophants?"

Uriel made a sound of impatience. "Our minions aren't the only ones who are restless. It feels like the entire world is sitting on a powder keg. Your arrival . . ." Uriel bit off his words, shock widening his eyes. "What the hell? Is that a Jinn? And gargoyle?" He glanced over Tane's shoulder. "Shit, do you have a death wish? Victor is going to kill you."

"Many have tried." Tane stepped forward, done with the polite chitchat. He needed to get Laylah to safety. "I seek asylum. Will you offer it?"

"As if I have a choice," Uriel muttered. "Styx has commanded that his Charons be given whatever they request. That's a pretty big trump card to carry around."

Tane curled back his lips to flash his fangs. "I have bigger."

"Fine," the younger vampire grudgingly conceded. "You can stay in the dungeons."

"Uriel . . ."

"Hear me out."

Tane narrowed his gaze. "Talk fast."

"As I've said, the natives have been rumbling and it's my duty to keep complete chaos from erupting," Uriel pointed out. "The dungeons are wrapped in illusions and protected by hexes. It should keep your presence in London concealed. At least until Victor returns."

"And an effective means of locking me in an inescapable cell."

Uriel's sharp laugh echoed through the cramped tunnel. "And risk the wrath of our Anasso?"

Tane allowed his power to bite through the air. "Styx's wrath would be the least of your worries."

"Bloody hell, I got it." Uriel held up a hand. "Trust me."

Tane shoved aside his initial reaction and forced himself to consider the suggestion. He truly didn't fear that Uriel would try and trap a Charon. Despite his skirmish in the cave, few vampires were that stupid. And the dungeons would offer Laylah the concealment she so desperately needed.

For now he could put aside his massive pride.

"I suppose they would provide a temporary protection. Are there any prisoners?"

"Not currently."

He nodded, his decision made. "I want a room with suitable comforts."

"Of course."

A sudden smile curved his mouth. "And privacy."

"Privacy?"

"Thick walls, convenient chains on the wall, sound-proof privacy."

Uriel's expression was unreadable. "I assume you'll be sharing the room with the Jinn?"

Oh, he intended to share more than a room with the Jinn.

He'd been suffering with a primitive need to claim Laylah from the moment he'd caught her scent in the tunnels. Now his all consuming need threatened to overwhelm everything, including his sense of self-preservation.

He had to get her in his bed.

And soon.

"I will."

"And the gargoyle?" Uriel demanded.

Tane shrugged. Laylah was done babysitting the obnoxious little demon. Even if she didn't know it yet.

"That's your call, although I highly suggest the bottom of the Thames."

Uriel shuddered. "Why do I have a nasty suspicion that I'm acquainted with this particular gargoyle?"

Laylah glanced uneasily over her shoulder, cursing Tane for abandoning her in the dank tunnels.

With every passing second her scent was spreading through London, attracting demons like a homing beacon. The knowledge was making her itch. As if there was a pair of unseen eyes watching her from the dark.

And if that wasn't bad enough, her arms were beginning to ache from carrying the unconscious Levet.

It was like toting around a cement truck.

Thankfully, just when she was considering the possibility of finding her own shelter, she watched as Tane stepped out of a side tunnel along with a tall vampire with the face of an angel.

"Laylah. This is Uriel." Tane moved to stand at her side. "Victor's second in command."

Uriel's gaze remained averted, as if he couldn't bear to glance in her direction.

"I have arranged for your privacy."

She frowned in confusion. "Privacy?"

Without warning Tane plucked the sleeping gargoyle and shoved him at the reluctant vampire.

"Here."

She watched in confusion as Uriel grasped a stunted horn, allowing the gargoyle to hang at his side.

"What are you doing with Levet?"

"He's an old friend of Uriel's," Tane assured her. "The two of them have a lot of catching up to do."

Uriel flashed Tane a glance that should have struck him dead.

"You're in my debt, Charon."

With his warning delivered, the vampire took off down the opposite tunnel while Tane steered her through the tunnel he'd just exited.

"What's going on?"

"I have negotiated the safe haven you demanded of me," Tane explained, pausing to shove open a heavy lead door that blocked the passageway.

Laylah grimaced as she stepped into the vast dungeon that held a number of iron-lined cells.

"Here?"

He grabbed her hand to urge her past the cells. "Were you expecting the Ritz?"

"Of course not." She shivered, not prepared to confess the dungeon forcibly reminded her of the nightmarish months spent as the mage's prisoner.

A smart demon didn't flash childhood traumas in front of sinfully gorgeous vampires. Not when they were masters of emotional manipulation.

Besides, she hated looking weak.

At last reaching the far side of the dungeon, Tane pushed open a door and stepped aside for her to enter.

Warily she entered the room, relieved to discover an effort had been made to add a few comforts.

There was a wide bed with a hand-stitched quilt, and two wingchairs set near a brick fireplace. There was even a bookcase with leather-bound volumes stacked on the shelves.

It was either a room used by a guard, or for . . .

Conjugal visits.

A stab of excitement pierced through her. Sweet, treacherous excitement that made her long to forget she was in a damp dungeon with a vampire who would haul her to her waiting death the moment he slipped his leash.

She slowly turned to discover Tane closing the heavy door and leaning against it with a negligence that mocked her own tightly clenched muscles. The breath was wrenched from her lungs.

He was magnificent. From the raven satin of his mohawk, to the bare chest and flat stomach that rippled with muscles, to the thrust of his powerful legs, he oozed with male potency.

And sex.

He oozed lots and lots of sex.

Her stomach clenched as his honey gaze traveled down her stiff body with slow appreciation, lingering on her hardening nipples that were visible beneath her T-shirt.

Gods. She wanted to toss him on the bed and rub against that hard golden body until he pinned her beneath him and took her with raw hunger.

Easily aware of her surging arousal, Tane pushed from the door, uncoiling like a predatory cat who was on the scent of his prey.

Laylah instinctively backed away, her mouth dry and her heart thundering in her chest.

"Are you . . ."

"Yes?" Tane prompted as her words faltered.

"Do you have rooms nearby?"

With a liquid grace, he tossed the dagger onto the floor beside the bed, then with a tug of a button, dropped the khaki shorts to reveal his male glory that was already fully erect and anxious to please.

"You could say that."

Heat seared through her veins, pooling in the pit of her stomach. She had pathetic little experience when it came to men, but she was fairly certain Tane knew precisely what to do with that fine, fine instrument.

And how to make a woman beg for more.

"What are you doing?"

He smiled to reveal the fully extended fangs that gleamed in the darkness.

"Changing into something more comfortable."

Comfortable? There wasn't a damned thing comfortable in the sensations assaulting Laylah.

Her skin was too tight for her body, her breasts were heavy and her nipples aroused to painfully sensitive peaks. And there was a hollow ache between her legs that was demanding to be filled.

She swallowed a moan.

A damned shame he was her enemy.

Otherwise . . .

Otherwise he'd be on that bed and she would be fulfilling a few dozen fantasies.

"Well, go and do your striptease in your own rooms," she muttered.

"What's the point of a striptease if there's no one to enjoy it?" he drawled, abruptly wrapping her in his arms and smiling down at her wary expression. "Besides, I intend to have my wish granted."

Chapter 6

Skimming his hands down Laylah's back, Tane savored the rich scent of her arousal that spiced the air.

She could huff and puff and glare all she wanted, but she couldn't disguise the truth. She desired him with a fury she couldn't contain.

"What are you talking about?" she demanded, her breathless voice making Tane smile. He was a vampire famous for his sexual prowess, but this demon managed to make him feel as uncertain as a fledgling. "I got you out of the mists."

He lowered his head to fill his senses with her scent of fresh rain.

"But that wasn't my wish."

She trembled. "You . . ."

"I wished to be at your side."

"Tane." There was another tremble as he found the spot at the curve of her neck that made her pulse pound and her breath ragged. "I command you to go to your rooms."

"Your wish is my command," he murmured, scooping her off her feet to lay her on the nearby bed.

Her eyes widened as he followed her down, stretching out beside her reclined form.

"Why aren't you going away?"

"It could be because these *are* my rooms." He traced the outline of one puckered nipple through her T-shirt. "But more likely it's because you don't truly want me to leave."

"Arrogant ass," she husked, even as her back arched in silent invitation.

He chuckled, burying his face against the heat of her throat.

"Stubborn mongrel."

Hunger spiked through him and his cock gave a painful jerk. He could smell the sweet blood that rushed just beneath the satin heat of her skin. It was maddening.

Murmuring encouragements in his ancient language, he abruptly grabbed the neckline of her T-shirt and with one jerk had it ripped from her body.

Her lips parted in protest, but before she could punish him with her sharp-edged tongue, he loosened a trickle of his power as his fingers cupped the soft curve of her breast.

She gasped as she bucked in helpless pleasure, her beautiful eyes wide with shock.

"What the hell was that?" she breathed.

He smiled. He had several specialized talents. His kick-ass hunting skills. His raw strength. His cunning. And a rare ability to concentrate his power until it was just on the right side of pleasure as it raced through his partner.

He shifted over her, his tongue outlining the lush curve of her lips.

"I do have talents beyond killing, my sweet."

"Oh."

Her eyes fluttered shut as he crushed her lips in a kiss of utter possession. Tane groaned as he tasted her sweet fire, struck by an odd regret that they were in a damp dungeon rather than surrounded by the elegant luxury Laylah deserved.

She should be stretched across satin sheets with velvet pillows beneath her head and champagne spilled across that magnificent ivory skin.

Later, he silently promised himself, completely ignoring the fact the only plans he should be making for the future was turning the renegade female over to the Commission.

He was a vampire in lust.

He wasn't supposed to be thinking clearly.

Plundering her parted lips over and over, he teased her nipple with the pad of his thumb, his cock pressed against her slender hip.

"Again?" he murmured.

She shivered in anticipation. "Yes."

With care he released a flare of power, covering her mouth with a fierce kiss as she cried out in passion. He growled in warning as she squirmed against him, rubbing his erection and threatening to hurry matters along in a quicker pace than he'd anticipated.

"Laylah."

With an effort he gentled his kiss, his hands skimming down the dip of her waist and the flare of her hip. His fingers curled into her soft flesh, attempting to hold her still. Holy shit. Who would've thought after so many centuries a tiny mongrel could threaten to unman him?

His lips swept over her cheek, tasting her perfect skin with a slow appreciation. His tongue traced the outline of her ear, nipping the lobe before seeking the tiny hollow below. She felt perfect in his arms. Slender, but with a hidden strength that made him throb in painful anticipation.

Already he could imagine her legs wrapped around his waist, holding him prisoner as he drove deep into her willing body, sending them both to paradise.

His fangs scraped over her shoulder, sharply reminding him that he had more than one hunger he ached to satisfy.

Not yet, a voice cautioned from the back of his mind.

Feeding during sex was an intimacy that took absolute trust.

Something sadly lacking as far as Laylah was concerned.

With a groan he resisted the compulsion to slide his fangs through the silken skin, and instead shifted to suck one of her straining nipples between his lips, using his tongue to make her arch and moan in rising passion.

He would eventually have the sweet taste of her blood on his tongue.

Until then, he could sate at least one craving.

Using the tip of his tongue to circle her tightly budded nipple, Tane allowed his fingers to loosen their grip on her hip and stroked down her thigh. He shuddered as she readily parted her legs, allowing him full access. She was already wet and slick, in preparation of his entry.

Thank the gods.

On the point of rolling her onto her back so he could mount her, Tane was caught by surprise when he instead found himself being shoved backward with Laylah straddling him.

"Dammit," she muttered, her spiked hair a crimson halo about her beautiful face and her eyes smoldering with a savage desire. "Let's do this."

He studied flushed cheeks with a narrowed gaze.

His body was screaming with outright approval at her wicked impatience. He rarely bedded aggressive women, but the sight of Laylah perched naked above him, her firm breasts within easy reach of his mouth and the entrance to her body pressed tantalizingly against his fully aroused cock, was enough to make him grit his teeth against the looming climax.

The slightest shift and this would be a wham-bam-thank-you-ma'am kind of deal.

"Easy, my sweet," he coaxed, his fingers cupping her ass as she squirmed against him.

"Easy?" She glared into his tightly clenched expression. "Do you know how long it's been for me?"

He frowned, something primitive and possessive stirring deep inside him. He didn't recognize the emotion, but it violently protested the thought of any hand but his touching this woman.

"The cur?" he demanded. He'd intended to leave Caine for Salvatore to kill, but if he'd had his hands on Laylah, then he would drain the bastard himself.

"A convenient partner in crime, but not in bed." She shivered, her breath coming in tiny pants. "God, I . . . ache."

His fingers tightened on her hips. "Hold on."

"She frowned with impatience. "What?"

"You're not going to pretend you want me just because you've been going through a dry spell."

"What's wrong, Tane?" she taunted. "Did I hurt your fragile ego?"

"You shouldn't challenge me, sweet Laylah," he growled in warning.

"Or what?"

A slow smile curved his lips. "I promised I would make you beg."

"Not even in your wildest . . . oh . . . oh . . ." Her head fell back, her eyes squeezing shut as he released a jolt of power. Her nails dug into his chest, the tiny pain making his hips jerk upward in pleasure. "Dammit," she muttered. "That's not fair."

Gripping her hips he stroked her over the hard length of his erection, hissing at the exquisite sensation.

"But you like it," he said, his hand skimming up the curve of her waist to cup her breast.

"I didn't say that."

His smile widened as her soft sigh of encouragement filled the room.

"Your moans of pleasure gave it away."

She sucked in a deep breath, her eyes opening to reveal a dangerous sparkle in the dark depths.

"Did they? Well, maybe we should discover what you like."

Before he could guess her intent she was bending forward, deliberately rubbing her breasts against his chest before brushing her mouth over his lips.

The caress was as soft as a feather, but Tane jerked as if he'd been punched in the gut. It was *this* woman. Her touch, her scent, her soft sounds of pleasure. It all combined to send his lust into hyperdrive.

Just as gently she parted his lips, running her tongue down the length of his massive fang. He groaned, wondering if she knew what the hell she was doing to him.

"Be careful that you're not starting something you're not prepared to finish," he husked.

"I'm making sure you're prepared." She laughed, spreading kisses down his clenched jaw. Then, with an evil disregard for his shattered restraint, she forged a brazen path over his chest and journeyed southward.

His hands clutched the sheet beneath him as she tormented him with light nips and nibbles, touching him everywhere but where he most ached.

Sadist.

Lifting his head off the pillow, he glared down at his tormentor, his words of protest dying on his lips as he caught sight of her beautiful features intent as she concentrated on her self-imposed task and her brilliant hair shimmering like fire.

The mere sight was nearly enough to make him come.

Then her tiny tongue peeked out and she licked him from root to tip.

Tane roared in pleasure, his fingers threading through her hair as her lips parted and she closed around his head, her tongue doing things that threatened to enslave him far more effectively than her Jinn magic.

With an obvious intent to punish him, she explored him with her lips and tongue, her caresses a slow, deliberate exercise in torment.

He moaned, at last grasping her shoulders and hauling her up his body.

"You prepare me anymore and our fun will be over before it's begun," he muttered.

She gazed down at him, a smug hint of amusement shimmering in her dark eyes as she straddled his hips.

"What about the famed stamina of vampires? I suppose it was too good to be true?"

His predatory instincts flared. A direct challenge.

With a motion too swift for her to anticipate, Tane rolled so her slender body was trapped beneath him, her hands pressed to his chest and her eyes wide.

"You want stamina?" He brushed his lips along the stubborn line of her jaw and scraped his fangs down the length of her neck. He smiled as she shuddered in reaction. "I can give you all the stamina you'll ever need."

"Tane . . ."

Her words broke off with a sigh as his lips closed over the tip of her breast, his tongue teasing the puckered nipple before trailing down the center of her body, pausing to dip into her belly button before he was arranging himself between her spread legs for the most delectable feast.

Drowning in the scent of her arousal, Tane nibbled at her inner thigh, a smile curving his lips as her soft whimper filled the air.

With deliberate care, he turned his head to slide his tongue gently into the waiting heat of her body. He stroked through her slick honey, once and then twice, his hands pressed against her legs as she bowed beneath the fierce pleasure. Tane had barely found the tiny nub he'd been searching for before Laylah had reached down to grasp his mohawk and struggled to yank him upward.

"Please."

Tane had every intention of making her suffer as he had, but his cock was ready to explode, threatening to embarrass him.

Rising upward, he studied the woman spread below him, her eyes dark with passion and her lips parted in anticipation. His gaze slid down the perfect ivory form, with the rose-crested breasts and softly flaring hips.

A stunningly beautiful creature.

That was his.

All his.

"Your wish is my command," he softly swore, his hands shifting beneath her legs to tilt her upward.

Their gazes locked as he slid into her welcoming heat with one smooth stroke.

Tane froze as a stunning ecstasy combined with a sense of . . . rightness blazed through him.

God almighty. He would have sworn that he knew everything there was to know about sex.

The women he'd bedded had been entertaining companions for a few hours and he'd done everything in his considerable power to make sure they both enjoyed their time together.

But this . . .

This was touching him in dangerous places. Places he had deliberately kept shut off since the night of the god awful bloodbath.

Ignoring the perilous sensations, Tane softly groaned as he pulled back his hips before pushing slowly back into her tight channel. His hands cupped her ass as he watched her dark lashes lower, her teeth biting into her lower lips as he pressed back into her body.

Magic. There was no other word for what was shimmering through his body.

Pure Laylah magic.

His slow, deliberate pace gradually quickened as her hips rolled upward to meet his thrusts, his initial desire to make this last the entire night being undone by the looming promise of paradise.

Laylah stretched her arms over her head, her soft pants as beautiful as any music as she climaxed.

His fangs ached as he felt the ripples tug at his cock, the compulsion to claim her with his bite almost overwhelming.

Then his own orgasm overtook him, making him forget everything but the shattering pleasure.

They were left to cool their heels in the dungeon until the following evening.

Not that Tane protested.

He was recklessly content to share the tiny cell with his beautiful mongrel.

An attitude that might have made sense if he'd spent

the past hours sating his persistent lust. What vamp wouldn't enjoy several hours of uninterrupted sex?

Especially when it was mind-blowing, balls-to-the-wall, best-sex-ever sex.

Instead, Tane had held Laylah tightly in his arms as she had tumbled into a deep slumber, clearly exhausted by the past few days.

Hour after hour, he had watched over her, refusing to allow anyone to enter the dungeon, including Uriel, in case they disturbed her.

Dusk was falling when he sensed that Laylah was beginning to stir and realizing she might feel awkward at having him hover over her, he left the cell so she would have privacy to pull on the jeans and T-shirt that Uriel had sent down earlier.

Offering such tender care was an unfamiliar experience for him.

He was a cold-hearted assassin, not a babysitter for vulnerable half-breeds.

Not that the pigheaded female appreciated his efforts, he acknowledged as he moved to block the door of the cell, glaring down at her stubborn expression with a surge of annoyance.

"We're not going to argue about this, Laylah."

"You're the one arguing, not me." She stabbed him in the middle of the chest with her finger, no doubt wishing it was a stake. Ungrateful wench. "I'm going with you to speak with the clan chief and that's final."

"Damn you, Laylah." His hands curled into tight fists. "Victor isn't a lame-ass cur like Caine who you can manipulate with a smile and too-tight shirt."

Her face flushed as they both glanced down at the stretchy shirt that lovingly clung to every curve.

"Hey, this wasn't my idea."

Tane's jaw clenched. "Believe me, I intend to have a long talk with Uriel the first chance I get."

"As if you have a say in what I wear."

It was a ridiculous argument.

What did it matter what she was wearing so long as she could easily run or even fight if necessary in the clothes?

Hell, his only interest in female clothing was how quickly he could get her out of them.

Now, however, the thought of any other male seeing so much of Laylah's ivory skin and soft curves was making him homicidal.

"I'm your lover," he said with an arrogance that brought a glitter of anger to her eyes. "I intend to have a say in everything that concerns you, sweet Laylah." He shrugged off his gray hoodie, leaving him wearing nothing more than a pair of cargo pants. Not that it mattered. The chill in the air didn't bother him. Wrapping her in the soft jersey, he tugged up the zipper and stepped back to regard her with satisfaction. The hoodie was too large, but it at least covered her from neck to well below her hips. "Much better."

She held out her arms to display the cuffs that fell past her hands.

"Seriously?"

He reached out to tug the hood over her head, hiding her face in shadows.

"The fewer people who can describe you once we leave this lair, the better," he smoothly improvised.

With a roll of her eyes, she shoved the arms of the sweatshirt up and over her elbows before regarding him with impatience.

"Fine. Can we just go?"

"As I was saying before you distracted me, Victor is a vicious clan chief who is notorious for striking first and asking questions later." He resisted the urge to shake some sense into her. "If it's true he holds a prejudice against Jinn he will attack before I can protect you."

"I don't want your protection," she snapped. "I want answers."

"Then perhaps I can be of assistance," a soft female voice said from behind Tane.

Whirling on his heel, Tane silently cursed his inattention, his fangs on full display as he watched the small female with a long mane of reddish gold curls and faintly slanted eyes that were the palest shade of green halt mere steps away. It was the towering vampire with long black hair, and silver eyes rimmed with black, however, that held his attention.

Victor's power was a tangible force in the air, challenging Tane's aggressive need to prove his superiority. It was never comfortable having two alphas in the same place.

"Easy boys," the female murmured.

Tane sent Victor a tight smile. "Boys?"

The clan chief of London gave a small shrug. "My mate has a challenging sense of humor."

There was a brief pause as the two predators became familiar with one another. Tane used the opportunity to run a practiced glance over the female's slender body attired in jeans and short sleeved sweater before moving to the towering Victor who wore a dark pair of chinos matched with a charcoal silk shirt.

He could easily detect the silver dagger hidden beneath Victor's shirt and catch the scent of the handgun tucked in an ankle holster. So far as he could determine the female didn't carry any weapons.

At least not the mundane sort of weapons.

She had witch's blood running through her veins,

which made her more of a danger than any dagger or handgun.

"Charon," Victor drawled, the silver eyes narrowed. "And a Jinn." He tested the air. "No. Half Jinn."

"As you say," Tane growled, bristling in warning.

There was the sound of footsteps behind him, then a completely unprovoked blow to the center of his back as Laylah felt the need to vent her displeasure.

Meeting Victor's amused gaze, he grudgingly shifted to the side so Laylah could step out of the cell, her face still concealed by the hood.

"My name is Laylah."

"A beautiful name," Victor's mate was swift to step into the tense silence, her smile kind. "I'm Juliet and this is Victor." She sent the vampire at her side a wry grimace. "My mate when I choose to claim him."

Tane stepped toward the clan chief, his body rigid with the compulsion to put as much distance as possible between Victor and Laylah.

"I must speak with you in private," he demanded.

Laylah grabbed his arm. "Tane . . ."

"I must warn you, Laylah, that it's a waste of breath to argue with vampires," Juliet murmured, moving to place an arm around Laylah's shoulders.

"But I have questions."

"So I heard. Come with me." Juliet urged Laylah down the opening between cells, obviously headed for the nearby stairs. "I think I have the answers you want."

Tane's brows snapped together in disbelief as he watched the two women disappear. Dammit, was Laylah trying to drive him nuts?

Victor snapped his fingers in front of his face. "Earth to Tane."

He jerked to meet Victor's amused gaze. "Where the hell are they going?"

Victor arched a brow. "Does it matter?"

"Laylah is a creature banned by the Commission. As soon as she leaves the tunnels she will be vulnerable."

"So? It'll save you the trouble of . . . shit." Victor's humor was replaced with cold fury as Tane grabbed him by the neck and slammed him against the wall of the cell. "Unless you have an overwhelming itch for your grave I suggest you release me."

Tane was rarely stupid.

He'd learned a brutal lesson in ever allowing his emotions to overcome his senses.

Until Laylah.

Now he was making a perilous habit of charging from one bad decision to another.

A pity there wasn't a damned thing he could do about it.

"The Jinn is mine," he hissed, grudgingly releasing his hold on the older vampire.

Victor smoothed his silk shirt, his sardonic expression disguising the lingering fury that Tane could scent in the air.

"I doubt the Oracles would agree."

"I will deal with them later."

Victor folded his arms over his chest, a speculative expression on his noble features.

"What's going on, Tane?" he demanded. "You have a reputation as a ruthless bastard who does your duty and disappears back to your hidden lair. Like Batman, without the creepy butler."

He hesitated. He wasn't about to share his strange obsession with Laylah, but he was going to have to offer some explanation if he wanted Victor's help.

"Would you believe me if I told you that I'm playing a hunch?" he at last said.

"Yes," he agreed with a remarkable sincerity. "Let's go somewhere more comfortable."

Victor headed toward the door leading out of the dungeon, his Italian leather shoes clicking against the stone floor. Tane was barefoot as usual. Who gave a rat's ass for expensive leather? Silence trumped fashion any day of the week.

Tane hurried to catch up with the clan chief, reaching his side as they climbed the narrow steps to enter the grand mansion above.

"Laylah," he gritted.

"She'll be safe with Juliet," Victor promised with an offhand tone that made Tane's jaw clench. The vampire was lucky that Tane had need of him.

"Not if half the demons in London are trying to capture her."

"Don't worry." Victor smiled with smug confidence. "My mate has a collection of magical artifacts that could fill the Louvre. Somewhere among the cache are a hundred amulets, charms, and crystals that will keep Laylah hidden from nosy demons."

They passed through the black and white foyer of the Palladian masterpiece and up an imposing staircase with a gilded balustrade. From there Victor led him through the marble hall that held a priceless collection of Greek statues set in shallow alcoves and a coved ceiling painted with fierce angels battling a horde of demons and into the formal salon.

The towering walls were covered by crimson silk panels, the rich color echoed in the upholstery of the traditional English furnishings and heavy velvet curtains that had been pulled aside to reveal a line of arched windows that overlooked a sunken garden.

It looked and smelled of ancient wealth.

The sort of stuffed shirt, grandiose, don't-touch-anything place that made Tane itch.

Although he had no memory of his life as a human, he retained his people's preference for being surrounded by nature.

Moving toward a heavy sideboard, Victor tugged open a scrolled panel to reveal a mini fridge tucked inside. There was the tinkle of glass, then he turned to cross the Oriental carpet and shoved a glass of fresh blood into his hand.

"Here."

Tane wrinkled his nose. "I don't want . . ."

"I know what you want," Victor interrupted in a tone that defied argument. "But for now you'll settle for this. Tell me how you came into contact with a mongrel Jinn."

Tane concisely explained the events leading up to his pursuit of Laylah and her desperate attempts to elude him that had eventually landed them both in London.

Victor listened in silence, his expression unreadable. "So you've had her in your powers twice and failed to take her to the Oracles? A dangerous game."

He grimaced, downing the blood in one gulp. Immediately he felt his strength increasing, although it was flat and tasteless.

For the first time in his long existence, he hungered for one blood in particular.

"This stopped being a game days ago."

Victor nodded. In understanding or sympathy? Impossible to say.

"What of your hunch?" he prompted.

"She's hiding something," Tane confessed.

"Something?"

"A baby."

Victor revealed the first hint of surprise. "Hers?"

"No." Tane made a sound of frustration. "But that's all I'm certain of."

Victor took his empty glass and returned to the sideboard. When he turned he held two glasses of whiskey. He crossed to offer one of the shots to Tane.

"Then what's your interest in the child?"

Tane tossed the fine Irish spirits down his throat, savoring the burn.

"Laylah was willing to give her life to protect the babe. I want to know why."

Victor studied him with a piercing gaze. "Tane, are you certain you aren't just inventing reasons to keep Laylah with you rather than turning her over to the Commission?"

Tane paced toward the gardens drenched in a silvery fog, annoyed by the intrusion into his privacy.

Like every vampire he answered to Styx, the Anasso, but as a Charon he had no clan and no chief. Which meant he didn't have to explain himself or his decisions to anyone.

Or perhaps he was annoyed by the possibility the clan chief was right on the money.

"I'm not damned well sure of anything beyond the fact the woman has crawled beneath my skin," he muttered. "But I sense . . ."

"What?"

"I sense the babe is important." He studied his companion with a stubborn expression. "And so is Laylah."

Chapter 7

Laylah had never had a female friend. Not even when she'd been in the comforting care of her foster mother.

The need for secrecy had always overridden her aching desire for companionship.

Loneliness was the price for her freedom.

Now she found herself . . . what was a good word? Discombobulated, yeah that fit perfect, as Juliet hustled her to a vast guest bedroom that was decorated in shades of ivory and lavender, barely allowing Laylah to get a word in edgewise as she draped an amulet of disguise about her neck before urging her into the attached bathroom that was a woman's wet dream.

A sunken marble tub the size of Rhode Island was smack dab in the center of the room and already filled with steaming hot water. A line of bottles that held bath oils, soaps, shampoos, and soothing crystals were set on the glass shelves. And lit candles filled the air with a soft vanilla scent.

Left alone, Laylah gave in to temptation and soaked away the dirt and tension of the past days, only leaving the water when she began to resemble a prune. Why not linger? For now the amulet would hide her presence from even the most persistent demon.

At last returning to the guest room she discovered clean jeans and a pretty yellow shirt, as well as lacy underwear and tennis shoes laid out on the canopy bed.

She shook her head as she pulled on the clothes and ran a brush through her spiky crimson hair. She didn't know what she'd expected when Tane had brought her to the lair of London's clan chief, but it certainly wasn't to be treated like a welcomed guest.

There was a knock on the door. "Can I get you anything else, Laylah?" Juliet demanded.

With a smile, Laylah crossed to pull open the door, stepping hurriedly aside as the tiny woman bustled in with a silver tray that she carried directly to the cherry wood table.

"No, I believe you've thought of everything," she said dryly.

"Sorry." Juliet laughed, occupied with unloading the various plates of sandwiches, scones, fresh cream and . . . Laylah's nose twitched, her mouth watering. Cake. German chocolate cake. "It's so rare that I have visitors who aren't here to kiss Victor's ass or to try and assassinate him that I don't remember how to treat a normal guest."

Laylah snorted as she closed the door. "Don't sweat it, there's nothing normal about me."

"Poor choice of words." Juliet poured two cups of hot tea. "Did you know I'm a mongrel? Witch and imp. Or imp and witch, depending on who I'm trying to shock."

Lured by her companion's friendly chatter, and of course, the temptation of cake, Laylah crossed the room to join her next to the bay window that overlooked the sprawling parkland.

"I think the half-Jinn thing has you beat on the whole shock factor."

"Fair enough. I hope you . . ." Juliet's words faltered to a halt as she lifted her head and studied Laylah with wide, startled eyes. "Bloody hell."

"What is it?" Laylah raised a hand and brushed at her cheek. "Do I have something on my face?"

Juliet shook her head. "Do you have relatives in London?"

Laylah's heart slammed against her ribs. So this wasn't just a wild goose chase.

"That's what I'm here to discover. Levet said that he ran into a Jinn in London. Oh." Laylah grimaced, belatedly realizing she hadn't given the poor little demon a thought since she'd awoken. "Where is the gargoyle?"

"Hunting." Juliet shuddered. "Don't ask."

Reassured Levet was safe, Laylah returned her attention to the reason she'd traveled to London.

"So, do you know about the Jinn?"

Juliet cleared her throat, abruptly turning to pace across the room in obvious discomfort.

"I'm afraid I do."

Laylah frowned. "How?"

"I suppose it must have been two hundred years ago, maybe a bit more," Juliet said, keeping her back to Laylah. "It was before I was mated to Victor, although he was already making a pest of himself."

"Obviously a vampire trait," Laylah muttered, ignoring the pang that tugged at her heart.

She was doing her best not to think of the wild, frenzied sex she'd shared with Tane. After all, what was there to think about?

He'd rocked her world. Hell, he'd sent her into orbit.

And now he was back to being her enemy.

End of story.

"Yes," Juliet readily agreed. "Anyway, Levet had become a squatter of my current master and one of my few friends. So when he was kidnapped I went to rescue him. I had no idea that he'd managed to piss off a Jinn or I might have reconsidered."

"You actually met the Jinn?"

"Not precisely." With a sigh, Juliet turned, her expression rueful. "He wasn't in a chatty mood. In fact, when we crossed paths he was doing his best to kill me."

"It was a male?" Laylah stepped forward, unable to believe she could actually find the truth of her past. Not after waiting for so long. "You're certain of that?"

"Absolutely certain."

So. Her Jinn blood must come from her father's side. It was a beginning.

"But you don't know why he was in London?"

"No." Juliet spread her hands. "All I really know is that he was beautiful and terrifying and so powerful I truly thought he was going to kill me, not to mention Victor and Levet."

Laylah heaved a sigh of disappointment. She'd hoped that Levet's mention of running into a Jinn had included more than a brief moment of violence.

"Damn."

"Laylah."

"Hmmm?"

Lost in her thoughts, Laylah didn't realize her companion had returned to her side until she laid a hand on her arm.

"There's no easy way to say this. I killed him," Juliet softly confessed. "I'm so sorry."

Laylah made a choked sound. Not in distress. How did she mourn a complete stranger, even if that stranger did happen to be her long lost father? But in shock that the slender witch could possibly have survived an encounter with a powerful Jinn, let alone be responsible for his death.

"*You* killed him?"

Juliet looked miserable. "I swear it was in self-defense."

Laylah grabbed Juliet's hand, giving her fingers a gentle squeeze.

"You don't have to explain, Juliet," she assured the woman. "I've done enough research to know that full-blooded Jinns are deceitful, immoral creatures who have loyalty to no one but themselves."

Her eyes darkened with regret. "That doesn't matter if he was a part of your family."

Laylah shrugged, not entirely certain how she felt.

If she were a wide-eyed innocent she might try to convince herself that the Jinn had indeed been her father and that she now had a perfect explanation for why she'd been abandoned. After all, not even the most devoted father could overcome death to keep his child protected.

Well, not unless he happened to be a ghoul.

But she was a demon that had been smacked around by the world and as far as she was concerned fairy tales were for suckers.

"I suppose he must have been if I look enough like him for you to notice," she said.

"Oh, no." Juliet blinked in surprise. "You don't look like the Jinn. Well, maybe a little around the nose and mouth, but you could be the daughter of Lady Havassy." Her gaze swept over Laylah's pale face. "It's downright uncanny."

Laylah was momentarily speechless.

She'd been so focused on discovering information on

the Jinn that she'd never considered the possibility that
she might have other relatives dangling about London.

"Who is Lady Havassy?" she at last managed to
choke out.

"A local vampire with a nasty temper and dislike for
Victor." Juliet grimaced, clearly not a huge fan of Lady
Havassy. "Thankfully she rarely leaves her house near
Buckingham Palace."

"Vampire." Laylah frowned in confusion. "They can't
reproduce, can they?"

"No, but they're human before they're turned," Juliet
pointed out. "Obviously they would have families."

"But then I would be mortal."

"Yes. If she mated with a Jinn and had you, then became a vampire."

"Oh."

Laylah had never considered the possibility that one of
her parents could be mortal. After all, she had talents that
had nothing to do with Jinn magic.

She shoved her hand through her still damp hair. She'd
come to London for answers, but so far all she'd discovered was more questions.

As if sensing Laylah's frustration, Juliet gave a hasty
wave of her hand, her fey blood evident in her expressive
movements.

"It could also be a mere fluke," she assured Laylah.
"We're all supposed to have a twin out there somewhere,
right?"

Laylah nodded, not at all convinced. "I suppose."

The door flew open, banging against the wall with
enough force to make both women turn in surprise. At the
same moment, the small gargoyle waddled into the room,
his ugly face twisted into an expression of disgust.

"Fog, fog, fog. Who does a gargoyle have to sleep with

to get off this soggy island?" he complained, his eyes abruptly widening as he caught sight of Laylah standing near the window. "*Ma cherie,* you are well?"

"I'm more worried about you," Laylah said, guilt tugging at her heart as the miniature demon hurried toward her. She'd simply forced the gargoyle to come with her to London. How selfish could she possibly be? "I'm so sorry. I didn't realize the shadow walk would knock you out."

"Knock me out?" Levet sniffed, his wings twitching in outrage. "Absurd. I was merely resting my eyes. Being a Knight in Shining Armor is a tiresome business."

"Of course," Laylah instantly soothed.

Levet tilted back his head, sniffing the air. "Cake. I smell cake."

Hurrying past the women, the gargoyle set about demolishing the large amount of food left on the tray, ignoring Juliet's futile attempt to rescue a piece of cake for Laylah.

Grateful for the distraction, Laylah wandered across the room, absently halting at the marble mantel that was lined with priceless Faberge eggs.

She was seemingly at a dead end when it came to the Jinn. At least she was until she could find someone in London who had managed to have an actual conversation with the volatile creature two hundred years ago.

But the vampire . . .

Juliet had said the similarity between them was remarkable. Surely there must be *some* family connection? Laylah didn't believe in coincidences.

There was a light touch on her arm as Juliet joined her, a concerned expression on her pretty face.

"Laylah?"

"Yes?"

"Is everything okay?"

Laylah hesitated. She already liked Juliet. In fact, she already considered her a friend.

Her *only* friend.

And how pathetic was that?

But the desperation to discover where she'd come from, who her parents were, and why she'd been abandoned was an overwhelming compulsion.

"Actually I have a headache," she said with a stiff smile, hating herself for the lie. "Do you happen to have any aspirin?"

Juliet couldn't entirely hide her surprise at the hasty excuse. Demons, even of the mongrel variety, tended to be impervious to the usual human ailments. But, swiftly hiding her confusion, she gave Laylah a comforting pat.

"I have a healing crystal that should do the trick much quicker."

"That would be fantastic."

"I'll be back in a sec."

Laylah watched Juliet hurry from the room before she jogged into the bathroom where she'd left the oversized sweatshirt. Gods, she felt like a jerk. Juliet had every reason to treat her as a dangerous, unstable beast who should be locked away.

It was how most people reacted once they discovered she was half Jinn.

Instead she'd been kind and welcoming and . . .

"Um, Laylah?"

She turned her head to discover Levet standing in the door to the bathroom. "Where are you going?"

She shoved up the overlong sleeves before hurrying toward the window. "To see if I can find Mommie Dearest."

"You're leaving?"

"I know . . . I feel terrible." She threw open the window, climbing onto the stool to sling her leg over the sill. "Please tell Juliet I'm sorry."

Levet hurried forward, halting only long enough to grab one of the disguise amulets that Juliet had left on a table.

"*Mon Dieu.* Wait for me."

Laylah was a little touched. And a lot embarrassed.

As nice as it was to have the demon offer his companionship, she couldn't afford to have him tagging along, drawing unwanted attention.

"I appreciate your concern, but there's no need for you to go with me."

"Do you have pigeons in your belfry?" Levet demanded, climbing onto the sill next to her.

"I beg your pardon?"

"I'm not going to be anywhere near a Charon when he's discovered his prisoner has escaped."

"Good point." She grimaced. Tane was going to be livid when he discovered she'd slipped away. Again. "Maybe we should hurry."

The lower kitchens of the London town house had long ago been given over to Sergei. Marika had no use for them, and while she insisted the blood sacrifices be made in the cellar, there were always potions to brew and spells to prepare.

She made a point of avoiding the cavernous rooms that were lined with odd hieroglyphics scribbled on the brick walls and dried plants that hung from the open timbered ceiling. A circle had been etched into the stone floor, where a wooden altar stood holding an ancient book that made Marika shiver in disgust.

Like any vampire she hated magic.

Almost as much as she hated magic users.

And the fact that she was forced to depend on one to achieve her glorious fate only inflamed her already seething temper.

Tugging off the veiled hat she'd matched with her black Valentino gown for her evening at the opera, she carelessly tossed it aside and allowed her heavy curls to tumble about her shoulders.

The evening had begun with such promise.

She had dined on two tender wood sprites that had strayed into Green Park and a lovely Turkish businessman in Covent Garden. From there she'd made her entrance at the Royal Opera House, causing her usual stir as she made her way to her private box.

Then, in the middle of the second act of *La Traviata*, one of her numerous minions had intruded into her box, whispering in her ear that there were rumors of a Jinn being scented near London.

Her lips twisted with fury.

The rumors had been true enough.

She'd instantly been able to detect the lingering female scent in the tunnels.

But she'd been too late.

The Jinn was gone. Seemingly vanished into thin air.

Turning from the counter that was overflowing with a variety of nasty ingredients used in his spells, Sergei frowned at her entrance.

"Did you find her?" he stupidly demanded.

"Does it look as if I found her?" She threw her arms wide. "Twit."

The mage shrugged off his protective cloak, revealing the elegant gray suit beneath.

"You said the Jinn was scented last evening," he said,

crossing to stand directly before her. A display of his sheer arrogance considering her foul mood. She'd been known to rip out throats when she was slightly peeved. "She can't have disappeared so quickly. Not unless . . ."

Her eyes narrowed. "Unless what?"

"Unless it wasn't the Jinn we're searching for." He grimaced. "Or she possesses far more Jinn powers than we originally suspected."

"You should be intimately familiar with the female's various talents considering you held her hostage for months," she hissed.

"I kept her locked in an iron cell that muted her powers." He abruptly glanced over his shoulder, as if searching for an unseen watcher in the shadows of the attached pantry, then with a shake of his head he turned back to meet her icy gaze. "Besides, she will continue to gain powers for the next five hundred years or so."

A frigid blast of energy swirled through the kitchen, stirring Sergei's silver hair and tumbling clay bowls and copper pans from the shelves.

She'd wasted years searching for the Jinn bitch and the babe she was hiding, constantly denied the power and glory that should be hers.

And now, just when she had been teased with the promise of her scent, she'd once again been denied.

Her bloodlust was at a fever pitch.

"Assuming she lives that long," she growled.

Sergei lifted his hand, as if he intended to touch her, only to hastily step back at the sight of her fully elongated fangs.

"Marika, don't forget that for now we need her alive," he attempted to soothe. "At least until we get our hands on the child."

With a flick of her hand, the drying plants crumbled to dust. "Don't you dare presume to lecture me."

Sergei's lips tightened at the loss of his rare ingredients, but he wasn't suicidal enough to complain.

"I merely want to prevent any mistakes you might regret later."

"Regrets?" She had wrapped her fingers around his throat, squeezing until his face turned an interesting shade of puce. "My greatest regret is ever choosing a treacherous mage whose only contribution so far has been to deceive me."

Sergei wheezed, his blue eyes darkening with a mixture of pain and impotent fury.

"If you will release me I can try to scry for the female," he choked out.

"You've tried it before only to fail."

"She's obviously lost the veil of protection that has kept her hidden from me." He struggled to speak, a hint of genuine fear beginning to perfume the air. Tasty. There was nothing like terror to whet her appetite. "If nothing else I might discover a trail that will lead us to her."

Distracted by his words, Marika tossed the mage aside, her violent fury morphing to curiosity.

"Yes," she said slowly, "why would she be so careless after so long?"

Sergei straightened, his hand instinctively smoothing his black silk tie.

"Perhaps the greatest question is what brings her to London," he muttered.

She smiled with mocking amusement, the fey blood she'd consumed earlier still bubbling like champagne through her veins.

She'd intended to find a partner at the Opera to screw

her senseless while she was still high, but watching Sergei squirm was almost as fun.

"Ah. Poor Sergei." She clicked her tongue. "Are you worried she's come into her powers and decided to seek revenge on the mage who tore her from her Sunnybrook Farm and kept her caged like an animal?"

He again glanced over his shoulder, rubbing the back of his neck.

"She couldn't possibly know I'm here. I kept my scent disguised while she was in my care."

"In your care?" she drawled. "I doubt she recalls your hospitality so kindly."

Sergei shifted uneasily, returning his attention to Marika.

"I also shrouded myself in illusion when I allowed her out of her cell. She has no means to recognize me."

She lifted her hand to toy with the perfect strand of pearls about her neck.

"Something brought her to London."

The mage abruptly tensed. "You don't suppose . . ."

"What?"

"Could Kata be calling to her?"

"Laylah," Marika breathed. "Is that the female's name?"

"How would I know?" He waved a dismissive hand. "I never bothered to ask."

"Such an idiot," she snarled, longing to drain the fool dry.

It was bad enough that Sergei's greed had put her plans to return the Dark Lord and stand at his side as his reigning queen on hold, but his brutal treatment of the female had ensured the mongrel would go to any lengths to avoid being found.

"Kata's connection to the girl is remarkable," he hastily said, anxious for a distraction.

"Yes," she agreed. She'd sensed Kata's ability to speak mind to mind with her child from the moment the brat was born. Unfortunately Marika had been left out of the loop, despite her own lingering connection to Kata. "And the only reason dearest sister is still breathing."

"If she thought her daughter was in danger she might be able to summon the necessary strength to shake off the spells that hold her," Sergei said, scowling as Marika tilted back her head to laugh with rich amusement. "Did I say something funny?"

"I was savoring the irony."

"Irony?"

"Kata has endured centuries of torture to protect her precious daughter." Anticipation warmed her dead heart. Kata's stirring. The scent of Jinn. The growing unrest among the demon world. Surely they had to be premonitions that her glorious destiny was at hand? "How brilliant would it be if she were the one to lead her straight into our hands?"

"It would be even more brilliant if the female has the child with her," Sergei muttered.

"It doesn't matter. Once I have her in my hands she will reveal the location of the babe. I can be . . ." She glanced down at her long nails painted the rich color of blood. "Quite persuasive."

Sergei grimaced in memory of what those nails could do to tender flesh. Then, with a tiny shudder he moved across the room to a locked cabinet protected by a series of symbols etched into the wooden door.

He waved his hand over the heavy, old-fashioned lock, muttering soft words that made Marika's skin crawl.

"What are you doing?" she snapped. The mage knew she hated having spells performed in her presence.

"I need a piece of the female." He opened the cabinet

to withdraw a small, cedar box. Flipping open the lid he pulled out a strand of crimson hair he'd clipped from the mongrel's head while he kept her as his prisoner. "This should be enough for a simple scrying."

Arrogant bastard.

Whirling on her heel Marika led the way to the lower cellar. Soon, she tried to soothe her irritated nerves. Soon she would have her niece in her clutches and her need for the mage would be at an end.

She intended to savor his slow, painful death with a bottle of 1787 *Chateau Margaux* she had hidden in her private lair.

In silence they moved down the narrow stairs, crossing the cellar to the back chamber. Marika gave the altar a wide berth, halting beside the shallow depression in the floor.

Sergei followed her, bending down to toss the hair into the depression, watching as the crimson strand floated on top of the water.

He did his usual hand waving and muttered his strange words, his handsome face settled in lines of concentration and his silver hair floating about his shoulders as his power filled the air.

No doubt such a sight impressed the hell out of the Russian Czars who'd kept Sergei in luxurious style before Marika had decided she had need of his services. She, however, wanted him to be done with stupid mumbo jumbo and tell her where the hell she could find the Jinn mongrel.

"Well?" she gritted.

Sergei straightened, a smile curving his lips.

"Your niece has been here. Recently."

Marika clenched her hands, her nails drawing blood that dripped onto the stone floor.

Close. So close.

"Where is she now?"

Sergei shrugged, pointing toward the water. "That's where she disappeared."

Marika leaned forward, studying the image that had formed on the surface. It took only a moment to recognize the tunnels.

"Victor's lair."

Sergei cursed, his face paling. Every creature in the demon world knew it was easier to escape the pits of hell than the clan chief's dungeons.

"That makes no sense," he rasped. "Why would she seek out a vampire?"

Marika shrugged, headed toward the door. "It's more likely that Victor realized a Jinn had invaded his territory and took steps to capture her. It would explain why I lost track of her so swiftly."

Sergei hurried to keep pace beside her. "Where are you going?"

She entered the outer cellar and headed toward a door hidden by a spell of illusion. Victor wasn't the only one with private tunnels to move about the city.

"There's only one way to discover if our beloved chief is holding the female."

"And if he is?"

She tossed her companion a cold smile. "Then you're going to make certain my property is returned to me."

Sergei's face went from pale to downright gray.

"Shit."

Chapter 8

Laylah stepped from behind the stairs as the scary mage and even scarier vampire disappeared through the back door.

Halting in the middle of the damp cellar, she absently rubbed her aching temples.

It seemed to be an evening for shocks, she ruefully concluded.

First had been her astonishment at the sight of the elegant vampire she'd followed into the town house. Juliet hadn't been exaggerating. The two of them could have passed as twins. Well, except for the other woman's long, dark hair. And the lethal fangs. And the psycho temper.

And then, of course, had been the shock of being so close to the mage who had brutally kidnapped her from her foster mother's home and held her captive in Russia. The arrogant son of a bitch. It had taken every bit of her willpower not to charge into the kitchen and rip out his black heart.

Laylah shivered, trying to concentrate on what she'd discovered.

It wasn't every day a girl found out she had an aunt who was a vampire and that the bitch was not only in cahoots with the mage who had imprisoned her for months, but that she was still on the hunt for her.

Her thoughts, however, kept slipping away as she was distracted by the soft sound of her name being called.

Where the hell was it coming from?

Barely aware of her surroundings, she headed toward the room where the vampire and mage had so recently left.

"Laylah, there is some ridiculous saying about 'getting out while the getting is good,'" Levet muttered as he hastily followed in her wake. "I believe this is an appropriate moment for the getting out part."

"Don't you hear that?" she asked, grimacing as she entered the adjoining chamber to catch sight of the stone altar that dominated the dank space. Were those bloodstains?

She circled around the disgusting object, the voice still ringing in her ears.

"Hear what?"

She frowned. Levet couldn't hear the voice? Which meant she was either going mad or some unknown creature had zapped her with a Vulcan mind-meld.

Neither option held any appeal.

"Someone's calling my name."

Levet's tail snapped and twitched with growing agitation. "I can tell you from painful experience that a mysterious creature calling your name inside your head is never a good thing."

She ignored his warning, slowly approaching the pool of water in the floor that shimmered with a strange glow.

"I have to know."

Levet stomped to stand at her side. "Of course you do."

"Laylah," the soft voice crooned. "My beautiful Laylah."

Halting at the edge of the pool she glanced into the

still water, her heart jerking in shock at the image of a woman stretched on a cot in some sort of dark cell.

For a mystified moment she thought it was Marika.

Understandable.

They could have been clones, until the woman in the image abruptly opened her eyes.

The eyes might have matched in shape and color, but there the resemblance ended.

Marika was a cold, cunning predator without conscience.

The woman reflected in the water possessed dark eyes that smoldered with the heat of her fierce emotions.

"Who are you?" Laylah breathed, ignoring Levet's dire warning of speaking to strange women who magically appeared in water.

"Kata," the woman offered, her lips moving as her voice left Laylah's head and filled the cavern. "Your mother."

Mother.

Laylah licked her lips, her heart ricocheting painfully around her rib cage.

Of all the scenarios she had envisioned of meeting her mother, this one had never popped into her mind.

"What's happened to you?" she managed to rasp. "Are you being held captive?"

Kata shook her head, her body trembling beneath the shroud as if she were struggling against unseen bonds.

"It doesn't matter, you must listen to me."

"I can help you."

"No." Kata gave a frantic shake of her head. "You must protect the child."

"Child?" Levet squeaked. "What child?"

Laylah waved a silencing hand toward the gargoyle. "He's safe, I promise. But you . . ."

"My fate has no meaning," the woman protested.

Laylah unconsciously sank to her knees beside the small pool of water.

"It does to me."

"Oh, my darling daughter." Kata's expression softened and Laylah would have sworn she could feel a warmth settle deep in her heart. "I knew you were destined for greatness from the first moment I held you in my arms."

Yeah, right.

Laylah knew she could be gullible, but she wasn't stupid.

"Then why did you throw me away?"

The dark eyes softened with distress. "Never, *kicsim*. It broke my heart to leave you in the care of Sadira."

Laylah frowned. Sadira was her foster mother. A gentle witch with a messy thatch of silver curls and round face that was pretty in a grandmotherly sort of way.

She was the one person in the entire world she truly trusted.

Now she was supposed to believe that she'd lied to her?

"How do you know about Sadira?"

"She was my dearest friend when we were both just children in the old country."

Laylah didn't know or care what the hell the 'old country' meant. She was far more interested in the implication that she hadn't been tossed out like rotting trash.

"But . . ." Laylah was forced to clear her throat. "She told me that she found me abandoned in the sewers of London and that she knew nothing about me or my parents."

"I know, and I'm sorry for that," the woman said, her voice thick with regret. "I made her swear never to tell you anything about your past."

"Why?"

"I could not risk having you come in search of me. I

had to keep Marika and her pet mage from using you to bring evil into the world."

Laylah jerked in pain. Even accustomed to people assuming she was a cross between the boogieman and Rosemary's Baby, it hurt.

"I'm not evil."

"No, of course you are not. Anyone can sense your heart is pure," her supposed mother protested. "But you are blessed with the ability to enter the mists."

"Oh." Comprehension slammed into her. "The babe."

"Yes."

She stiffened, a wave of emotions zigzagging through her. Fear, possession, and a shockingly maternal need to protect.

"But he's an innocent. I swear to you."

"He possesses the blood of the Dark Lord."

Oh . . . shit.

"His son?"

"His vessel."

Levet leaned forward. "Vessel? Are you certain?"

Laylah shot him a suspicious glance. "Do you know something?"

"I know you never want to be a vessel for an evil god," the gargoyle stated the obvious. "Very bad karma."

Laylah tilted her chin.

She didn't care what blood might flow through her baby. Or why he'd been created.

She would kill to keep him safe.

"The babe is trapped in a spell, but I refuse to believe he's evil," she said. "I can sense his purity."

The woman hesitated, as if troubled by Laylah's obvious concern for the child.

"Not evil, but . . . empty."

"I don't understand."

"He has been created by magic to be filled with the soul of another."

Laylah bit back her words of protest. She didn't intend to share her intimate knowledge of the child.

Not with anyone.

"The Dark Lord's soul?" she instead asked.

"Yes." Despite the invisible bonds that held her, Kata shivered in horror. "A genuine rebirth that will shred the veils between worlds and allow hell to spew forth."

"Mon Dieu." Levet poked her on the leg. "I particularly dislike hell spewing forth. Laylah, you must do something."

"I'm working on it." Her gaze never wavered from the vision of her mother. Gods. She'd always sensed the child was important. Perhaps even dangerous. But she'd never thought he was an apocalypse waiting to happen. "What can I do?"

The woman stared toward Laylah with a desperation that was nearly tangible.

"You must keep the child out of the hands of Marika," she said, her eyes flashing with a fierce intensity. "She will use him for her own vile purpose."

"Really, Kata, is that any way to speak of your only sister?" a cold, horrifyingly familiar voice sliced through the chamber.

Laylah stumbled to her feet, turning to watch the elegant vampire cross the room to peer at the water.

"Laylah . . ." Kata cried out.

With a terrifying laugh, Marika used the toe of her Manolo to stir the water, dissolving the vision of Kata.

"Toodles, dear sister."

There was the scrape of footsteps and Laylah turned to watch the mage stroll to join the vampire. She reminded herself to breathe as her gut clenched with an age-old fury.

The bastard had caged her like an animal and forced her to enter the frozen Siberian cave without giving a damn if the spell that protected the entrance would kill her.

Thankfully her stark, raving fear overcame any ridiculous urge to seek vengeance on the man who'd caused her such misery.

"I told you that I sensed a rat spying from the shadows," Sergei drawled, his pale blue gaze lingering on the gargoyle at her side.

"A rat?" Levet sputtered. "*Sacrebleu.* I shall turn you into . . ."

Laylah hastily grabbed a delicate wing to keep her companion from becoming a pile of gravel.

"Levet, no."

Sergei laughed with cruel amusement. "Did you have him shrunken or did he come in this size?"

"Now Sergei, it's not polite to mock our guests." Marika flashed her pearly fangs, stepping forward. "I have waited so very long for this family reunion."

Laylah grimaced.

Had she actually been stupid enough to pray she would one day find her relatives?

Yeah. That was a mistake she wouldn't be making again.

"Stay away from me."

The woman continued forward, reaching out to run a crimson nail down Laylah's cheek. It might have been affectionate if she hadn't used enough force to draw blood.

"Surely you're not afraid of your auntie?"

An icy dread clutched at her stomach, her latent powers stirring at the unmistakable threat.

"Yes."

Sergei reached out to lightly touch his companion's shoulder.

"Careful, Marika, we don't yet know the extent of her powers."

The dark eyes narrowed, the slender nose curling with a fastidious disgust.

"True. She has the look of her gypsy mother, but her blood stinks of Jinn."

Laylah wiped away the stinky Jinn blood that dripped down her cheek. "You knew my father?"

Marika's sharp laugh echoed through the cavern. "No one is foolish enough to actually become acquainted with a Jinn, but we did have a brief encounter before Sergei locked him in the room with your mother so he could impregnate her. He was . . ." She deliberately paused, a reminiscent smile curving her lips. "Delectable."

Outrage overwhelmed her fear. She never doubted for a moment the mage was without conscience or morals. But Marika obviously took the prize in being an evil bitch.

"You trapped your own sister in a room to be raped by a powerful Jinn?"

Marika shrugged. "Who can say what happened behind closed doors? It was," she paused, glancing toward the smirking mage. "What do they say in America, Sergei?"

"Don't ask, don't tell."

"In any event, you were born nine months later." She waved her slender hand. "That's all that matters."

She took an impulsive step forward. "You are . . ."

Icy power lashed through the air, striking Laylah like a sledgehammer to the chest.

"Careful, Laylah, I sometimes allow my temper to get the better of me," Marika purred, her eyes glowing with a lust for pain. "Neither of us wants me to forget I still have need of you."

Damn. Laylah rubbed her cracked rib. That hurt.

"What do you want of me?"

Marika regained command of her composure. "The child, of course."

"To sacrifice for the Dark Lord?"

The vampire appeared genuinely startled by the blunt question.

She glanced toward the obediently silent Sergei. "Obviously brains do not run in the family. A pity." She returned her attention to Laylah. "Why would I destroy my perfect means of ruling the world?"

Levet snorted. "Your aunt might be a raving lunatic, but at least she is ambitious."

Laylah gave his wing a warning pinch. Did the silly creature have a death wish?

"Levet."

"Lunatic?" Marika gave a throaty chuckle. "Geniuses are always misunderstood." Seeming to relish being the center of attention, Marika strolled across the cavern, her hand running over the expensive material of her designer gown. "For centuries the Dark Lord's disciples have sought to return their deity to the world. Altars have run red with the blood of sacrifices and mages have grown rich beyond their wildest fantasies as demons seek their services to part the veils between worlds." She halted to toss her pet mage a condescending smile. "Is that not true, Sergei?"

The man shrugged. "Fools."

"More than fools," Marika countered. "They offer their blood and magic and most precious possessions, all in the hopes of summoning a god who will reward their loyalty with a brutal death."

Laylah grimaced. It'd never been a secret that the Dark Lord was a bad guy on an epic scale. Thankfully, the scary ass Lord of Demons had been banished beyond the mists centuries ago. And while his minions, along with his minion wannabes, were constantly trying to bring him back from the other side, so far they'd been batting zero.

So what the hell was this crazy vampire and her slimy sidekick of a mage up to?

"So you don't want the Dark Lord returned?"

"Of course I want him returned, but not as a pissed off, fully functioning deity who is anxious for revenge," Marika snapped. "I want him . . . malleable."

"Mon Dieu." Levet's wings quivered as he pressed against Laylah's leg. "Have you ever met the Dark Lord? He is even less malleable than my great Aunt Zepharina who hasn't budged from Notre Dame cathedral since 1163."

Marika moved to stand directly in front of Levet, her expression sending a jolt of revulsion skittering down Laylah's spine.

Reaching out, the vampire stroked her fingers over Levet's stunted horn, her power altering to become something far more lethal than mere brute strength.

A dark, sweetly potent force that concealed a sickening rot.

"A clever woman always has the means to control a man whether he is a deformed gargoyle or a god," she husked.

"Ah," Levet's tail twitched as Marika tugged on his horn. *"Oui."*

Laylah rolled her eyes. Men. They were all the same. No matter what their size.

"How do you intend . . ." Her words broke off as she was hit with a terrifying suspicion. "Oh my gods. The baby."

Marika shot her a mocking glance. "Perhaps you're not so stupid as I thought."

"What?" Levet shook off the sensual spell, absently scrubbing his horn as if trying to rid himself of the lingering feel of the vampire's hand. "What is it?"

Her stomach clenched with guilt. Dammit. She'd been an idiot. A selfish idiot.

In her haste to come to London and track some vague rumor of a Jinn (who hadn't been spotted for over two hundred years), she'd not only left the baby to be protected by mere wood sprites, but after years of keeping them both hidden, she'd now alerted the world there was a mongrel Jinn roaming around and then proceeded to waltz straight into the hands of her family, who also happened to be her worst enemies.

A record screw-up, even for her.

"Somehow she intends to have the Dark Lord resurrected into the child," she told Levet, her gaze never wavering from the cold perfection of Marika's face.

"Sergei has promised he possesses the necessary talent for such a miracle." The vampire turned toward the mage with a taunting smile. "Let us hope he has not exaggerated his skills."

Sergei shrugged, looking his usual smug self. But Laylah didn't miss the unease in the back of the pale blue eyes.

Either the bastard wasn't nearly so confident in his ability to resurrect evil deities as he pretended, or he was intelligent enough to be terrified of his partner.

Laylah was betting on the terrified option.

"I never promise more than I can deliver," he drawled.

"Even if you did manage to resurrect the Dark Lord what good would he be to you as a mere child?" Laylah demanded.

If she did survive this encounter, then she needed all the information she could scrape together. She'd been stumbling through the dark for far too long.

How could she protect the baby if she didn't understand the dangers?

"Children eventually mature." She gave a toss of her

raven curls. "Carefully protected by their devoted mother, of course."

"Mother?" Laylah twitched at the mere thought. She wasn't sure even the Dark Lord deserved such a hideous fate. "You?"

"How better to mold a god to suit my purpose?" Marika threw her arms wide. "When he at last regains his rightful place as the master of this world, I will stand at his side."

Laylah swallowed the urge to laugh as the image of Leonardo DiCaprio standing at the rail of the Titanic shouting 'I'm king of the world' flashed through her mind.

There was nothing amusing in the thought of a demented vampire and an evil god taking over the world.

She turned toward the mage, bristling with anger at the memory of his deliberate cruelty. One day she was going to knock that cocky smile from his lips.

"That's why you kidnapped me? To get the child?"

"Only a Jinn could enter the veil surrounding the cavern and since there's no mage insane enough to trust such a rare treasure in the hands of a full-blooded Jinn, it was obvious we would need a mongrel."

Her mind shied from the thought of what her mother must have suffered at the hands of the Jinn.

She would deal with the depraved method of her conception when she didn't have an Armageddon hanging over her head.

Instead she concentrated on the child she'd sworn to protect.

"Did the Dark Lord create the baby or just donate the DNA?"

"What does it matter?" There was a peevish edge to Marika's voice, as if annoyed by the question. Odd. She'd answered the others readily enough. "I heard rumors of its existence and knew it would be the perfect means to take my rightful place."

Laylah swallowed the lump in her throat.

The only rightful place for Auntie Marika was in the nearest looney bin.

"Where are you keeping my mother?"

The vampire slowly blinked, caught off guard by the abrupt change in subject.

Unfortunately, Laylah's hope she might blurt out the truth was doomed to failure. Instead, a calculating expression hardened her delicate features.

"Ah. Poor Kata," she purred. "I can't tell you how it's broken my heart to have kept her locked away. But really, she gave me no choice." She slid forward, the scent of expensive perfume and cold malice wrapping around Laylah. "Of course, now that we have you, there's no longer a need for her to remain my prisoner. With the proper incentive I might be convinced to release her."

Laylah's throat threatened to seal shut as the vampire cupped her cheek with icy fingers.

She'd never tested the limits of her ability to heal.

She preferred not to start now.

"Incentive?" she managed to choke out.

The fingers on her face tightened, the nails digging into her flesh.

"The child."

"Laylah . . ." Levet tugged on her jeans. "No."

"Shut up, gargoyle," Sergei snarled.

Marika ignored the peanut gallery, her dark eyes boring into Laylah with the flat, soulless gaze of a snake.

"What do you say, niece?" she urged. "Surely we can come to an agreement that's mutually beneficial? After all, the child is worthless to you."

Laylah swallowed her words of protest. At the moment

the baby was her only bargaining chip. And her only means out of the cellar alive.

"Hardly worthless."

Marika studied her with undisguised suspicion. "You want to barter?"

Laylah forced a smile. "You did claim that I have gypsy blood."

Levet tugged on her jeans. "Laylah."

Sergei lifted his hand, sending an invisible blast of energy slamming into the tiny gargoyle.

"I said shut up," the mage thundered.

Laylah glared at the towering bully. "That's not the best way to start negotiations."

Marika's grip threatened to crush Laylah's jaw as she jerked her back to meet the vicious craving that lurked deep in the brown eyes.

The vampire's lust for power had become a dangerous addiction.

One that might very well be the death of Laylah.

"I want the child."

"Yeah." Laylah tried to swallow, her bones beginning to crack beneath the pressure of those slender fingers. "I got that."

"And I'll do whatever necessary to get my hands on the brat," Marika hissed. "Beginning with the sacrifice of Kata if you don't give me what I want."

Visions of death danced before Laylah's eyes, but before the demented vampire could snap and slaughter them all, Sergei was laying a restraining hand on Marika's arm.

Brave mage.

"Marika," he murmured softly. "We're no longer alone."

There was a tense moment as the female battled back her bloodlust, her punishing grip on Laylah's face easing as she tilted back her head to test the air.

Her beautiful face twisted with frustrated fury.

"Victor."

"And his entire clan." Sergei was already headed for the door. "We have to leave."

Marika shook her head. "Not without my prize."

Taking advantage of the vampire's momentary distraction, Laylah jerked free of her grasp, then gathering Levet close she held up a warning hand, more surprised than anyone when the earth trembled and a large chunk of rock fell from the ceiling to knock Marika to the ground.

"Stay back," she gritted.

"You bitch. Do you have no respect for a Valentino original?" Rising to her feet, Marika brushed off the clinging dust, more concerned with the gown than the jagged wound on her shoulder. Of course, the wound would heal. The gown? It might be a write-off. "You'll pay for that."

Laylah braced herself for the looming attack, but with remarkable speed Sergei was grabbing the infuriated vampire's arm and tugging her toward the door.

"Marika, let's go."

Frigid hatred hung in the air, but Laylah's powers once again lashed out, cracking the stone floor and filling the air with the prickle of an approaching lightning strike.

An impressive display of powers.

A pity that they spent most of their time in hibernation. And when they did decide to appear they usually created more trouble than they were worth.

Thankfully, Marika was suitably freaked by tremors that continued to rock the cavern, and backing toward the entrance, she sent Laylah a glare of venomous warning.

"Bring the child to me or I will make your mother suffer unimaginable pain."

Laylah tilted her chin. "Go to hell."

The woman hissed. "Then spend the rest of your life knowing that she's screaming in agony and that you have no one to blame but yourself."

Smiling at the fear that Laylah couldn't entirely hide, Marika allowed Sergei to pull her out of the cavern.

Alone with Levet, Laylah dropped to her knees, her power switched off as abruptly as it had switched on.

Dammit. She'd survived the encounter with her aunt-from-hell, but at what cost?

"Laylah."

The distant sound of Tane calling her name echoed through the cellar. So distant that she could almost pretend that the edge in the dark, smoky voice was fear instead of fury.

She tried to rise to her feet.

Within moments the cavern would be filled with vampires and she didn't want anyone seeing her on her knees.

Not again.

But her body refused to cooperate. Instead a tide of darkness began to creep relentlessly through her mind.

Obviously even mini-earthquakes took their toll on her strength.

She trembled, her head spinning. Then, as the cool, exotically male scent of Tane filled the cavern, she found herself tumbling into a pair of waiting arms.

Chapter 9

Tane was vaguely aware of the wary vampires who scurried to clear him a path as he stormed his way from the London town house to Victor's lair. And the curious glances at the sight of him cradling the unconscious woman in his arms as he headed up the stairs to the privacy of the ivory and lavender bedroom.

But beyond demanding that Levet reveal precisely what had occurred from the moment Laylah had left the country estate until she'd fainted in his arms, he'd been indifferent to all but overriding need to have this woman safely hidden from those who would harm her.

And far away from prying eyes so he could personally demonstrate his opinion of impetuous, pigheaded Jinn mongrels who didn't have the sense of a drunken dew fairy.

Entering the vast room that was softly lit by a fire in the marble fireplace, he kicked shut the door with enough force to rattle the windows. Then, crossing the floor he ruined his splendid display of bad temper by settling her slender body on the canopied bed with a gentleness that was utterly foreign to him.

On the point of straightening, Tane was halted as

Laylah's thick tangle of lashes slowly lifted to expose the weary amusement shimmering in her dark eyes.

"Feel better?"

"No," he growled, his throat tightening with a terrifying relief as Laylah struggled back to consciousness. "The next time you try to take off without me I'll have you locked in chains and thrown into Victor's dungeon."

"You're not the boss of me."

He snorted as he settled on the mattress next to her, his hand instinctively reaching to brush over her pale cheek.

"You sound like a spoiled human."

"It doesn't make it any less true." Her voice was weak, but her magnificent eyes flashed with stubborn independence. "I don't have to take orders from you."

His frigid power blasted through the air as he recalled his alarm when he'd discovered she'd slipped away.

Victor had been forced to physically restrain him from charging through the dark in pursuit, and it was only because Juliet assured him she knew exactly where to find Laylah and the obnoxious gargoyle that he wasn't currently ripping London apart brick by soggy brick.

"You're not that naïve, Laylah." He leaned down until they were nose to nose, absorbing her scent that was becoming fatally addictive. "There's no way in hell I'm going to let you blindly charge into danger."

Her hands lifted to press against his chest. He shuddered as the heat of her palms seared against his skin, melting his icy fury and replacing it with a far more pleasurable sensation.

"It's none of your business."

He stole a brief, starkly possessive kiss. "Have you forgotten that you're my prisoner?"

She flexed her fingers, digging into his flesh with just enough pain to bring pleasure.

Tane groaned, lust slamming into him with an intensity that might have been shocking if he'd been in his right senses.

But he wasn't.

And he hadn't been since he'd gone on the chase of a mongrel Jinn.

"I think you have that backward. You're my prisoner." She sucked in a startled breath as he grabbed the hoodie and with one smooth motion had it yanked off her body and tossed on a dainty Louis XIV chair across the room. "What the hell are you doing?"

He curled back his lips to reveal his elongated fangs that throbbed with need.

Gods, he *ached* to taste her.

Never had his hunger been so acute.

Not even during those dark days when he'd retreated from the world, feeding only when his body compelled him to seek substance.

But he'd just watched her collapse in his arms after a brutal skirmish with a vicious vampire and a mage who had some mysterious connection to her past.

His primal need to protect her overcame the lust for her blood on his tongue.

Amazing.

Of course, there was more than one way of satisfying his hunger.

Lowering his head he used his fangs to slice through the thin top, liquid heat pouring through him as the yellow fabric fell to the side, revealing the bit of lace that did nothing to hide the swell of her breasts.

"If we're going to fight then we might as well do it in comfort."

Her eyes widened, but it wasn't fear that flared in the

midnight depths. He smiled as her ready arousal filled the air with a heady perfume.

"No, Tane," she breathed. "We can't."

"We've already proven we can," he said, his voice deepening, thick with need. "With spectacular results."

Around him he sensed Victor's clan bustling through the manor house, no doubt discussing the best strategy of dealing with the traitorous Lady Havassy and her mage sidekick. Not to mention the threat of a looming apocalypse.

Discussions Tane should be a part of.

Instead he was wholly focused on the woman who challenged him on every level.

He needed . . . what?

To prove his dominance? To mark his territory? To reassure himself that she was unharmed and back in his arms where she belonged?

Something knotted in his chest.

Something that was too dangerous to contemplate.

As if battling her own inner demons, Laylah lifted her hands to knot her fingers in his hair, attempting to hide the raw need he could sense spreading through her body.

"I have . . ." She caught the betraying words. "Things I have to do."

His lips twisted. Would she ever trust him with her secrets?

"Collecting the child?"

Her breath caught at his blunt question. "How did you know?"

"Levet was urged to confess what happened after you snuck away."

Her eyes narrowed. "Urged or forced?"

He shrugged, his fingers skimming along the lacy line of her bra before headed down the warm satin of her stomach. Pure male satisfaction raced through him as he felt her muscles contract in pleasure beneath his light caress, even as he growled in frustration at the amulet that hung around her neck.

He could savor her delectable heat and her rising passion, but the unique aroma of fresh spring rain was hidden by the witch's spell.

For reasons he couldn't explain, he wanted to be wrapped in her distinctive smell.

"I've made preparations for our return to the States," he assured her, his fingers making short work of the button fly so he could tug off her jeans. With a toss they landed next to the sweatshirt.

Her eyes flashed with annoyance, but she made no effort to halt the soft brush of his hand over her bare thigh.

"I don't need you making my travel plans. I'll return the same way I came."

"Brave talk, but you forget that we're bound together." He leaned down to nip at the lobe of her ear, not bothering to mention his awareness of her had nothing to do with her magical powers, and everything to do with a male fascinated with a particular woman. "I can feel your lingering weakness."

She stiffened, as if troubled by the knowledge he could so easily detect her vulnerabilities.

"I'm not powerless."

"No," he was swift to agree, his lips tasting a path down the temptation of her throat. Laylah was fragile. Not only had she exhausted herself fighting off the bitch vampire and mage, but she was mentally traumatized by her introduction to her supposed family from hell. Tane, however, understood her need to appear strong. It was a part of who she was. And for all his sins, he would never crush her spirit. "Never powerless, but you're drained and in need of rest."

She stirred as his fingers found the edge of her panties, her hip pressing against the thickening length of his erection as her lips parted on a soft moan of anticipation.

Still, she struggled against her body's need.

"I don't have the luxury of resting. If those freaks get their hands on the baby . . ."

"Laylah, Victor has a fleet of private jets at his disposal," he interrupted in rough tones, abruptly rolling to press her into the mattress. He didn't want her able to think when he was seducing her. He wanted her consumed by her lust. Consumed by him. He buried his face in the tender curve where her neck met her shoulder. "One is currently being prepared for us."

She gripped his shoulders, arching in silent invitation as he jerked off his khakis before settling between her legs.

"Vampires fly?" she husked.

He lightly scraped his fangs down her collarbone, using his centuries of experience to unhook her lacy bra and pull it away without her realizing it was missing.

"Only on planes that are built to protect us and with loyal servants that can stand guard," he absently answered, his attention fully intent on the soft mounds of her breasts that were crested with dusky pink nipples already beaded in anticipation. "We'll be in Chicago within a matter of hours."

"Fine . . ."

Her words ended in a breathy sigh as he took one of the nipples in his mouth, a groan of approval rumbling through him as her hands skimmed down his back, filling an aching need deep inside him.

Gods, he was a vampire not a Were.

Why the hell did he crave her touch with such intensity?

"Of course, it will be another hour before it's ready to depart," he said, tracing the underside of her breast with his tongue before heading lower.

So far as he was concerned the private plane could wait an eternity.

She lifted herself onto her elbows, a flush of desire staining her ivory skin as she watched him kiss his way down the curve of her hip, pulling her tiny panties out of his path.

"I need to speak with Victor," she said, her voice a strangled gasp.

He settled between her legs, nibbling the satin skin of her inner thigh.

"Why?"

She swallowed a scream as he shifted to run his tongue through her damp heat.

"My . . ." She gripped the bedspread, her breath coming in shallow pants. "My reasons don't concern you."

Tane chuckled. His hands shifted to press against her lower stomach, keeping her locked in place as he licked and nibbled and at last sucked on the tiny jewel that hid the source of her pleasure.

She moaned, flopping back on the pillows with a boneless motion.

Still he continued to tease her. Only when he sensed she was on the edge of her climax did he surge upward, looming over her with the tip of his cock nestled at her entrance.

"Do you find it a moral imperative to argue with everyone or is it just me?" he demanded.

She reached up to wrap his hair around her hand, jerking him down for a kiss that was raw with feminine need.

"I don't like being bullied."

With one smooth thrust he buried himself deep inside her, their matching groans of satisfaction filling the air.

"There will be no mistake if I decide to bully you, my sweet Laylah," he rasped.

He devoured her lips in a kiss of unrestrained urgency, slowly arching his hips before sliding back into her tight sheathe. He shuddered as her hips lifted to meet his thrust, her tongue tangling with his in a dance of erotic pleasure.

Someday he intended to spend hours seducing this complex, impossible female.

No, not hours . . . weeks, perhaps months.

But for now the lust was too new, too potent.

It was a fire that threatened to consume him.

Crushing the urge to sink his fangs deep in her tender flesh, Tane instead concentrated on the exquisite sensation of plunging into the welcoming heat of her body. Muttering words in the language of his ancestors that he hadn't used in centuries, he set a driving pace that had them both spiraling toward an explosive release.

Savoring Laylah's rasping attempts to regain her breath, he waited for her tiny shudders to ease before rolling to the side, gathering her tightly in his arms.

He wasn't cuddling.

Unmated vampires didn't do cuddling.

They had sex. Period. End of story.

But, Laylah was not like his usual lovers and he wouldn't put it past her to try and bolt despite the staggering pleasure they'd just shared. He didn't have the time or energy to chase her down.

Satisfied with the dubious explanation, Tane pressed her head into the curve of his shoulder, once again ruing the amulet that disguised her sweet scent.

"Now, tell me why you want to speak with Victor," he commanded.

She stiffened, but astonishingly she didn't try to struggle out of his possessive grip.

Not that he was stupid enough to believe she'd conceded defeat. No. This was merely a temporary reprieve. One that would last only as long as she believed she needed him.

Tilting back her head, she met his searching gaze.

"My . . ." She halted, considering her words. "A woman claiming to be my mother is being held captive. She must be found and released."

"I know." He cupped her cheek in his hand. "Victor has promised to send Uriel in search of the female."

He didn't add that it would be several days before Victor could negotiate with the local coven to cast a spell to find where the female was hidden.

Her brows snapped together. "Without even asking if I might want to join in the hunt? Typical." Her expression made Tane glad there wasn't a sharpened stake handy. "She's my mother."

He met her accusing glare without flinching, refusing to apologize. She could have her pride, but he'd learned a brutal lesson in allowing emotions to overcome common sense. Until Laylah had the opportunity to calm down and fully investigate what she'd discovered in the cellar of the London town house she wasn't going to be making the decisions.

"No, you had it right the first time," he said. "She's a strange female who claims to be your mother."

Her lips thinned. "Do you have a point?"

"There's a good chance the woman is nothing more than clever bait."

"Bait for what?"

"You."

She shook her head. "That's impossible."

"Why? Boris and Natasha made it clear they were willing to go to any lengths to get their grubby hands on the child." He smiled at the surprise etched on her face at his reference to Bullwinkle. No doubt she assumed he spent his leisure hours sharpening swords and eating children for breakfast. She wouldn't be alone. "How better than to blackmail you into simply handing the babe over in exchange for your long lost mother?"

"Maybe, but unless they're prophets, they couldn't have known I would be coming to the town house," she countered. "Let alone hiding in their cellar so they could spring the trap."

"The gargoyle admitted that the mage sensed your presence."

"Only after we were there. They didn't know we were coming," she stubbornly insisted, a part of her obviously wanting to believe in the vision of her mother. "There was no way they could have set up such an elaborate hoax."

His thumb brushed her cheek. Eventually they would have to discuss the child she was protecting. And of course, the Oracles who were still a threat (and who might very well castrate him when they discovered he'd kept a Jinn mongrel hidden), but one problem at a time.

For now he had to make certain she didn't slip away on some wild goose chase for the promise of a mother, who more than likely was a trap waiting to happen.

"A powerful mage can create any number of illusions with a wave of his hand. It would be easy to fool you."

Her hand landed against his chest with enough force to have broken a rib if he weren't a vampire.

"So now I'm stupid as well as impulsive?"

He scrambled for damage control.

Dammit. For centuries he'd chosen women who wanted one thing from him.

And it didn't include charm.

He shifted his hand to cup her chin, holding her gaze as he leaned down to brush his lips over her mouth.

"You haven't learned not to care," he husked. "A dangerous weakness that others will eagerly exploit."

She shivered, her lips melting in ready response, but she firmly pushed against his chest, her eyes dark with a concern he sensed she didn't want to feel.

"How does Uriel intend to discover if she's real or not?"

Happy to offer a distraction from her troubles, Tane stroked his lips down the line of her jaw.

"Juliet cast some sort of spell over the scrying bowl that allowed Uriel to catch the female's scent. Once he's close enough, he'll find her."

The hand that pressed against his chest softened, exploring the rigid line of his muscles as his tongue discovered the sensitive spot at the base of her throat.

"And what of Marika and the mage?" she managed to husk.

"Victor has his finest warriors searching for them, but I doubt they'll find more than smoke and mirrors. The damned mage will be able to cover his escape with magic." He lifted his head, studying her pale face with a brooding gaze. "They'll be looking for you."

"They've been looking for me for a long time. And they aren't alone." She sent him a deliberate frown. "I could lead a freaking demon parade down Fifth Avenue."

The truth of her words stirred his temper.

Logically he understood.

She was a dangerous mongrel that had been banned by the Commission. She was harboring some mysterious child that held the blood of the Dark Lord and the potential to bring the world to a crashing halt.

On top of it, she was a gorgeous, sensually alluring female who would cause every unmated demon in her vicinity to trail after her like dogs in heat.

Yeah, he got the whole parade thing, but it royally pissed him off.

"They can't have you." His hand stroked down her back, pressing her against his hardening cock in a display of blatant male possession. "You're mine now."

Her eyes narrowed to dangerous slits, then, with one smooth motion she rolled him onto his back so she could perch on top of him.

"Yours?"

His hands clamped on her hips, potent heat spreading through him at her brazen challenge.

"Mine."

Deliberately she rubbed her sex along the granite length of his erection, smiling as a groan was wrenched from his throat. His fingers dug into her flesh. He'd never seen anything so beautiful as the sight of her poised above him, her cheeks flushed with desire and her expression one of defiance.

"Even in England the feudal system is long gone," she warned, shifting until the tip of him barely penetrated her hot, slick channel. "Females are no longer property to be purchased and traded among the men folk."

His hand skimmed up the arch of her back, urging her down so he could suckle one of her puckered nipples. A voice in the back of his mind was whispering a warning at his endless craving for this female.

It was a voice that was easily drowned by the tidal wave of exquisite pleasure as she slowly impaled herself on his aching erection. Scorching heat blasted through him and his eyes rolled into the back of his head.

Shit.

Nothing should ever feel this good.

"Human laws have no meaning for a vampire," he muttered, lashing the tip of her nipple with his tongue, careful not to break her skin with his fully erect fangs.

That business of claiming her as his own . . .

That was a little too close to the whole mating thing.

And while he might be deeply in lust, he wasn't stupid enough to risk becoming permanently entangled with any woman, let alone one that was destined to get herself, and anyone standing next to her, in a shitload of trouble.

She rolled her hips, taking him even deeper. "What about the laws of common decency?"

He moaned, his hands shifting to frame her face so he could capture her lips in a branding kiss.

"I prefer indecency."

She laughed softly, obviously pleased with her sexual power over him.

"I thought there was a plane waiting for us?"

He traced her lower lip with the tip of his tongue, his back arching as she rode him with a slow, deliberate pace.

"Victor will send word when it's prepared for takeoff."

She caught her breath as he lifted his hips to meet her downward stroke.

"Do they have coffins in first class?" she taunted.

"No, but I'm hoping they have tiny genie bottles for your comfort. I intend to devote the entire flight imagining you in a pair of those flimsy harem pants and tiny top sprawled on a round velvet divan."

He growled in approval as her carnal pace quickened, her fingers scratching down his chest in punishment for his fantasy of *I Dream of Jeannie*.

But who could blame him?

She was a Jinn. What male wouldn't imagine her locked in a conveniently portable bottle, dressed to seduce, and devoting her existence to waiting for him to conjure her?

"It will be a cold day in hell before you ever see me in harem pants," she snarled, her back arching as her climax began to build.

His eyes smoldered with wicked promise, his tongue following the tantalizing shadow of her jugular vein.

"I can wait."

Caine's lair outside of Chicago had been abandoned for years, but thanks to the large fortune he'd paid the local coven the spells of illusion were still firmly intact, shrouding the two story brick farmhouse with a vision of a decaying barn. There were also a number of revulsion hexes planted around the yard to deter unwelcomed intruders, and a few curses for those who ignored the various "no trespassing" signs.

As a result, the house was as pristine as the day he had walked out and locked the door behind him.

Not even a cobweb dared to mar the perfection.

Caine had intended to collapse once he'd reached his most private home.

Over the past few days he'd played a dangerous game of chicken with the King of Weres, battled a zombie Were who'd used and abused him for years, and been killed by a demon lord who had rammed through him with the force of a nuclear blast.

And if that wasn't enough, when he'd come back to life it was to realize that he was no longer a mere cur, but a full blooded Were and that he'd somehow become the default guardian for a genetically altered female Were who'd been held prisoner by the demon lord and was a priceless prophet. The rarest, most coveted creature in the world.

Yeah, no real shocker he needed some serious R and R.

But, throwing away the empty sacks of fast food he'd consumed on the way to the lair, Caine made no effort to head for his bedroom.

Instead he scrubbed his hands through the short blond hair that when combined with his pale blue eyes and naturally bronzed skin (that was currently revealed to full advantage by his lack of a shirt and the worn jeans that rode low on his slender hips) made most people think of him as a harmless surfer dude.

It was an image he encouraged until his wolf was ready to come out and play.

Smiling wryly, he watched the slender female who prowled through the kitchen with an intensity that was scaring the shit out of him.

Not that she wasn't worth eyeballing.

Her hair wasn't just blond, it shimmered like the purest silver despite being annoyingly wrenched into a braid that fell nearly to her waist. Her skin was a perfect alabaster, so smooth and satin it would tempt a saint to sin. And her wide, innocent eyes were the shade of summer grass, astonishingly flecked with gold.

Then there was that flawless body.

Even covered by frayed jeans and shapeless sweatshirt there was no mistaking the slender curves and lean, well-toned muscles that assured him she was no delicate flower.

She was a woman who could handle a wolf in full heat.

His nose flared as he sucked in her sweet lavender scent, his body tense with the urge to pounce.

Ah, the things he could do . . .

Instead he leaned against the counter, his arms folded over his chest as he watched her tentatively stroke her hand over the toaster before moving onto the microwave, absently pushing the buttons on the control panel.

There was nothing fancy about the farmhouse. The kitchen was decorated with blue and white tiles with the mandatory gingham curtains and a plain wooden table and chairs in the center of the floor. The sort of homey atmosphere prized in the Midwest.

Cassandra, however, was inspecting her surroundings with a fascination that should have been reserved for a trip to the space station.

Understandable.

She'd been trapped in a dark, dank cave for God knew how many years. Even the simplest technology had to seem astonishing.

So why did he find her distraction with his home perilously close to an insult?

Because he wanted all that feminine fascination reserved solely for him?

Giving a sharp jerk of his head, Caine forced himself away from the counter, moving to stand directly in Cassandra's path.

"Do you intend to spend the entire night pacing the floors?"

With her peculiar habit of taking the world, and everyone in it, at face value, she paused to consider his question.

"I'm not certain. Do I need to inform you of my decision now?"

He rubbed the back of his neck, vaguely recalling his mother's bitter predictions.

"I was warned my sins would land me in hell," he muttered.

The green eyes studied him with an unwavering interest. "You're upset."

"Dying tends to sour my mood."

"You were only dead a few minutes and now you have what you've always desired," she pointed out with perfect logic. "You're a full-blooded Were."

"Yeah, I got the memo."

He shuddered, still adjusting to the sensations that crashed through him. It was like the floodgates had been jerked open to release a torrent of raw power. It would be days, if not weeks before he could become accustomed to his newly heightened senses and the strange cravings that gripped him.

"Then why aren't you pleased?" she softly demanded.

He grimaced at her puzzlement. It was true he had never made a secret of his lust to gain the gifts of a Were. What creature wouldn't want to be stronger and faster and downright superior?

And, of course, there was always the whole immortality thing.

But when he'd received the visions that had promised he was destined to become a pureblood, he hadn't counted on the sacrifice.

"Because it . . ."

"What?"

He squeezed his hands into tight balls of frustration. "I thought my destiny was to unlock the secret of transforming cur blood into pure Were," he bit out. "Not being genetically altered because a whacked-out demon lord rammed through me in an attempt to escape into another dimension."

She tilted her head to the side, somberly considering his words.

"You regret that you won't be able to share your wondrous transformation with others?"

He snorted at the naïve question. Obviously Cassandra hadn't figured out yet that he was a selfish bastard who'd never done a thing in his life that didn't benefit him in one way or another.

"I'm not Gandhi."

"Who?"

He heaved a pained sigh. "Never mind."

"I still don't understand why you're upset.

"I wanted to fulfill my visions with science, not magic."

"Why?"

"A gift given by magic is never without cost. The universe always manages to extract a payment. Christ." He shuddered. "I can't even imagine what the cosmic debt for immortality will be."

"It's too late for regrets." She frowned at his sharp laugh. "Did I say something funny? I'm never sure."

"I've been saying that it's too late for regrets for the past decade," he muttered.

"Ah." She turned to wander toward the nearby window, studying the untamed nature that surrounded them. "And yet you still have them."

"I . . ." His mouth dropped in shock as Cassandra absently pulled the sweatshirt over her head and dropped it on the floor. The jeans swiftly followed, leaving her standing in nothing more than a plain white bra and matching panties. "Holy shit, what are you doing?"

She turned to meet his eyes that glowed with the fire of his wolf, seemingly surprised by his strangled question.

"My clothes smell bad." She wrinkled her nose. "And I need a bath."

Hot, savage lust slammed into Caine, nearly sending him to his knees.

The kind of lust that could drive a man to madness.

Which was the only reason he was spinning away from the slender elegance of her near naked form and was gripping the counter with enough force to crack the marble top.

He'd made one bad decision after another over the past few decades.

It was time he started thinking with his actual brain.

"Yeah, well, as much as I appreciate an impromptu strip-tease by a gorgeous female, my self-control is non-existent, so I suggest you head upstairs," he growled.

He heard her sniff the air, easily scenting his arousal. "You want me?"

Want?

His cock was pressing against his jeans with enough force to cut off his blood supply.

With one fluid motion he was whirling, crossing the floor to press the provoking woman against the wall. He distantly remembered to temper his newfound strength, rubbing his face along the curve of her neck as he absorbed her unique scent.

"Correction, I fucking ache for you," he rasped, his body on fire with need. "But right now we're both in a crazy place. When I take you as my lover it will be when I have nothing on my mind but how much I want to please you."

Caine wasn't sure what he'd expected, but it certainly wasn't to discover himself lying flat on his back, with Cassandra bending over him with a smug smile.

"You'll become my lover when I say and not a minute sooner," she assured him.

Caine rolled over just in time to watch her sashay from

the room, the sway of her tight little ass sending his blood pressure through the roof.

Shit.

Who the hell was Cassandra?

An isolated, cave-dwelling prophet who'd been irrevocably damaged by a demented demon lord?

Or a ruthlessly seductive female who'd just given him a smack down with frightening ease?

Rolling to his feet, Caine rubbed the lump on the back of his throbbing skull. Karma was definitely a bitch, he decided, heading toward the guest bedroom upstairs.

Entering the room decorated in shades of yellow, Caine opened the walnut armoire and pulled out a pair of jeans and plain T-shirt.

Like every other cur, Caine always kept a surplus of clothing available in his various lairs.

Who knew when he might feel the urge to shift?

Of course now, all that was in the past.

As a Were he would have the ability to control his shifts.

Shaking his head at the disturbing thought, Caine entered the attached bathroom and stripped off his grubby jeans before stepping into the shower.

After hours spent digging out of the tunnels that had collapsed on top of him and Cassandra, he was in dire need of hot water and soap that was made to scrub off the filth, not make him smell like flowers.

He'd just dried off and was in the process of pulling on a pair of jeans when the door to the bedroom was thrown open and his houseguest entered with a scowl.

"Dammit, Cassie." He jerked up his jeans, his body hardening at the sight of the tight jeans that clung lovingly to her slender curves and the casual tank top that hinted at the soft swell of her breasts. Her damp silver hair tumbled freely down her back, making his fingers curl with the need to stroke through the silken length. "If we're going to be sharing a house we obviously need to establish a few ground rules."

She ignored his chiding, her expression distracted. "We need to go."

"Go? Go where?"

Her hand lifted in a vague wave. "East."

A chill inched down his spine. He hadn't saved this female's life only to have her toss it aside on a whim.

"No way. Until I figure out how to keep hidden the fact you're a prophet, you're staying here."

She shook her head, her hand unconsciously pressing against her stomach.

Caine's heart twisted at the memory of the small mark of the demon lord that marred the satin skin just below her belly button. The shimmering tattoo made him long to howl in fury.

Cassandra belonged to him.

No one else could have her.

"I have to . . ."

Crossing the carpet, he took her shoulders in a gentle grasp. "To what?"

Without warning she headed toward the door. "Come with me."

Caine paused long enough to pull on his T-shirt. Usually he made it a rule never to keep a woman waiting, but he already knew he wasn't going to like what was coming.

Stepping into the hall he padded down the hardwood floor and entered the master bedroom, not at all surprised his guest had taken command of the finest room in the house. She might have been a prisoner for the past several years, but she was all woman.

She skirted past the heavy, walnut bed that had been carved by wood sprites and pointed at the wall painted a soft shade of ivory.

"Look," she commanded.

Caine swore at the sight of the shimmering hieroglyphic that swirled just above the surface of the wall.

He didn't know a damned thing about prophecies, but he had seen the peculiar symbols lining the walls of Cassandra's cave. They were visions of the future.

Visions that powerful demons would commit wholesale slaughter to get their greedy hands on.

"Already? You couldn't take a few days off?"

Her lips tightened at his impulsive words. "It's not a faucet. I can't turn it on and off."

He bit back a sigh. Of course she couldn't.

No more than he could head for the front door and run as far as possible from this woman who was destined to lead him straight to disaster.

Hell, he'd already died.

What could be worse?

Shutting his mind to the numerous, unpleasant answers to his question, Caine reached out to touch the swirling symbol.

"What is it?"

Cassie shifted closer, as if unconsciously seeking his comfort. Without hesitation he wrapped his arm around her shoulder and tucked her against him.

"Gemini," she whispered.

"The zodiac sign?"

"The alpha and the omega."

"Still too vague."

She shivered. "A child."

"Yeah, that would've been my next guess." He brushed

a reassuring kiss over the top of her head, the tender gesture disturbingly natural. "What does it mean?"

"A warning." The stunning green eyes held a fear that twisted Caine's gut. "The child must be protected."

"Protected from what?"

"The darkness." She shuddered. "Evil."

"Where is the mysterious child?"

"I'm not sure."

His lips twisted. Exactly what he'd expected.

"Great."

Tilting back her head, Cassie stabbed him with a fierce gaze. "Caine, he *must* be protected."

Chapter 10

It was the middle of the night when the small jet landed on the private airstrip in a remote field south of Chicago.

With a smooth efficiency it was quickly whisked into the small hangar, and the landing lights switched off before attracting unwanted curiosity.

Vampires made drug runners look like amateurs when it came to "flying below the radar."

Laylah tossed aside the glossy magazine that had been filled with painfully gaunt females who were dressed in ridiculous outfits and wearing shoes that looked like torture devises. Of course, the spiked heels would come in handy if she had to spend any more time in the company of vampires. So long as the heels were made of wood.

Something to consider.

The wheels came to a halt, and Laylah was on her feet, moving past the low leather seats that were arranged around small tables and set to easily view the flat screen monitor on the wall.

The elegant décor was carried into the gourmet kitchen and cocktail bar that was fully stocked with delicacies to tempt the most discerning demon. No doubt the bedrooms where Tane was safely tucked in a sealed compartment were equally lavish, but she'd sternly refused to allow herself to leave the forward cabin.

She wasn't a hypocrite.

Sex with Tane had been . . .

She shifted through a number of adjectives, but none of them came close to describing the explosive pleasure of Tane's touch.

The man had serious skills between the sheets.

No, she couldn't make herself regret giving into temptation, but she also couldn't ignore her problems that were piling up with frightening speed.

A woman who might or might not be her mother who was being held captive in an unknown location.

A crazy-ass aunt in league with a demented mage who were no doubt hot on her trail.

A child that was soon going to be considered the freaking jackpot for every demon hoping to curry favor with the Dark Lord.

And a ruthless vampire who she suspected intended to turn her over to the Commission the minute she let down her guard.

Yep, it all added up to problems with a capital P.

The door to the jet was tugged open by a uniformed vampire and without missing a step she was headed down the metal stairs and glancing about the hangar. It was larger than she'd first suspected and as bright as day with fluorescent lights running the length of the curved ceiling. It was also immaculate. A testament to Victor's control over his servants, even an ocean away.

Which meant they'd already been ordered not to let her escape.

She grimaced, ignoring the nearby exit as the intoxicating scent of Tane spiced the air. On some level she'd known she would never have time to flee, even with him locked in the private compartment.

It was still annoying as hell.

There was the sound of flapping wings as Levet landed at her side, his ugly little face pinched with displeasure.

"Worst. Airline. Ever," he muttered, waving his pudgy arms. "No drinks, no peanuts, no in-flight movie. Not even a sexy stewardess waiting to induct me into the Mile High Club."

Laylah smiled despite her bad mood. "You were a statue for most of the flight."

Levet sniffed. "All the more reason to have suitable accommodations when I awoke."

"I warned you to leave him in London," Tane's dark voice wrapped around her, making her flesh prickle with awareness. Damned vampire. "Of course, Victor did warn me not to even consider slipping away without him."

Laylah stubbornly refused to turn and watch Tane's approach.

What was the point?

Her body was already giving her a play-by-play.

The soft tread of his bare feet against the cement floor. The cool wash of his power that filled the air. The male scent that made her think of things that were illegal in some states.

Then he was standing at her side, his golden skin glowing in the overhead lights, and his face impossibly beautiful.

Her heart gave an odd, dangerous lurch before she was squashing the sensation.

The vampire was drop-dead, heart-stopping, Johnny Depp gorgeous. And of course, there was that whole bad-boy thing with the mohawk and huge dagger stuck in the waistband of his shorts.

Not that he needed either to be a badass.

It was chiseled into his DNA.

Was it any wonder when he strolled around wearing nothing more than a pair of khaki shorts her hormones were shot into hyperdrive?

Heat washed through her as she met the liquid honey gaze, but before she could make a complete fool of herself, Tane was abruptly whirling toward the back of the hangar, shifting to stand between her and whatever he'd sensed approaching.

"What is that stench?" Levet complained, his eyes widening in sudden surprise. "Ah, I should have known. The King of I-have-a-bigger-stick-stuck-up-my-derrière-than-you is approaching."

Laylah frowned. "Who?"

"The Anasso." Tane shot a warning glare at the gargoyle. "You'll show proper respect or I'll have your head mounted on my wall, gargoyle."

"Shit." Laylah didn't think. She whirled on her heel and took off.

Two steps later, Tane had her by the arm and spinning about to meet his searching gaze.

"Where are you going?"

"Anywhere that isn't here." She gritted, futilely struggling against his hold. "Maybe you've forgotten I'm considered the equivalent of Typhoid Mary among the demon world, but I can promise you the King of Vampires hasn't. He'll consider it his duty to hand me over to the Oracles."

"Laylah, it's too late to run."

Her eyes narrowed. "Damn you. You led me straight into a trap."

His brows snapped together, like he was offended. "No, Laylah. I didn't contact Styx."

"Yeah right. You expect me to believe he just happened

to make a royal appearance at a tiny airport in the middle of nowhere?"

"Tane speaks the truth."

A voice echoed through the hangar, the air so thick with frigid power Laylah could barely breathe.

Holy shit.

Talk about making an entrance.

With her heart lodged in her throat, Laylah forced herself to turn. And was terrified all over again.

But who wouldn't be?

Styx, King of all the Vampires, was a towering brute. He easily topped six foot five, with shoulders that looked like they should be registered in different counties. He was dressed in black leather matched with heavy shit-kickers that would have given Tim Gunn an ulcer, and his raven hair was pulled into a braid that fell to the back of his knees.

But it wasn't the whole *Blade*-vibe that made the hair on the back of her neck stand up and her innate powers stir in warning.

It was the grim, bronzed face that hinted of Aztec ancestors and the dark eyes that held an ancient knowledge. There was a cruelty etched in his handsome features that warned this vampire hadn't earned his position as Anasso because of some stupid popularity contest.

He was the biggest, baddest, most ruthless demon going. Period.

Strolling to stand directly in front of her, Styx turned his head toward Tane, a raven brow flicking upward as the younger vampire placed a protective arm around her shoulders.

"He was not the one to inform me of your imminent arrival, nor did he warn me that he intended to journey to Victor's territory with a creature he was commanded to capture," the Anasso drawled. "Something we'll discuss in full detail at a more appropriate moment."

Laylah stiffened. Dammit. It was moronic to be offended, but she was freaking sick of being treated as if she didn't have feelings. Or pride.

"Creature?"

Tane's arm tightened around her. "Laylah, maybe you should let me handle this."

Styx's power thickened until Laylah felt as if it might flay the skin from her body.

"You seek to challenge me, Charon?" he asked, oh so softly.

To his credit, Tane didn't flinch. His manner, however, was one of wary respect.

Smart vampire.

"I request the opportunity for an audience."

Styx shot a brief glance toward Laylah. "Intriguing." He paused before returning his attention to Tane. "And impressive. Not many vampires are suicidal enough to dangle a forbidden half-breed beneath the noses of the Oracles."

"That wasn't my intention."

"I'm relieved to hear it."

Laylah parted her lips to inform the offensive duo that it was rude to talk about her as if she weren't there, but before she could descend into complete madness, Levet charged forward, his wings flapping.

"Hey, where's the Starbucks? A gargoyle cannot be expected to be civilized before his vanilla *dolce latte*." He planted his fists on his hip. "And what about my Cinnabon? Where are the Cinnabons?"

Styx snapped humongous fangs at the gargoyle, but without warning the biting power eased and something that might have been resigned amusement flashed in the Anasso's dark eyes.

"You really do enjoy living on the edge," he told Tane in dry tones.

Tane snorted. "Victor threatened an international incident if I left him in London."

Styx shook his head. "Why me?"

There was the unmistakable scent of Were before a tiny woman with short blonde hair and green eyes that dominated her heart-shaped face entered the hangar and crossed to stand at Styx's side.

"Because you love me," she said with a dimpled smile.

The towering vampire scowled, but not even the dimmest demon could fail to notice the warm adoration that softened his expression.

"I do, but I thought I asked you to wait in the car?"

"You didn't ask, you commanded. And we both know how well I obey orders," she said pertly, turning to grab Laylah's hand. "Hi, you must be Laylah."

Laylah struggled to find her voice. Although she knew that she'd never met the pretty Were, for a moment she'd been convinced that it was Harley walking toward her.

Up close she could see the subtle differences between this woman and the female Were that Caine kept as a heavily protected guest at his home, but the resemblance was still stunning.

"You're . . ."

"Darcy," the woman supplied, her smile filled with a friendliness that put Laylah on instant guard. She had ample experience at being feared, loathed, and kicked when she was down. But kindness? Not so much. "Harley's twin sister."

"Where is she?" she asked. Harley had been left behind when Caine and Laylah had headed to Hannibal, but since the cur had been stupid enough to try and kidnap the King of Weres, Laylah was fairly certain everything had gone to hell. "Is she okay?"

"She's in Chicago." Darcy chuckled. "And I suppose she's okay considering she's just accepted the position as the Queen of Weres."

Laylah's mouth fell open.

Now that was a shocker.

Caine had always been careful to keep Laylah isolated from his pack, but she'd heard the rumors that the King of Weres had murdered Harley's family and intended to include Harley in his path of destruction once he found her.

Obviously the rumors were wrong, or Harley was a thrill-seeker on a massive scale.

"She mated with Salvatore?"

Darcy nodded. "Crazy, isn't it? But, she's convinced she loves the arrogant pureblood."

"I'm very happy for her," Laylah murmured, telling herself the pang in the center of her heart wasn't envy.

Didn't she just do an inventory of her pile of problems?

Having a mate would only be the cherry on the top.

"She's been worried about you."

Laylah blinked. She and Harley had an odd, distant connection. But they hadn't been BFFs.

"Really?"

"She made me promise that I would make sure that you weren't being bullied by a bunch of overzealous vampires."

"I have done my best to protect her," Levet announced, waddling to lean against Laylah's leg in a strangely touching gesture. "But you know how impossible vampires can be."

Darcy glanced toward her mate. "Intimately."

Styx reached to brush a tender hand down Darcy's cheek. "My dear, perhaps we can finish this conversation in a more secure location?"

Laylah took an impulsive step backward, her momentary pleasure in knowing there were actually those who cared about her in the world forgotten in a tidal wave of fear.

"No."

Tane tugged her back to his side, his body tightly coiled as if preparing to strike.

"Where do you intend to take her?" he growled.

"Easy, Tane." Styx lifted a hand, the motion making the medallion that hung around his neck glow in the overhead lights. "For now I merely have a few questions for Laylah. She will be safe in my lair."

Tane wasn't satisfied. "Have you contacted the Oracles?"

Styx narrowed his gaze, ready and willing for a pissing match.

"Don't press your luck, Charon."

"Oh, for goodness sake, come with me Laylah." Muttering under her breath at the stunning lack of intelligence among the male gender, Darcy hooked her arm through Laylah's and tugged her toward the nearest door. "We'll let the men huff and puff in privacy."

Laylah allowed herself to be led away. Any distance between her and the King of Vampires was welcome. But as soon as they stepped out of the hangar, she gently tried to pull free.

"I can't go with you." She absently glanced around the isolated field that had been carved out of a thick tangle of oak trees. It was a perfect spring night with a sky filled with stars, but Laylah was more interested in the stretch limo waiting near the road and three combat-ready vampires that stood guard. Hell, she knew there were ridiculous rumors that she was dangerous. But seriously? She returned her attention to Darcy. "I have . . ." She stopped to consider her words. "Someone is waiting for me."

Darcy smiled even as she hauled Laylah steadily toward the waiting car.

"At least join us for dinner," she urged. "I'm afraid it will be vegetarian, but I have a fabulous cook who makes a veggie lasagna to die for."

Before she could mouth a protest, Laylah found herself seated in the back of the elegant limo that could easily have hauled the Green Bay Packers.

"And to think I was afraid the Anasso would be ruthless," she muttered in resignation.

The Anasso's private study wasn't what Tane had been expecting.

Not that he'd been thinking the room would be lined with the heads of his enemies and decorated with medieval torture devises. But the polished mahogany furniture and delicate Persian carpet seemed way too civilized for the most powerful vampire in the world.

On the plus side, the vast estate on the outskirts of Chicago was wrapped in a dozen spells and hexes with an entire horde of vampires patrolling the grounds.

Nothing and nobody was coming in or out without Styx's say so.

For the moment Laylah was safe.

So why the hell was he pacing the pansy-ass carpet while battling the crazy impulse to tear through the monstrous house in search of the female?

Dammit. He'd encouraged Darcy to cart the reluctant Laylah off to enjoy a hot bath and dinner. He had business to discuss with Styx that was best done in private.

But now that they were alone in the study that was lead-lined and heavily shrouded in a cloaking spell, Tane couldn't concentrate on anything other than the fact he couldn't sense Laylah.

Even with her amulet on he'd been able to feel their strange connection. As if a part of her had burrowed someplace deep inside him.

He instantly jerked away from the unnerving thought. Nope. Not going there.

"Damn Tane, I feel like I'm standing in the middle of an electrical storm," Styx growled, breaking into his dangerous thoughts.

With a grimace Tane turned to watch the large vampire scrub a hand over the back of his neck. Christ. He hadn't realized his powers had been leaking.

"Sorry."

Styx leaned against the reinforced desk, folding his arms over his chest.

"It wouldn't be so disturbing if it didn't border on pleasure," he complained. "Even if I wasn't mated, you're not my type."

"Right back at you, chief."

Styx snorted, his fixed stare making Tane twitch. "I can hazard a guess at what your type is," he at last said.

"Don't go there."

"Pretty."

Tane's brows snapped together. "Gorgeous."

"Spunky."

"A pain-in-the-ass."

There was a deliberate pause. "Forbidden."

A cold dread settled in Tane's gut. "Is the Commission aware of her presence?"

Styx's expression tightened with concern. "Not from me, but that's not to say they haven't heard rumors of a half-breed. They won't be pleased to discover a vampire has helped to keep her hidden from them."

"I understand the risk."

"I doubt that."

Tane narrowed his gaze. "Just what are you implying?"

"Your mind is clouded."

"Ridiculous."

"Trust me, Tane, I recognize a vampire whose judgment is being compromised by his obsession for a certain female."

Tane had long ago learned to leash his hot temper. Nothing good happened when he let his anger control him. But, having his companion laying bare his uncharacteristic weakness was setting his teeth on edge.

"My judgment is not open for discussion."

Styx straightened from the desk, moving with blinding speed to pin Tane against the towering bookcase.

"I decide what's open for discussion, Charon," he growled. "Don't ever forget that."

Intent on their private power play, neither vampire noticed the door being opened. Not until a strange sizzle filled the air. With synchronized curses, both males whirled toward the door. The sizzle was the same sensation that warned of a lightning strike.

And vampires and lightning didn't mix.

Indifferent to the danger, Laylah stormed forward, her power making the lights flicker.

"What are you doing?" she demanded, facing the King of Vampires without fear.

Tane growled in appreciation, his gaze lingering on the soft flush that stained her ivory skin and the fire burning in her dark eyes.

She'd never been so beautiful.

A fiery warrior who charged to the rescue.

His rescue.

Astonishing.

He was feared, hated, and occasionally desired.

But never, ever protected.

Not surprisingly Styx shot him a disbelieving glance before the scent of burnt wiring had him crossing to his desk.

"Damn, that computer was brand new." He scowled at Tane, not hesitating to hold him responsible. "Her power isn't nearly so fun as yours."

Laylah blushed, but she refused to back down.

Typical.

"Why were you hurting Tane?"

Styx tossed the computer in the trash, his expression unreadable as he studied the bristling female.

"I need answers, Jinn," he said slowly. "If I can't get them from you then I'll get them from Tane. Whether he's willing or not."

Tane waited for Laylah to tell the Anasso to go to hell.

What did she care if he got a bully-beatdown?

She'd threatened to do it herself on more than one occasion.

Instead she folded her arms over her chest and glowered at Styx.

"Fine. What do you want to know?"

"Tell me what you know of your past."

Tane clenched his hands. With Laylah in the room he could once again feel the connection between them. A double-edged sword as it turned out. While his fierce impulse to make sure she was unharmed had eased, he was acutely aware of her pain at Styx's demand.

Still he kept his trap shut. As much as he might want to protect Laylah, he understood that the only means to keep her safe was to discover the truth of the child she sheltered.

"The first memories I have are of living on a farm in Australia with my foster mother," she grudgingly revealed.

"A demon?"

"Witch."

Styx narrowed his gaze at her clipped tone. "She was unkind to you?"

Tane edged closer as he sensed the sadness settle in Laylah's heart.

"No, she loved me as if I truly was her daughter," she said, her voice so soft it could barely be heard. "But if what I learned in London is true, then everything she said to me was a lie."

Styx perched on the edge of the desk. "The most dangerous creature in the world is a mother protecting her cub. She will lie, cheat, kill, and even die if necessary. Wouldn't you do the same?"

She frowned, as if considering Styx's blunt words. At last she gave a nod, a portion of her betrayal seeming to ease.

"I suppose."

"What happened to her?"

"One day I was collecting the herbs that Sadira used in her spells of illusion when I heard her scream." Her very lack of emotion revealed the depth of her wounds. Any healing was a long way off. "I rushed back to our house but I was too late. She was . . ." She was forced to halt and clear her throat. "She was lying on the porch with her throat sliced open."

"Dead?"

Laylah shuddered. "I've always assumed she was, there was so much blood, but I was captured by the mage before I could reach her."

Styx shot Tane a warning glare as he instinctively stepped toward Laylah.

Reluctantly Tane came to a halt. They were at the mercy of the Anasso. For whatever reason, he was willing to at least listen to Laylah, but Tane didn't fool himself. The moment Styx decided that she posed a danger to his vampires she would be sacrificed to the Oracles.

No fuss. No muss.

"Victor said the wizard goes by the name Sergei," Styx said.

Anger replaced her painful memories. "He never told me his name."

"What did he do to you?"

"Styx," Tane growled.

A sharp pain lashed through Tane as Styx punished him for his interference.

Just a tiny taste of what could be.

"The truth is all that will save her, Tane," the king warned. Then, he snapped his attention back to Laylah. "Well?"

Laylah stiffened, but she stubbornly refused to cower beneath the chilling gaze.

"I don't know exactly how the mage knocked me out, but when I woke up I was locked in a cell in northern Siberia."

"Siberia?" Tane echoed in surprise. "That's a little remote, isn't it?"

"Actually, it confirms what Victor has discovered about the mage," Styx answered.

"Victor already has intel on the bastard?" Tane was impressed. "That was quick."

"Victor is nothing if not efficient."

Efficient?

Yeah. He was also a brutal, ruthless, stone-cold killer.

It was no wonder the info superhighway had a direct route to his desk.

"What did he learn?"

"Sergei Krakov made his first appearance as a mystic in the royal court of Peter the Great." Styx's voice held the contempt all vampires held toward magic-users. "He provided himself with a life of luxury by producing a few minor 'miracles' and acting as a spiritual advisor, but from what Victor could uncover his true interest was in the ancient prophecies. His library is said to rival Jagr's."

"That's saying something," Tane murmured. It was rumored the ancient Goth's library had over twenty thousand books and scrolls.

"The mage is convinced he's destined to lead the world into a new era," Styx continued with a grimace. "Whatever the hell that means."

Tane rolled his eyes. Every half baked tyrant claimed to possess the ability to lead the world into a new era.

Laylah, however, pressed a hand to her chest, the scent of her fear spiking the air.

"The baby," she breathed. "He and my bat-shit crazy aunt think they can use the child to reincarnate the Dark Lord."

Styx nodded, clearly having been given a blow by blow account of Laylah's encounter with Marika from Victor.

"Where did the child come from?"

"I'm not entirely certain." She lifted a hand as Styx's eyes flashed with frustration. "Chill."

Styx arched a brow. "Chill?"

"You have that look that says you're planning to lecture me on keeping secrets . . . yadda, yadda, yadda."

"I never lecture," Styx tried to deny, only to backtrack at Tane's sharp burst of laughter. "I may *encourage* others to see things from my point of view."

"Well don't bother with your encouragements," Laylah said. "I spent my time with the mage either locked in a cell or so tightly wrapped in spells I could barely sense my surroundings."

"There must be something you remember," Styx prompted.

"I remember the mage entering the cell one morning and then the world went black." She rubbed her hands over her bare arms, as if she were suddenly cold. "When I woke up I was in a dark, frozen cave."

"A cave?" Styx frowned. "Where?"

Laylah lifted a shoulder. "I think it was north of where we were staying, but I can't say how far. I could probably find it if I shadow walked."

Styx and Tane exchanged silent glances. No one would leave a child that was rumored to possess a part of the Dark Lord lying around a cave.

No matter how remote.

"Were there any markings in the cave?" Styx asked.

She shook her head. "No, nothing but the mist."

Tane absently stroked the hilt of his dagger. "The same mist you used to take us to London?"

"In a way. When I enter the mists I sense a . . ." She halted, wrinkling her brow as she struggled for the right word. "Corridor. Like a highway at the edge of different worlds. This was more a bubble."

"As if it was self-contained?" Styx demanded.

"Exactly," Laylah agreed, clearly surprised by Styx's accurate description.

Tane didn't blame her.

Styx was so good at flexing his brawn that it was easy to forget he had a brain.

He did it on purpose, of course.

He liked for others to underestimate him.

Tane turned toward Styx. "Do you know where it is?"

"No, but I suspect I know *what* it is."

"Are you going to share?"

Styx shrugged. "I've only heard rumors, but it's said that full-blooded Jinn are capable of creating small fissures between worlds to hide their treasures."

Chapter 11

Laylah pressed a hand to her churning stomach. She didn't want to discuss the child. Especially not with a vampire who had yet to prove he wasn't preparing to hand her over to the Oracles.

Still, she had to admit that she needed information if she were going to protect the baby.

"It would explain why they needed a Jinn mongrel," Tane said, crossing his arms over his bare chest.

Styx nodded, his gaze never wavering from Laylah. Did the Anasso suspect she would disappear the moment she had the strength to shadow walk?

If he didn't he was an idiot.

"Was there anything but the child in the mist?"

She forced herself to think back to her time in the cave. She remembered the cold. The sort of cold that made her lungs ache. And the sense of barren emptiness, as if they were a great distance from the nearest town.

Then the mage had shoved her forward and she had tumbled into the swirling mist.

At the time she'd been terrified. She'd only shadow walked a handful of times and she'd briefly thought he had shoved her through the corridor and into another world.

"No." She shuddered, knowing that it probably would have been best if she'd left the baby where it had been hidden.

But how could she?

Even now she was convinced the child had reached out to touch her heart.

Either that or she was a raving lunatic.

A distinct possibility.

"Pity," Styx murmured, his brow furrowed. "It would have been nice if we had a clue to who stashed the child in the fissure."

"Surely it was a Jinn?" Tane challenged.

"Not necessarily." Styx held Laylah's gaze. "The Dark Lord . . ."

"The child is not evil," she interrupted, her hands clenched at her side.

"How can you be so certain?"

"I just know."

Styx didn't roll his eyes, but then again, he looked far from convinced. Big shocker there. *"I just know"* wasn't exactly a foolproof guarantee.

Thankfully he didn't press.

"So you took the babe from the mists." He picked up the previous thread of conversation. "Then what happened?"

"Sergei returned us to his home and locked me back in my cell with the child."

Styx pushed from the desk, not seeming to notice how he towered over her.

At least she assumed the looming was unintentional. Who knew with vampires?

"After going to such an effort to get his hands on the babe why would he leave it with you?" he rasped.

Laylah hesitated before grudgingly revealing the truth. "Because he's afraid of the stasis spell that's wrapped around the baby. As far as I know I'm the only one who can touch it."

Tane moved to stand next to Styx. Laylah's breath tangled in her throat.

Talk about an overabundance of riches.

Even furious with the vampires for their interfering, she was female enough to appreciate the sight of two of the finest beefcakes to ever walk the earth.

The tall Aztec with his forbidding beauty and unnerving power. And the bronzed, honey-eyed hunk who made a woman think of hot, tropical nights and exotic sex.

Lots and lots and lots of sex.

Tane shot her a knowing glance, but he was smart enough to keep any smartass comments to himself.

"It could have been a trigger," he said instead.

"Yes," Styx agreed.

Laylah shook off her strange fascination. "What's a trigger?"

"The most powerful demons can twist a spell to either recognize a specific person or a specific occurrence," Tane explained. "It could be that the spell was woven to bind the child to the first person to enter the mists."

Laylah had never heard of such a power, but then again, her foster mother had kept a lot of things hidden.

She thrust aside the memory of Sadira's pretense as she attempted to teach Laylah magic. All along she knew that her powers were that of a gypsy, not a witch.

Later she would sort through her tangled emotions.

"Whatever the cause, it made the mage nuts," she said. "I could hear his tantrum through the solid iron walls."

A cold smile touched Styx's mouth. "Is that when he let you go?"

"Are you kidding me?" Laylah scoffed. "The bastard never let me go. A few weeks after I found the baby

Sergei suddenly got spooked." She abruptly held up her hand as his lips parted with the predictable questions. "Don't ask me why. We weren't best buds who spent our nights braiding each others' hair and sharing our intimate secrets. One night he came into the cell and knocked me out." She shrugged. "I woke up in Rome."

"Rome?" Styx lifted a brow. "He took a risk choosing a city so heavily populated by demons."

She gave a sharp laugh as she remembered Sergei's panicked flight from his lair.

"I think his choice was made in haste rather than a well thought out escape plan." She shivered. "And I can't say that I blame him if it was my charming Aunt Marika on his tail. That woman would make anyone flee in horror."

Tane nodded in grim agreement, but Styx remained focused on his interrogation.

No doubt he was trained during the Spanish Inquisition.

"Did he have a private lair in Rome?"

Laylah shook her head. Her brief time in Rome hadn't been any more pleasant than being held hostage in the Siberian lair. She'd traded an iron cell for a spellbound closet and silver shackles that had come close to driving her over the edge.

"No, we stayed with the local witches," she said, her voice thick with remembered pain.

Styx's expression tightened as Tane moved to place a protective arm around Laylah's shoulders.

She didn't know if he disapproved of Tane touching a nasty mongrel, or if he didn't like public displays of affection.

And she didn't care. It felt good to have a little support.

"They allowed a forbidden demon into the coven?" the older vampire asked, indifferent to her feelings.

Hey, what was new?

"Sergei was careful to keep me hidden in his private rooms. Besides they were terrified of him. If it wasn't for Caine I would no doubt still be locked in that damned closet."

Tane shot her a startled frown. "The cur rescued you?"

She wrinkled her nose. "I'm not sure if rescue is the proper word. Let's say that we made a mutually beneficial bargain."

Tane's finger brushed her cheek, his touch comforting. "How did he find you?"

"One of the witches was his lover and she hoped to impress him with the 'Jeannie in the Closet.' Caine returned the next morning to offer me the chance to escape Sergei if I would agree to be his . . ." Her lips twisted as she remembered the handsome cur's description. "Secret weapon."

"Arrogant dog." Tane growled.

She tilted back her head, startled by the raw fury that glowed in the honey eyes.

"I thought you didn't know Caine?"

It was Styx who answered. "The vampires have yet to claim the pleasure, but I'm confident he will soon be my guest."

Eek.

"Why do I suspect that's not a good thing for Caine?" Laylah muttered.

"The dog held my mate's sister as a prisoner." Styx's dark tone warned of pain for anyone stupid enough to hurt his mate. Ridiculously, Laylah briefly wondered what it must feel like to be loved by such an overwhelming demon. Darcy must feel . . . what? Cherished? Empowered? Smothered? Perhaps a combination of all three? "A crime he will eventually pay for," Styx continued, unaware of her inane thoughts. "But for now I think we have more important matters to discuss. How did Caine manage to get you away from the mage?"

"Caine has a talent for creating pharmaceuticals," she admitted. Over the years the cur had made a fortune off his ability to create designer drugs that humans craved. "He slipped Sergei a rophy in his orange juice and while he was knocked unconscious we slipped away."

Styx looked surprised. "The mage was done in by a rophy?"

"Trust me, it was supercharged."

Tane narrowed his eyes. "Did you stay with Caine in Rome?"

"No, Caine sent me to his lair in America so his private witches could keep me hidden." She smiled. When she'd arrived in Caine's lair outside of St. Louis it had seemed almost paradise. Sure she had to live in an outbuilding that was heavily wrapped in disguise spells, and she often went years without speaking to another. But her rooms were comfortable enough, and best of all, she and the baby were safely hidden from the world.

Oh, and a wide screen TV and five hundred channels of free cable.

Not bad.

"I didn't see him again until he arrived in St. Louis with a baby Were."

"Harley," Styx said.

"Yes, but he refused to speak of where she came from or why he was so protective of her," Laylah hastily informed him. Darcy had already spent the past hour grilling her on any information on how Caine had gotten his hands on Harley and if he'd said anything that involved Darcy's other sisters. Apparently one of the quadruplets was still missing. "I'm sorry, I don't know any more."

Styx studied her in silence, weighing the truth of her words.

"Tell me about the child," he at last said abruptly.

She swallowed a sigh. The King of Vampires was nothing if not relentless.

Like Chinese water torture.

"There's nothing to tell. The baby's wrapped in a stasis spell that I can't penetrate. I'm not even truly sure if it's a boy or a girl."

Tane tilted her chin back to study her with an unreadable expression.

"Are you sure it's alive?"

Ah, he thought her loneliness had driven her to carrying around the magical equivalent of an empty shell.

She might have been insulted if there wasn't a real possibility she would have gone stark raving mad without the baby to concentrate on instead of her miserable existence.

"I can sense its essence, but it's not conscious," she said, her tone firm enough to warn she wasn't going to debate what she knew in her heart.

The child was alive and it belonged to her.

Styx stepped forward. "And it hasn't altered over the years?"

"No."

"Where is the child now?"

The abrupt question came without warning, but Laylah was prepared. Folding her arms over her chest, she met Styx's dark gaze without flinching.

"Safely hidden."

"You must . . ."

"No."

"Perhaps it would be better if I spoke with Laylah in private," Tane interrupted, wisely preventing Laylah from provoking the most dangerous demon on the face of the earth.

* * *

Tane waited until Styx had left the room and closed the door behind him before turning to meet Laylah's mulish expression.

She lifted a hand and pointed a finger in his face.

"Don't even think it."

"Think what?"

"That just because you've gotten into my pants you can manipulate me."

A flare of anger seared through him. *Gotten into her pants?*

She made him sound like a frat boy anxious for an easy lay. The truth of the matter was that he'd had the most beautiful and powerful women in the world beg to share his bed.

But it wasn't male pride that made him yank her hard against his body, or glare down at her wide eyes.

"Don't ever dismiss what burns between us," he rasped.

Her pulse hammered at the base of her throat, but she stubbornly refused to yield.

"Nothing burns between us. We had sex. End of story."

He leaned down, scraping a fully extended fang down the line of her jugular, his gut twisting with a primitive need to taste the rich nectar of her blood.

"If I truly thought you believed that I would take you right here and prove just how wrong you are," he said, his lips moving against the satin of her skin.

"Tane." She shivered, the scent of her excitement teasing at his senses, but her hands lifted to press against his chest. "Stop."

He pulled back to study the flush of arousal staining her cheeks with smug satisfaction.

"You belong to me."

Her eyes flashed, but she was wise enough not to try and continue the ridiculous argument.

"I thought you wanted to discuss the baby?"

His lips twitched. "And I thought you didn't."

Without warning, she twisted out of his arms, shaking her head as she backed away.

"You're not going to trick me."

Ignoring the urge to tug her back into his embrace, Tane instead allowed his gaze to skim over her pale face and stiffly held body.

She was as beautiful as ever.

The crimson hair that shimmered like fire in the overhead light. The ivory features carved with a delicate perfection. The slender body that was a tantalizing combination of hard muscles and feminine curves.

But, his searching eyes didn't miss the shadows in the dark eyes and the tension that hummed around her.

She was anxious to return to her child and suspicious he intended to halt her.

A well-founded suspicion, unfortunately.

Every damned demon in the world would soon be on the hunt for the latest, greatest hope to return the Dark Lord. Either for the glory of returning their god, or to destroy the potential threat.

Tane wouldn't allow Laylah to be standing in the firing line.

"Trick you?" he said with a stab at innocence.

Her chin jutted, not buying his pretense for a minute. "I'm not handing over the child."

He swore in frustration. He'd hoped to avoid an outright confrontation.

"What choice do you have, Laylah?" He planted his hands on his hips. "You aren't a fool."

"That's open to debate."

He ignored her muttered sidebar.

"You've been outed, my sweet. Far too many demons now know that there's a mongrel Jinn on the loose with a child that has the potential to resurrect the Dark Lord." He cupped her face in his hands, holding her gaze as he sought to make his point. No matter how ruthless he had to be. "There's nowhere you can hide the baby that it will be safe."

Fear flashed through her eyes before she was stubbornly hiding it behind her ready temper.

"If there's nowhere safe then why would the vampires want to get involved? Or can I guess?" Her eyes narrowed. "As soon as I'm stupid enough to reveal where the baby is hidden you'll turn the both of us over to the Commission. Tell me, Tane, do you get a bonus for a package deal?"

"You must have an addiction for playing with fire," he warned, his voice soft.

"Just the opposite." She knocked away his hands. "All I want is peace and quiet and a place where I can keep the baby safe."

He clenched his teeth. He wouldn't let that hint of wistful yearning tug at his heart.

"An impossible dream."

"Perhaps for the moment, but eventually I'll manage to provide us with a home. I'm not helpless."

His lips twisted in a humorless smile. "I'm painfully aware of your powers, but I'm not willing to turn a blind eye to the dangers that stalk you. I'll bet my favorite Rolex that Marika and her mage are in search of the child."

Without warning she turned on her heel and paced across the office, her beautiful features set in lines of grim determination.

"No, they're looking for me," she corrected. "I'm the only one who can touch the baby. They need me."

Fear feathered down his spine.

"Stop right there, Laylah."

She glanced over her shoulder. "What?"

"I'm beginning to recognize that expression."

She abruptly returned to her pacing. "I don't know what you're talking about."

With a blinding speed he was across the room, yanking her around so she wouldn't miss his don't-screw-with-me frown.

"You're hatching some insane scheme and I won't allow it."

"Won't allow it?" The air filled with dangerous prickles. "I ought to fry you just for being an arrogant ass."

"And I ought to lock you in the nearest dungeon." With an effort he loosened his grip on her arm, leashing his Neanderthal urges. "Laylah, you aren't going to make yourself bait."

She paused. Perhaps weighing the pleasure of zapping him with lightning against the less lethal, yet more terrifying delight of trapping him in the mists between worlds.

"It will only be long enough to lead Marika and Sergei away," she at last broke the silence. "Once they've lost my trail I can return to collect the baby and disappear for good."

His power blasted through the room, knocking priceless first editions off the shelves and making the lights flicker.

"Is that supposed to be a joke?"

She paled, but held her ground. "I'll admit it's not the best plan . . ."

"It's a suicide mission and you know it," he snapped.

"There's no need to be so melodramatic. I've survived on my own for a long time."

"Shit ass luck that's bound to run out eventually."

She sucked in a furious breath as she surged onto her tiptoes and stabbed a finger into the center of his chest.

"I wasn't asking your permission, He-man."

He grasped her arms and lifted her until they were nose to nose. Glare to glare.

"Then obviously you've forgotten you're my prisoner. You're not going anywhere."

"Don't you have that backward?" she ground out, drowning him in the delicious sensation of heat and furious woman. Even when she was frustrating the hell out of him the image of spreading her across Styx's desk and thrusting deep into her body was searing into his brain. "You're in my power and I command that you let me go."

He claimed her lips in a kiss of blatant ownership. "Checkmate."

Her lips softened in a brief moment of madness, then she was pressing her hands against his chest.

"Tane . . ."

"No Laylah, you won't be charging off alone." He returned her feet to the fancy carpet, but he held onto her arms, unable to let go. Dammit. There weren't any good choices. Not so long as the Commission considered her a danger. What he needed was time to convince the damned Oracles this female was not a threat. And more importantly, the ability to keep her from getting herself killed before he could do it. "There's nowhere you can go that I won't follow."

She frowned at the harsh warning in his voice. "Why?"

"I don't know."

Chapter 12

It was his simple honesty that stole her breath.

Along with her higher brain functions.

I don't know . . .

She could return the sentiment.

The damned vampire had her so twisted in knots she didn't know if she was coming or going.

One minute she wanted to zap him into a little pile of dust and the next she wanted to back him against the nearest wall and do wicked things to his hard, perfect body.

Lost in the honey gaze, Laylah nearly came out of her skin when Styx's voice boomed through the intercom.

"Tane. I need you upstairs."

Tane stiffened, his grip tightening on her arms.

"Not now," he growled.

"Now," the ancient vampire snapped back.

"Damn." Tane abruptly stepped back, his expression tight with frustration. "I won't be long."

"I'll come with . . ."

"No, my sweet." Tane firmly overrode her words, folding his arms over his chest. "If Styx wanted you to join us then he would have asked for you."

She frowned, her mood tilting toward the whole turning him into toast rather than licking him from head to toe.

"So I'm supposed to wait here like a good girl while you decide my future?"

"It's much more likely that this has nothing to do with you, Laylah."

Her hands clenched at her sides. "Yeah, right."

"Have you forgotten that Styx is the King of Vampires and I'm his Charon?" He held her gaze, his painfully beautiful face impossible to read. "Stay here."

Her heart forgot to beat.

Shit. Did he think that made things better?

"Tane," she said as he headed toward the door.

He halted and turned to meet her worried gaze. "Yes?"

"What if this is vampire business?"

He shrugged. "Then I'll do my duty."

She was standing directly in front of him without knowing how she got there.

"A Charon's duty?"

Another shrug. "Yes."

Let him go, a voice whispered in the back of her mind.

With Styx and Tane distracted she would have the perfect opportunity to escape. Perhaps the *only* opportunity.

But instead she grabbed his arm, her gaze glued to his face as if she were desperate to memorize every elegant line and curve.

"What does that mean?"

"Now is not the time . . ."

"Please, I need to know." She tightened her grip until her nails dug into his flesh, already suspecting that his position among vampires not only was one of power, but of intense danger. "What exactly does a Charon do?"

She felt him tense, as if he were startled by her fierce reaction.

Hell, he couldn't be any more startled than she was.

Minutes ticked by until at last he brushed his fingers through her spiked hair.

"It's not common knowledge, but there are vampires who become addicted to the blood of alcoholics and drug users," he said, his voice instinctively lowering as he shared the private weakness of vampires. "It eventually drives them mad. If I don't track them down and kill them before it's too late they will go into complete bloodlust."

A ball of ice formed in the pit of her stomach. "What happens?"

"They will go on a mindless rampage and they will destroy everything and everyone in their path."

She sucked in a shocked breath.

She was prepared for dangerous.

Not for mindless rampages.

"And it's your job to stop them?" Her voice was thick.

"There's no choice." His fingers absently outlined the shell of her ear. "Once a vampire's crossed the threshold into madness they won't stop the massacre until they run out of victims or they're decapitated."

His touch held its usual magic, sending tiny jolts of pleasure through her, but she was consumed by the terror at the insane risks this vampire took with his life.

"Why you?"

His honey gaze bored deep into her wide eyes, seeming to seek the truth of her tangled emotions.

Yeah, good luck on that.

"Me?" he rasped.

"Why do you have to be the one to hunt down the mass-murdering psychos?"

"Because I'm a Charon."

Her breath hissed through her clenched teeth. He was being deliberately evasive.

Which meant he was hiding something.

"Were you drafted or was it a volunteer program?"

"Styx approached me about the position and I accepted."

"Just like that?"

"Why do you sound so skeptical?"

"Because I don't think anyone would willingly put themselves in a position of being an executioner."

He dropped his hand, his expression closing up like the proverbial clam.

"It has to be done."

Her dread deepened at his flat statement. It was the sort of thing a man said when he didn't intend to be reasonable.

"I'm not arguing the legitimacy of the job, just why you would choose to do it."

"Why not?" The honey gaze shifted to somewhere over her shoulder. "Every vampire loves the thrill of the hunt. Styx has tried his best to civilize us, so it's a rare treat to pit my skills against a worthy opponent."

She snorted. Only an idiot would doubt that Tane was aggressive enough to enjoy ripping the throat out of an enemy. But there was no way she could be convinced that he would take pleasure in putting down a brother who was crazed with bloodlust.

Besides, no one would deliberately take a position that would have them shunned by their own family.

"You love the hunt so much you're willing to be feared and ostracized by your family?" she challenged.

His brows lifted. "What makes you think I'm an outcast?"

"I'm not stupid, Tane." She folded her arms around her waist, a familiar ache settling in the center of her heart. She knew all about shunning. And the pain of always being seen as a threat, no matter how hard she tried to prove herself. "I could see how Victor's clan treated you.

Half of them looked like they wanted to crawl in the nearest hole when you walked into the room and the other half looked like they wanted to plant a stake in your back."

With a smooth motion he turned to pace toward the heavy desk, but not before Laylah glimpsed the wounds that darkened the beautiful honey eyes.

Wounds so raw she shuddered in horror.

"My power is great enough I'll always be feared regardless if I'm a Charon or not." He kept his back turned, his voice stripped of the emotions that festered deep inside him. "And to be honest, I don't give a shit about the assholes who want to see me dead. I'm not here to win friends and influence vampires."

Laylah ignored the rigid stiffness of his shoulders and the don't-screw-with-me vibe he was throwing off in pulses of frigid air.

She'd been pissing Tane off since the moment they met. Why stop now?

"Don't do this." She moved to stand directly before him. "Not to me."

He refused to meet her gaze. "Do what?"

"Pretend that it doesn't matter that you're treated like a leper by those who have no right to judge you." She reached up to touch the hard line of his jaw. "That you hide away from the world that doesn't want you. That you're so alone it makes your soul ache."

He froze at her light touch, his expression wary. "Laylah?"

"I don't have any say in my fate, but you . . ." She slowly shook her head. "You could be a part of a clan. Even have a mate."

"Mate?" His sharp laugh rasped across her nerves. "Can you see me in a cottage with a white picket fence?"

She lowered her hand, pretending she didn't give a shit he was shutting her out.

"Fine, keep your secrets," she snapped. "It's not like it matters to me."

She was taking her first step away when Tane reached out to lightly touch her shoulder.

"She was my maker."

She turned back, meeting Tane's bleak gaze. "What?"

"Sung Li." His hand absently stroked over the bare skin of her shoulder, but she sensed his thoughts were far away. "She transformed me into a vampire."

"So she's your mother?" she asked, a queasy sensation rolling through her stomach.

She'd insisted that he reveal his pain.

As if she had the right to share his deepest secrets.

Now she realized that she was forcing him to stir up memories he'd fought to bury.

"Every relationship between a foundling and his maker is different. Sometimes it can be a parent and child connection, other times it can be sexual." His voice was ruthlessly controlled. "Usually there's nothing that holds them together. Until the past century most vampire foundlings were abandoned by their maker and rarely made it past their first year. Now Styx is trying to make certain any new vampire is brought directly into a clan."

At any other time Laylah would have been fascinated by the glimpse into vampire politics.

For all their power, they were careful to keep their world shrouded in secrecy.

But there were far more important matters to occupy her mind.

"What about you and Sung Li?"

"She was my lover."

"Your mate?" she rasped.

"No, but we were . . . close."

Even braced for the revelation, Laylah jerked as if she'd been slapped.

Sung Li.

She sounded . . . exotic.

And no doubt beautiful, like all vampires.

She wanted to slap the bitch without knowing another thing about her.

"You said *were*."

"She's dead."

"How?"

"I cut off her head."

Regret slammed into her. "Shit. I'm sorry. I should never have pushed." She lifted her hand to touch him, only to pull it back at his tight expression. He was hanging on by a thread and she didn't want to be the one to snap it. She'd done enough damage for one night, thank you very much. "It's none of my business."

A choking tension filled the room. "Don't you want to know why?"

She shuddered. Not out of shock at his confession, but in horror at the anguish he must have suffered at being forced to kill his lover.

"I . . ." She licked her dry lips. "I don't want to make you go back there."

His hand slid to cup the back of her neck, his thumb stroking the line of her jugular. Almost as if it comforted him.

"Sung Li was ancient even before she made me," he said, his voice a rough whisper. "And like many she had grown bored with her existence."

Laylah frowned. "She changed you for entertainment?"

"I suppose that's one way of putting it."

Yep. Super bitch.

"How long were you together?"

"Almost three hundred years."

The stinging pain she felt was not jealousy. That would be . . . insane. Freaking nuts.

It was something else. Something not jealousy.

"Well no one can claim you aren't in it for the long haul," she muttered.

An emotion that might have been satisfaction ghosted over his beautiful face at the edge in her voice. Then, the bitter memories returned, shadowing his eyes.

"Time has little meaning for an immortal."

"Maybe not, but you must have loved her very much to have stayed together so long."

"Love?" He grimaced. "No. I was her disciple who worshipped at her feet. There was no true affection. If there had been I might have . . ."

That strange emotion gripping her heart eased, only to be replaced with a deeper, more worrisome desire to wrap herself tight against Tane and offer him . . . what? A comfort she didn't understand and that he would no doubt reject?

She cleared her throat. "You might have what?"

"I might have accepted the truth of her growing instability."

It took a minute for his words to sink into her brain. "Oh." She gave herself a mental head slap. She should have seen this coming a mile away. "She was . . ."

"An addict."

She frowned at the regret that burned in the honey eyes. "That's not your fault."

"Not her addiction, but I was certainly her enabler."

"She was a powerful vampire, Tane, not a second rate celebrity on Dr. Drew. I doubt any intervention in the world could have helped."

With a muttered curse he paced across the room, his movements jerky.

"There's only one intervention when a vampire goes rogue and it sure the hell doesn't include any touchy-feely shit." His voice was rough with ancient pain. "But I was weak. I cleaned up her 'accidents' and pretended I didn't notice her erratic mood swings. I didn't want to admit, even to myself, she was spiraling into bloodlust."

Laylah bit her bottom lip. She didn't need to be a mind reader to know this story didn't have a happy ending.

"What happened?"

His head bent downward, his body held so rigidly it looked like it might shatter.

"Exactly what you would expect."

"How many?"

She shivered, the terrifying image of a crazed vampire drenched in the blood of others making her stomach roll.

"She wiped out our entire clan and several human villages before I managed to corner her in the mountains of Peru."

She hesitated before moving to stand directly behind him. She didn't want to push, but it was obvious that his habit of keeping his memories buried hadn't helped him heal. Maybe if he shared the horror he could lance the festering pain.

"Why didn't she kill you with the rest of the clan?"

His sharp laugh bounced off the walls. "In her demented mind she wanted someone to admire her glorious path of destruction."

Gods. Tane not only witnessed the woman he loved plunge into madness, but he had to watch her gory meltdown in full living color.

That would scar anyone.

"And it never occurred to her that you might put a stop to her rampage?"

"Why should she?" He slowly turned, revealing his stark expression. "I had been her loyal sycophant for countless years."

She reached up and framed his face in her hands. His skin was cool and deliciously smooth. Perfect.

But his eyes were filled with a pain that made her heart bleed.

"And now you carry the guilt of those she killed?"

"Not killed." He grasped her forearms, gripping her as if caught between the urge to shove her away or haul her against his chest. "They were slaughtered, Laylah. Ruthlessly, savagely slaughtered."

She welcomed the pressure of his fingers that dug into her flesh. He'd been smothering his emotions for so long. It was a wonder he hadn't exploded.

"You're not to blame."

"That's my call to make."

Laylah swallowed her words of protest. He'd decided it was his fault, and for now there was no arguing with him.

Typical male.

"Did Styx know your history when he asked you to become a Charon?" she instead demanded.

He hesitated, his gaze narrowing with suspicion at her abrupt change of subject.

"Yes."

"Bastard."

He tugged her close, his gaze instinctively flashing toward the closed door.

"Take care, my sweet, Styx has played the gracious host so far, but make no mistake he is a very bad enemy," he warned.

She leaned against the broad strength of his chest, feeling the usual flare of excitement stirring in the pit of her stomach. Along with far more dangerous sensations.

The sort of sensations a wise woman pretended didn't exist.

"It seems that he makes a very bad friend as well," she muttered.

He pressed a finger to her lips. "Laylah."

"No, he deliberately used your guilt to manipulate you into a position that not only has made you a leper among vampires, but puts your life at constant risk," she insisted.

He stilled, his gaze sweeping over her face as if seeking an answer to an unspoken question.

"Hardly constant."

She made a sound of impatience. "Have you forgotten you were attacked by your precious brothers the same day we met?"

His eyes blazed with a sudden heat as his arms wrapped around her.

"I've forgotten nothing of the day we met," he said, his husky tone making her heart slam against her ribs. "Nothing."

Yeah well . . . ditto.

Her eyes drifted to the hard curve of his mouth, memories of the sensual devastation of those lips sliding over her skin jolting through her before she was sternly squashing her flare of arousal.

No.

She wouldn't be distracted.

"He had no right to ask you to sacrifice so much."

"Styx isn't a benevolent leader." He snorted. "Hell, he's a son of a bitch who wouldn't hesitate to do what he thought necessary to protect his people. But, he didn't manipulate or compel me to become a Charon."

She scowled. Tane's loyalty to the terrifying Anasso was admirable, but it blinded him.

"Are you so certain?"

His hands lightly skimmed up her back, as if offering her comfort.

"Actually, he's the only one who truly understands."

She shook her head, far from convinced. "Understands what?"

"He had his own history with guilt and the scars of a twisted relationship." His jaw muscles knotted. "He knew I needed a tangible means of righting the wrongs of my past."

Laylah bit back a sigh of frustration.

She wanted to insist that Styx was using Tane's guilt to manipulate him into being a Charon. That way she might have a chance of convincing the stubborn fool that it wasn't worth the danger.

But if his position was a personal holy war . . .

She shook her head. Dammit. She didn't want to be concerned.

It implied that she cared.

And hadn't she already decided that was a very bad idea?

There was a click from the direction of the desk, then Styx's voice once again filled the room.

"Tane, you won't like what happens if I have to fetch you."

They both flinched at the icy edge in the voice.

With a low curse, Tane bent down to snatch a searing kiss before striding toward the door.

"We'll speak later."

"Tane."

He shot a glance over his shoulder. "Yes?"

"Don't . . ."

"Don't what?"

She clenched her teeth. "Don't do anything stupid."

Chapter 13

Over the years Tane had developed a finely honed sense of self-preservation.

A vampire assassin learned to stay on guard or he died. That simple.

But, Laylah was proving to be a dangerous distraction. He barely noted the priceless statues that lined the marble halls or the framed masterpieces that would no doubt make a collector wet himself. Which meant he barely noted the shadowed alcove where an enemy might be hidden and the coved ceiling where a trap might have been set.

His thoughts remained on Laylah's unexpected anger. She didn't like that he was a Charon. But why?

Because she was worried about him?

Because she . . . cared?

A dangerous warmth stirred in his heart.

A warmth that was still stirring and even spreading when he was abruptly jerked out of his inane thoughts by a wave of crushing energy that nearly sent him to his knees.

Shit. Shit. Shit.

Nothing but an Oracle could throw out voltage power that high.

He hesitated outside the library where he could sense Styx impatiently awaiting his arrival.

The savage urge to rush back to Laylah and carry her away blazed through him. Stupid, of course. He didn't stand a chance in hell of getting her out of here. Not before they could be stopped by Styx's Ravens.

Or worse.

Still, it was only the years of self-discipline that gave him the strength to step over the threshold into the vast library rather than rushing off like some newbie vampire with a hero-complex.

He was going to convince the Oracle that Laylah wasn't a danger.

Or die trying.

Belatedly on full alert, Tane took a cautious glance about the long room with its soaring windows that overlooked the sunken garden bathed in moonlight.

There were the expected shelves with a portion of Styx's enormous collection of books, and a heavy desk set near a marble fireplace. Across the room there were various leather chairs dotted about the expensive carpet and a glass case that held a variety of ancient scrolls.

His gaze briefly skimmed over Styx who was currently leaning against the desk, a thunderous scowl on his face, before shifting toward the female creature who stood in the center of the room.

Astonishment raced through him. Christ. She was as tiny as a human child with delicate features. At the moment she was simply attired in a white robe with her silvery-gray hair pulled in a long braid that hung down her back.

It would be easy to dismiss her as harmless if one didn't notice the ancient knowledge that smoldered in the black, oblong eyes. And, oh yeah, the razor sharp teeth that were obviously made for tearing flesh.

And of course, there was the power.

It beat against him with all the subtly of a sledgehammer.

The woman gestured for Tane to approach with a gnarled hand. "This is the Charon."

Her voice was low, hypnotic.

"Yes, mistress," Styx answered, although the words hadn't been a question.

She watched Tane halt directly before her with an unblinking gaze.

"I am Siljar."

Tane managed a stiff bow. "Tane."

Amusement flared through the dark eyes. "Yes, I know."

Tane swallowed a curse. The Oracle could read his mind.

She gave another lift of her hand. This one in dismissal.

"We will speak alone."

"As you wish." Styx readily headed toward the door, although he paused long enough to send Tane a warning frown.

Right. Like he needed a reminder not to poke the lethal rattlesnake with a stick.

Waiting until Styx had shut the door behind him, Siljar folded her arms over her chest.

"You have been a very naughty vampire."

"I can't deny I've broken the law."

"Hmmm. I can guess why."

Tane sent her a puzzled frown. "Mistress?"

She smiled. Not a particularly comforting sight with a set of pearly whites that a shark would envy.

"I have evolved beyond the weaknesses of the flesh, but that does not mean I have forgotten the temptation." The smile disappeared as fast as it had arrived. "Still, you have interfered in Commission business and that cannot be tolerated. Are you acquainted with Cezar?"

Tane grimaced. The vampire had been condemned to becoming a slave to the Commission for two centuries for bedding a potential Oracle.

"Not personally."

"You should make a point to meet him," the demon informed him. "He can tell you what happens to vampires who taste of forbidden fruit."

Tane bent his head. "I will accept whatever punishment you feel appropriate, but Laylah is innocent."

"She is an abomination."

His fury flared through the room, knocking out the electricity and shattering a lamp on the mantel.

"Through no fault of her own," he gritted.

She faced him without flinching despite the fact she was half his height and outweighed by two hundred pounds.

Of course, she could probably toss his ass against the wall with a flick of her finger.

"It is not the fault of an Urlenal demon that he drains the life of humans by simply being near them, but we keep them isolated."

"Laylah is not dangerous."

"She is unstable, like all Jinn mongrels."

His lips parted to argue only to snap shut as he remembered the Oracle could see into his mind. She would already know that Laylah had accidentally killed the cur in Hannibal. It might have been self-defense, but it still proved she couldn't control her powers.

Without thought he sank to his knees.

Screw pride.

He had to do something to keep Laylah from being exterminated.

"Please," he whispered.

There was the rustle of the satin robe as Siljar stepped forward. "You would plead for the female?"

"Yes."

"You are not mated." She peered into Tane's eyes that were nearly level with hers. "Not yet."

Not yet?

Okay. Tane quickly filed away that potential time bomb with things not to think about.

He bent his head, doing his best to look humble. Not one of his finer talents.

"I only ask that she not be destroyed without being offered an opportunity to prove she means no harm."

The dark eyes narrowed. "She makes you vulnerable and yet you would protect her. Fascinating."

More like suicidal, but he couldn't seem to stop the insanity.

"May I ask what you intend to do with her?" he demanded, proving his point.

"What we intended to do from the beginning."

"But . . ."

"Silence."

His forehead hit the carpet as pain drilled into his brain. Holy . . . shit. It felt like someone had lit a blowtorch inside his skull.

"Yes, mistress," he managed to rasp.

The pain abruptly disappeared and Tane groaned in bone deep gratitude. He might have suffered worse, but he couldn't remember when. Not that he was given an opportunity to appreciate the shocking relief.

Siljar's small hand grabbed his mohawk and yanked his head up to meet her creepily pleasant smile.

"Do you truly believe the Commission was not aware of the Jinn mongrel from the moment she was conceived?"

He faltered. What the hell? Was she toying with him?

Or was this a more dangerous game?

"The law states they are to be destroyed."

Her gray brows lifted. "You seek to lecture me on the laws I proclaimed?"

Careful, Tane.

He wouldn't be any use to Laylah dead.

"No, only to understand."

She hesitated, as if debating whether to continue with the mind-splitting pain or simply rip open his throat. At last she released her grip on his hair and stepped back, neatly folding her hands in front of her.

"It was determined that she is a *principium*."

He frowned as he met her fathomless gaze. "A what?"

"A rare soul who is destined to play a pivotal role in the future of the world."

The floor seemed to shift beneath his knees.

Damn.

His strange sense of . . . premonition when he was with Laylah hadn't been a delusion that he'd invented for an excuse to keep her near.

He should be leaping for freaking joy.

The Oracles had decided that Laylah was fated to be of use to them. Which meant that they had no intention of killing her. At least not until she'd fulfilled her mysterious destiny.

Instead a cold ball of dread was lodged in the pit of his stomach.

In his long life he'd learned that being important to the future of the world was never, ever a good thing.

Martyrdom sucked for the actual martyr.

"What does this pivotal role entail?" he rasped.

"Do not take that tone with me."

He flinched at the trickle of power that stabbed through his brain, but he couldn't back down.

"Forgive me. I just . . ." He struggled and failed to find the words. "Need to know."

The pain faded until it was only a vague warning that he was treading near the edge of the Oracle's goodwill.

"Only a true prophet can read the future," she said in that low, hypnotic voice. "But the importance of her birth was written in the stars."

"So you don't intend to destroy her?"

"Of course not. She is vital to our future."

His muscles twitched with the need to return to Laylah. "Then may I ask why you wished to meet with me?"

"My reasons are twofold."

"Damn," he muttered.

She thankfully ignored his impatient outburst. "The first reason is to remind the vampires that the Commission is not to be trifled with. It was your duty to inform us of the mongrel, but instead you attempted to keep her hidden. You willfully ignored our laws and endangered others for your own pleasure. Obviously you need a reminder of the dangers of flaunting our authority."

"And the second?" he asked, trying not to consider his looming punishment.

"To make sure you do not intend to interfere in Laylah's destiny."

He was on his feet before he even realized he was moving. "Interfere?"

"Precisely."

"I've done nothing but try to keep her pretty head attached to her neck," he argued. "A job that should come with a sainthood, believe me."

Siljar wasn't impressed. "You have imposed your will upon her, have you not?"

He frowned, oddly offended by the accusation. "You don't have to make me sound like Kim Jong-il."

"I beg your pardon?"

"Never mind." Tane hunched a defensive shoulder. "I was only trying to protect her."

"She must be allowed to make her choices freely."

"Even if they put her in an early grave?"

"If that is to be her fate." The female held up a warning hand as Tane's growl trickled through the room. "Do not be rash, vampire. The female is necessary to the world. You, however, are disposable."

His jaw clenched. He might be disposable, but he'd be damned if he was going to let Laylah be some sacrificial pawn.

"You want me to abandon her to her fate?"

Siljar tilted her head to the side. Like an inquisitive bird. Only with pointed teeth and enough power to destroy the world.

"If I say yes?" she murmured.

"Then I will admit that you'll have to chain me to the wall or kill me to keep me away."

The demon heaved a sigh that sounded remarkably like the one all females heaved when confronted by a determined male.

Or as they would say—a pigheaded, unreasonable, obstinate male.

"Vampires."

"I can offer a compromise."

"You aren't in a position to negotiate."

"Then I would ask a favor."

She stilled, as if intrigued by his words. "And you would be in my debt?"

He should have hesitated. To be in the debt of this female was bound to come back and bite him in the ass.

But, he nodded his head without missing a beat. "Yes."

"An intriguing thought." She tapped a finger against

the tip of her chin. "Of course, I could always command you to do whatever I want."

"You could."

There was a nerve-wracking silence before she gave a dip of her head. "I will hear your request."

"Allow me to remain with Laylah and I will swear not to . . . interfere."

Siljar made a sound of disbelief. "You cannot halt your obsessive need to protect her."

Okay. Valid point.

There wasn't a power in this world, or the next, that could force him to stand aside and watch Laylah being harmed.

"Perhaps not, but you said that I was not to impose my will on her," he plunged onward. "Not that I couldn't keep her safe."

Her lower lip jutted as she considered his words. Then she gave a decisive shake of her head.

"True, but it is doubtful you could recall the distinction. Should the female choose a path of danger you would feel compelled to halt her."

Desperate, Tane dropped to his knees once again. Dammit. He would beg until he lost his voice.

"Mistress, I give my word."

"Yes."

Without warning, Siljar popped out of sight and reappeared a mere inch from his face. Tane jerked in surprise.

"What the . . . ?" Before he could react, the Oracle reached out to lay her tiny hand against his upper chest. An agonizing heat seared through his flesh, seeming to scorch to his very bones. Then a strange sensation of . . . well, there was no way to explain it but to say that something had shifted and locked into place. When at last she pulled back Tane glanced down to find his skin marred by a shimmering black tattoo that looked remarkably like a bolt of lightning. "Shit," he breathed in shock. "What did you do?"

"Nothing more than strengthen the ties that already bind you to Laylah." She stepped back to study him with a hint of surprise. "Really, vampire, you should know better than to make a wish with a Jinn."

With a hiss he pressed a hand to the mark on his chest. It was one thing to have a tenuous connection to Laylah and another to be at her mercy.

"You've enslaved me?"

She flashed her terrifying teeth. "No, Tane. You did that all by yourself."

He so didn't want to consider that disturbing tidbit.

"Can the bond be broken?"

"That is for Laylah to decide."

With a low growl, he rose to his feet. He hated to be jerked around. And he was beginning to suspect he'd just been played by an expert.

"Are we finished?"

Siljar's smile widened as she calmly headed toward the door. "For now."

"What of my punishment?"

The female never slowed. "I suspect the Jinn will offer a greater torture than I could ever devise."

Well, wasn't that the god-awful truth?

"Amen," he muttered.

"Of course if you do intend to stand as her protector I would suggest that you hurry."

"Hurry?"

"She and her tiny companion left the estate just after we began our conversation."

"Shit." Tane charged toward the door, yanking his dagger from the leather sheath at his lower back. "I'm going to kill that damned gargoyle."

Chapter 14

"I'm going to kill that damned vampire," Laylah muttered, jogging along the dirt path that was leading her away from Chicago.

And Tane.

The rat bastard.

Gods. She had believed him. He'd assured her that she wasn't in danger and like a gullible idiot she'd accepted his word.

If it hadn't been for Levet she would still be sitting in Styx's office, meekly waiting to be handed over to the Oracle.

Half an hour ago the tiny gargoyle had rushed into the room, his wings flapping and his tail twitching. A sure sign he was in a mood.

But even prepared for some new disaster, Laylah was shaken when he'd started babbling about an Oracle and danger and shoving her disguise amulet into her hand as he told her to run.

Laylah hadn't hesitated. A good thing considering the moment she'd left Styx's highly protected office she'd been nearly squashed by the thick power pulsing through the air. The Oracle was indeed there and no doubt waiting for her to be turned over.

Putting her trust in Levet, she'd allowed the gargoyle to lead her out a hidden tunnel that had opened into the open fields behind the froufrou neighborhood. And since then she'd set a blistering pace, unable to do anything more than run and hope she could escape.

Levet struggled to keep pace at her side. "Not that I do not fully share the need to exterminate the vampire race with extreme . . . what is the word?"

"Prejudice?"

"*Oui,* prejudice, but I thought you were fond of the cold-hearted leech?"

Her gaze skimmed over the passing fields and distant farm homes that slumbered beneath the moonlight. It wasn't yet midnight but the locals were already safely tucked in their beds.

They were hardworking humans who believed in the theory that the "early bird" got the worm.

"I suppose he's proved himself useful on occasion," she muttered.

"Useful?" Levet waggled his thick brow. "*Ooh la la,* I wish I had such a useful companion."

Heat stained her cheeks at the vivid image of Tane poised above her as he thrust deep inside her. It had been *ooh la la* and then some.

"Yeah, it's all fun and games until they betray you," she said, not bothering to hide her bitterness.

Levet sent her a startled glance. "You believe he sent for the Oracle?"

"I don't know if he did it personally, but someone in the vampire lair must have contacted the Commission." She tried and failed to smother the sharp jab of disappointment. "How else would they know I was here?"

"I doubt a mere amulet would hide you from the

Commission, *ma petite*," Levet said, seeming oblivious to Laylah's shock. "Their powers are *formidable*."

Laylah stumbled to an abrupt halt, her hand lifting to the small medallion hung about her neck. She'd been waltzing around with the assumption that the disguise amulet was keeping her hidden from all the nasties that prowled through the dark.

Now Levet was revealing she wasn't nearly as protected as she had assumed.

"Are you saying that I'm out here hanging in the breeze?" she demanded, watching as Levet came to a reluctant halt and turned to meet her worried gaze.

"It would depend upon the magical abilities of the one casting the spell," he hedged. "Some are more powerful than others."

She shook her head. She would have to worry about the amulet later. For now she wanted to be pissed off at Tane.

"Even if he didn't call for the Oracle he should have done something to warn me I was in danger."

There was a rustle from a nearby tree and then a black shadow dropped into the center of the path. Laylah instinctively jerked backward, her power gathering as she prepared to strike out at the unexpected threat.

Before she could launch her attack, however, the shadows dropped to reveal her personal pain-in-the-ass.

"I clearly remember being told that I was an unnecessary interference in your life and that you were quite capable of taking care of yourself," Tane drawled, twirling a large dagger in his hands.

"*Sacrebleu*. I nearly turned you into a newt," Levet snapped, waving a clenched fist in Tane's direction. "A neutered newt."

Muttering a number of inventive names for vampires who rudely dropped into private conversations, Laylah's powers dissipated as abruptly as they had arrived, leaving her with nothing more dangerous than a petulant scowl.

"Laylah?" he prompted, looking decidedly edible in nothing more than his khaki shorts with a massive sword strapped across his back.

She forced herself to meet the honey gaze, not bothering to ask how he managed to be waiting for her. She might be fast, but she was no match for vampire speed. And with his ability to wrap himself in shadows, she had no warning he was lurking like a damned vulture.

"You could have at least given me a heads up that one of the Board of Directors from hell was in the house."

He shrugged. "There is no way to outrun the Commission, my sweet."

Fury raced through her. Didn't he even have the decency to *pretend* regret?

"I've been doing a pretty damned good job of it until you came along," she gritted. "Over two hundred years and not one Oracle sighting."

"Only because they allowed you to believe you had escaped their notice."

Her anger faltered. "What are you saying?"

He slowly moved toward her, the dagger held loosely in his hand and bare feet barely stirring the dirt of the path.

"They've known of you from the moment of your conception."

"But . . ." She cleared the sudden lump from her throat. "That's impossible."

"Nothing is impossible for the Commission." He held her gaze, willing her to believe his soft words. "They possess powers that make a sane demon shudder in horror."

The world tilted on its axis.

She'd lived in fear of the Oracles since the day she was born.

They were the boogiemen who gave her nightmares and ruined any hope of a "normal" life.

To think that they hadn't been after her at all . . .

Trying to wrap her mind around the enormous implications, Laylah was distracted as he stepped into a pool of moonlight and a strange mark shimmered on his chest.

"Shit." She reached out to touch the tattoo that pulsed with obvious magic. "What did they do to you?"

"It's a . . ." He grimaced. "Reminder."

"A reminder of what?"

"That I can't control everything."

She slowly shook her head, a wrenching pain twisting her heart.

"No. You were punished." Her gaze lifted to meet the honey gaze that was shielded by his thick tangle of lashes. In that moment she hated the Commission more than she ever had. "You were punished because you helped me."

His hand pressed her fingers against the tattoo, his beautiful features impossible to read.

"It doesn't matter."

"If the Oracles knew of my existence then why did they hurt you?"

In answer he lifted her hand, brushing her palm with his lips before stepping back with an expression that warned he didn't intend to reveal what had happened between him and the Oracle.

Stubborn, infuriating vampire.

"Where were you going, Laylah?"

She sniffed. Fine. He didn't want her to feel bad he was tortured because of her, then she wouldn't.

"I was trying to escape." She shrugged. "I didn't have the time or inclination to make out a full itinerary."

"Don't try it." His lips twisted. "For better or worse you've bound us together. Lying is a waste of breath."

Bound them together? Ha. He'd just acted like she had some control over him to lure her into a false sense of security.

"I don't trust you."

"Yes, you do." Holding her gaze, his hand skimmed down her cheek before circling her upper arm in a possessive grasp. "You're just not ready to admit it."

She snorted. "Arrogant."

He leaned down until they were nose to nose. "You're going to the child, aren't you, my sweet?"

"No one invited you along, vampire," Levet muttered.

The golden gaze never shifted from her face. "Your assistance is no longer required, gargoyle."

The shocking desire to close the small distance and press her lips to his had Laylah stepping backward.

Gods. He was making her crazy.

"I will decide whose assistance I want," she snapped. "Levet is coming with me."

"Merci, ma petite." Levet's wings fluttered as he flashed Tane a smug smile. "There are some who lack the taste to appreciate my exquisite charm."

Tane's eyes narrowed. "I also lack the taste to appreciate chewing on glass, being skinned alive, and reruns of the Rosanne Barr show. Call me crazy."

Laylah heaved a resigned sigh.

Obviously there was no getting rid of the damned vamp.

Why not give into the inevitable and take advantage of his presence?

He was, after all, a powerful warrior who could protect her from most demons.

Even her crazy-ass aunt.

"Can we just go?" she demanded.

Smart enough not to press for a precise destination, Tane glanced toward a nearby farmhouse.

"We'll need transportation." He headed toward the surrounding field. "This way."

They moved in silence, bypassing the barn painted a bright red with a tin roof, and the attached corral that held the pungent odor of pigs.

Laylah was swift to grab Levet's wing, ignoring his squeal of protest. A gargoyle was like a teenage boy . . . always hungry and willing to eat whatever crossed his path. Even if it was still rutting in the mud.

She maintained her grip as they passed the henhouse and dog kennel, not releasing him until they entered a long shed that housed the tractors, combines, bulldozer, and shiny new Ford Expedition.

Tane yanked open the driver's door, but before Laylah could protest his typical male assumption that he would be driving, he laid his hand on the steering column. Instantly the engine fired to life. Laylah lifted her brows. Nice trick.

"Shotgun," Levet called, scrambling into the passenger's seat.

His butt never hit the leather seat as Tane grabbed him by the horn and tossed him in the back.

"Don't even think about it."

There was a flurry of French curses and Laylah was forced to hide her smile as she climbed into the seat Levet had nearly claimed and shut the door. The tiny gargoyle could always be counted on to lighten the mood.

Not nearly so amused, Tane gunned the engine and pulled out of the garage at a speed that made Laylah happy she had the blood of an immortal running through her veins. He slowed as they reached the road.

"Which way?"

She hesitated. For years she'd sacrificed everything to keep the child hidden. It wasn't easy to risk revealing his location to anyone.

"South," she at last forced herself to say, instinctively tugging on the seat belt as Tane stomped on the gas.

Laylah clenched her teeth to keep them from banging together as they hurtled down the rough road. The three of them off to save the world.

Or at least one helpless baby.

Not quite the Justice League, she wryly accepted. A brooding vampire, a stunted gargoyle, and a Jinn mongrel with trust issues.

Still, they had to be better than nothing.

Casting covert glances at Tane's elegant profile that was caught in the glow of the dashboard, Laylah was relieved when Levet suddenly stuck his head between the seats.

She didn't want time to consider whether or not she'd just made the greatest mistake of her life.

"You know, Laylah, if you intend to keep the child then you should really consider giving it a name," the gargoyle gently chastised her.

Tane flashed Levet an annoyed glare. "What does it matter?"

Levet sniffed. "Because a mother who cares about her child gives him a name."

If Laylah hadn't been looking directly at the gargoyle she would have missed the pain that flared through the gray eyes.

Her heart wrenched.

Oh, dear God. Levet was intimately familiar with a mother who didn't bother to name him. Perhaps she had even abandoned him.

Demons could be even more brutal than humans when it came to dealing with deformities.

"Yes," she breathed, reaching to run a comforting hand down his wing. "You're right."

A wistful smile touched his ugly face. "Then why have you hesitated?"

"Because I've always known there was the possibility that the child belonged to someone else. And that one day they would come for him," she tried to explain. "It wouldn't be fair if I had already named him."

"And less painful for you to give him away?" Levet asked softly.

She grimaced, knowing she must sound like an idiot. "That was the thought."

"And now?" Levet prompted.

"Now I'll kill anyone who tries to take him from me."

Tane sent her a knowing smile. "Spoken like a true mother."

Marika prowled along the wrought iron fence that framed the elegant estate.

Out of necessity she'd swapped her Valentino gown for black silk pants and matching top that snuggly outlined her perfect figure and allowed her to blend into the shadows. She'd also tugged her hair into a simple knot at her nape to keep it from being caught on the nasty trees and bushes that cluttered the godforsaken country.

Her lips pinched.

At least Sergei had managed to cast a Spell of Finding on Laylah before Victor and his henchmen had forced her from her lair. The interfering bastards. It meant that it was only a matter of time before she had her hands on her niece and they could return to civilization.

And in the meantime she intended to keep a very detailed tally on every indignity she was forced to suffer. She was going to take payment out of Laylah's flesh.

Tapping a manicured nail against her chin, she considered the distant house, her impatience to track down her niece briefly overshadowed by the waves of power that filled the air.

"You are certain she is no longer inside?" she demanded.

Sergei nodded. Like her, he had changed from his designer clothing into a pair of casual chinos and a loose black silk shirt. His hair was pulled into a tail at his nape.

"I can sense her heading south."

"Is she alone?"

"It's impossible to say." The mage sent her a warning frown. "The spell I cast on her is fading. We should hurry before I lose all connection to her." He muttered a curse as Marika stepped toward the fence, her head tilted back as she tested the air. "What are you doing?"

"Do you know what this place is?"

Sergei shrugged. "A vampire's lair."

"Much more than that." A humorless smile curved her lips. "My niece moves in elevated company."

The mage shifted uneasily, sensing something was wrong but unable to detect the power that choked the air.

"A clan chief?"

"The King of all Vampires."

"The Anasso?" Stark disbelief was laced through Sergei's voice. "I thought he was a myth."

"You are welcome to ring the doorbell and discover the truth for yourself."

"No, thank you." There was a tense pause before the mage moved to stand at her side, his expression suspicious. "You are remarkably indifferent to the fact that the Anasso is now aware that you defied demon law to create a Jinn half-breed for the sole purpose of returning the Dark Lord to this world and crowning yourself queen."

Marika waved aside his words. Why should she care that her plans had been revealed to the Anasso? There was no point in being superior to those who claimed positions of power if no one appreciated her brilliance.

"It was bound to be revealed eventually."

The pale blue eyes glittered with annoyance. "Not until we had the Jinn and babe in our possession. A task that now will be considerably more difficult if we are being hunted by your brethren."

"I do not fear the fools," she said, scorn dripping from her words. "But there is something else."

"Something worse than the Anasso?"

"Yes."

"Lovely." The mage reached to grasp the crystal hung about his neck. Marika sneered at the instinctive reaction. His human magic would be worthless against the demon inside the mansion. "What is it?"

"An Oracle."

Sergei backed away from the fence with a string of Russian curses.

"Then this is the end." He halted at the edge of the tree line, perhaps stupid enough to believe the shadows could hide him from the danger. "If the Commission knows of the female then they'll kill her."

Marika turned, taking a malicious pleasure in her companion's fear.

"That would have been my assumption and yet you claim Laylah escaped."

He scowled. "She did, unless they have managed to lay a false trail."

It was the same thought that had crossed her mind.

Rumor was that Styx wasn't the Anasso simply because he was the strongest vampire. He was just as infamous for his cunning.

"A trail leading to a trap," she murmured. "It is something to be considered."

"Something to be *considered?*" Sergei shook his head in incredulity. "*Nyet.* The only thing to be considered is the fastest means to return to London."

"We are not leaving without Laylah and the child."

"You might consider the glorious return of the Dark Lord worthy of a few thousand years of torture in the hands of the Commission, but I do not."

Marika flowed forward, grabbing him by the hair and bending him backward.

She could forgive his treachery.

But never his cowardice.

"I have not come this far to have your lack of guts ruin this for me."

His eyes bulged in pain. "Marika."

She leaned close to whisper directly in his ear. "If you have no use for your spine I can snap it in two."

"No . . ." he panted. "Please. You have made your point. Release me."

Marika pursed her lips.

The desire to break Sergei in half was nearly overwhelming.

She had sated her hunger for blood before leaving London, but it had been too long since she'd indulged her lust for pain.

For a moment she reveled in his pulsing agony, then recalling she needed the cretin to track Laylah, she loosened her grip. He fell heavily to the ground. With a smile, she bent over his sprawled body.

"Don't test my patience again, Sergei." The words were a deadly whisper. "You won't like the consequences."

"I am, as always, your humble servant," he choked out, waiting until she stepped back before he cautiously rose to his feet. "What do you desire of me?"

She turned back toward the mansion, dismissing her

brief distraction. Instead she coldly calculated their options.

"There's no means to discover why the Oracle allowed Laylah to escape," she finally decided. "We have no choice but to follow the trail."

"Even if it leads us into a trap?"

"I am not so easily caught." Marika waved a distant hand toward the woods where her tiny army was hidden. "And I do have my new allies."

Sergei shuddered. He wasn't nearly so fond of her servants.

"Do not remind me."

"They have proved quite useful," she reminded the mage. "We could never have followed Laylah so swiftly without their skill with portals. And they are exquisitely beautiful." Without warning she was hit by a wave of dizziness, the image of her sister dancing before her eyes. "Damn."

Sergei stepped forward. "What's wrong?"

"Kata." She furiously pressed a hand to her forehead. Why would the bitch not leave her in peace? "She is . . . troubled."

"Is she awakening?"

Reluctantly, Marika forced herself to concentrate on her bond with Kata. She could sense a strange fluttering, as if her sister was being disturbed by an outside force, but the fog of unconsciousness was intact.

"No." She tried to shake off the tug of awareness. "You are certain no one can find her?"

"Even if they could locate her there is no way that they could penetrate the layers of protection I've set around the tomb."

Her icy power swirled through the air. "Pray you are right, mage."

Chapter 15

They arrived at the hidden copse of trees south of Hannibal only a few hours after they left the outskirts of Chicago.

The benefit of Tane's indifference to the laws of traffic. And occasionally those of physics.

Climbing out of the vehicle, Laylah breathed a sigh of relief. Jeez. Those people who mocked women drivers had never ridden with a vampire in a hurry.

Talk about a freaking death wish.

Steadying her weak knees, she headed toward the narrow path that led into the trees. Over the past hour she'd been plagued by a deepening sense of urgency to get her hands on the child.

As if it was calling out to her.

Nearly reaching the outer fringe of oak trees, Laylah was brought to an abrupt halt when Tane grabbed her upper arm.

"Wood sprites?" he muttered, his tension filling the air with a frigid bite. "You trusted them with a child?"

She didn't blame him for his skepticism. Sprites were as unpredictable as they were beautiful.

"They owe me."

He blinked in surprised. "A wish?"

"No, I . . ." She instinctively cut off her words.

He tugged her around to meet his searching gaze. "What?"

She blew out a resigned sigh. There was no point in hiding anything now.

Tane knew everything. The good, the bad, and the ugly.

"The Queen was poisoned by a jealous rival," she confessed. "I was able to save her life."

Something that might have been respect flared through the honey eyes.

"You're a healer?"

Gods, was that a blush heating her cheeks?

Next thing she knew she would be batting her lashes and simpering like an idiot.

"I don't perform miracles, but I can heal most injuries."

He brushed the back of his hand over that revealing blush. "A rare talent."

She cleared her throat, trying to sound brisk. "I've always assumed it came from my mother's side of the family since Jinns are a lot happier destroying things than fixing them."

"Oui," Levet chimed in, moving to her side. "Gypsies are coveted for their skills in healing."

Tane scowled at the gargoyle. "We have yet to determine if the vision Laylah was given in London was real."

Levet sniffed. "Do you think that I would not recognize a *faux* vision? *Moi?* The great connoisseur of magic? The . . ." He came to a sudden halt, a dreamy expression settling on his tiny face. "Mmmmm. Sprites." With a burst of unexpected speed he was rushing into the trees. "Sorry, *ma belle*, I will join you later. Much later."

Laylah rolled her eyes.

So much for the Justice League.

Not that she needed his help . . .

As if she'd deliberately jinxed herself, the thought had barely whispered through her mind when a dozen sprites stepped out of the shadows.

Her breath snared in her throat, her gaze skimming over the combination of males and females that were attired in the traditional robes that took camo to a whole new level. Even looking at them straight on, the flowing fabric melded perfectly with their background, giving the queasy illusion that they were floating in and out of focus.

She might have been amused if it weren't for the deadly expressions on the beautiful faces. Oh, and the crossbows that were currently pointed at her heart.

Her gaze never wavered from the line of sprites as Tane cautiously moved to her side. These weren't the flighty, unpredictable fey that they readily revealed to the demon world. These creatures stood at confident attention with their long hair, that ranged in hues from pure gold to dark red, tightly braided so they could easily reach the swords strapped to their backs.

Warriors.

And prepared to attack.

"I thought they were friends of yours?" Tane muttered.

"Yeah, me too." She squared her shoulders, meeting the steady gaze of the nearest sprite. "I have been granted safe passage by Eirinn."

The male sprite shifted his crossbow toward Tane. "The vampire doesn't have such privileges."

Tane's low growl filled the air, sending lesser demons fleeing in fear and causing even the hardened warriors to shudder.

"You really don't want to play this game."

"It's no game, Charon."

The high, musical voice was the only warning before a tall, slender female stepped into view. Like her warriors, Eirinn, Queen of the Wood Sprites, was attired in a loose robe, although her dark golden hair was left free to cascade down her back and held back with a delicate crown set with an emerald the size of a quail's egg.

She halted in a pool of moonlight, her beauty so perfect that Laylah would have thrown herself off the cliff if she was stupid enough to consider the numerous ways she failed in comparison.

With a lift of her hand, Eirinn spoke a few words in a foreign tongue. As one the warriors lowered their crossbows. Not that Laylah was reassured.

One wrong twitch and she was fairly certain she would be pinned to the nearest tree with an arrow through her heart.

Tane seemed to come to the same conclusion, and with his typical arrogance shifted until he was standing directly in front of her.

"Is the Welcoming Committee specifically for me or do you share the love with all vampires?" he mocked.

"These are dangerous times," the Queen said.

"That they are," Tane agreed, glaring at Laylah as she firmly stepped to his side.

Did he really think she would cower behind him?

Watching them with a narrowed gaze, Eirinn abruptly chuckled, moving forward to link her arm with Laylah's.

"Come with me, Laylah. Your vampire is distracting my warriors," she purred, tugging Laylah past her guards with just enough force to warn she wasn't going to take no for an answer. A faint smile curved her lips. "Unless you're willing to share?"

Share?

Not even when hell froze over.

"Forget it."

"A pity." Eirinn's perfect smile widened as Tane firmly pulled Laylah from her grip and he tucked a protective arm around her shoulders. "He is a fine specimen."

"Did you hear, my sweet?" He leaned to speak directly into Laylah's ear. "I'm a fine specimen."

She rolled her eyes, but she didn't pull away from his possessive hold.

Only because it wasn't worth the struggle, and not because she wanted the damned Queen of Sprites to know the vampire was off limits.

"Don't let it go to your head," she sniffed. "Sprites have a notorious appetite for sex."

She could have kicked herself as he flashed a smug smile.

"Yes, I know," he said. "Intimately."

"My point is they would think a drunken cur with the mange a fine specimen." In the distance the sound of Levet's laughter filled the air. It was Laylah's turn to smile. "Or a diminutive gargoyle."

His lips brushed the curve of her ear. "You, thankfully, have an insatiable appetite for only one male. An appetite I'm more than happy to sate."

She narrowed her gaze. "And your appetite?"

"Starving for a taste of a Jinn half-breed. The sooner the better." The force of his desire blasted through her, making them both shudder. His eyes flared with frustrated heat. "Damn."

They fell silent, both shaken by the brutal need that flared so abruptly between them. It didn't feel like the natural response of two individuals who were attracted to one another. It felt like . . .

Destiny.

She shook off the dangerous thought as Eirinn led them between two ancient trees.

Laylah grimaced as they passed through an invisible barrier. It felt like spiders crawling over her skin.

"The glade is my sanctuary and guarded by my personal magic," the Queen murmured. "We can speak in privacy here."

Once past the spell of protection, Laylah paused to appreciate the small glade.

It wasn't the cartoon version of a fey meadow with unicorns and rainbows, but there was a tiny stream that cut through the lush grass and clumps of wild flowers that added splashes of color.

At her side Tane folded his arms over his chest, clearly indifferent to their charming surroundings.

"Who is threatening you?"

"Ah, vampires." Eirinn slid an appreciative glance over Tane's body, blithely unaware how close she was to Laylah beating her senseless with her own crown. "Always so deliciously sexy and yet so lacking in manners."

Tane remained grimly indifferent to the open invitation in the woman's voice.

"We don't have the time for proper etiquette."

"I suppose that's true." The Queen tossed Laylah a taunting glance. "And I doubt Laylah would agree to a formal ceremony of greeting. She is astonishingly prudish for a Jinn."

"She is perfect," Tane snapped before Laylah could respond.

"So I see." The Queen chuckled. "And yours?"

"Yes."

Laylah flashed him a disgruntled frown. She didn't have a clue what was going on between her and Tane, but she was absolutely certain she didn't want it discussed with Eirinn the Queen of Tramps.

"Do you mind?"

His gaze slid with slow deliberation down her body. "Not at all."

Eirinn's eyes sparkled. "If you would prefer privacy . . ."

Yes, yes, please yes.

"No," Laylah forced herself to snap.

"Very wise, my dear. Never allow a vampire to believe he has you completely enthralled. They're so tediously full of themselves."

"Preaching to the choir," Laylah muttered.

"Enough." Tane stepped forward. "Tell me why your warriors are armed and twitchy as hell."

The Queen's amusement fled as she reached beneath the neckline of her robe to pull out a crystal that was hung on a golden chain around her neck.

"Because of this."

Laylah frowned at the oval stone that glowed with a soft, bluish light.

"A glowing rock?"

"A *Ciomach*," the sprite said.

"A what?"

"It's like an early warning system," Tane clarified.

"Convenient." Laylah watched as the stone pulsed with the strange blue glow. "What does it warn against?"

"Ancient enemies."

Well that was nice and vague.

"Can you be more specific?"

"The Sylvermyst."

She felt Tane jerk in surprise.

"Shit," he muttered.

Laylah's heart sank. Her spotty education didn't include much about the Sylvermyst. Nothing beyond the fact that they were related to the fey and were as notorious for their irresistible beauty as they were for their cruelty.

And of course, the most pertinent fact, that they were supposed to be long gone from the world.

Now she sensed she was about to find out more than she ever wanted.

"Tane, what's going on?" she demanded.

"When we first arrived in London Uriel mentioned that Victor was meeting with the Prince of Fairies in Dublin." He shook his head in disgust. "I assumed the Prince had been eating too many funny mushrooms."

"There is nothing amusing about the Sylvermyst," Eirinn said, dropping her image of frivolous flirtation to reveal the powerful leader beneath.

"No," Tane readily agreed.

Laylah frowned in confusion. "I thought they were banished?"

Tane grimaced. "A lot of unpleasant nasties are crawling out of the shadows these days."

The Queen shivered, clutching the stone around her neck. "Yes, the wind whispers of evil."

"When did your *Ciomach* start with its Christmas tree routine?" Tane asked.

"Early this evening."

Tane cursed and pulled his large dagger from its sheath.

Laylah instinctively glanced toward the nearby trees. "Tane?"

"It can't be a coincidence," he said.

"What can't?"

"The Sylvermyst first appearing in England and now here."

Perfect. Absolutely perfect.

Like her schizoid aunt and Sergei weren't bad enough?

"You think they followed us?"

His eyes glowed with a deadly intent. "Or they were led."

Laylah swallowed a sigh. Had she actually spent years wishing she had a family?

"Marika, I assume?"

"A possibility." He clutched the dagger as if wishing there was someone around he could stick it into. "One of too god damn many. We need to get moving."

"But it's almost sunrise. It would be safer to remain here until . . ."

"No, Laylah," Eirinn interrupted. "My debt is paid and I won't risk my people to defend you against the death that stalks you. You will collect the child and leave."

Laylah didn't argue. She didn't want anyone put in danger because of her. But even as she turned to make her way out of the glade, Tane was at her side.

"Too late," he whispered.

She paused, concentrating on her surroundings.

The magical barrier muted the outside world, but suddenly she was aware of the distant sounds of shouts and an unfamiliar smell of tangy herbs that blended with the fruity scent of fey.

Sylvermyst.

It had to be.

She didn't hesitate.

Charging toward the barrier, her only thought was to get to the child as swiftly as possible.

Several miles away, Caine cursed and yanked his Jeep to a halt next to the abandoned gas station that was the only building for miles.

Dammit. He should never have left the top off. Of

course, he hadn't expected his companion to leap from a vehicle traveling sixty miles an hour.

It wasn't the sort of thing most people did.

Clearly he needed to turn off his sane dial.

Throwing the damned thing into park, he vaulted over the door and headed toward the back of the parking lot. He cursed as he stubbed his toe on a rusting crow bar and nearly landed on his face. He was still trying to become accustomed to his newfound strength and speed.

Which was a nice way of saying he was as clumsy as hell.

"Cassie, wait."

She stood at the edge of the crumbling pavement, staring across the empty fields.

Despite her heavy sweatshirt and jeans, Cassie shivered. "I sense them."

He sniffed the air, picking up the earthy scent of fresh herbs. Not fey . . . but close.

"What the hell are they?"

"They are from . . . distant lands."

He growled, the wolf inside him snapping at the savage need to toss Cassie over his shoulder and haul her far away from the danger.

It didn't matter that she'd been a pureblood Were a hell of a lot longer than he had. Or that the danger was too far away to pose an immediate threat.

"I'm going out on a limb and guess that you don't mean illegal aliens," he said dryly.

The pale green eyes shifted in his direction. "Why are aliens illegal?"

"Never mind." When would he learn? He gave a shake of his head, considering the distant sense of violence that stained the air. "It seems we need a detour. How do you feel about Mexico?"

He didn't expect her to agree. She was OCD when it came to her visions.

Not even death would stop her from her self-imposed task.

"No, we must wait," she abruptly announced.

"Here?"

"Yes."

"Wait for what?"

Her eyes flared white and with a wave of her hand a glowing symbol hovered in the air.

"This."

"Dammit, would you stop doing that?" he growled.

Her eyes returned to their astonishing shade of green, a serene smile curving her lips.

"Did you bring dinner?"

Chapter 16

Cursing, Tane was in swift pursuit of Laylah, managing to catch her arm as she headed deeper into the trees.

"Laylah, stop," he commanded.

She jerked her arm free, her expression one of pure panic. "The baby."

"No."

"Wait here. It will only take a minute."

With a swift motion she darted beneath a low hanging branch and disappeared through a large bush.

"Damn," Tane clenched his hands, helpless against the compulsion that forced him to remain where he was.

Given enough incentive he might be capable of breaking the urge to give in to Laylah's request, but he couldn't ignore the warning given by Siljar.

Like it or not, Laylah was a *principium* and if he tried to screw with fate the Oracles would have him hanging by his balls and Laylah would be left on her own.

Or worse than alone, he silently corrected as the ridiculous gargoyle crashed through the underbrush, his wings flapping and his eyes wide as he was chased by two tall pursuers.

"By my father's stone balls," the tiny demon gasped, "who invited the Sylvermyst to the party?"

Tane shifted into a fighter's stance, the dagger held loosely in his hand as he watched the warriors approach.

They looked like fey.

Tall and lithe with long hair in varying shades of red and gold. All of them were dressed in jeans and T-shirts, no doubt hoping to avoid unwanted attention from the humans.

A wasted effort.

Generic jeans and T-shirts didn't disguise the liquid grace of their movements or the perfection of their faces that could never belong to a mere mortal.

Oh, and of course there were the enormous crossbows that were currently pointed in his direction.

Dead giveaway.

A swift count revealed four Sylvermyst approaching from the east and two more from the south.

Too many to defeat without risking a wooden arrow through the heart.

"Make yourself useful, gargoyle," he commanded.

Levet sniffed, but thankfully he lifted his hands and pointed them toward the advancing Sylvermyst.

"Watch in wonder, vampire."

There was a sputter of sparkles that shimmered in the air before they fell harmlessly to the ground.

Just his luck.

The gargoyle was shooting blanks.

Accustomed to fighting impossible odds without backup, Tane charged toward the two nearest attackers, taking an arrow in his shoulder and another in his upper chest before he was near enough to grab the first Sylvermyst and rip open his throat.

The potent taste of fairy blood slid down his throat. Not

the sparkling sweetness of most fey, but a dark explosion of power that burned a path to his gut.

Sucking the bastard dry, he stuck a dagger into the fey's heart and gave it a twist before tossing him to the ground and reaching for his partner.

The second fey had already dropped his crossbow and reached for the sword strapped to his back.

Tane ducked as the blade swiped a mere inch above his head. Wisely he kept low as he took out the warrior's legs and drove him hard into the ground.

The Sylvermyst spoke in a language that grated harshly on Tane's ears, but even as the words formed Tane was slicing his throat.

He wasn't in the mood to be hexed or cursed or hit with any other nasty spell.

Once assured there weren't going to be any surprises, Tane kicked the sword out of the fey's hand and efficiently cut out his heart.

The eyes, a strange, metallic shade of copper, widened in shock. As if he hadn't expected to be killed by an enraged vampire.

Fool.

With the two nearest warriors dispatched, Tane grabbed the Sylvermyst's sword and straightened. If the magic filling the air wasn't screwing with his senses there were plenty more where those came from.

He was kicking aside the nearest corpse to make sure it didn't impede his movements when the explosion rocked the ground from beneath his feet.

He flowed upright, his startled gaze sweeping his surroundings.

The trees in front of him were flattened, the massive trunks still smoking, and the dirt that filled the air settling on top of them.

More impressive, the four fey who had been approaching were now scattered across the ground in a dozen different pieces.

"Holy mother . . ." he breathed, tugging out the arrows stuck in his flesh.

Levet's wings flapped in embarrassment. "Oops."

Oops?

The gargoyle had released the equivalent of a minor nuclear bomb and all he said was "oops"?

"I said make yourself useful, not cataclysmic," he snapped, terrified by the knowledge that Laylah was somewhere in the trees and that she could easily have been harmed.

"Hey, I do not critique your battle techniques," the tiny gargoyle protested.

The ridiculous squabble was brought to a thankful end as Laylah appeared behind them, holding a small child in her arms.

He grimaced at the protective ward that surrounded the baby. Despite being transparent it visibly shifted, distorting and obscuring the image of the child. He doubted even Laylah had ever had a clear view of what she was carrying around.

Not that she seemed to give a damn.

His heart clenched with an odd ache as her expression softened and she cradled the baby against her with maternal care.

Her short, crimson hair was mussed. Her jeans and T-shirt were marred with grass stains. And there was a streak of dirt on her cheek.

And she'd never looked more content.

Unaware of his fascination, she lifted her head, the tender expression hardened as she glanced toward the charred trees decorated with bits and pieces of Sylver-mysts.

"Gods." She shuddered. "Where did they come from?"

Levet waddled toward her, his gaze taking a cautious inventory of the child in her arms.

He wasn't as stupid as he looked.

Tane couldn't sense the stasis spell that bound the baby, but he was wise enough to give it a wide berth.

"I don't know where they came from," the gargoyle said, "but I know who they're traveling with."

"Marika?" she asked.

"And the mage," Levet confirmed Tane's suspicions. "I am going to turn him into a pile of fairy dung."

She shook her head. "No, we have to get out of here."

Tane moved to grasp her arm, tugging her away from the carnage.

"Levet, keep watch," he ordered, his narrowed glance warning he wouldn't take "no" for an answer.

Perhaps sensing Tane's hidden motive, the gargoyle gave a ready nod.

"Oui."

He maneuvered Laylah behind a large oak before she dug in her heels and narrowed her gaze.

The gargoyle wasn't the only one to guess his motive.

"Don't even think about it."

He held her furious gaze. "Laylah, you must shadow walk."

"And leave you and Levet here to die?"

"Your faith in my skills is always heartwarming," he said wryly.

"You're surrounded, outnumbered, and my lunatic aunt is out there with a powerful mage," she said without apology. "What do you think your odds are?"

"They would be considerably better if you weren't here."

She winced at his brutal honesty. "What?" she muttered. "I pricked your pride now you have to insult me?"

He released his grip on her, folding his arms over his chest. He refused to back down.

He couldn't force Laylah to obey him, but he was happy to use whatever emotional blackmail necessary.

"Think, Laylah. Your aunt and her horde from hell are searching for you. Once you're gone she won't have any reason to continue her attack."

She frowned. "You can't be certain."

"Marika's crazy, not stupid."

"What does that mean?"

"She's not going to risk her warriors on a bunch of wood sprites and a vampire who has no value to her."

She caught her bottom lip between her teeth, unable to deny the truth of his words.

"I . . . I can't."

"You have no choice," he ruthlessly pressed. "You claimed the child as your own. Now you must protect him."

Her lips tightened as a battle between loyalties raged inside her. At last, her fierce need to protect the innocent child in her arms overwhelmed all else.

"Damn you," she muttered, stepping back as she prepared to enter the mists.

Relief blasted through him, but his primitive instincts had him moving forward to kiss her with a stark promise.

"Laylah," he whispered, careful to avoid contact with the child in her arms.

"What?"

"Don't think this is over." He pulled back, his face hard with resolve. "I'll find you."

She met him glare for glare. "If you get yourself killed . . ."

"Go."

With one last kiss, he spun away and headed back to Levet, but even with his back turned he felt the moment she disappeared.

It wasn't the absence of her soft breath. Or the prickling heat of awareness he felt when she was near.

It was the gaping hole in the center of his chest.

He absently rubbed the mark that Siljar had seared onto his skin, as if it might ease the icy emptiness.

God almighty.

He was in deep shit.

As if to emphasize the point, he stepped through an opening in the trees to be greeted by a half dozen Sylvermyst warriors advancing with their crossbows raised.

"Arrows." Levet heaved a tragic sigh. "Must they be so predictable?"

Tane wasn't nearly so dismissive. A wooden arrow through the heart would make for a very bad night. Besides, they hurt like a bitch coming out.

"Hard to beat the classics," he said, halting a step behind the gargoyle as the tiny demon lifted his hands to launch a fireball at the encroaching enemy.

"True." Levet glanced over his shoulder with a smirk. "And they are most effective against vampires. Always the mark of a fine weapon."

"Not only vampires." He bared his fangs. "The Sylvermyst are rumored to hex their arrows with spells that make demons impotent."

The gray eyes widened in pure male horror. "That is not a matter to jest about."

Tane gave a twirl of his Sylvermyst sword, knocking aside a flurry of arrows.

"Who says I'm jesting?"

"You are truly a wicked man," Levet muttered.

"So I've been told."

With a flick of his tail, Levet turned back toward their attackers, lobbing another fireball among the trees. The sudden light revealed a tall form standing in the shadows, watching the battle in silence.

The leader.

Tane was certain of it.

Not that he had much opportunity to assess the danger. Dodging the flames, two of the Sylvermyst leapt directly at him, their swords slashing toward his head.

With a speed that no fey could follow, Tane spun to the side, striking out with his sword.

His blow was blocked by a matching sword, the sparks flying through the air. Sensing movement behind him, Tane used his superior strength to shove the fey off balance, turning to meet the second sword thrust.

The blade moved smoothly through the air, speaking of the craftsmanship of the sword. Obviously the Sylvermyst were well armed.

And well trained . . .

He growled as the opponent behind him jabbed his sword through the fleshy part of his shoulder, obviously hoping to disable him long enough to strike a killing blow. A wise strategy if he was battling anything but a vampire.

Gritting his teeth, Tane grasped the end of the sword sticking out of his shoulder, pulling it deeper into his body.

The Sylvermyst breathed a sound of shock, but grimly held onto his weapon. A lethal mistake.

With a last yank, Tane had the warrior close enough to

his back that he could reach over his wounded shoulder and grab him by his long braid.

A cry was ripped from the fey's throat as he found himself flying over Tane's head and landing on his partner had grimly been attempting to get past Tane's sword.

The two went down in a pile of flailing limbs and curses, and Tane didn't hesitate as he sliced off the head of one Sylvermyst and then the other.

A potent scent of herbs filled the air as the blood of the fey soaked into the mossy ground, but Tane didn't pause to admire the gory victory. Spinning the sword, he turned, not at all surprised to discover yet another fey barreling through the trees in his direction.

Dammit. Enough was enough. He was tired of playing pincushion for the bastards. Yanking his dagger from its sheath he sent it sailing in one smooth motion.

The fey tried to dodge to the side, but the blade sank deep in his throat, slicing through a major artery. For a minute the warrior remained indifferent to the blood pouring down his chest. It wasn't until his knees buckled and he fell forward that he realized the danger of the gaping wound.

Tane was on him before he could try to stem the flow, sinking his fangs into his flesh and draining the last of the blood from his limp body.

The power of the fey flowed through his veins, helping to heal his wounds.

Straightening, he was prepared for the next attack.

An attack that never came.

Instead the remaining fey sank back into the shadows. All but the tall warrior that Tane had already tagged as the leader.

He reached down to pull the dagger from the fallen

warrior as the Sylvermyst strolled through the underbrush,
a large crossbow pointed at Tane's chest.

He was taller than the others and built with more bulk
than most fey, but he had the same oddly metallic eyes of
the other Sylvermyst that shimmered with a pure bronze
in the moonlight. His long hair was a dark shade of chestnut and his delicate features held an arrogant sneer.

Tane narrowed his gaze. Ah, the pleasure of knocking
that sneer from the too-pretty face.

A pity he needed answers more than he needed the
pleasure of slicing and dicing another fey.

Obviously the Sylvermyst came to the same conclusion
as he stepped into the small clearing, his crossbow aimed,
but his finger off the trigger.

"Where is the child?" the Sylvermyst demanded, his
voice holding a power that filled the air.

Tane's fingers tightened on the sword. Damn. This
Sylvermyst was different.

Dangerous.

"Why don't you come and find out?" he invited, wanting the creature close enough he could rip out his heart if
necessary.

There was a rustle in the undergrowth as Levet sidled
to stand at his side.

"Tane, do you truly think it wise to taunt the Sylvermyst with the hexed arrows?"

The bronze gaze dipped to the tiny gargoyle, his lips
pulling into a mocking smile.

"Is that your wingman?" He shifted his attention back
to Tane. "Pathetic even for a leech."

"Hey!" Levet protested.

Tane, on the other hand, couldn't argue.

It really was pathetic.

Instead he narrowed his gaze. "Wingman? You don't

speak like a fairy who has been banished from this world for centuries."

"I'll admit my cable service was shitty in hell, but . . ."

"No," Tane growled. "You're lying."

"Probably. I'm evil, after all," the fey taunted. "It's what we do."

"I don't need an owner's manual for evil."

The fey's smile widened. "No, I don't suppose you do, vampire."

Tane paused. Did the bastard have a sense of humor or a death wish?

Either way he was setting off alarms that Tane wasn't willing to ignore.

"Who are you?"

"Isn't it enough to know I'm the man who is going to kill you?"

Tane lifted a brow. "Are you scared to give me your name or embarrassed?"

There was a moment of hesitation before the creature shrugged.

"Ariyal," he revealed, his gaze flicking dismissively over Tane. "And you are the infamous Tane. Scourge of rogue vampires around the world. Now that we have the introductions out of the way, tell me where the child is."

Tane's question was answered.

A death wish.

Now that was cleared up, he wanted to know how the fey had discovered he was a Charon.

"Where have you been hiding?"

"Now, now. Don't be rude, leech," Ariyal drawled. "I asked my question first."

"You sure the hell haven't been sharing a dimension with the Dark Lord."

The bronze eyes glittered, a prickling pressure filling the air.

"Did you miss the story about the overly curious cat?" he asked smoothly. "He got his head chopped off."

"Damn." Tane came to a sudden decision. Ariyal annoyed the hell out of him, but he wasn't stupid enough to underestimate him. When he realized the babe was long gone he was going to release whatever magic he was keeping leashed. Tane didn't want to be around when that happened. "Levet."

"Oui?"

"Can you hide our scents long enough for us to escape?"

"I thought you would never ask," the gargoyle muttered. He waved a hand toward the Sylvermyst. "What about Tinker Bell?"

Ariyal glanced toward Levet, smiling with a cruel anticipation.

"Oh, I'm going to enjoy grinding you into dust."

"He's coming with us," Tane muttered.

Levet squeaked in dismay. "Are you *complètement fou?*"

Was he completely mad?

A question for later.

Moving with a speed not even a fey on steroids could track, Tane halted directly before Ariyal, knocking the crossbow out of his hand.

"Arrogant bast . . ."

The fey's furious words were brought to a sharp end as Tane's fist connected with his chin.

There was a satisfying crunch as Tane felt the man's jaw shatter beneath the impact of his blow. Then, catching the fey's limp body before it hit the ground, Tane slung him over his shoulder and turned toward the wide-eyed gargoyle.

"Let's go."

It all started out so well.

Laylah entered the mists without problem, even carrying the child.

It had taken a minute or two to shake off the draining dizziness that always plagued her after a shift into the corridor between worlds, and another few minutes to determine a direction.

She could go anywhere.

She could disappear with her child and never be found.

But even as the thought fluttered through her mind, she deliberately focused on Chicago and Styx's elegant lair.

For years she'd believed that she'd managed to disappear, but she wasn't nearly so clever as she'd thought. The Commission had always known about her, and God only knew who else.

Besides, the only true means of keeping the baby safe was to kill off those who hunted him. Bloodthirsty, but true.

And the vampires were her best bet.

She was busy convincing herself that her decision had nothing to do with Tane when she felt an archway forming in the mists.

On instant alert, she clutched the baby tightly in her arms, backing away from the shimmering veil that was growing at a rapid rate.

Shit.

This was something she'd always feared when she shadow walked.

Either something was about to enter the mists with her or . . .

It turned out to be the "or" as the veil swelled forward and wrapped around her, sucking her into another dimension.

She screamed as she was yanked from the mists and tumbling through the veil to land with painful force on her back.

Black flecks danced before her eyes as the air was slammed from her lungs. Gods. It felt like she'd landed on a brick wall.

Holding the baby in a death grip, she sucked in a deep breath and took stock of her surroundings.

It didn't feel like hell. Or even a foreign dimension, she slowly concluded.

In fact . . .

Scrabbling to her feet, Laylah glanced around the familiar countryside, her heart sinking.

Dammit. She'd gone less than twenty miles from where she'd started. And worse, she wasn't alone.

Whirling around, she was prepared for anything.

Oracles, mages, a full-bred Jinn. Something powerful enough to yank her from the mists.

Instead her gaze landed on a slender man with surfer-boy good looks who she easily recognized.

"Holy crap. Caine?" she breathed in shock, her gaze skimming the abandoned gas station and empty pumps before returning to the cur. "What the hell did you do to me?"

He held up his hands, his slender face and blue eyes revealing a grim maturity that hadn't been there only a few days ago.

He grimaced, walking toward her. "Don't blame me."

Laylah froze, the air charged with the electric pulse of her energy.

"Wait."

Caine halted on a dime. He'd known her long enough to realize bad things happened when she was threatened.

He lifted his slender hands in a gesture of peace. "What is it?"

"Stay right there," she warned. "Who are you?"

"Who am I? Are you tripping?" His brows snapped together. "You just said my name."

"I know what I said, but there's something wrong with you."

His sharp laugh echoed through the darkness. "I can't argue with that. You want the long list or short?"

"I want to know why you smell like a pureblood."

He shoved his hands into the pockets of his faded jeans. "Believe it or not a demented demon lord, who had been sucking the magic from Weres for centuries, slammed through me on his way back to hell, killing me in the process before I was mysteriously resurrected as a pureblooded Were."

Laylah blinked, struggling to process the clipped words.

Good . . . lord. Had his bizarre visions actually come true?

Unbelievable.

She had a thousand questions, but Caine's rigid lack of emotion warned he wasn't ready to discuss his mindblowing experience.

She could relate.

She wasn't much into sharing.

"I believe you," she said. "No one could make up that story."

"I actually have a witness."

He waved a hand and a female Were who had been hidden in a nearby Jeep slowly approached.

Laylah was momentarily disconcerted. She looked like Harley and Darcy, only with longer hair and lighter eyes.

"Gods, not another one," she muttered. "How many are there?"

The woman studied her with an unconcealed curiosity that might have been rude if Laylah hadn't sensed the remarkable innocence of her heart.

"If you refer to my sisters there are four of us in total." She tilted her head to the side, her pale hair shimmering in the moonlight. "At least, that was what I was told."

"This is Cassandra." Caine moved to place a protective arm around the Were's shoulders. "Cassie, this is Laylah."

Laylah flashed a strained smile. Now wasn't the time for chitchat.

She didn't have a clue what had yanked her from the mists, but she did know she wasn't near far enough from her aunt and the attacking Sylvermysts.

"Well, it's great to meet you, Cassie, but I'm kind of in a hurry."

"Wait." Without warning, Cassie reached out to grasp her upper arm, her grip astonishingly strong. "You're meant to be here."

Laylah's eyes narrowed in anger. Obviously the Were had wanted her at this godforsaken gas station in the middle of nowhere.

"Are you the one who pulled me out of the mists?"

"Easy, Laylah," Caine growled. "Cassie is just the messenger."

"For my aunt?"

"Aunt?" Caine looked genuinely confused. "Where the hell did you get an aunt?"

"I ordered her off eBay," Laylah snapped, tugging away

from the Were. She didn't trust either one of them. "Who sent you?"

"Fate," Cassie murmured.

A flash of lightning struck the steel pole that supported the rusting sign in the shape of a hamburger.

With an awkward movement, Caine pushed himself between Laylah and his companion.

"Dammit, Laylah, don't wig out, she really does mean fate."

She grit her teeth. "Caine, I'm not in the mood to be jerked around. Tell me what's going on or I swear I'll fry you."

"She's . . ." He hesitated before the words were seemingly ripped from his lips. "A prophet."

Prophet?

Well, that was a conversation ender.

Laylah sucked in a startled breath, her powers faltering. "She sees the future?"

"Only in glimpses," Caine warily admitted, clearly driven by a primitive need to protect the beautiful Were.

A dangerous position.

If she truly were a prophet then she would be considered a holy grail among the demon world.

"I thought they were extinct," she said.

"Most people thought the same of Jinn mongrels," Caine pointed out dryly.

Laylah grimaced.

Couldn't argue with that.

She turned toward the Were who possessed such an eerie resemblance to Harley.

"So if you're not completely out of your mind, why has some mystical fate brought me here?"

She shrugged. "I don't have a clue."

"Great. Then fate's out of luck . . ."

"No," Cassie hastily interrupted. "It's the child."

Laylah's gut twisted in fear. "What about him?"

"He's in danger."

Laylah frowned. That was the prophecy?

"Not really a newsflash. Why do you think I was trying to get away? If you hadn't interfered . . ."

Caine's growl trickled through the air. "Careful, Jinn."

Cassie waved aside her champion, her expression troubled as she touched Laylah's arm, insanely indifferent to the danger of being so close to the stasis spell that surrounded the baby.

"Don't be blinded by the obvious threats. There are more than you suspect."

"Perfect," Laylah muttered, then she jerked back in alarm when the crazy Were placed a hand directly over the spell surrounding the baby. "Hey. What are you doing?"

The woman's eyes flared with a blinding white light. "The Gemini."

Laylah stepped back, cradling the child tight against her chest. Hidden threats? Gemini?

It was the sort of babble that she would expect from a fake prophet, not the real deal.

"I don't know what that means."

"The alpha and the omega." Cassie shrugged, her eyes returning to normal. "To find the end you must return to the beginning."

Chapter 17

A cold prickle filled the air, sharply reminding Laylah she already had enough known enemies to worry about without adding mysterious ones.

"Okay. I really need to be on my way."

Cassie shook her head. "Not yet."

Caine spun toward the empty fields, catching the unmistakable scent of vampire the same moment as Laylah.

"Cassie, someone's coming."

"Tane," Laylah breathed, relief slamming through her that he was safe.

Caine lifted his brows in surprise. "A friend of yours?"

"He's not alone," Cassie said, thankfully diverting Laylah from the need of explaining her complicated relationship with Tane.

"That damned gargoyle," Caine muttered, his head tilted back as he sniffed the air. "And . . . what?"

"Darkness," Cassie breathed.

Caine swore. "We're out of here."

Cassie lifted a restraining hand as Caine reached to toss her over his shoulder.

"No, Caine. I must speak with the vampire."

Laylah might have admired the tiny woman's ability to

tame the once rebellious cur if she hadn't been consumed
with the sight of the infuriated vampire who was barreling toward her with a strange fey tossed over his shoulder
and a gargoyle on his heels.

It wasn't a sight you ran across every day.

"Damn you, Laylah, you're supposed to be . . ."

"Don't start with me, He-man," she warned, wisely
shifting backward as Tane tossed aside the unconscious
fey and glared toward Caine. Two alphas in the same
space was never, ever a good thing. "It wasn't my choice
to be here."

Tane moved to stand directly between Laylah and
Caine, his frigid power lashing through the air.

"I thought I caught the stench of dog."

Caine's eyes glowed with the inner light of a pureblood.
"You want a piece of me, bloodsucker?"

Laylah grabbed Tane's arm. "No, Tane. We don't have
time for a pissing contest."

With a blithe disregard for life and limb, Levet waddled
between the two predators, studying Caine with a puzzled
expression.

"Hey, I know you." He rubbed his stub of a nose. "*Mon
Dieu,* what have you done to yourself?"

Tane scowled. "What's going on?"

Laylah and Cassie shared a glance of mutual female
exasperation.

"Long story short, this is Caine who had a run-in with
a demon lord who transformed him into a pureblood,"
Laylah said.

Tane stiffened. "The cur who held you captive?"

"She was never my prisoner," Caine snapped, as if offended by the accusation.

"Please, we have little time." Cassie stepped forward,
belatedly capturing Tane's attention.

"God . . . damn," he muttered in shock.

Levet was equally astonished. "The last of Darcy's sisters."

Tane nodded. "Styx must be told."

"No fucking way . . ."

"Caine." Cassie hastily halted Caine with a hand to his chest. She glanced toward Laylah, as if hoping for a little "women versus men" cooperation. "I am only here to deliver a warning."

Tane predictably ignored what he didn't want to hear. "I'll take you to your sister and you can deliver all the warnings you want."

Caine's scent was musky as his wolf prowled to the surface.

"Touch her and die, vampire."

"Tane, you must listen to her," Laylah commanded. "She's a prophet."

Dead silence greeted her little announcement.

Even Levet was speechless.

Nothing less than a miracle.

At last, Tane shook his head. "Impossible."

"Cassie, you're wasting your time," Caine snapped, firmly scooping her into his arms and heading for the Jeep. "A vampire's ego is too bloated to listen to advice, no matter who's offering it."

Cassie didn't struggle, but she did pop her head over Caine's shoulder.

"Vampire, you must not kill your prisoner."

Tane glanced toward the forgotten fey lying on the ground. "Why not?"

"You will have need of him."

"I will have need of him? Wait." Tane clenched his hands as Caine settled Cassie in the passenger seat and then leaped behind the wheel, taking off in a cloud of dust. "This mystical future shit is pissing me off," he muttered.

Laylah parted her lips to demand an explanation of why Tane was carrying around an unconscious Sylvermyst, when all three of them froze in alarm.

The scent of herbs carried on the breeze, and something much worse.

A deranged vampire.

"Umm . . ." Levet cleared his throat. "Can you be pissed off somewhere far away from here?"

Tane glanced toward the horizon. "Damn. It's too close to dawn to make it to my lair."

"Hand over the Sylvermyst and I will consider offering you shelter."

The female voice came without warning, nearly making Laylah jump out of her shoes. Tane, on the other hand, had his dagger flying toward the gas station and the sword pulled from the scabbard he'd strapped to his back.

With the calm arrogance only a vampire could claim, the woman snatched the dagger from midair and stepped out of the decrepit building.

"Hunter," Tane rasped in a low tone.

"Hunter?" Laylah questioned, not sure whether she should be relieved or screaming in horror.

"They're vampires who are born with the rare ability to wrap themselves in such deep shadows that no one can detect their presence," he explained. "Traditionally they hire themselves out to hunt down demons who don't want to be found. Very exclusive and very expensive."

Laylah wondered if Tane was mistaken.

The female looked like a fashion model with the exotic beauty that only a mixture of races could achieve.

Tall and slender, her glossy black hair that hinted at her

Asian ancestry was contained in a tight braid that hung down her back. There was also a touch of the East in her faintly slanted eyes, although they were a dark shade of blue that revealed a European heritage. Her skin was as pale as alabaster and her lips a lush shade of pink.

She was drop-dead gorgeous.

Of course, she was dressed in black spandex from head to foot that gave off a whole *Mission Impossible* vibe and the sawed-off shotgun holstered at her side did warn she might not be just another pretty face.

Twirling the dagger, she approached with a bold nonchalance that Laylah could only envy.

"You must be Jaelyn," Tane said.

"And you must be Tane, the Charon," the female drawled.

Laylah frowned. "Are the two of you acquainted?"

"No, but I recognize her skills. What do you want with the Sylvermyst?"

The vampire glanced toward the unconscious fey. "I've been tracking him for days."

"Why?"

She smiled, flashing her fangs.

Nope, no fashion model.

"Not your biz."

Tane narrowed his gaze. "Considering he's currently my prisoner, I'd say it's very much my biz."

"Ah, but I'm the one with the solarproof digs."

Laylah reluctantly stepped into the fray. What choice did she have? Tane was just stubborn enough to ignore the offer of shelter because he was annoyed by the vampire's attitude.

"Tane, we don't have much time to debate the issue."

He slid a smoldering glance in her direction, his

expression softening as he took in the weariness she couldn't hide.

She was discovering that being pulled out of the mists, no matter what the cause, was more draining than actually walking through them.

He returned his attention to Jaelyn.

"Your lair is secure?"

The indigo eyes narrowed. "I'm the wrong vampire to insult, Charon."

Laylah swallowed a sigh. Did all vampires have anger management issues?

Levet tugged on her pant leg. "I assume that means it's secure?"

Laylah grimaced. "I'm thinking we want to stay out of the family squabble."

Levet shuddered with ready revulsion. "*Oui*, there is nothing more dangerous than families."

Laylah glanced toward the distant fields where her aunt had brought an evil army to search for her.

"No shit."

Tane didn't like putting his trust in a vampire he knew only for her reputation of being overly aggressive with a short fuse.

Especially not when Laylah was with him.

But with the sun less than a half an hour from rising and Marika and her Sylvermysts on their trail, he didn't have a lot of choice.

Allowing Jaelyn to lead them to a small town settled between a patchwork of farms, Tane wrapped himself in shadows as they moved across the small park in the center of town. Country folk tended to be up early and the last thing he needed was someone to spot him carrying the still unconscious Sylvermyst.

The hunter at last waved them into a crumbling brick building on the corner of the downtown square. Entering, Tane realized that it had once been a local bank, but now the teller windows were shuttered and the tile floor was covered in dust.

They passed through the narrow lobby and moved down a short flight of stairs that led to the bank vault below.

Laylah briefly faltered, perhaps fearing they were all expected to squeeze into the small space for the next twelve hours.

He didn't blame her.

Two vampires, a Sylvermyst, a gargoyle, and a half-breed Jinn shoved in a tiny, steel-lined vault . . . yeah, bad idea all the way around.

With a gentle pressure he urged her inside. No vampire had a lair without a few hidden doors.

To prove his point, Jaelyn brushed past them, shoving aside the shelves of safety deposit boxes to reveal a door cut into the steel. She paused, whispering soft words that released the hexes that guarded the entrance and the door sprung open, revealing a wooden staircase that led to the underground tunnels.

In silence they moved into the darkness below. Tane could feel the heavy weight of the approaching dawn, but it was his concern for Laylah that made him urge Jaelyn to a faster pace. The stubborn Jinn would rather collapse than ask for help, but he could sense she was barely able to put one foot in front of the other.

The short tunnel ended at another door that opened into a large room. Tane studied the leather seats scattered across the crimson carpet and the tools of S & M hung on the walls. Not that he gave a crap about the décor. His only interest was in potential dangers and, of course, the nearest exits.

Laylah, however, grimaced, seemingly relieved when Jaelyn led her into a private bedroom with a simple bed and armoire with an attached room she could use to lay the child.

Grudgingly handing the Sylvermyst over to his hostess, Tane shooed Levet away and, waiting for Laylah to make the babe comfortable in the attached room, he at last settled her on the wide bed and tugged the covers over her.

Then, leaning against the headboard, he made himself comfortable and closed his eyes.

He was old enough that he could rest and regain his strength while still remaining on full-alert.

Several hours passed before the sound of approaching footsteps had him off the bed and wrenching open the door.

He might be forced to accept Jaelyn's hospitality, but he didn't trust her near Laylah.

Actually, he wasn't sure he trusted anyone near Laylah.

Wisely halting several feet from the door, Jaelyn lifted a hand in a gesture of peace.

"Easy, Charon," she said, still dressed in the spandex although she'd replaced the shotgun with a Glock 18. "I'm no threat to your female."

His lips twisted at his fierce rush to protect Laylah. Especially considering she could destroy this entire lair with a single thought.

"My female can take care of herself," he said wryly.

Jaelyn rolled her eyes. "Yeah, she can, but I doubt you're willing to give her the opportunity."

"What do you want?"

"My prisoner is awake."

"*Your* prisoner?" He arched a brow. "Having trouble with your pronouns, Hunter?"

"My only trouble at the moment is you." The female pointed a finger toward the ceiling protecting them from the late afternoon sun. "I held up my end of the bargain."

Not sure what Jaelyn intended for the Sylvermyst, Tane turned to retrieve the sword he'd leaned against the wall near the door.

"Fine," he said, "but I need to question him before you do any damage."

She gave a lift of her shoulder, turning to walk down the narrow hallway.

"Come with me."

Tane readily followed. "Are you going to tell me why you've been hunting the Sylvermyst?"

The vampire paused to tug open the trapdoor set in the center of the hallway. Tane smiled. The lead door had to weigh a ton, but Jaelyn had lifted it with ease.

A testament that the rumors of her innate powers weren't inflated.

A pity she was still so young. He would have sponsored her in the battles of Durotriges, the gladiator-type games that were for the most elite of demon warriors. The few vampires who survived walked out with the mark of CuChulainn, a dragon-shaped tattoo that earned them the right to challenge for clan chief.

She lifted her head to stab him with an impatient glare. "I was hired by the Oracles, that's all you get."

Tane grimaced. It was more than he wanted.

He had enough trouble with Oracles without adding more.

Jaelyn could keep her damned reason for wanting the Sylvermyst to herself.

She disappeared through the hole and Tane was swiftly

dropping into the darkness behind her. His feet had barely touched the hard floor when Jaelyn flicked a switch and he studied his surroundings.

He wasn't entirely surprised to discover they were standing in the center of a dungeon. Where else did you keep a prisoner?

But he was a little startled by just how elaborate the dungeon was.

Ten cells lined the walls, each of them custom constructed to hold different species of demons. Some made of silver, some of iron, some of wood, and even one of solid gold. But it was the large room at the far side of the dungeon that captured his attention.

Had Jaelyn gone to a close-out sale for Torture-R-Us?

There were racks, branding irons, enormous pinchers, spiked clubs, and the always popular electric chair that did nasty things to a vampire. There were even a few devices that Tane didn't recognize.

And in the air the scent of disinfectant hung like a cloud. As if someone spent a lot of time cleaning up gory messes.

"Nice," he murmured, shooting his companion a mocking glance. "Yours?"

She flipped him off, headed toward one of the lead cells. "I'm subletting the place."

"From Marquis de Sade?"

"I have a strict policy of not putting my nose where it doesn't belong."

"I can imagine."

A haunted expression briefly darkened her eyes. "No, you really can't."

She opened the cell door, before Tane could press her for an answer. Not that he was sure he wanted to. She didn't seem like the kind of vampire who wanted to share.

Exactly like he used to be.

He paused, then hastily squashed just what his stray thought had revealed.

Instead he turned his attention to the Sylvermyst seated in a wooden chair.

Ariyal looked decidedly worse for the wear.

His hair had come loose from his braid to fall about his face streaked with dirt, and his clothes were stained and ripped. At some point, Jaelyn had tied his arms together behind his back and shackled them to the wall with iron cuffs.

He had to be in considerable pain, but his expression was mocking as they entered.

"Ah, the fanged Bobbsey Twins. How cute," he drawled, stretching out his long legs and crossing them at the ankle. "Are we going to play games?"

"If that's what you want. Let me explain the rules." Tane strolled casually forward, touching the tip of his stolen sword to the bastard's throat. "I'm going to ask you a number of questions. If you refuse to answer or try to lie I will carve a strip of flesh from your body. We'll continue until I have the answers I want or you run out of flesh."

The bronze gaze shifted to Jaelyn who had closed the door and strolled to stand at Tane's side.

"If we're going to play rough I'd rather have the female. No offense, but she's more to my taste."

"You'd never survive me." She leaned down to grab his chin, only to release it with a hiss, shaking her hand as if she'd been scalded. "Shit."

Tane frowned. "What's wrong?"

With a scowl at the Sylvermyst who'd lost his smirk, Jaelyn backed away until she was leaning against the door.

"Nothing."

Tane took a step toward her, sensing something important had just happened.

"Hunter . . ."

"Get on with your interrogation," Jaelyn snapped. "I expect you to be gone at nightfall."

"Is she always so charming?" Ariyal taunted, although Tane didn't miss the edge in his voice. Whatever had occurred between the two of them had been as unwelcome to the Sylvermyst as to Jaelyn.

Turning back to the prisoner, Tane sliced two cuts into the fey's shoulder and peeled off a small piece of flesh.

"You forgot the rules," he said.

With a foreign curse, Ariyal leaned away from the hovering sword.

Tane watched in fascination as the blood on the blade sizzled and then melted into steel, as if the sword was absorbing power from the blood.

Interesting.

"Ask what you want," Ariyal gritted.

"How did you avoid being banished with the other Sylvermyst?"

His jaw clenched, but he grudgingly answered. "Our Prince bartered with Morgana le Fay to remain hidden in her sanctuary."

Hell. Talk about a deal with the devil.

Tane jerked back in shock. "Avalon?"

Ariyal shrugged. "What better place? Nothing could penetrate the shroud of magic."

Tane could think of a shitload of better places.

Beginning with the fiery pits of hell.

Morgana le Fay was a cruel megalomaniac who had terrorized the fey, and every other demon too weak to withstand her magic, until her seer had predicted that she would be condemned to hell by a descendent of her brother, Arthur.

She'd predictably retreated to her private island and shrouded it in a thick layer of magic that was impossible to penetrate, although she occasionally returned to the world in the hopes of killing off Arthur's descendents.

A poor choice in the end.

"What did you barter?" he asked.

Ariyal smirked, but Tane sensed the surge in his pulse and the sudden sweating of his palms. Whatever happened on Avalon hadn't been good.

"We were slaves in her harem." He ground his teeth so hard it was a wonder they didn't shatter. "Sex slaves."

Tane grimaced. He wouldn't wish that on his worst enemy.

"From what I've heard of Morgana I'm surprised you survived."

"Many didn't."

"Then you were fortunate that the vampires managed to destroy her."

The Sylvermyst snorted, but the horror faded from his eyes as he reacted to Tane's deliberate taunt.

"She was defeated by the descendent of King Arthur."

"Anna is the mate of a vampire, and it was only with the assistance of my brothers that she survived to battle Morgana le Fey," Tane said with cool logic. "It would seem you are in our debt."

"What makes you think I wanted her dead?"

"A lie," Jaelyn said from the door, her tone stripped of emotions.

Tane smiled. He'd forgotten a hunter's skill often included being able to sense a lie.

"You didn't ask me a direct question," Ariyal said,

refusing to glance in her direction. "I have broken no rules of the game."

Yep. Definitely something going on there.

But none of his concern.

Hallelujah.

"What is your interest in the child?" he instead demanded.

"We were hired by the vampire and her wizard to find the child."

Tane glanced toward Jaelyn. She nodded. "He speaks the truth, but not the full truth."

"You're a mercenary?"

Ariyal paused, choosing his words with care. "I'm willing to sell our services with the proper incentive."

"And what incentive did Marika offer you?"

"The opportunity to locate the supposed child of the Dark Lord."

"Supposed?" Tane latched onto the word, certain that it had been a slip. "Is there some question to the child's identity?"

The Sylvermyst quickly recovered. "Only a fool accepts rumors and obscured folktale as truth."

Tane shifted with impatience. Ariyal was too cunning. He answered the question with just enough truth to avoid a painful mutilation, but without telling Tane a damned thing.

"You hope to return the Dark Lord to the world?" he pressed.

"The Sylvermyst have worshipped him before vampires ever crawled from their caves."

Another evasion.

But if he didn't want to return the Dark Lord, then why was he searching for the baby?

It made no sense.

"How does Marika intend to use the child to return the bastard?"

Ariyal shrugged. "She claims the mage has a spell that will resurrect his essence within the child."

With a growl, Tane shoved the sword back against the fey's neck, frustration boiling through him.

How the hell could he keep Laylah safe if he was stumbling around blind?

"What are you really up to, Ariyal?"

The Sylvermyst met his blazing gaze without fear. "I've answered your questions."

Deciding that he was going to have to beat the answers out of the bastard, Tane felt a sharp pang of fear slice through him.

He stepped backward, momentarily confused.

Then, his heart slammed against his chest as he realized he was feeling Laylah's fear, not his own.

"Damn. Laylah needs me." He was across the cell and pulling open the door just as Jaelyn scrambled out of his path. "Don't kill him yet, I'm not finished with him."

"No guarantees," he heard her mutter before he was charging back to Laylah's side.

Chapter 18

It was the sensation of strong arms tugging her into a comforting embrace that woke Laylah from her nightmare.

Even then she continued to tremble as she struggled to banish the horrific visions of demons feasting on raw flesh as cities burned.

"Hush Laylah," Tane murmured, stroking a soft hand down her back. "You're safe."

"The child," she choked out.

Tane reluctantly released his hold on her to peek into the adjoining room, returning so swiftly that Laylah barely had time to untangle herself from the sweat-drenched covers before she was tugged firmly back into his arms.

"He appears well."

She breathed a sigh of relief, laying her head against his bare chest.

"Gods, it was horrible."

"It was only a dream, my sweet," he soothed, his exotic male scent teasing at her nose and easing the knot of fear in the pit of her stomach.

"There was blood," she husked, snuggling against his hard body. "The world was drowning in blood."

"Let it go," he whispered.

"It felt so real."

"I have you." He pressed a kiss to the top of her head. "You're safe."

Laylah calmed as she realized that for the first time in her life she actually did feel safe.

It was . . . lunacy.

She was being hunted by a power-hungry vampire, an immoral mage, a horde of evil fairies, and enemies who still lurked in the shadows, if the prophet was to be believed.

But when she was in Tane's arms, she felt as if there was nothing that could harm her.

She savored the amazing sensation for a moment.

A pity they couldn't lock out the world and remain together for eternity.

With a grudging sigh she pulled back to meet Tane's concerned gaze.

"Did you question the Sylvermyst?"

He made a noise of disgust. "For what it was worth."

"He wouldn't answer?"

"On the contrary, he gave me any number of answers," he said dryly. "None of which told me a damned thing."

She hid her smile at the edge in his voice. Tane was accustomed to striking fear into the hearts of everyone he encountered. It obviously pissed him off that he hadn't managed to bully the information he wanted from the Sylvermyst.

"Do they work for my aunt?"

"So Ariyal claims."

Ariyal. Laylah had only had a brief glance at the supposedly evil fey, but she'd been startled by his astonishing beauty.

Not that beauty meant a crap.

Jinn were notorious for possessing the faces of angels and the malevolent hearts of the devil.

Still she'd expected something . . . else.

"You don't believe him?"

Tane shrugged. "I believe he has his own reasons for wanting the child and he's willing to use Marika to locate the babe."

"Maluhia," Laylah said softly.

"What?"

"I've named the baby," she explained. "It means peace."

Tane froze, doing a perfect imitation of a mannequin. "I know what it means. It's a name of my ancestors," he at last rasped. "Why?"

Laylah chewed her lip.

He looked like he'd just been hit with a baseball bat.

So, was that a good or bad thing?

"I told you I was going to give the child a name," she hedged.

"Why that name?"

"I liked it."

Without warning Laylah found herself lying flat on her back with a very large, very delicious vampire pinning her to the mattress.

Her bones melted at the feel of his hard body pressed on top of her, glad she'd taken the time to remove everything but her panties and bra before crawling into the bed.

Now if she could just get rid of his khaki shorts . . .

"Laylah, tell me why."

She met the honey gaze, sensing her answer was somehow important.

"It reminded me of you."

His fingers threaded through her hair. "No one could call me peaceful."

"That is my wish for his future," she said gently, "but my hope for him as a man is that he will possess a sense of honor, with the strength to protect those he loves, and loyalty to those he claims as his family."

With a groan, Tane lowered his head to press a kiss to her forehead.

"You're killing me."

She frowned in confusion. "I thought . . ."

"What, my sweet?"

"I thought you would be pleased."

He pulled back, revealing an aching vulnerability that made Laylah's heart forget to beat.

"I'm humbled," he whispered.

Reaching up, she framed his beautiful face in her hands. "Never."

His fingers brushed through her hair and down the side of her throat, his thumb lingering at the pulse beating at the base.

"Laylah, you asked why the Oracle marked me."

She winced, lifting her hand to press it to the strange mark on his chest.

"To punish you."

"No. It was to bind me to you."

Oh . . . gods.

Laylah shook her head in horrified disbelief. For such a proud, independent vampire it must have been torture to be forcibly bound to another.

"Why would they do such a thing?" she breathed.

He didn't look horrified. In fact, there was something that resembled anticipation smoldering in his eyes.

"It doesn't matter, I was already in your power."

She narrowed her gaze in suspicion. She'd been a fool

in London to think her magic was strong enough to control a vampire.

"I don't believe you were ever in my supposed power."

With a shift of his hips he managed to part her legs, settling between them with a wicked smile.

"I have become your slave, but it has nothing to do with Jinn magic and everything to do with pure female bewitchment."

Heat curled through her body at the feel of his thick erection pressing against her inner thigh. Oh, it was so close to perfect. All she needed was a wiggle or two and she could have him settled exactly where he needed to be.

"Your slave, huh?" she husked.

"It's the truth, my sweet." He stroked his lips down her cheek, pausing to nibble at the corner of her mouth. Her arms instinctively circled his broad shoulders, skimming down his back. Pleasure hummed through her. Nice. She could spend hours exploring the hard muscles that rippled with encouragement beneath her touch. "With or without spells you're a part of me," he said, his voice thick with a fierce intensity.

She pulled back to study his somber expression with a searching gaze.

"What are you saying?"

"You're already the mate of my soul. I want to make it official."

Laylah's mind shut down at the same time her heart went into overdrive, ricocheting around her ribs like a pinball.

"Mate?"

His lips twisted. "Are you shocked or horrified?"

"I'm stunned," she readily admitted.

He frowned, as if puzzled by her reaction to his little stunner.

"Did you actually think I would chase after you for days, defy the Commission and my own Anasso by keeping you hidden, and risk my neck because I had nothing better to do?"

"But, I'm a Jinn mongrel," she said, those words explaining everything.

Jinn mongrels didn't mate.

End of story.

Or at least it should be.

Tane, however, seemed to be out of the loop as he flashed a smile filled with dangerous intent.

"I hate to disappoint you, my sweet, but I managed to figure that out all by myself."

"I'm an outcast."

"And I'm not?"

She made a sound of impatience. "I'm unstable."

"You're a female." His smile widened. "It's expected."

"Jerk." She curled a fist and hit his back with enough force to make him grunt. Dammit. Was he completely insane? Or was his fascination with her a part of his guilt-complex? She was, after all, the go-to gal for a vampire with a self-destructive urge. "You won't think it's so funny if I accidentally strike you with a bolt of lightning or collapse your lair into a pile of rubble."

He captured her lips in a kiss that blazed through her, searing away her self-righteous impulse.

Making her toes curl in the process.

"So long as you are next to me it won't matter," he said against her lips.

She gave a tug on his mohawk. "You must know this is crazy."

"Be my mate, Laylah," he coaxed, his eyes glowing. "Say yes."

She should say no.

Had she forgotten the horrible accidents over the years? For God's sake, she'd killed more than one demon when her powers had slipped her control.

Of course, it had only been in self-defense, a voice whispered in the back of her mind. And none of the demons were anywhere near as indestructible as a vampire.

And . . .

And she loved him.

The pure simplicity of her emotion brought an end to her inner dialogue.

"Yes," she said.

He groaned, pressing his forehead to hers. "Thank God."

Laylah stroked the tense muscles of his neck, bracing herself for his strike. She wasn't afraid. Excitement bubbled through her, as intoxicating as champagne. But, she'd had an up close and personal view of his fangs. It seemed impossible they wouldn't at least sting.

Tane, however, caught her off guard, crushing her lips with slow, drugging kisses that had her arching in ready response. He tasted of wildfire. And sex. And power.

A lethal combination.

His hands skimmed down her body, removing her bra and panties with skillful ease, then returning for another intimate exploration that made her tremble with pleasure. He stroked the line of her shoulders, and down her collarbone. He cupped her breasts, his thumbs teasing her nipples to aching peaks. And all the while he kissed her with a deep urgency that made her blood race.

Desire swelled inside her, as well as something new.

A hunger to feel him at her throat, his fangs buried deep in her flesh.

Perhaps sensing she was too impatient for a marathon seduction, Tane lifted himself off her long enough to shed his shorts before returning to cover her, his mouth seeking the pointed tip of her breast.

He groaned in approval as her hands scraped down his back, digging into his hips with her nails.

Using his tongue and teeth, he tormented the swollen bud, his cock rubbing against her clit until she was ready to plead for release. He shifted his attention to her other breast, his hand sliding between them to slip a finger between her folds, finding the pinpoint of her desire with remarkable ease.

"Tane . . ." she choked.

"Yes, my sweet."

"I need you."

As if her words snapped the last thread of his composure, Tane gave a low growl and with one hard thrust was buried deep inside her.

Laylah gasped, feeling stretched to the very limit. Then, with a throaty moan she wrapped her legs around his hips in blatant appreciation.

"Mine," he rasped, burying his face in the curve of her neck. "My mate."

She quivered as his tongue ran a wet path down the line of her jugular, arching her head back to offer what he desired. Tane didn't hesitate. With a harsh groan, he plunged his fangs through her skin, his hands holding her hips steady as she bucked from the pleasure slamming into her.

Gods.

She wrapped her arms around him, holding on tight as he began to pump his hips in rhythm that matched the sucking of her blood.

The combined sensations were . . .

Earth shattering.

Happily tossing herself into the maelstrom of bliss,

Laylah met him stroke for stroke, rushing toward an orgasm even before he released a trickle of his power. She screamed as the tiny jolt of electricity threw them both over the edge and she exploded into a million pieces.

Lost in the shattering pleasure, she felt him withdraw his fangs and gently close the puncture wounds. She floated in a daze of paradise, already sensing the deepening connection between them.

He nuzzled a path of kisses toward the hollow beneath her ear, his hands stroking up the curve of her waist to cup her swollen breasts.

"Your turn," he whispered.

Laylah readily threaded her fingers through his mohawk, excitement shimmering through her. She was no expert on vampire relationships, but she did know that the mating was only half complete. It was only after she took his blood that they would be truly bound together.

Not giving herself time to consider the pain she was bound to cause, she raised her head to sink her teeth deep into the flesh of his neck. She didn't have fangs, but she was able to draw enough blood to trickle down her throat.

Tane groaned in satisfaction. "Laylah."

The breath was snatched from her lungs as the awareness of Tane flowed through her with a shocking intimacy. It was like . . .

She sucked in a shaky breath.

It was like he was a part of her, so deeply ingrained it was impossible to know where one began and the other ended.

And buried deep in her heart were the threads of his love that shimmered as brilliant as the finest gold.

She lowered her head and met the fierce honey gaze. "You're mine."

His hips began to thrust at a slow, delectable pace. "Forever."

Lying entangled with Laylah in the middle of the bed, Tane ran gentle fingers over the crimson tattoo that was scrolled beneath the skin of her forearm.

It was the mark of their mating.

His mark.

Just as he had an answering mark on his arm that revealed Laylah's claim.

Not that he needed any tattoo to prove their mating.

She was the other half of his soul.

Cheesy, but true.

His lips twitched. If someone had told him two weeks ago that he'd be as smug as a Pheral demon with a harem of harpies at being mated to a Jinn mongrel, he would have laughed. Or sliced out their hearts.

Lifting her arm, he pressed his lips to her palm, his body readily stirring despite the past four hours he'd spent making love to this woman. It was fairly certain he'd never, ever get enough of Laylah.

He ignored the sensation of night falling, instead savoring the scent of spring rain that wrapped around him like a warm blanket.

For this rare moment, he wanted to forget the world beyond the closed door . . .

A hand slammed against the door with perfect timing, the cold chill of Jaelyn's power swirling through the air.

So much for forgetting the world.

"Open the door, Charon," the Hunter ordered.

"Go away," he growled, wrapping protective arms around his mate.

There was a pause, as if the vampire wanted nothing more than to disappear, then he heard her low curses.

"The Sylvermyst escaped," she at last confessed.

"Damn."

Tane slid from the bed, his gaze ruefully watching Laylah pull on a pair of jeans and stretchy T-shirt before looping the disguise amulet over her head.

The Sylvermyst bastard was going to pay for interrupting his mating night.

Once he had tugged on his shorts, he strapped the stolen sword to his back and tucked two daggers into his waistband. Then, tugging Laylah into his arms, he kissed her with a fierce promise of pleasures delayed.

She returned his kiss before pushing him away, chuckling at his undisguised frustration.

"Later," she said softly.

He moved to pull open the door, reminding himself that the sooner they'd destroyed Marika and her happy band of misfits, the sooner he could have Laylah all to himself.

What better motivation?

"What happened?" he demanded as Jaelyn stepped into the room, still dressed in black spandex and carrying her favorite shotgun.

Her expression hardened. "That's still under investigation."

Tane's brows snapped together. Was she evading his question?

"Did you let him out of the cell?"

She growled, her eyes glowing with fury. "Stupid questions piss me off."

Moving a speed only an ancient vampire could follow, Tane had a dagger pressed beneath her chin, his expression grim.

"And petulant foundlings who have to constantly prove how tough they are piss me off."

Jaelyn trembled, battling not to be stupid enough to provoke a vampire bigger, badder, and older than herself.

"I'm not a foundling," she gritted.

Tane narrowed his eyes. "You're barely out of the nursery and if you think . . ."

"Yeah, yeah," Laylah abruptly interrupted, moving to stand at his side. "You're both super scary." She turned her attention to Jaelyn. "How did he escape?"

Something that might have been embarrassment rippled over the young vampire's face before she was stepping away from Tane's dagger and gathering her composure.

"The surveillance camera caught him just . . ." She grimaced. "Disappearing."

Laylah frowned. "A portal?"

"It shouldn't be possible," Jaelyn muttered. "The cell was lined with lead."

Tane shrugged. "We don't know what magic the Sylvermyst possess. Especially Ariyal."

Jaelyn's eyes flashed with blue fire. "He won't get far."

Tane lifted his brows. It was a Hunter's cardinal rule to remain impervious to their prey. Any emotion, whether it was anger or hatred or attraction, would only cloud their considerable skills.

The Sylvermyst had clearly gotten under her skin.

"It doesn't matter, the damage has been done," he said.

Laylah sent him a startled glance. "What damage?"

"He knows where we are."

She shivered. "Which means he's going to tell my aunt."

Tane wasn't nearly so certain, but now wasn't the time

to discuss his suspicions of the Sylvermyst. Not when it was nothing more than a gut feeling.

"That's certainly a risk," he said.

Jaelyn stepped back, her shotgun resting against her shoulder.

"I'll do my best to keep them off your trail."

Tane dipped his head. "We're in your debt."

"Don't worry, I have every intention of collecting."

With a taunting smile, Jaelyn turned on her heel and jogged down the hall, swiftly disappearing from view.

Tane shook his head. How did so much bitch get into such a small package?

At his side, Laylah heaved a sigh. "Now that is a woman who can take care of herself."

Tane glanced at her in shock. "You can't be envious."

"I am," she said, her lips twisted in a wistful smile. "I've depended on others to protect me my entire life."

He framed her face in his hands. "There are times when we all depend on others. That's why there are clans and families and packs." His thumb brushed the sensuous curve of her lower lip. "And mates."

"But . . ."

"Laylah, you not only survived despite being hunted from the day you were born, but you've protected the world from a potential Armageddon." He studied her beautiful face, wondering how she couldn't realize just how astonishing she truly was. "Not bad."

Her lips twitched into a rueful smile. "I suppose when you put it that way."

He leaned down to whisper in her ear. "Of course, I wouldn't mind seeing you in that spandex."

"Hmmm." She nipped his throat, sending jolts of white-hot desire directly to his cock. "Only if you're very, very good."

"I prefer to be very, very bad," he growled, barely resisting the urge to topple her back onto the bed. Oh, for another hour. Or ten. "Unfortunately we don't have time. We have to get out of here."

"My thoughts exactly," an aggravatingly familiar voice said from behind. "Where are we going?"

He turned, regarding the tiny gargoyle with a steady gaze. "Levet, we need a distraction."

Laylah grabbed his arm. "Why do we need a distraction?"

"If Ariyal is capable of forming portals then it won't take him long to collect your aunt and return."

She shook her head. "There's something you're not telling me."

Tane sighed. He'd forgotten the side effects of the mating. He'd never be able to lie to Laylah again.

Not always a good thing.

"I have a feeling that Ariyal was willing to use your aunt to track the child," he confessed, "but now that he's found you, he plans to take matters into his own hands."

"What matters?"

"I don't intend to find out." He glanced toward the gargoyle. "But I need your help."

Levet folded his arms over his narrow chest. "Ah, so I am to remain behind and become a martyr?"

"That's what heroes do."

The gargoyle hesitated, no doubt debating between his desire to remain with Laylah and his oddly quixotic nature.

"True," he finally conceded, heaving a tragic sigh. "I am, after all, a Knight in Shining Armor."

Laylah moved to kneel in front of the demon. "Just promise me you'll be a knight who doesn't take foolish chances."

Levet glanced toward Tane with a sly grin before placing a kiss on Laylah's cheek.

"For you, I promise."

Tane reached down to grab his mate's arm, gently pulling her back to her feet.

Damned gargoyle.

"We must go," he muttered.

Levet snapped his wings. "How will I find you?"

Tane parted his lips to inform the beast he could start his search in hell, when Laylah caught them both by surprise.

"We'll be in Siberia."

He flashed her a puzzled frown. "Why the hell are we going to Siberia?"

"Cassie told me, 'to find the end you must return to the beginning.'"

Chapter 19

Just before dawn they found themselves in Styx's lair.

Laylah hadn't been pleased, but he'd convinced her they needed to share the information they'd learned with the Anasso, not to mention the fact that she could use another day of rest before trying to shadow walk with a baby and vampire as passengers.

Now she was settled in an upstairs bedroom and he had sought out his king in his private study so she could actually get some sleep.

Damn.

Just the thought of her stretched on the massive bed with satin gold sheets draped over her naked body was making him hard. She wouldn't get any rest if he didn't control his libido.

He leaned against the massive desk, watching Styx pace the floor as he processed Tane's account of what had happened since they had last met in this room.

"Darcy's sister is a prophet?" he at last muttered, tugging on the amulet that hung around his neck while the turquoise ornaments in his long braid filled the air with a musical tinkle. "Damn."

Tane grinned. "You have interesting in-laws."

"Tell me about it." Styx came to a halt in the middle of the office, his arms folded across his massive chest. "We just had a visit from Darcy's mother."

Tane's smile widened. Darcy's mother was a pureblood Were who liked her sex rough and often. The more often the better. Styx usually had to give his Ravens an entire week off after a visit from his mother-in-law just to recover.

Then he recalled the date and he doubled over in laughter. "She visited during a full moon?"

Styx failed to find the humor. "She was . . . terrifying."

Tane straightened, his amusement fading. "Speaking of mothers. Have you heard from Uriel?"

"Victor sent word that Uriel had located the tomb where the gypsy was being held, but there was some difficulty in the escape."

That didn't sound good.

"Difficulty?"

"He didn't go into detail, but he did promise to send word once she'd been brought to his lair and he'd determined she wasn't a threat to Laylah."

"Good." Tane nodded. If it was up to him the gypsy wouldn't be allowed near Laylah until it was proven beyond a shadow of a doubt that she was her mother. Unfortunately, he sensed his mate might have her own opinion. "She doesn't need any unnecessary distractions. Not now."

Styx studied him with a somber expression. "She is determined?"

"You have no idea."

"Is that a joke?" Styx demanded in incredulous tones. "I'm a walking testament at having a mate who is determined to risk her neck at every opportunity in the name of truth."

Tane grimaced. "Does it get any easier?"

"No."

"Thanks."

Styx shrugged. "Would you prefer I lie?"

Hmmm. Was ignorance bliss?

Tane didn't have an answer.

And in the end, it didn't matter.

Laylah was his. And no amount of future aggravation, annoyance, and downright terror would convince him that it was anything but a miracle.

Time for a new conversation.

"Have you discovered any information on the Sylvermyst?"

"Not much." Styx's expression hardened. He didn't like the fact the evil fey had managed to keep their presence hidden. Or the fact that they weren't sure just how much a danger they posed. "Jagr has been studying what little information he has in his library."

"And?"

"From what he read they share the same magic of other fey. They can form portals, cast hexes, and enchant objects. They can also create the usual illusions."

Tane straightened from the desk. That was next to worthless.

"Styx, these were no typical fey."

"No, they aren't," he agreed, his eyes darkening with frustration. "But they were always secretive and rarely mixed with other demons, so the truth of their powers is hid in obscurity. Now there's nothing more than nearly forgotten rumors."

"What are they?" Tane demanded. Rumors were better than nothing.

"One claims that they have a much higher tolerance to iron than their cousins."

"That's no rumor. The bastard disappeared out of a cell made entirely of iron and lined with lead while shackled. I've never heard of another fey who could do that." He shook off his regret they hadn't kept a constant guard on the bastard. How could they have known he could create a portal through enough lead to kill most fey? "What else?"

"They can speak with the dead."

Tane shuddered at the unexpected revelation. "Charming."

"More than charming," Styx said. "They can compel spirits into their service."

"Are you saying they have ghost slaves?"

Styx held up a warning hand. "Don't dismiss the danger, Tane. There are spirits who can cause damage even to a vampire. And the more powerful shades are capable of pulling souls into the underworld."

Tane had heard of demons who possessed the talent of necromancy, but they could rarely do more than communicate with those who'd passed to the underworld.

To actually be able to take command of a shade . . .

He abruptly stiffened. "Damn."

"What is it?"

"Jaelyn must be warned," he said.

"Don't worry," Styx soothed. "I've sent DeAngelo and Xander to track her."

Tane shook his head. Jaelyn was a genuine pain in the ass, but she was a true born Hunter.

"They'll never find her."

Styx regarded him with a curious expression. "She's that good?"

"The best I've ever encountered."

"Excellent." The Anasso smiled. "I have need of a Hunter. Perhaps I'll invite her to join my Ravens."

Tane snorted, trying to imagine the prickly female trying to make nice with the massive, overly arrogant vampires that made up Styx's bodyguard.

Blood would most certainly flow.

"Better you than me."

"Why?"

"She has the attitude of a rabid badger."

Styx was unfazed. "I remember another vampire with impressive skills and a nasty attitude," he murmured. "I had to kick his ass on a regular basis, but eventually I managed to tame him." He shrugged. "Or maybe I just found the means to focus his feral nature."

Tane grimaced. He rarely thought back to those days. After he was forced to kill Sung Li, he'd retreated from the world, living as little better than a rabid animal in the caves of northern Mongolia.

He wasn't sure how much time passed when Styx made his first appearance, but he did know that he'd done his best to kill the massive Aztec. He didn't know that Styx was a servant of the previous Anasso, and wouldn't have given a shit if he did. He would have been happy if the unknown vampire had managed to put an end to his miserable existence.

But Styx didn't strike the killing blow.

Instead he retreated, only to return the next night, sitting on a rock near Tane's cave and eventually leaving behind a blanket. The next night he had settled a few feet closer and left behind a stack of books. The next night it had been clean clothing.

His patience had been remarkable, and slowly he'd earned enough of Tane's trust to lead him back into civilization. And eventually he'd trained him to become his Charon.

At the time Tane hadn't known why the vampire would make such an effort.

It was only in the past months that he'd discovered that two of them had committed the same fatal sin.

Styx had covered the madness of the previous Anasso until it was nearly too late.

They shared a sense of gnawing guilt and regret that no one else could truly understand.

"I have never . . ."

"Hell, no," Styx cut in, his brows snapping together in a scowl of warning. "If you start with any touchy-feely crap I'm tossing your ass out of here."

"I owe you my life," Tane pressed. "It won't be forgotten."

"You have repaid any debt several times over." Styx paused, as if struck by a sudden thought. "Of course, now I suppose I shall have to choose a new Charon."

"Yes." Tane smiled, realizing he no longer had the driving need to purge his guilt. Laylah had healed the wounds that plagued him for so long. "I intend to devote myself to my mate once we're done with this mess."

A mysterious smile touched Styx's lips. "We'll see."

Tane froze. "I don't like the sound of that."

"I always have need of loyal vampires."

"I don't think Laylah would be any happier with me becoming one of your Ravens."

An evil glint entered the ancient vampire's eyes. "I was thinking more as a liaison to the Commission."

Tane made a sound of choked disbelief. Styx wanted him to negotiate with a group of powerful demons who could turn him into a toad on a whim?

No. Way.

"I'd rather have my head chopped off," he said, meaning every word.

Styx shrugged. "We can discuss it later."

"We can discuss it never," he growled, heading for the door. Obviously the Anasso had lost his damned mind. "Now I'm going to join my mate before you suggest I become a translator for the hellhounds."

Styx chuckled. "I'll have dinner sent to your room at dusk."

Tane glanced over his shoulder. "Make sure there's German chocolate cake. Laylah loves cake."

"I did not become the most powerful mage in the world to tromp through damp woods," Sergei whined, looking decidedly worse for the wear with his hair hanging loosely around his thin face and his expensive clothing stained beyond repair. "My shoes are completely ruined."

Marika was no happier when Sergei's spell finally picked up Laylah's trail only to discover it led her straight back to the lair of the Anasso.

The one place certain Marika couldn't follow.

Aggravating little bitch.

But whatever her annoyance, she was too wise to reveal any lack of confidence in her ultimate glory in front of the Sylvermyst that she'd commanded to surround and keep watch on the Chicago estate.

It was bad enough that their leader, Ariyal, had disappeared during their battle with the wood sprites. The ridiculous fey had been convinced that it was a bad omen. She wasn't going to have Sergei's petulant behavior further undermine their belief in her leadership.

A pity she still had need of the idiot.

She would take great pleasure in offering him as a public sacrifice.

"Shut up, you moron," she hissed, standing near the edge of the tree line, trusting that Sergei's cloak of concealment would keep them hidden from the Anasso's Ravens. "You have done nothing but complain since leaving London."

His lips thinned with childish resentment. "I possess a fragile constitution."

"You are an embarrassment to mages everywhere," Marika mocked. "Even the fey consider you a spineless fool."

"Ah yes, your precious Sylvermyst." He glanced toward the slender warriors who were nearly impossible to see among the dark shadows of the trees. "Tell me, Marika, just where is Ariyal?"

Her expression revealed none of her fury at Ariyal's vanishing act.

Or the suspicion he wasn't as dedicated to the cause as he pretended to be.

"He was obviously captured or killed."

"Or he switched sides."

Her tongue toyed with the tip of her fang. A reminder that for all of Sergei's magical abilities, she could kill him with one strike.

"Jealous, Sergei?"

"Jealous of a fey who spent endless centuries playing whore to Morgana le Fey?" His disdainful tone didn't entirely hide his edge of envy. Ariyal hadn't bothered to conceal his amusement at the mage's superior attitude. The fey was a natural leader of his people who had no need of magical tricks to gain respect. "Not hardly."

Marika laughed with cruel enjoyment. "He's more of a man than you'll ever be."

"He's a demon whose loyalty is for sale to the highest bidder," the mage snapped. "Be careful, my dear. He might be using your own army to betray you."

The fact that the fear had crossed her mind more than once infuriated Marika.

She regarded him with a cold glare. "The only traitor in my employ is you, mage."

Sergei was an arrogant ass, but he wasn't suicidal. Dropping the subject he instead glanced toward the house that was guarded by a dozen vampires.

"How long do you intend to wait here?"

"As long as Laylah and the babe remain."

"They could stay in the Anasso's lair for the rest of eternity."

"Then we wait."

Biting back his angry words, Sergei turned to pace through the thick undergrowth, his hands clenched at his side.

Marika left him to his pouting, returning her attention to the Anasso's lair. If Laylah had any sense she would remain in the protection of the King of Vampires, but she'd already proven she was willing to take ridiculous risks when it came to protecting the child.

Eventually she would find some need to leave.

And when she did, Marika would be prepared.

She wouldn't escape again.

It was nearing midnight when Sergei abruptly fell to his knees, shaking his head as if trying to clear it.

"Bloody hell," he gritted.

Marika whirled to study him with displeasure. "What is it now?"

"Someone just entered the cave in Siberia."

"What cave?"

Slowly he lifted his head. "The one where I found the child."

Marika watched the mage climb to his feet, unease stirring in her heart.

"How do you know?"

"I set alarms in case there was any unwanted interest."

"It could be an animal or an overly curious human."

He shook his head. "No, the spell was cast to ignore the mundane intruders, even if they could penetrate the natural barriers."

"So it's a demon?"

She paced across the uneven ground, the sense of foreboding knotting her stomach.

There was no reason for a demon to be roaming in such a frozen, desolate cave. Even those who preferred the cold avoided the area that was riddled with active volcanoes and a barren lack of prey.

"Or a magic user," Sergei added.

She halted, a dark suspicion spreading through her like poison.

"Laylah," she breathed.

Sergei frowned. "I have no way of knowing for sure."

Marika had no doubts.

The worthless bit of baggage was just like her mother.

Stubborn, rebellious, and refusing to concede gracefully to her inevitable fate.

Thankfully, Marika would soon have the mongrel in her hands. Then she would teach the child how to obey her betters. No matter how much pain it took.

A smile of anticipation curled her lips.

She liked teaching people to obey her.

"It's her," she said with absolute confidence.

"It makes no sense." Sergei waved his hands in confusion. "Why would she travel to an empty cave in the frozen mountains of Siberia?"

"She must have discovered some information of the child," Marika reasoned, glaring toward the mansion. It was infuriating that Laylah could use her powers to sneak away. "What if the bitch seeks to call the Dark Lord herself?" Turning her back on Sergei, she headed toward the nearest Sylvermyst. "We must go."

The mage stumbled to catch up to her long strides. "Marika, wait."

"We have no time to lose."

"Have you considered the possibility this is a trap."

Marika came to an abrupt halt, stabbing Sergei with a suspicious glare.

"Trap?"

"How better to get you off the trail than to send you half a world away?" he said, clearly desperate to avoid an uncomfortable journey to northern Siberia.

She tapped her tongue on the point of one fang, considering his logic. She hadn't lived so long by being impulsive.

Or stupid.

At last she continued her path to the copper-haired Sylvermyst she'd taken as her most recent lover. He was second to Ariyal, but far more . . . malleable.

Her steps faltered at the stinging memory of Ariyal's rejection of her advances. He hadn't even pretended that he found her anything but a means to an end.

Angrily she squashed the image.

The bastard was no doubt in his grave.

A pity considering he was by far the most powerful of the Sylvermyst and their undoubted leader, but hardly a disaster.

Marika was a master at turning any situation to her advantage.

"No, they couldn't possibly have known that you had cast a spell to alert you to trespassers," she said, her firm tone revealing she wasn't going to argue the point.

Sergei swore, hurrying to catch up. "Then what if it's a

random demon who strayed into the cave?" he demanded. "By the time we realize our mistake the Jinn could leave this lair and be long gone."

"Not with our newfound friends." She halted directly before Tearloch, her fingers stroking down the smooth skin the color of rich cream. "We can search the cavern and return before Laylah could possibly escape."

"We're going to regret this," Sergei muttered.

"Remain here if you wish, coward." With a firm grip Marika led the impassive Tearloch deeper into the woods, away from any prying eyes. She didn't intend to give Laylah the opportunity to realize that she was about to have surprise visitors. "I won't allow anyone to steal the glory that should be mine."

Leading her companion toward the small clearing, Marika ignored Sergei as he trailed behind them, tripping over the underbrush as he struggled through the dark.

"Marika, wait," he urged as she linked her hand with the Sylvermyst and prepared to travel through his portal. "I thought I saw that idiotic gargoyle . . ."

At the end of her patience, Marika turned to grab him by the hair, yanking him close as a shimmering hole formed in front of them.

"Another word and I'll rip out your tongue."

Chapter 20

Tane didn't have memories of his life before waking up as a vampire.

His body, however, had retained an instinctive love for the warm beaches and tropical scents of the South Pacific. Who wouldn't prefer to swim in a moon-drenched ocean than huddle by a fire in a damp lair?

Which made the arrival at the frozen cavern in the Kamchatka Peninsula all the more unpleasant.

Gods. He thought nothing could be worse than traveling through the strange mists between worlds. Until Laylah had tugged his hand, and they'd landed on the narrow ledge of a mountain that overlooked . . .

A frozen wasteland.

That smelled of sulfur.

His nose wrinkled at the pungent aroma of distant geysers that warned of volcanic activity. It would be just his luck one of the damned things would blow while they were there.

At least he was impervious to the cold.

Unlike Laylah who had wrapped herself in a dark cloak that provided cover for the baby she held in her arms.

She'd also pulled on fur-lined boots that protected her feet from the ice-covered ground.

Tane's only concession was a T-shirt that was tight enough not to impede his movements and khaki pants that covered the daggers he had holstered at both ankles, one at his side, and another at his lower back. He'd also strapped the Sylvermyst sword to his back and had a handgun tucked in his pocket.

He hated to be underdressed when he came to a fight.

Of course, there was always the tiny hope that he could convince Laylah to return to Styx's lair before they were attacked yet again.

His lips twisted.

Naw.

His luck wasn't that good.

A blast of frigid air slammed into them, whipping at Laylah's cloak and nearly tumbling her over the edge of the sharp cliff.

Cursing the godforsaken mountain, the cold, and the stubbornness of Jinn mongrels, he grabbed her shoulders and hauled her backward, careful not to disturb the bundle in her arms.

"Are you sure you didn't take us into a hell dimension," he accused directly into her ear.

Pulling free of his grasp, she turned with a wry smile. "It's bleak, but there's a harsh beauty if you look for it."

Much like him. She didn't have to say the words out loud.

"And you're an expert at finding beauty in the most unlikely places, are you not, my sweet?"

She flashed a smug smile. "I know a good thing when I see it."

"Only after I held you captive and forced you to accept that I was destined to be yours."

Her magnificent eyes sparkled with a teasing glow. "How do you know I wasn't playing hard to get?"

A poignant warmth tugged at his heart. When he'd first encountered Laylah she'd been filled with a bitter resentment and a fear that was grinding her into a mere shell of herself.

A portion of the fear remained, of course. It wouldn't go away until the child was safe.

But the bitterness had faded, replaced with a contentment that made Tane preen with a smug pleasure.

He was willing to take full credit for her budding happiness.

"Because what I admire most about you is your refusal to be anything or anyone but who you are. Your honesty is . . ." He shuddered at the endless years of lies and deceptions that had marked his relationship with Sung Li. "A blessing."

"Really?" Her expression was wicked. "I have other blessings to offer."

He growled low in his throat. "Haven't you learned that it's dangerous to tease a vampire?"

"But it's so much fun."

He captured her lips in a fierce, painfully brief kiss before pulling back and glancing toward the narrow opening of the cave.

Beyond the entrance, he could sense several tunnels that zigzagged down into the depths of the mountain.

"We have to do this?"

"Yes."

"There's nothing for miles not even a frost fairy."

With a grimace she headed toward the cave, slipping through the entrance.

"This is where I'm supposed to be."

Staying close to her side, Tane pulled his sword free, prepared for the inevitable attack.

"I don't like it."

"I can't say I'm crazy to be back here either, but I have to find the truth of Maluhia."

"And then what?"

She headed straight for the nearest tunnel, leading him down the roughly carved steps.

"If it's safe I intend to find someone to release him from the stasis spell."

Tane stumbled to a halt as they entered another small cavern. This one just as bleak and frigidly unwelcoming as the one above.

"Hell," he muttered.

Laylah turned to regard him with concern. "What's wrong?"

"I just realized I'm going to be a . . ." His tongue faltered over the unfamiliar word. "Dad." He scowled as her laughter broke the ominous atmosphere that shrouded the long forgotten caves. "What's so funny?"

"I'm trying to imagine you coaching the T-ball team."

He smiled, tugging open Laylah's cloak to reveal the child she held in her arms.

Vampires could procreate in their own way. Some even felt a parent/child bond with the "offspring" they created, but Tane had never considered creating a foundling.

Hell, he hadn't wanted a mate.

He'd already royally screwed up one relationship; he didn't feel the need for a repeat performance.

Until Laylah.

And now Maluhia.

They were a family.

His family.

And he would die to protect them.

"Perhaps not T-ball," he grudgingly admitted. What was T-ball? "But, I can teach him to hide his presence when he's stalking his prey and how to kill with his bare hands and . . ."

"Enough," she laughingly protested, shaking her head. "What?"

She glanced down at the child. "We might have to seek assistance in our parenting skills."

He moved to gently press his lips to her forehead. "So long as we love and protect the child, what else matters?"

Laylah lifted her head, her eyes shimmering with the warm affection that he could feel flowing between them.

"Nothing at all," she said softly. Then, visibly squaring her shoulders, she headed toward the small antechamber at the back of the cavern. "Let's do this."

She'd taken only a few steps when she came to an abrupt halt. "What happened?"

She shivered. "I felt . . ."

"What?"

"I think we tripped a spell."

"Damn." Holding his sword ready, Tane turned in a slow circle, scanning the cavern. When nothing happened he muttered a curse. He'd rather battle a rabid Were during a full moon than walk into a magical trap. How do you kill something you can't see? "Why isn't something happening?"

"It doesn't necessarily have to be an offensive spell." She grimaced. "It could be an alarm."

"Sergei," he growled.

"Probably," she admitted. "He always was a paranoid ass."

"If he knows we're here then it won't be long before he makes an unwanted appearance with your aunt." He glanced in her direction. "We must leave."

"He can't know who or what tripped his spell. Besides it will take them hours, if not days, to travel here."

"Not with the Sylvermyst."

"Oh." She made a sour face. "Portals."

"Exactly. We can't risk remaining here."

She bit her lower lip, her expression troubled. "I'm sorry, Tane. I don't know why, but we have to stay. The baby needs to be here."

"Laylah." He clenched his teeth as she headed directly into the antechamber, and then squeezed through a narrow crack in the wall. "Where are you going?"

"I don't know."

"Perfect." Squeezing through the rocks, Tane was forced to sacrifice skin off several parts of his body, and a chunk of his hair. "This wasn't exactly the honeymoon I was hoping for."

She glanced over her shoulder, her wicked smile making him forget his stinging wounds and overall aggravation.

Hell, a smile like that could make him forget a nuclear attack.

"Once we've made certain Maluhia is safe and freed of the stasis spell I intend to give you a honeymoon you'll never forget."

He groaned at her throaty voice. "Christ, woman. You're killing me."

They squeezed through another curve in the passageway before it spilled into a wide opening. Laylah gave a sudden gasp, hurrying across the stone floor to stand before a visible rift in the air.

"Here," she breathed.

Tane stood before the shimmering mist, his flesh crawling at the sight.

Very few things scared an ancient vampire.

This was one.

"You found the child here?"

"Yes. He was hidden within the mists."

Tane stiffened as the air pressure in the cavern changed. It was the only warning before a portal was about to open.

"Shit."

The instant Tane turned, waving his big sword, Laylah knew there was trouble.

A suspicion that was swiftly confirmed as she sensed a portal opening in the cavern overhead.

"Laylah, run," Tane gritted, moving to place himself between her and the tunnel where they entered.

For once, Laylah wasn't going to argue.

As much as she might hate leaving Tane in danger, he had forced her to realize that the child came first. She had taken on the duty to protect Maluhia from his enemies.

She couldn't waver. Not even when the thought of abandoning Tane was like a dagger through her heart.

Unfortunately, she was no match for vampire speed.

Even as she sprinted toward the opening, she was stumbling to a halt as a blast of frigid air hit her with the force of a blow.

Marika.

Looking like she'd just stepped off the pages of Vogue, the beautiful vampire stepped into the cavern, her dark hair cascading down her back with perfect curls and her slender body attired in black silk slacks and matching top. Hell, she was even wearing black heels.

"She's not going anywhere," the vampire purred, holding up a slender hand as Sergei and a copper-haired Sylvermyst suddenly appeared behind her. "Not when

I've gone to such trouble to arrange this long overdue family reunion." Her eyes narrowed as she studied Laylah, then her gaze snapped toward Laylah's inner arm that now carried the mark of her mating with Tane. "What have you done, child?"

There was a rush of air as Tane moved to stand directly in Marika's path.

"Laylah, go."

Marika growled, her dark eyes smoldering as she stabbed a finger toward Laylah.

"Take a step and Sergei will destroy your mate."

Laylah snorted. At least Marika wasn't stupid enough to threaten to kill the massive vampire herself. Even Laylah could sense Tane would crush her with little effort.

"Don't listen to her." Tane pointed his sword directly at the mage who turned a pasty shade of gray. "I intend to cut out the mage's heart and shove it down his throat."

Laylah licked her lips, a crazy idea forming in the back of her mind.

She didn't have Tane's raw power, or her aunt's evil cunning, but she did know all about survival against the odds. And sometimes crazy was all she had.

"How can I ignore her?" she mocked, ignoring Tane's furious glare. Instead she deliberately glanced down at the child in her arms. "You sound like a broken record, Auntie Marika. First my mother and now my mate. If you want me, why don't you just come and get me?"

The dark eyes predictably flared with fury. Really, the female was embarrassingly easy to provoke.

"Bitch."

Marika flowed forward, but Laylah had already scoped out her escape route.

Trusting that Tane would buy her time, Laylah hauled ass toward the small tunnel at the back of the cavern.

Swinging his sword, Tane forced Marika to dance backward as Laylah disappeared down a small passageway.

She hissed in frustration, chopping her hand through the air. Tane felt a stinging pain and he glanced down to discover a deep gash marring his chest. It wasn't an unusual talent in vampires and, thankfully, Marika's power wasn't capable of more than flesh wounds, but it briefly weakened his sword arm.

He tossed the sword to the other hand, but the vampire was already slipping past him in pursuit of Laylah. He turned to follow, only to grunt in shock when he found himself flying through the air and slamming into the wall of the cave. He dropped the sword as he was held with crushing force against the cold rocks.

Goddamn magic.

"Release me, mage," he roared, his voice causing the Sylvermyst to bolt in terror and Sergei to sway in fear. "Or I swear you will regret it for all of eternity."

"I regret the moment I ever met Marika, vampire," the mage said, his voice thick with sincerity. "There's nothing you could threaten me with that would be worse than what she would do to me if I betrayed her again."

Tane bit back the urge to explain in detail just how wrong the mage was. The things he could do would give the mage nightmares for an eternity.

Instead he opted for the good cop routine. Hey, it worked on *CSI Miami*.

"Then let's negotiate what I can offer you."

Sergei nervously glanced around the empty cavern. "I'm listening," he at last said.

"What do you want?"

"Marika dead."

"Done."

He shifted, a sly glint replacing the terror in his eyes. "And the child?"

Tane swallowed a growl. "Out of the question."

"It's no good to you. Without my ability to release it from the stasis spell it's nothing more than a paper-weight."

Tane strained against the invisible bonds that held him, desperate to rip out the throat of the mage before hunting down Marika and chopping off her head.

"What do you intend to do with it?"

"Are you kidding?" The mage regarded him in genuine shock at the question. "That brat would be worth a for-tune to me on the black market. I could finally retire in the luxury I intend to become accustomed to."

Now that was unexpected.

Tane frowned. "You don't intend to resurrect the Dark Lord?"

Sergei shrugged. "Not if I have a better offer."

"I have money if that's what you want."

"How much?"

"Name your price," Tane said without thinking.

A mistake.

A man willing to sell a child on the black market could have no understanding of Tane's utter indifference to the enormous fortune he'd accumulated over the centuries. He would naturally assume that Tane had no intention of paying unless he bargained a deal.

Sergei backed away, shaking his head. "No, I don't trust you."

Tane cursed his stupidity.

"And you trust Marika?" he snapped.

"Better the devil you know," the mage muttered, heading in the same direction as Marika.

And Laylah.

Briefly halting his attempts to escape, Tane closed his eyes and sent his senses flowing outward.

He easily located Laylah rushing through a tunnel headed deeper into the bowels of the mountain with Marika in pursuit. A violent fury screamed through him, but he grimly turned his attention to the fleeing Sergei.

He couldn't stop Marika from such a distance, but he could keep the mage from following them.

Calling on his abilities, Tane allowed a tiny pulse of power to flow through the air, aiming it in the opposite direction of Laylah. The mage didn't have the ability to use his sense of smell to follow the females, but he no doubt had learned to associate Laylah with the tiny prickles of electricity she released when she was mad or upset.

If Tane could lead the bastard away, then Laylah would have a chance to escape from Marika.

He continued to send out the tiny pulses, a cold smile curving his lips as he sensed the mage becoming lost among the vast spiderweb of tunnels.

He hoped the bastard rotted among the frozen rocks.

Concentrating on his self-imposed task, Tane abruptly snapped open his eyes, watching in disbelief as the tiny gargoyle waddled into the cavern.

"Well, well." Levet came to a halt, his eyes widening before a satisfied smile spread across his ugly mug. "I would have gone in another direction, but there is a piquant charm in decorating frozen caverns with vampires."

Tane's brows snapped together. "How the hell did you get here?"

Levet shrugged. "I hitched a ride with Cruella de Vil through the portal."

Hitched a ride?

Well . . . hell.

Tane had to admit the gargoyle was nothing if not resourceful. He was also Tane's only visible means of escape.

Dammit.

He was never going to live down the shame of being rescued by a stunted gargoyle if word got out.

A thought that did nothing to improve his already foul mood.

"Get me down," he barked.

Levet folded his arms over his narrow chest. "And destroy the lovely picture you make?"

A blast of frigid air tumbled the gargoyle backward as Tane's temper flared.

"Levet."

"Oui, oui." Climbing to his feet, Levet made a show of brushing off a bit of nonexistent dust, before moving toward him with a deliberately superior expression. "I am rushing to the rescue yet again."

Tane clenched his teeth until they threatened to crack beneath the strain.

"Why me?" he muttered.

Levet lifted his hands in a grand gesture, then he paused, as if struck by a sudden thought.

"You might wish to turn your head and close your eyes."

Recalling the fireball that had taken out a good chunk of forest, Tane gave a sharp shake of his head. He'd rather freeze to the wall than be blown into a million pieces.

"Wait, gargoyle, if you . . ." His words lodged in his throat as there was a brilliant flash of light.

Braced to be barbecued by the unpredictable gargoyle, Tane was totally unprepared when he felt nothing more than a warm breeze before the invisible shackles were disappearing and he was hitting the ground with enough force to rattle his spine.

Surging upright, he snatched the sword off the ground, feeling like an awkward fool. He glared at his aggravating companion, not entirely convinced that Levet hadn't intentionally ensured he dropped like a sack of potatoes.

Now, however, wasn't the time to slice and dice his only ally.

He'd save that particular pleasure until later.

"Come on," he ordered, headed toward the back of the cavern.

"What? Not even a thank you," Levet grumbled. "Next occasion I'll leave you to the bats."

Tane never slowed. "Laylah needs us."

"Oh." There was a flutter of wings as Levet hurried to catch up. "Why did you not say so in the first place?"

Chapter 21

Laylah turned down yet another passageway, the chill brushing over the back of her neck becoming more pronounced as Marika steadily closed the distance between them.

She could have escaped.

She had halted only moments after entering the tunnel to shadow walk. But rather than disappearing into the corridor, she'd shoved Maluhia into the mists and returned to the frozen mountain.

It hadn't been easy to leave her child behind.

Even knowing that she'd never encountered another demon in the mists, not to mention the fact no one but herself could touch the babe, had made it easier.

Still, only the grim determination to bring an end to danger, once and for all, gave her the strength to leave Maluhia behind as she resumed her terrified flight.

"You can't outrun me, Laylah," Marika's mocking voice floated through the air.

Laylah shivered.

Turned out that being chased through dark caves was just as creepy the second time around.

Just like when Tane was hunting her, there was no

sound of approaching footsteps, no heavy breathing, not even the accidental kick of a pebble.

There was only thick silence and a relentless cold that froze her heart.

On this occasion, however, she wasn't running blindly.

She had a plan.

A wild, insane, please-God-let-it-work plan.

But a plan.

Entering the small cavern she'd been seeking, she slowed to a halt and turned to watch her aunt surge into the space behind her.

With an eerie ability, the vampire came to a precise stop. Laylah grimaced. One minute Marika had been charging forward at full speed and the next she was frozen in place. Not even a strand of hair moved.

Too weird.

The woman's dark gaze scanned the cavern, searching for hidden enemies or a stash of weapons.

Thankfully, Marika was too much a vampire to consider that the cavern itself might be the trap.

Once confident she had her prey cornered, the older woman allowed a sneer to twist her lips.

"I warned you that you couldn't escape."

Laylah tilted her chin, but she didn't bother to try and hide her fear.

If she'd learned nothing else, it was that it was impossible to hide emotions from a vampire.

Besides, she wanted Marika to believe she had conceded defeat.

The longer she could keep the woman off guard, the longer she could slowly build her power. If she did it too quickly the revealing sparks of electricity would warn the vamp of danger. She was certain to strike out and try to disable her.

And truthfully, she was still aching from her trip through the mists while hauling along a very large vampire, not to mention her side trip to hide the baby.

"Then I suppose I'll have to kill you," she said, knowing the arrogant bitch was bound to think it was a bluff.

Marika stepped forward. "You really are the most ungrateful brat. If it weren't for me you wouldn't even exist."

"You want me to thank you for arranging to have my mother raped by a Jinn just so you could use me to sate your lust for power?"

She shrugged. "Not everyone is perfect."

Laylah snorted. "Yeah well, not everyone's a psychopath either."

A frozen fury slammed through the cavern as Marika's gaze lowered to Laylah's arms.

"Where's the child?"

Laylah grit her teeth.

Obviously the pleasant small talk portion of the encounter was over.

Things were bound to get ugly in a hurry.

"Somewhere you can't reach him."

"We didn't have to do this the hard way, Laylah." Certain that Laylah was no threat, Marika slowly circled her, like a shark sizing up its prey. "We are family, after all, even if you don't approve of my . . . methods."

"Family?" Laylah shook her head. "You know, there was a time when I would have done anything to find my family."

"If my bitch of a sister hadn't given you away you would have been properly raised to understand your duties." Marika halted in front of her, a cruel smile curving her lips. "In fact, one could claim this entire mess is her fault."

Laylah suppressed the suicidal urge to punch the bitch in the nose.

She was very close to having the necessary power gathered. She wasn't going to screw up her plan for a momentary sense of satisfaction.

"Why did you choose your own sister to sacrifice to the Jinn?" she demanded. "There must have been demons more suitable?"

Marika waved a dismissive hand. So much for sisterly concern.

"She was beautiful enough to tempt the fastidious demon and more important we share a telepathic link."

"You can read her mind?"

"We share thoughts."

Laylah recalled her brief contact with the woman claiming to be her mother. She had assumed there had been a spell that allowed her to hear her mother's voice in her head. The thought she could share such an intimate connection with the woman who had given birth to her was oddly comforting.

It also reminded her to send up yet another prayer that the vampire Uriel had managed to rescue her.

"Then how did she keep me hidden from you?"

Marika looked like she'd just bitten into a lemon. "She shouldn't have been able to. It was the only block she ever managed to put between us, and no amount of torture could force her to confess the truth." Her lips thinned, not seeming to notice Laylah's soft gasp at the thought of what her mother must have endured to keep her safe. Dammit, she'd been so hung up on the thought she'd been lied to and deceived that she hadn't truly taken time to appreciate the sacrifices that had been made to keep her safe. Her mother had endured God knew what hideous torture. Her foster mother had given up her very life.

Even Tane was willing to risk everything to protect her. It was her turn for sacrifice. "It was most annoying."

"Obviously you underestimated the love of a mother for her child," Laylah said softly.

"Such a human emotion," Marika scoffed.

"And yet more powerful than a vampire and her stooge of a mage. Remarkable."

"She's a stubborn fool who has sacrificed her life for no reason."

Laylah lifted her hands, allowing her power to flow through her body.

"You don't get it, do you?"

Suddenly wary, Marika took a step backward. "Get what?"

"A mother will do whatever necessary to protect her children."

Glancing upward, she concentrated on the fissures that ran through the thick stones.

With Jinn blood running through her veins, she was intimately connected to nature. She could feel the age of the stone, smell the droplets of ice in the air, and sense the raging inferno that was churning deep in the earth.

The entire area was a powder keg waiting to blow and the numerous quakes had left several of the tunnels dangerously unstable.

Which was perfect for her needs.

Releasing her powers, she leaped backward, scrambling toward the small opening hidden behind a stalagmite as the entire cavern began to shake.

Belatedly realizing the danger, Marika tried to follow Laylah, only to be stunned as a large chunk of rock tumbled from the ceiling and struck her with a glancing blow. She fell to her knees, blood streaming down her face as she watched Laylah shoving herself through the narrow opening.

"No," she screamed, flowing back to her feet, her hand slashing through the air.

Laylah felt a cut slicing through her chest, but she didn't allow her concentration to falter. Exhausting the last of her powers she widened the fissures, ripping them apart with enough force to send several tons of rubble into the cavern.

The impact of the collapse thankfully tossed her backward rather than tumbling her into the lethal avalanche. She smacked her head against a low-hanging rock, and she choked on the cloud of dust that filled her lungs, but she was able to crawl away from the cave-in.

Which was more than Marika could say.

Or at least, that was the hope.

A grim smile touched her lips at the thought of the vicious bitch squashed beneath half the mountain.

It would be a fitting end.

Of course, there was always the less pleasant prospect that the vampire had survived the crush of rocks and was even now clawing her way free to wreck horrible vengeance.

The thought was enough to make her curse the cramped passageway that forced her to squeeze through on her hands and knees.

She traveled several hundred feet before she at last crossed paths with a larger tunnel that led upward.

With a sigh, she straightened, only to lurch to the side, banging her head yet again.

Crap.

She hadn't realized how much energy she'd drained. Now it was an effort to stand upright.

Ignoring her exhaustion, the throbbing cut across her

chest, and the various head wounds, Laylah forced her legs to hold her weight. Then, one slow step after another, she moved up the tunnel.

She lost track of time. It felt like an eternity had passed since she'd first fled with Marika hot on her heels, although she suspected that it had been less than a half hour. Funny how time could drag when she was battling a lunatic vampire.

At last she managed to stumble her way back to the original passageway. Then, finding the spot she'd been searching for, she lowered herself to her knees, her head bent as she struggled to dredge up the last of her failing strength.

Distantly she was aware of the mini-tremors that shook the mountain and the fine dust billowing through the air. You couldn't create a cave-in without repercussions. But, so far the upper chambers hadn't collapsed.

Which meant that Tane should be fine.

Always assuming the mage hadn't . . .

No. She shook her head. She had to trust he could keep himself safe.

For now her duty was to her child.

Scrubbing her fingers through her short strands of hair, Laylah rose to her feet and squared her shoulders. Then, lifting her hand, she carefully searched until she'd found the exact spot where she'd left Maluhia before opening the veil.

She trembled from the effort, sweat dripping down her face as she reached into the mists and wrapped her arms around the baby.

It would, of course, be safest to simply remain in the corridor and travel as far and fast away from the mountain as possible. But, the very fact she could barely hold open the smallest doorway warned she was far too weary to make the attempt.

She would need hours, if not days, of rest before she could shadow walk again.

Allowing her cloak to drape around the babe, Laylah closed the veil and turned to continue her path through the dark tunnels.

For the moment her only thought was finding Tane. And then curling up in the nearest corner to rest.

After that . . .

Any fuzzy plans beginning to stew in the back of her mind were forgotten as the unmistakable scent of fresh herbs mixed with the thick dust in the air.

A Sylvermyst.

Heading in her direction at a rapid pace.

She glanced over her shoulder, as if she hoped a magic door had suddenly appeared. What she saw instead was a whole lot of nothing.

No magic door, no quick escape route, no fairy god-mother.

Just the cramped passageway that led back to the crumbling caves below.

Effectively trapped, she clutched the baby tight against her and watched the Sylvermyst with long chestnut hair and bronze eyes round the corner and step into view.

Ariyal.

"Don't move, Jinn."

The fey kept his crossbow at his side, but he didn't have to wave his weapon around to make his point. He screamed danger from the coiled muscles of his slender body to the lethal intent etched onto his beautiful face.

Laylah tried to swallow the lump in her throat. Judging by the Sylvermyst's ripped T-shirt and the blood staining his jeans, his past few hours had been about as much fun as hers, but unlike her, he didn't look like he was running on empty.

Just her luck.

"What do you want?" she demanded.

His lips twisted in a parody of a smile. "We have unfinished business."

Great. She gave a shake of her head.

"Is there a freaking demon who isn't lurking in this cave?"

The odd, metallic gaze lowered to the child she had tucked beneath her cloak.

"You hold the fate of the world in your arms."

"And that's exactly where he's going to stay."

He took a step forward. "No, I'm afraid that's not possible."

"Stop," she gritted. "You'd better keep your distance . . ." She deliberately allowed the threat to dangle.

He didn't look particularly intimidated.

Big shocker.

"Or?"

"I'm not helpless."

He took several more steps toward her. "Neither are you at your full . . ." He jumped backward as she released a bolt of energy that hit him square in the chest. He glanced down in shock at the singed hole in his T-shirt. "Shit."

"I warned you," she rasped, praying he wouldn't suspect that she was as astonished as he was. "Next time I won't be so nice."

For once her prayer seemed to work.

Or maybe the fey just assumed he could talk her into handing over her baby.

"Easy, female." He lifted a hand, his tone patronizing.

"There's no reason we can't discuss this in a rational manner."

"My name is Laylah, not female," she snapped. "And this is Maluhia."

"Laylah," he grit between clenched teeth. "This isn't your battle. Give me the child."

"You're wrong. It's very much my battle."

"Why?" He appeared genuinely perplexed by her refusal to toss aside Maluhia as if he were no more than some trash she'd found. "That babe has no connection to you. Unless Marika lied and claimed . . ."

"Maluhia became my child the moment I took him from the mists," she fiercely interrupted.

"Admirable." His tone revealed he found her anything but admirable. "But don't you think it's unforgivably self-indulgent to condemn the world to hell because you want to play mommy to a creature born of sin?"

Her spine stiffened at his accusation.

Maluhia was an innocent. And there was nothing self-indulgent in her desire to protect him.

Schmuck.

"I'm not the one who wants to return the Dark Lord."

"Neither do I."

The stark words brought the conversation to a screeching halt.

She blinked, trying to figure out what new game he was playing. Did he really think she was stupid enough to believe he had become her aunt's henchman, not to mention chased her and the baby halfway around the world, for shits and grins?

"I don't believe you. You're . . ."

"Evil is no doubt the word you're searching for," he smoothly completed her sentence.

Her chin tilted. "That's exactly the word I want. It's no

secret the Sylvermyst willingly worshipped the Dark Lord and were banished from this world."

"*Most* were banished, Laylah," he corrected, anger flaring in his beautiful eyes. "Get your facts straight. Some of us chose to become slaves rather than continue to follow the Dark Lord."

She frowned at the throbbing sincerity in his voice. "Only because you didn't want to be cast out."

"A fey does not put himself in the hands of Morgana le Fay just to avoid banishment." An ancient, unimaginable pain twisted his features. "Trust me."

Against her will, Laylah found herself wondering if he could be speaking the truth.

Not that she trusted him. A man like Ariyal would always have his own agenda.

But, it wouldn't hurt to hear him out.

After all, the longer she could keep him occupied, the better chance that Tane would come riding to the rescue.

And she didn't doubt for a minute that her mate was already on the hunt.

"Fine, I'll play," she said. "If you don't plan to use Maluhia to return the Dark Lord, then what do you intend to do with him."

He pulled a large, indecently sharp sword from the scabbard strapped to his back.

"I intend to kill him."

Tane flowed with silent speed through the tunnels, only distantly aware of the tiny gargoyle struggling to keep pace.

His mating bond with Laylah assured him that she was alive and somewhere in the lower chambers of the mountain, but his vampire senses warned him that the tremors shaking the ground beneath his feet were warming up for something truly catastrophic. Within the next few hours this whole damned mountain was coming down.

Time to pack up and move on.

The sooner the better.

If only he could convince his stubborn mate.

Rounding a sharp curve in the tunnel, Tane and Levet came to a matching halt, both glancing toward the entrance to a nearby opening in the stone wall.

"Why do I smell female vampire?" Levet demanded, a sly smile curving his lips. "And does Laylah know you are keeping a secret stash?"

Tane tested the air, a dagger clenched in his hand. "It isn't Marika."

"No." Levet frowned. "But it is familiar."

It was familiar. Tane's brows snapped together as he realized why.

"Jaelyn."

"Oui." The gargoyle was equally confused. "I thought she was hunting the Sylvermyst?"

Tane carefully inched forward, peering inside the narrow opening.

"She was."

"Then what . . ." Levet squeezed beside Tane to get a glimpse of the female vampire who was bound and gagged in the center of the hard stone floor. "Oh. Kinky, but I like it."

Tane snorted as Jaelyn glared at the gargoyle with a promise of pain to come.

"Do you have a death wish, gargoyle?" he demanded.

"Non." Indifferent to the danger, the tiny demon gave a flap of his wings. "But I do have several birthday wishes if you would like to hear them. My party is to be held next month."

"I can't think of anything I want less."

"Fine." Levet gave a wounded sniff. "See if you get an invitation."

Tane shook his head, turning his attention to the female vampire.

He could make out the cuts and bruises that were visibly healing, but he couldn't detect any serious wounds. Which meant there was no way she should be held captive by the simple leather straps.

Something else was going on.

"Stay here and keep your mouth shut," he muttered, stepping through the opening and pressing himself against the jagged wall.

"Hey. I saved your worthless . . ."

"Do you want to walk into a trap?" Tane hissed.

Levet looked sulky. "Not particularly."

"Then let me concentrate."

"*Oui*, concentrate to your heart's content."

Remaining against the wall, Tane caught and held the other vampire's gaze.

"Jaelyn, do you know what happened to you?" He waited for her nod. "Was it the Sylvermyst?" Her eyes flared with fury. Okay, he was going to take that as a yes. "Bastard," he muttered, his lips twisting as she gave a fervent nod of agreement. He paused, his gaze skimming around the darkness. "Can I come to you?" He wasn't surprised when she shook her head. "Is there a spell?" She deliberately tilted back her head, gazing upward. He leaned forward to follow her gaze, his gut twisting at the sight of the black shadow hovering near the ceiling. "Shit. Levet."

"Oh, now you need me . . . eek."

The demon screeched as Tane reached to grab him by the horn and dragged him into the cave.

"Can you control spooks?"

Levet struggled against Tane's ruthless grip, his wary glance heading upward.

"Only evil dabbles with the dead. *Sacrebleu.*" He shuddered. "Spirits, zombies, vampires. They should stay in their graves where they belong."

Tane ignored the insult, swinging the gargoyle toward the strange symbols surrounded by a circle that had been burnt into the rock floor.

"What's that?"

Levet continued to thrash around, his tail twitching in agitation.

"It must be where the Sylvermyst cast the spell that is holding the spirit."

"What happens if you disturb the symbols?"

"It's possible that it will release the ghost. Not that pleasant of a thought," Levet said, his tone sour. "Or it might return it to the Underworld."

Tane silently debated. He hated specters. How did you kill something that was already technically dead?

Hell, you couldn't even injure them.

Good news was, they rarely bothered vampires. Bad news was, he didn't know a damned thing about them.

His gaze flicked from the circle to the shadow spinning above. Time to roll the dice.

"At the very least it should keep the creature distracted," he said aloud.

"More likely it will just piss him off."

Tane set the gargoyle on the ground. "We're about to find out."

Levet scrambled for the opening. "It is your baptism."

"Funeral," Tane muttered, grabbing the twitching tale and tugging the coward back into the cave. "It's my funeral."

"Whatever." Levet folded his arms over his chest. "I will wait here."

"What you're going to do is give me enough time to get Jaelyn free," Tane corrected in frigid tones.

"Why do you not play decoy for the ghost and I will rescue the maiden?"

"Do I really have to state the obvious?" Tane asked, casting a meaningful gaze over the stunted three-foot form.

Levet called him jackass in several languages before conceding defeat.

"If I get eaten by a ravenous, flesh-eating specter I am going to haunt you for the rest of eternity."

"Shit, don't even joke about it." Tane held up three fingers. "On the count of three."

One by one he lowered his fingers, then trusting the gargoyle to keep up his end of the rescue mission, he rushed across the floor, tossing Jaelyn over his shoulder and heading back across the cave. Once at the entrance he lowered her to the ground and easily sliced through the leather straps. She took care of the gag herself, tossing it aside with a foul curse.

There was a flash of light and Tane turned his head to see Levet using his magic to destroy the symbols.

A loud shriek cut through the air, and Levet fell to the floor, his arms folded over his head and his tail between his legs as the dark shadow arrowed straight for him.

"Help," the demon screamed. "Tane, get it away."

Ignoring the urge to leave the annoying gargoyle to his fate, Tane shoved his dagger back into its sheath and stepped toward the center of the cave.

A blade, no matter how sharp, wasn't going to help against a spirit.

The shadow continued downward, swooping over the

shivering gargoyle's wings before landing just outside the destroyed circle.

Tane growled in warning, but before he could charge to the rescue, the shadow was shifting and pulsing in an ominous manner.

He stilled, warily eyeballing the strange phenomenon.

Was the thing going to disappear? Or attack?

Turned out, it did neither.

Instead the darkness coalesced, changing from a formless blob into a tiny female barely four feet tall.

Fear jabbed through Tane's heart at the familiar sight of the small, heart-shaped face with the almond eyes that were entirely filled with black and the childishly small body that was covered by a plain white robe.

She looked so similar to Siljar that Tane briefly thought the powerful Oracle was haunting him.

A hideous thought.

Then he realized that the delicate features were cut on softer lines and the long hair that floated eerily around her shoulders was a pale gold rather than gray.

The female was obviously the same species as Siljar, but a younger version.

Oh, and dead.

Or at least he assumed she was a ghost.

He didn't know enough about the peculiar demons to know for sure.

Still cowering on the ground, Levet kicked his tiny feet, his head tucked beneath his arms.

"Get it away," he cried. "Get it away."

"For God's sake, open your eyes," Tane snapped.

"And have my soul sucked out? Do not be ridiculous."

Tane heaved a sigh. "Levet, open your damned eyes."

There was a long pause before the gargoyle at last removed his arms so he could peek at the tiny woman standing at his side.

"Oh." Almost as if he were embarrassed, Levet scrambled to his feet.

Tane felt a cold stir of air as Jaelyn stepped to his side. "Don't hurt her," she told Levet. "She was only doing as Ariyal commanded."

Levet's glance didn't stray from the specter, his expression . . . dumbfounded.

"Oh."

The female leaned toward the gargoyle, seeming to be as fascinated as Levet.

"Do I know you?" Her voice was sweetly musical, but filled with a surprising power considering she was a ghost.

"Levet, at your service." The gargoyle performed a formal bow. "And you are?"

"Yannah." With a tinkling laugh the female suddenly grabbed Levet's face between her hands and kissed him with a shocking intimacy.

When she finished, Levet's wings were flapping and his tail twitching.

"Yannah," he breathed. "You are . . . I am . . ."

His stammering words were brought to an end as the ghost reared back her arm and before anyone could guess her intent she had cold-cocked the gargoyle, sending him flying through the air to hit against the far wall. Then, taking a moment to wave a tiny hand in Jaelyn's direction, the ghost abruptly disappeared.

Tane's brows lifted as Levet peeled himself off the wall and marched toward the opening with a grim expression.

Talk about bizarre encounters.

"Levet, where are you going?"

"I am French," the demon muttered, his steps never slowing.

"Your point?"

"No woman kisses me like that and then disappears."

Tane didn't halt the gargoyle's grim exit. He was honest enough to admit that he owed the annoying demon a debt of honor.

But that didn't mean he had to like it.

Besides, he didn't have time to waste trailing after the fool. Every instinct he possessed screamed he had to get to Laylah.

Now.

Turning his head, he assessed his companion. "Are you hurt?"

Jaelyn shrugged, her gaze lowered to effectively hide her emotions.

"My pride has been brutalized and my manicure will never be the same, but otherwise I'm fine."

Tane studied the female's stark profile, sensing there was more than wounded pride churning beneath her don't-press-the-issue attitude. Thankfully, it wasn't his concern.

"How did you get here?" he instead asked.

She turned to meet his searching gaze. "I caught the trail of Ariyal as he followed the female vampire and mage to Chicago."

Tane blinked in surprise. He'd have bet good money the bastard planned to double-cross the female vampire.

"He returned to Marika?"

"No, he was hiding in the woods when he overheard them discussing your Jinn's journey to this frozen little slice of heaven."

"Ah." That made much more sense.

She grimaced. "I tried to stop him."

"So I see." Tane's narrowed gaze roamed over the healing scrapes and bruises, his hands clenching in anticipation of carving punishment out of Ariyal's fey hide. "Don't worry, payback's a bitch."

"No," Jaelyn fiercely refused his unspoken offer of a Sylvermyst smack down. "He . . ."

"What?"

She hunched her shoulder. "He could have killed me. Instead he brought me through the portal and left me here guarded by that spirit."

"Guarded or held prisoner?"

"Both I suppose," she muttered.

Was Jaelyn trying to excuse the son of a bitch? How long did it take for that whole Stockholm syndrome to kick in?

"If he kept you alive it was because he thought he could use you as a bargaining chip."

"Vampires don't bargain."

"Do you have a better explanation?" he bluntly challenged.

She gave a very feminine sniff. "Off the top of my head I would guess he simply enjoys torturing me." She instinctively reached for the gun she kept holstered on her hip, only to come up empty. Ariyal had obviously relieved her of her weapons. "Bastard."

Tane shook his head. "He's up to something."

"Whatever it is, he's desperate to get his hands on that baby."

Tane's fangs extended to their full limit and with a fluid speed he was out of the cave and running through the tunnels.

"Laylah."

Chapter 22

I intend to kill him . . .

Laylah took a stumbled step backward, her heart frozen in her chest as she stared in disbelief at the Sylvermyst.

She expected to find hatred etched on that beautiful face. Or fury. Or fanaticism.

Instead there was nothing more than a calm determination that was more terrifying than any amount of ranting and raving.

"Are you demented?" she hissed, hugging Maluhia to her chest. "You can't kill a helpless baby."

His lips twisted. "I thought we had already established my evil credentials."

"Why?"

He pointed the sword at the child in her arms. "It's the spawn of the Dark Lord."

She shook her head. "I don't believe that. It's innocent."

"What you believe doesn't matter. So long as the child exists there will be those determined to use him to return the Master." His expression hardened. "I can't allow that."

A cold prickle brushed the back of her neck, but

Laylah didn't dare glance around. One moment of distraction and the fey could have her head chopped off.

Not only would it make for a very bad day, but the child would be left at the mercy of this sword-wielding maniac.

"Why can't you allow it?" She covertly stepped to the side, her back feeling excessively exposed to whatever was rushing at her from the tunnel behind her. She could hope that it was Tane, but her luck wasn't that good. "Sylvermyst would surely rule at the Dark Lord's side if he is resurrected?"

"Not those who chose slavery rather than follow him into exile."

She had to admit he had a point.

The Dark Lord wasn't a forgive and forget kind of deity. Actually he was more of a use-any-excuse-to-maim-and-torture sort of guy.

"You think you would be punished?" she asked.

"Punished?" The Sylvermyst's laugh was edged with a painful bitterness. "The most we could hope for is utter destruction. The worst . . ." He shuddered in horror. "An eternity of endless torture."

"Let's find out, shall we, traitor?" a cold female voice drawled as Marika stepped into the room, accompanied by her frigid power and surprise, surprise . . . Sergei. Laylah's personal, magical, pain in the ass.

"Gods, why won't you stay dead," Laylah muttered, instinctively pressing against the far wall of the narrow passage as Marika strolled past her.

The female looked shockingly healthy considering she'd just had half a mountain land on her head.

Her dark hair was a perfect river of black flowing down her back, her pale skin unmarred by injury. But even the powerful vampire couldn't hide her ripped clothing or the dirt and blood that stained the fine silk.

She'd been gravely injured. Surely she couldn't be at full strength?

The vampire halted near the wary Sylvermyst, her mocking gaze flicking over Laylah's rigid body.

"You stupid child, my destiny has been written in the stars. I am not going to be thwarted by a common mongrel." Her attention returned to Ariyal, no doubt aware that the fey posed the greatest danger at the moment. "Or for that matter, by a treacherous fey who could have ruled the world at my side."

Ariyal held his sword at an angle, his feet spread wide as he prepared for an attack.

"I didn't escape becoming a whore for one crazy bitch just so I could take a position with another." His gaze briefly shot toward Sergei who was blocking the tunnel on one end while Marika deliberately halted to block the other end. "Besides, it's going to be a little crowded at your side with me and the Dark Lord and the mage and who knows what other gullible male you've managed to screw into blind faith."

Marika hissed, her elongated fangs proving just how lethal a woman scorned could truly be.

"You have sealed your fate, Ariyal."

The fey twirled his sword, a smile of anticipation curving his lips.

"Let's dance, vampire."

"Sergei, cast the spell while I enjoy my dinner," Marika commanded, advancing toward the fey with her hands curled into claws.

Laylah shuddered. She'd once seen a vampire rip through a brick building with nothing but his claws. It wasn't a fate she would wish on anyone.

As if sensing her unexpected flare of sympathy, the fey sent her a fierce glare.

"Laylah, get the hell out of here," he barked, swinging his massive sword as Marika attacked.

Laylah grit her teeth, turning toward the mage who was planted squarely in the middle of the tunnel.

"Do you really think I would still be here if that was an option?" she muttered.

Sergei smiled, stepping toward Laylah with his hands raised in a gesture of peace.

"You want to leave?" he asked. "Put the child down and walk away."

Behind her, there was a ghastly sound of a blade slicing through flesh, then a grunt of pain followed by the snapping of broken bones. Laylah didn't turn her head to watch the epic battle. What did it matter who won? They both intended very bad things for her and her baby.

Her best hope was that the two killed each other.

Besides, the approaching mage was her most pressing problem at the moment.

Everyone else would have to get in line.

"Right." She tucked the baby beneath her cloak, as if that would keep him safe. "And I, of course, have every reason to trust you after you kidnapped me, held me captive, and tortured me on several occasions."

Sergei shrugged. "It was business."

"Business is opening a Starbucks, not returning an evil god to destroy the world."

"Not everyone will be destroyed." His lips twisted with a self-derisive smile. "There are some who will rule."

"You can't be that stupid."

"Obviously I can." His gaze darted toward the fight behind her before returning to her, his face pale with . . . what? Resignation? Regret? "I've made my bed."

She frowned. "Don't do it, Sergei."

"I just told you, there's no longer any choice."

"I'll bring this entire mountain down on our heads," she warned. "I will survive, but do you think you will be so lucky?"

He didn't bother to flinch. Maybe he sensed she was barely strong enough to remain upright. Or maybe he was just beyond fear. In either case, it was obvious he wasn't going to be stopped.

"Your mate already tried the death threat route. It didn't work for him either."

Her heart missed a beat. "Tane, is he . . ."

Before she could finish her sentence, Sergei muttered a series of harsh words and stabbed a hand in her direction. Laylah tried to turn to protect the child from the spell, too late realizing it was intended for her.

A scream was wrenched from her throat as she was slammed against the wall. Not from the pain. She was becoming accustomed to being hit, smashed, and tossed around like she was a rag doll. And what did that say about her life?

No, her scream was that of pure terror as the baby was ripped from her arms by unseen hands and left hovering in midair.

Frantically she struggled to free herself from the invisible bonds that kept her pressed to the side of the tunnel. Gods. This couldn't be happening. She'd devoted so many years to keeping Maluhia hidden. How could fate be so cruel as to take him from her now?

Distantly she was aware that Tane was rushing in her direction, along with another vampire . . . Jaelyn? But, it didn't matter.

He wasn't going to arrive in time to stop Sergei.

Confirming her greatest fear, the mage stepped forward,

briefly glancing toward Marika, almost as if hoping to discover she'd been overcome by the Sylvermyst.

His lips twisted as the bitch vampire ignored her numerous wounds and lifted the battered fey over her head to launch him down the tunnel, laughing as his body landed in an awkward heap.

No need to guess who was winning that particular battle.

As if the sight was enough to prompt him into action, Sergei waved his hand toward the baby still floating in the air. Laylah swore as the shield that protected Maluhia pulsed and shimmered.

Whatever he was doing it was obviously disturbing the stasis spell.

Terror blasted through her, stirring her blood and pumping a much needed boost of adrenaline through her body.

With a fierce effort she strained against the power that held her captive. With a sudden wrench, she managed to break free and tumbled to the hard ground. She cursed as her knees cracked against the stone, but with one motion she was surging to her feet and heading toward the mage.

She had to stop whatever he was doing. She had to . . .

Taking less than a half dozen steps, Laylah was brought to a painful halt as a slender hand wrapped around her neck and she was jerked off her feet.

"Don't be a fool," her aunt warned. "If you disturb the spell the child will die."

Laylah reached up to grab Marika's arm, wrapping her fingers around the forearm that was deceptively delicate.

"I'd rather he be dead than used in your sick plans," she gasped, the crushing grip making it impossible to breathe.

"You're too late, dear Laylah." Her aunt's laughter brushed over her skin with a biting chill. "At last I shall have all that I deserve."

"Oh, you're definitely going to get what you deserve."

Laylah closed her eyes, concentrating on the feel of Marika's skin beneath her palm. She couldn't overpower the vampire even under the best of circumstances, but she could damned well make her regret squeezing her like she was an empty tube of toothpaste.

Gritting her teeth, she released the power she'd gathered.

She hadn't expected grand explosions, or point eight on the Richter scale. But the sparks of electricity that danced down her arm were barely enough to shock a dew fairy.

Desperately she struggled to dredge up the last of her strength, only to come up empty.

She was drained.

Empty.

Her heart faltered, her gaze shifting to where the baby was surrounded by a thousand shimmering lights.

Any moment the stasis spell would be destroyed and the child would become a helpless vessel to be filled with the evil spirit of the Dark Lord.

Screaming in frustration, Laylah dug her nails into Marika's flesh. It couldn't end this way. She wouldn't allow it.

She wouldn't.

Lost in her sickening sense of failure, it took a moment for Laylah to catch the scent of burning skin.

Bewildered, she glanced down to where she still clutched at the vampire's arm. Holy crap. The faint sparks were now small, jagged bolts of lightning that were spearing into Marika with devastating results.

She frowned.

What the heck?

The power wasn't coming from her. Or at least . . .

Laylah sucked in a shocked breath.

She was accustomed to the surge of energy coming from deep inside her. It was how her powers had always worked, no matter how unpredictable.

Now, however, she realized that she was *filtering* the power. There was no other means to describe it.

Just like a true Jinn she was absorbing the natural forces that surrounded her. The air, the earth, even the frozen water that clung to cracks and crevices, was seeping inside her, not precisely restoring her powers, but instead flowing out of her body and creating the electrical jolts that filled the air.

She shook her head, not taking time to ponder the unexpected turn of events.

It wasn't the first time a sudden ability had appeared, although rarely when she actually needed it. She wasn't going to look a gift horse in the mouth.

With no control, Laylah had no choice but to allow the power to flood through her, the intensity growing with every heartbeat.

Marika's fingers tightened on her throat, clearly attempting to snap her neck, but, with a direct reaction to the threat, Laylah's powers struck out. The female vampire cursed, forced to drop Laylah and retreat several steps.

"You can't defeat me," she hissed.

Laylah struggled to keep her balance, shocked by the sight of Marika.

The hand that held her captive was blackened and shriveled, as if it had been stuck in an industrial fire, while there were several other burns scattered over her body.

She'd managed to do a lot more damage than she'd initially realized.

Thank God.

She was so weary she could barely stand upright. She could only hope her spanking new abilities would be enough to put an end to the bitch.

"We're about to find out," she muttered.

"Stubborn," Marika snarled, her dark eyes smoldering with hatred. "So like your mother."

Her chin tilted. "I'll take that as a compliment."

Marika charged forward, slamming Laylah into the wall of the tunnel.

"Why?" the vampire gritted. "She lost. I broke her and now I'm going to break you."

Without considering the consequences, Laylah curled up her hand and punched the nasty woman directly in the nose.

She didn't possess a vampire's strength, but there was a satisfying crunch of cartilage and a spurt of blood as her fist connected.

That one was for her mother.

"No, she didn't lose," she hissed. "She will defy you to her dying breath. Just as I will."

Sharp claws sliced through Laylah's upper chest and raked down her stomach, ripping through her flesh with a painful ease.

"Continue to battle me and I will make certain that her dying breath happens sooner rather than later," Marika warned.

Laylah shook her head, gritting her teeth against the agony. Tane had already assured her that Victor's servant was in the process of rescuing her mother. There wasn't a damned thing Marika could do to halt him.

"I doubt that."

"I no longer have need of her. She is . . . expendable." Marika mockingly ran her tongue down the intimidating length of her fang. "Unless you concede defeat."

Laylah narrowed her eyes. The vampire had to be even weaker than she'd first suspected if she was trying to negotiate an end to their battle.

Lifting her hands toward her aunt's face, Laylah was profoundly relieved when the female hastily backed from her touch.

She could feel the blood dripping down her body from her wounds and she knew she would soon be on her knees. Or worse.

She would have to strike quickly if she intended to survive long enough to rescue her baby.

"Never," she swore, cautiously advancing.

Marika slashed her hand through the air, slicing open Laylah's forehead.

Laylah swiped away the blood, recognizing the wound wasn't deep. Yet another sign of the vamp's weakness?

"You are willing to sacrifice your mother for this hopeless attempt to save the child?"

"My mother is currently being rescued by a very handsome vampire."

Genuine outrage flared through the dark eyes. Marika didn't like the thought of her sister escaping her clutches.

"You lie."

"Well, Uriel can't compare to Tane, but what man does?" Laylah taunted. "Still, he's . . ."

With a screech, Marika launched herself forward. "You brat. You interfering, ill-bred mongrel."

"Ill-bred?" Laylah ducked, barely escaping the fangs that snapped a mere breath from her throat. She smacked her hands against Marika's chest, feeling the electrical current race through her and scorch the vampire's silk top. "I thought you went to a great deal of trouble to breed me?"

Marika cried out, once again forced to step back as her skin began to smoke.

"I created an abomination."

Laylah instinctively flinched, before lifting her chin in a gesture of defiance.

She didn't give a crap what this lunatic thought.

Or anyone else.

Tane loved her.

And nothing else mattered.

"You created nothing," she charged, discreetly leaning against the wall of the tunnel. Marika could no doubt sense her weakness, but pride demanded she at least make the attempt to disguise it. Besides, she was tired of getting smacked against the rocks. She had a vague hope if she were already pressed to the wall she could avoid a repeat performance. "Locking a lusty demon in the same room with a helpless female doesn't really justify your god complex. But then, you're desperate to use others to give you the power that you were denied." Her lips curled in disgust. "Your sister. Sergei. The Dark Lord. Pathetic really."

"Shut up."

"Why?" Laylah prodded. She wasn't overly excited about another round with the female, but stalling wasn't an option. She had to provoke the vampire into a reckless attack soon or it would be too late. Either she would pass out or Sergei would complete his spell. "Does the truth hurt?"

"You . . ."

Clearly preparing to rip out Laylah's throat, Marika was distracted when Sergei shouted in sudden alarm.

"Marika. Dear God." His voice was barely recognizable. "Two."

Compelled by the urgent fear in his words, both Marika

* * *

Tane rounded the corner of the tunnel just in time to witness Laylah slicing off Marika's head.

He skidded to a halt, his shock being quickly replaced by sheer pride.

That He-man part of him that drove Laylah crazy might regret not being the one to slay his mate's dragon, but damn if there wasn't something intensely exciting about a woman who could take care of business.

Stepping to his side, Jaelyn gave a low whistle, her gaze on the rapidly disintegrating vampire.

"You'd better watch yourself, Charon," she drawled. "Your mate's not a woman to screw with."

"No, she's not," he murmured in agreement, his hand absently rubbing the spot over his unbeating heart.

He was still adjusting to the intensity of his feelings for the tiny Jinn mongrel.

It was more than the mating bond, more than sexual attraction.

It was an all-consuming love for the one woman who completed his soul.

Lifting a hand, Jaelyn pointed down the tunnel. "The Ilvermyst is near."

With an effort, Tane turned his focus from his mate and owed his senses to flow through the frozen darkness, oring the mage who had his back turned toward . He could deal with the more obvious threats. For moment, he was more interested in making certain ing was trying to creep up on them.

e lives," Tane concluded, picking up the faint hint rbs.

ood." The kind of smile that made wise men run in r curled Jaelyn's lips. "No one kills him, but me."

and Laylah turned to where Sergei stood, one hand pressed to his chest and the other pointing at the child lying on the ground at his feet.

No.

Not *a* child.

Children.

As in more than one.

Laylah made a sound of choked disbelief. For years she had treated the babe as if it were her own. She had held him in her arms and slept with him in her bed.

Granted, the stasis spell made it impossible to truly touch Maluhia, but she had sensed him deep in her heart. Hadn't she?

She shook her head, refusing to believe that it had been part of the spell to compel her to care for the child. The stasis was broken after all, and she could still feel the connection to Maluhia. It was in every beat of his tiny heart.

Her baffled gaze shifted over two babies lying side by side.

They were both the size of a three-month-old human child and both naked to reveal that while one was male the other was undoubtedly female.

The alpha and the omega.

Cassie's words echoed through her head as the male, who she was convinced was Maluhia, turned as if sensing she was near. He had a bit of blond fuzz on his head and his blue eyes were filled with trust as they locked on her, a smile curving his lips.

The female lay still, although Laylah could see her chest move as she breathed. Her eyes were closed and her downy hair the same shade as her twin's, but she appeared unaware of the world around her.

As if she was still locked in the spell.

Laylah was jerked out of her fog of astonishment as Marika stepped toward the babies, a scowl marring her brow.

"What have you done?"

The mage took a step backward, bafflement etched on his lean face.

Yeah, bafflement seemed to be the word of the day.

At least she wasn't alone in feeling like an idiot that she had never suspected there was more than one child.

"There's two of them," Sergei stated the obvious.

Marika inched forward, her gaze locked on the babies. "How is that possible?"

Sergei shrugged, licking his dry lips. "I don't know. There's a boy and a girl."

Belatedly realizing she was wasting a perfect opportunity, Laylah cursed her stupidity and edged backward. What was wrong with her? The two were completely obsessed with the children. It was now or never.

Keeping her gaze trained on the vampire, Laylah bent downward, blindly searching for the large sword that Ariyal had been carrying before being tossed down the tunnel like a broken doll.

It took several swipes before her fingers brushed over the hilt. She swallowed her premature moan of relief. For the moment Marika was distracted. The last thing Laylah wanted was to remind the female vampire that she'd left unfinished business lurking behind her.

Clenching her hand around the leather-bound hilt, Laylah hefted the sword off the ground, nearly tumbling onto her face at the unexpected weight of the thing.

Gods.

Obviously size really did matter to the Sylvermyst.

Shifting to hold the sword with both hands, Laylah

straightened and with a slow, steady pace moved down the tunnel.

Oblivious to the approaching danger, Marika im⟨pervi⟩ously held out her hands.

"Pick up the children and give them to me."

Sergei dutifully bent, but Laylah didn't give hi⟨m⟩ opportunity to present his mistress with her long aw⟨aited⟩ trophies.

With the last of her strength she managed to lif⟨t the⟩ sword and with one smooth motion she was swingi⟨ng it⟩ through the air, hitting Marika on the side of her ne⟨ck.⟩

She was braced for the impact. She didn't have a lot of experience in decapitating vampires, but she assumed it would take considerable effort.

Instead the magnificent blade slid through the muscle and tendons and bone as if they were butter.

Laylah blinked in shock as Marika's head tumbled from her body.

It was . . . astonishing.

One minute it had been sitting on her neck, and the next it was rolling across the dirt ground.

A part of her was horrified.

Before that moment she'd only killed to prot⟨ect⟩ or her child. It had never been a premeditated⟨ . . .⟩

But a larger part of her was drowning in fie⟨rce⟩

The female had deliberately arranged for he⟨r⟩ to be raped and tortured for the sole purpose ⟨of bringing⟩ the Dark Lord to the world. She had hunte⟨d her as if⟩ she were an animal. And she'd used her pe⟨ople to try⟩ and kill Tane.

Unforgivable.

Dropping the too heavy sword, Layla⟨h⟩ dead eyes.

"Go to hell you evil bitch."

Personal, much?

Tane shrugged. "So long as he stays out of my way."

Keeping a close eye on the mage, Tane began to step toward Laylah, his sword held at the ready as Sergei belatedly sensed their presence and turned with a small cry of alarm.

Tane froze, his gaze lowering to the two naked babies that were squirming in the mage's hands.

"What the hell?" he breathed.

Jaelyn made a sound of astonishment. "Does your mate have a whole collection of babies?"

Stark fear was etched on Sergei's narrow face as he pressed his back to the side of the tunnel, dangling each of the children by one of their chubby arms.

"Stay back or I'll kill them," he rasped.

"No, you won't," Tane growled. "They're worth too much."

"I'm greedy, but I'm not stupid," the mage rasped. "Right now my only concern is getting off this mountain in one piece."

Laylah moved to his side, squeezing his arm. "Tane, please."

He turned to study her pale face, not missing the strain that tightened her expression. She was so exhausted she could barely stand and yet her only concern was for the children that whimpered in Sergei's rough grip.

Tenderness clutched his heart as he reached to brush a finger down her cheek.

"You've been busy, my sweet."

Her lips twisted as she glanced toward Marika's corpse that had turned to ash.

"I'm newly mated so I thought I would try a little housecleaning."

"A fine job, but it's not fair for you to do all the work.

I should at least take out the trash." He deliberately glanced toward the mage. "First, however, you might explain how you started with one child and now have two."

"When Sergei removed the spell it revealed there were twins," she said, clearly as baffled as he was.

"You never sensed the other child?"

"No."

He shook his head, a chill settling in the pit of his stomach.

"Why am I thinking that's not a good thing?"

"The alpha and the omega," a dark, musical voice said from the dark. "The Gemini."

With a rumble of warning deep in his throat, Tane turned to watch Ariyal stumble into view.

Shit. The Sylvermyst looked like he'd been put through a meat grinder. Compliments of Marika, no doubt. But Tane wasn't deceived. The fey had already made a fool out of Tane once.

He wasn't going to get a second chance.

"Wait, Tane," Laylah pleaded.

"Yeah, wait," Jaelyn snarled, shoving past them to stand directly in front of her personal nemesis. "I told you he's mine."

Ariyal flashed a smile that managed to be goading despite his mangled throat and the deep slashes that marred one side of his face.

"You haven't earned the right to claim me, vampire," he taunted. "Although I'll be happy to give you a taste when we're alone."

"You . . ."

Laylah was moving before the hunter could launch her attack, risking life and limb by grabbing the female vampire's upper arm.

"Jaelyn, I need answers first."

Jaelyn whipped her head to stab Laylah with a furious glare, her eyes glowing and her fangs fully extended.

"From him? You can't trust anything he says."

Ariyal blew a kiss in her direction. "You know me so well, pet."

"Don't call me that," she snapped.

Tane grit his teeth. The danger was so thick in the air he was chocking on it.

And not just between Ariyal and Jaelyn. Sergei's panicked fear bled through the tunnel, warning he was on the edge of doing something truly stupid.

With a gentle care, Tane tugged his mate away from Jaelyn, not wanting her in the firing line. In the same motion he managed to tuck her out of sight of the mage.

His little Jinn might be capable of kicking ass, but it would always be his duty to protect her.

"Laylah, what is it?"

She chewed her bottom lip, her brows furrowed. "Cassie called Maluhia the alpha and the omega." She turned her head back to Ariyal. "What does that mean?"

Tane pointed his stolen sword toward the fey in unspoken warning.

"The truth Sylvermyst."

Ariyal deliberately paused, as if to ensure Tane understood he was answering because he wanted to and not because he was intimidated.

"It's a prophecy," he at last admitted.

"Of course it is," Tane muttered.

Laylah pressed a hand to her throat. "What does it say?"

The Sylvermyst closed his eyes as he quoted the prophecy he'd obviously memorized:

"Flesh of flesh, blood of blood, bound in darkness.
The alpha and omega shall be torn asunder
and through the mist reunited.
Pathways that have been hidden will be found
and the veil parted to the faithful.
The Gemini will rise and
chaos shall rule for all eternity."

Tane snorted. Shit. He hated the mumbo-jumbo prophets spouted.

"The usual babble," he said in disgust. "Why can't they just say what the hell's going to happen?"

Ariyal narrowed his gaze. "Chaos ruling for all eternity seems pretty straightforward."

"Flesh of flesh?" Tane pointed out. "It's gibberish."

The fey nodded toward the mage who remained pressed against the far side of the tunnel.

"The Dark Lord created the brats out of his flesh."

Laylah cursed. "Stop saying that."

The bronzed gaze swung back to regard Laylah with a bleak gaze.

"Not saying it doesn't make it any less true."

"The children are innocent," Laylah insisted.

"They're vessels. With them the Dark Lord will be able to return."

"No." Laylah shook her head. "You don't know that."

"I'm not willing to risk it." The unnerving bronze gaze shifted to Tane. "Are you, vampire?"

Chapter 23

Laylah glared at the fey, wishing she had enough strength left to break his perfect nose.

What would it solve? Nothing. But it damned well would feel fantastic.

Instead she reached down to grab the sword she was too weary to lift and pretended that she wasn't about to fall flat on her face.

"Don't be looking to me for support, fey," Tane growled at her side. "You try to hurt my children and I'll cut your fucking head off."

Ariyal hissed in frustration. "You will sacrifice the world for them?"

"The world is already damned if it demands the blood of innocents," Laylah said. "You can't fight evil with evil."

"Are you bloody kidding me?" The Sylvermyst studied her as if she'd grown a second head. "No one is that naïve."

There was a low cry from one of the babies as Sergei stepped forward, sweat coating his forehead despite the brutal chill in the air.

"If you want the brats I'll give them to you." He looked directly at the fey. "Once I'm out of here."

Tane swung his sword in Sergei's direction, his low growl stopping the mage in his tracks.

"Take one more step and you're dead, mage."

Licking his lips, Sergei briefly glanced toward the lethal vampire before grimly turning his attention back to Ariyal.

"I'm not without power. If you'll join with me we can escape." He shook the babies dangling in his hands and it was only Tane's hand landing on her shoulder that kept Laylah from launching herself at the bastard. "Once we're away from here you can do whatever the hell you want with the babes."

"You wouldn't," Jaelyn muttered, studying Ariyal with an odd mixture of fury and . . . confusion. As if unable to accept the Sylvermyst could truly harm an innocent child.

The fey's beautiful features tightened, his gaze refusing to stray toward the female vampire.

"Someone has to stop the looming apocalypse. And if this Scooby-Doo gang doesn't have the stomach to make the tough choices then I'll do it for them."

"Don't pretend you have some altruistic motive for slaughtering children," Laylah snapped. "All you care about is saving your own worthless hide."

"Are you deaf?" The Sylvermyst pointed a finger toward the squirming babies. "They are not children, they're the spawn of the Dark Lord."

"He's right," Sergei parroted.

Laylah managed to force a small rock to drop onto his head. "Shut up, mage."

Sergei hissed, stabbing her with a furious glare. "They're creatures of dark magic, created by evil."

Laylah ignored the thick tension that blanketed the tunnel.

She wasn't stupid. She knew that the others suspected her overwhelming maternal instincts were blinding her to the truth of the babies. And in one sense they were right.

She refused to consider who or what had created the babies. Or what they intended to do with them. So far as she was concerned, they had been born the moment she'd taken them from the mist.

But it wasn't just blind hope.

To the very depths of her soul she believed the children were innocent.

After all, she was a creation of evil.

What else could you call the brutal rape of a helpless woman that had been orchestrated by her own sister?

She had to believe that it was possible for good to come out of such wickedness.

"It doesn't matter how they were created," she said, her voice thick.

Ariyal swore, the aroma of herbs so strong it overwhelmed every other scent. Not entirely a bad thing considering Marika had left behind the stench of burning flesh.

Nasty.

"Don't be a fool." The fey stabbed a finger toward the babies. "They are destined to open the path to the Dark Lord and his minions."

"Cousins of yours?" Jaelyn abruptly mocked.

"Yes." The furious bronze gaze swung toward the female vampire. "And trust me, they don't have my exquisite charm."

Jaelyn snorted. "Hard to believe they could be worse."

"You have no idea." Ariyal turned back to Laylah. "And

they wouldn't even be the worst of what would crawl out of hell."

She believed him.

She truly did.

Whatever his selfish motive in wanting to prevent the return of the Dark Lord, he wasn't lying when he spoke of the horrors that would engulf the world if the veil between worlds was ripped open.

That didn't mean, however, he wasn't a big fat liar when it came to the supposed fate of her beautiful children.

"Where did you hear this prophecy?" she demanded between clenched teeth.

He waved a slender hand. "It's taught to all Sylvermyst before they ever leave the cradle."

"Convenient." Ariyal intended to commit murder because of a vague bedtime story? She stuck out her chin. "Did you ever think it might have been a lie that was invented by the Dark Lord?"

He stuck out his own chin. "It couldn't have been."

Tane brushed a comforting hand up and down her back. "How do you know?" he challenged the Sylvermyst.

Ariyal muttered words in a harsh, foreign language, looking at them as if they were too stupid to endure.

"After the Dark Lord heard the prophecy he realized that he would eventually be banished from the world," he said, his tone indicating he was repeating something that should be obvious to the most dense creature. Jackass. "Everyone knows that it drove him crazy and he commanded that all prophets be slaughtered."

Tane and Laylah shared a brief glance. It was common knowledge that the Dark Lord had commanded that true prophets be destroyed. Still, Laylah had never heard that it was because he'd learned of a foretelling he didn't like.

Frowning, Tane swiftly came to the same conclusion.

"He could have twisted it to make sure you remained faithful even during his banishment." He continued to stroke Laylah's back, his steady touch keeping her volatile temper in check. A good thing considering she was too weak to do more than get herself killed. "So long as there was hope he would eventually return to this world, he could be certain you would continue to search for a means to open the veil."

The heat of Ariyal's anger swirled around them, only to be swiftly countered by Tane's blast of frigid power. The combination made the ground shift beneath them. Laylah grimaced. The mountain was unstable enough without adding the stress of two alpha demons flexing their muscles.

"The prophecy hasn't been altered by the Dark Lord or anyone else," the Sylvermyst said between clenched teeth.

Laylah shook her head at his stubborn refusal to accept he could be wrong.

"How can you be so certain?"

"Because it came from the lips of an Oracle."

Tane stiffened at her side. "What Oracle?"

"Siljar."

"Shit." Tane's hand gripped Laylah's shoulder and she turned to study his grim expression. "She's a prophet?"

Ariyal slowly nodded, easily reading Tane's shock. "The rumors are that it was her one and only foretelling and that when she spoke the words it unleashed such fury in the world that whole civilizations tumbled into dust."

Tane snorted, his hand shifting from Laylah to rub the tattoo marring the skin of his chest.

"Yeah, she does have a way of making her point," he muttered.

Laylah sent him a frown of astonishment. "Was she the one . . . ?"

"She was."

"Dammit." Ariyal moved forward until the silent Jaelyn stepped directly in his path. With a hiss of frustration, he stabbed Laylah with a fierce frown. "Then you understand this isn't a joke. You can save the world or destroy it." His hands clenched at his side. "Your choice."

"No." Laylah didn't even hesitate. "There is no choice."

The Sylvermyst turned his frown toward Tane. "Can't you control your female?" The words barely left his lips before he jerked in response to Laylah's infuriated bolt of electricity. "Shit."

Tane smirked in pleasure. "You want to try?"

Laylah ignored the byplay, just as she ignored the ball of dread in the pit of her stomach.

Okay, the prophecy hadn't been concocted by the Dark Lord, but that didn't mean it had anything to do with the children.

Dammit. She'd held Maluhia in her arms for years. She would know if he was evil.

Just as she'd known there was a second child? A ruthless voice whispered in the back of her mind. A child she still couldn't sense despite being only a few feet apart.

With a shake of her head she dismissed the troubling suspicions.

"You're taking an obscure prophecy and twisting it to suit your purpose," she accused. "The words could mean anything. Or nothing."

"You're being willfully blind, and you know it."

"You'll say anything to get what you want."

"I don't need your help to get what I want, Jinn." For some reason the Sylvermyst's attention turned toward the female vampire. "I can take care of that all on my own."

Jaelyn growled low in her throat. "Bring it on."

Laylah lifted her brows. Odd. But then, what wasn't odd about the entire encounter?

As if to add to the confusion, Sergei took a wary step forward.

"Dammit, why are you arguing with them?" he rasped. "Let's go."

Ariyal's expression hardened, his eyes remaining trained on the female who blocked his path.

"Stand aside," he commanded.

Jaelyn folded her arms over her chest. "No."

"Jaelyn," Tane warned softly, pointing a warning finger toward the mage who was chanting beneath his breath.

Laylah grasped Tane's arm as she felt the stirring of black magic in the air.

"Tane, please," she pleaded. "We can't let him escape."

Her mate lifted his sword, his beautiful face set in lethal lines.

"He won't."

Ariyal sidestepped toward Sergei, his arm held out as he clenched and unclenched his hand. Laylah braced herself, assuming he was conjuring a spell. Which just proved it was true about the whole "assume makes an ass out of you and me" thing.

Instead, a slender ash bow appeared in his hand, complete with a wooden arrow that she would bet her last nickel would be magically replaced the moment it was shot.

Hell of a trick.

And one he was swift to use to his advantage.

With one smooth motion the bastard had his weapon pointed at Tane.

"Stay back," he warned, his gaze narrowing as Laylah stepped in front of her mate.

A wooden arrow would hurt like a bitch, but it wouldn't be fatal. At least not to her.

"Laylah, be careful," Tane muttered.

"He's not leaving with my babies."

"I agree, but let's not provoke him into something stupid."

She shot a frustrated glance over her shoulder, meeting Tane's resolute gaze.

"If he takes the babies through a portal we'll never catch him."

"He's not going anywhere," Tane assured her.

"Arrogant leech," Ariyal mocked and Laylah turned back in time to see him reach for the mage.

Her heart came to an agonizing halt, but before he could create a portal there was a blast of icy power and Jaelyn was slamming into the Sylvermyst at full speed.

Although Tane had obviously been expecting the attack, Laylah was caught off guard. Unfortunate since the damned mage chose that moment to launch a spell in their direction.

A scream was wrenched from her throat as Tane grasped her arms and shoved her to the side, saving her and taking the full brunt of the spell.

She cursed, her knees making painful contact with the hard ground. Swiftly she scrambled to her feet, her heart in her throat as she caught sight of Tane flying through the air to land with a bone-rattling force against the side of the tunnel.

Muttering her opinion of vampires who always had to play the hero, Laylah stumbled to where he leaned heavily against the wall.

Distantly she was aware of Jaelyn battling with the Sylvermyst and the mage trying to edge toward escape, but Laylah couldn't concentrate on anything but her wounded mate.

"How badly are you hurt?"

He caught her hand that she was skimming down his chest in search of injuries, lifting it to his lips.

"Nothing that won't heal," he assured her, his voice thick with pain.

She gave a twist of her hand, pressing her inner wrist against his lips.

"Drink," she commanded.

He hissed, his head abruptly lifting. "No time, my sweet."

"What do you . . ."

Her words came to an abrupt end as she caught the scent of herbs.

Not Ariyal, but another Sylvermyst.

And close.

She reached to pull the handgun from Tane's pocket, sensing that Jaelyn and Ariyal had brought a sudden end to their battle as they too caught the scent of the approaching intruder.

Lifting the gun, she pointed it at the tall, copper-haired Sylvermyst that stepped into view, praying that Tane had loaded it with silver bullets.

"Tearloch," Ariyal growled, the shock in his voice genuine. "I thought you left."

The fey moved with liquid grace to wrap an arm around Sergei's neck, pressing a dagger to the mage's temple.

"I returned to right the wrongs of the past," the Sylvermyst said, his voice harsh and his gaze locked on Ariyal. "We were led astray by those who lost the faith, but we have paid our debt and it is not too late to return to the fold. Come with me, brother and we will free our kin."

Laylah's brows snapped together.

Tearloch sounded like a bad actor out of a B-rated movie, but she wasn't stupid enough to dismiss him. There was a fanatic glint in the sterling silver eyes and a savage expression on his slender face.

"You're not going anywhere," she informed the fey, giving a wave of her gun on the off chance he'd missed seeing it aimed at his head.

At the same time Ariyal stepped forward, his face a mask of arrogant command.

"There is no erasing the past, Tearloch. If you release the Dark Lord he will destroy us all."

The younger fey shook his head, obviously lost in his dangerous delusions.

"We will be his saviors," he breathed.

"No." Ariyal's voice held the authority of a natural leader. "We will be nothing more than traitors that he crushes beneath his heel. The Dark Lord never forgives or forgets."

Tearloch briefly wavered, his metallic eyes shifting from Ariyal to the others gathered in the tunnel. Then, with a sharp shake of his head, he was dragging the terrified mage down the tunnel.

Laylah's heart squeezed with terror as she belatedly caught sight of the shimmering portal the fey had already created. Shit. A few more steps and he would disappear with Sergei and the babies.

"You know nothing," the Sylvermyst was accusing Ariyal, his scent of herbs edged with the putrid taint of madness. "The Master has whispered the truth in my heart."

"The only truth is that we're doomed to a slow, painful

death if the veil is ever opened," Ariyal said with a grim certainty.

The fey gave another tug on the mage, one step closer to the portal.

"Then that will be our destiny."

Sergei gave a small moan, his face a pasty white. "Someone do something."

Ariyal lifted his bow, pointing the arrow at his fellow Sylvermyst.

"With pleasure."

"Stupid, mage," Tearloch hissed, pressing the dagger deep enough to draw blood. "Your only hope to get off this mountain is me."

Realization struck Sergei at the same moment that Ariyal launched the arrow. The mage squeaked, then muttering a swift spell, he managed to knock the speeding arrow aside at the last minute.

Laylah grit her teeth. Dammit. She felt like she was in a French farce. Only without the humor.

Keeping her gun trained on the Sylvermyst, she tracked his struggle to yank Sergei toward the portal, but she didn't pull the trigger. She was an excellent shot, but she wasn't perfect. What if she hit one of the babies?

Thankfully, Tane didn't have to hesitate.

With a hair-raising growl, he launched himself forward, his sword slicing through the air and his lips curled back to reveal his massive fangs.

Tearloch hissed in fear as he watched the very large, very pissed-off vampire barreling toward him, but once again Sergei was muttering frantic words of power.

Tane had nearly managed to reach them when he ran into an invisible wall. With a grunt of pain, he bounced backward, the sword flying from his hand.

"Tane." Laylah instinctively stepped forward, only to halt as the mage held the babies high over his head.

"No." His voice was harsh with fear as the fey continued to drag him toward the portal. "Stay back or I'll kill them."

"Dammit," Ariyal cried from behind her. "Stop him."

Yep, it had to be done.

Her gaze locked with the mage's and time seemed to halt.

Peripherally she was aware of Ariyal moving forward with Jaelyn hot on his heels. Of Tane slamming his hand against the invisible barriers. And most importantly, of Tearloch stepping through the portal, tugging Sergei in his wake.

But her concentration was centered on Sergei and the babes who screamed in his hands.

Fear slammed into her, making it impossible to breathe.

She had to act.

And she had to act now.

Sending up a prayer, Laylah squared her shoulders and pulled the trigger, aiming directly at the center of Sergei's chest.

Bam.

The sound of the gunshot was deafening as it echoed through the vast tunnels, making her ears ring and a shower of tiny stones land on her head. Holy crap. She'd never shot a gun in such a confined space. It wasn't an experience she intended to repeat.

Worse, Sergei managed to dart to one side, avoiding a direct shot to the heart.

Bastard.

Of course, in the nanosecond he had to move, he couldn't entirely avoid the speeding projectile. And it had at least managed to penetrate the invisible barrier.

He shouted in pain as the bullet ripped through the flesh of his shoulder, tearing his muscles and forcing him to drop one of the babies. Laylah's heart lodged in her throat, but the screams of the child assured her that it was still alive.

Grimly she aimed again, squeezing the trigger just as the mage disappeared into the shimmering swirl.

There was an unpleasant shift in the air pressure as the portal popped shut, and the magical barrier that the mage had conjured disappeared.

Cursing, Laylah scrambled forward to scoop the baby off the hard floor, cradling the child to her chest as Tane swiftly joined her, wrapping a protective arm around the both of them.

"Is he hurt?" Tane rasped, his large hand stroking with astonishing care over the baby's tiny head.

Laylah ran a frantic gaze over the delicate body, wincing at the small abrasions and numerous bruises that bloomed on the pale white skin. But she could detect no serious injuries and as the child snuggled into her arms, the tears slowly halted to be replaced by a smile that quite literally melted her heart.

Maluhia.

Her son.

She knew it with a certainty that nothing could change.

Just for a moment she savored the feel of his warm weight and sweet scent that had been disguised by the stasis spell. This was the baby she'd always sensed, but now she could physically feel. The steady beat of his heart, the soft, satin skin, the downy hair on his head.

Completing her.

Not that she was about to forget Maluhia's twin, she fiercely promised herself.

Somehow, someway they were going to track her down.

As if reading her mind, Tane gave her a gentle squeeze. "The mage won't be allowed to escape."

"He already has, genius," Ariyal snapped. "And it's entirely your fault."

"Watch your tongue, Sylvermyst, or I'll rip it out."

Laylah laid a restraining hand on Tane's arm. Not that she gave a crap if he ripped out the tongue of the Sylvermyst. But for now the most important thing was getting Maluhia to safety.

"Tane, we have to get out of here."

He returned his attention to the child in her arms. "Yes, you're right."

She grimaced. "I don't have the strength to enter the mists. We're going to have to walk."

A weary smile curved his lips as he leaned down to kiss the tip of her nose.

"Styx promised that word would be sent to the local clan chief that we would need a helicopter. It should be waiting nearby."

She readily leaned against his strength, brushing her lips over the top of Maluhia's head.

"Then let's go home."

"Home," he repeated softly, his expression remarkably tender. No one would recognize the terrifying Charon in this moment. Then, lifting his head, the lethal predator returned as he studied the Sylvermyst standing with proud dignity down the tunnel, the female vampire a step behind him. "But first we have some unfinished business."

"No." Jaelyn stepped to the fey's side, managing to look insanely beautiful despite her smudged face, her ripped clothing and the faint bruises. Laylah heaved a sigh. It had to be a vampire thing. "It's my duty."

Tane shrugged. "You'll get your bounty, hunter. But

only after he's been questioned. His—" A taunting smile curved his lips. "Clan has obviously turned against him and decided that they want the return of the Dark Lord. They need to be contained before they can do any further damage."

Jaelyn looked far from satisfied. In fact, she seemed downright pissy.

"The Sylvermyst belongs to me."

"You say the most charming things, vampire," Ariyal mocked, his eyes glowing with a sudden burst of power as he reached to clamp a hand around Jaelyn's arm.

The female vampire hissed in fury, but before any of them could react, the Sylvermyst had formed a portal and with a smooth motion disappeared into the shimmering void, hauling Jaelyn in with him.

And just like that, they were both gone.

Tane and Laylah exchanged shocked glances.

"Gods," Laylah breathed. "I didn't know it was possible for a fey to create a portal so quickly."

The muscle in Tane's jaw knotted, his body humming with a frustrated fury.

"Ariyal is no common fey," he bit out, the words clearly not a compliment. "Dammit. That's the second time I've allowed my guard to slip and the second time that Jaelyn has been forced to pay for my stupidity."

She placed a comforting hand on his cheek. "There was nothing you could have done."

His lips parted to argue. Alpha males were always eager to take the blame when they failed to protect another. But before he could assure her that he should have done something ridiculously impossible and heroic, the baby in her arms stirred, his plaintive cry warning that he was cold and no doubt hungry.

"Tane, we can't rescue Jaelyn without help. And we

can't forget that Sergei still has the other child." she pointed out softly. "The quicker we can get word to start searching for all of them the better."

His jaw remained clenched, but eventually he gave a grudging nod.

"You're right." He briefly laid his cheek on the top of her head, his arm tucking her and the baby close to his chest. "It's time to call in the cavalry."

She snuggled closer. "Let's go home."

Chapter 24

Two Weeks Later

As it turned out, they didn't go home.

Instead Styx invited them to join him and Darcy in his lair.

Well, invited wasn't exactly the word she would use.

It was more of a polite you-can-stay-here-of-your-own-free-will-or-I'll-toss-you-in-the-dungeon kind of deal.

Understandable, of course.

Not only was her son the supposed creation of the Dark Lord, but half the demon world was hoping to get their greedy hands on him.

And in truth, she didn't mind.

As much as she would love to have a secluded, private lair with only Tane and Maluhia as company, she'd found comfort in being surrounded by the odd collection of vampires and their mates who filled the elegant mansion.

She'd been isolated for her entire life. Now she had a mate, a son, and countless friends who filled her heart with joy.

It was more than she ever dreamed possible.

Lying in the bed that was as large as a football field,

Laylah stretched as she sensed Tane stepping into the private rooms that were nestled deep beneath the estate.

He had left nearly an hour before to meet with Styx and several of his brothers in a private powwow that Laylah was happy to skip. So far there'd been no trace found of Jaelyn and the Sylvermyst. Or of Sergei. Worse, the efforts to discover just how the missing child could be used to open the veil between worlds had turned up jack squat.

Which made for a very grumpy vampire clan.

Being in a closed room for hours on end with the frustrated warriors was enough to give her a headache.

Scooting up to lean against the carved headboard, Laylah smiled as she heard Tane opening the adjoining door to check on the baby.

She hadn't been surprised to discover Tane was a devoted, overly protective father. It was one of the many reasons she loved him with such ferocity.

But she'd been stunned by the reaction of the various creatures who were constant visitors to the Anasso's lair.

Perhaps she shouldn't have been. After all, babies were rare among demons, especially pureblooded Weres. And nonexistent to vampires.

Maluhia was an unexpected treat.

Still, nothing could have prepared her for the sight of massive warriors dressed in leather cradling the baby with exquisite care. Or the buzz of excitement among Darcy and her friends when Laylah brought Maluhia to the public rooms.

He was going to be spoiled rotten if she didn't take care.

A smile curved her lips as the door was pushed open and Tane crossed the room decorated in shades of green and cream with heavy furniture from the early Colonial period.

As always the sight of him made her heart flutter and her palms sweat.

Mmmm. He was yummy.

Savoring the sight of his broad, bare chest and the khaki shorts that rode low on his slender hips, Laylah was nearly purring by the time he climbed onto the bed with her and tugged her into his arms.

She would never, ever get enough of her beautiful mate.

"Maluhia?" she asked as he nuzzled her temple.

"Sleeping like a baby," he assured her. "And no wonder. The poor thing has been passed around like a soccer ball in the World Cup."

She chuckled at his disgruntled tone, planting a kiss on his upper chest.

"You're just mad because you haven't got to hold him in the past few nights."

"He is my son."

"And you're a wonderful father, but as we've discovered a baby is a beloved treasure to vampires." She tilted back her head to meet his honey gaze. "Besides, Maluhia is enchanting. Who could resist the temptation to cuddle him?"

"He needs his rest."

"Don't worry, once we are in our own lair we'll have Maluhia to ourselves."

"Our lair." His expression softened, the heat of his emotions flowing through her like the finest champagne. "I like the sound of that."

"Me too." She wrinkled her nose. "Unfortunately . . ."

He swooped down to claim a brief, all-consuming kiss. "I know, but as much as I hate to admit it, Styx is right. So long as there are those who believe Maluhia is the key to opening the Dark Lord's prison we must protect him, and there are few places safer than the Anasso's lair."

"Plus he wants to make certain Maluhia isn't a threat," she couldn't resist adding.

Tane snorted. "In the beginning, now I suspect he just wants an excuse to fuss over him."

Laylah's brief flare of annoyance swiftly faded. She hadn't been happy when she'd first arrived in Chicago, knowing that the vampires suspected Maluhia was some sort of Trojan horse.

But it hadn't taken long for her son to melt the hearts of even the most suspicious demons.

The last time she'd seen Styx he had Maluhia tucked in one arm and was pointing out the various constellations as they strolled through the rose garden.

She smiled. "I have to admit that it's an amazing sight."

His eyes darkened as he cupped her face in his hand, his thumb brushing her lower lip.

"Not nearly as amazing as you."

Ready heat rushed through her. Of course, just the thought of Tane was enough to make her hot and sweaty. But before she allowed him to properly distract her, she pressed a hand to his chest.

"Is there any word of Jaelyn or Ariyal?" she asked.

"None." His brows drew together in concern. "They have simply vanished."

"What of the other Sylvermyst?"

"Styx has sent out his Ravens, but they haven't had any luck."

Laylah shook her head. "They couldn't have just disappeared."

"And yet, that's exactly what they've done." His frustration was tangible.

It was echoed in Laylah.

She'd been so certain that it would be an easy matter for

the vampires to hunt down Ariyal. It was a surprisingly small world and there weren't many places to hide.

"And Sergei?" she pressed, even knowing the answer.

Tane knew she was desperate to know the fate of the baby girl. He would tell her the moment he discovered any clue of her whereabouts.

"Nothing," he confirmed.

Pain clenched her heart. As well as a healthy dose of guilt.

She'd gone over those last moments in the mountain a hundred times, trying to reassure herself that she'd done everything possible to rescue both babies and never quite convincing herself.

She wouldn't be at peace until the twins were reunited.

"That poor child," she breathed.

"Laylah, don't," Tane murmured, brushing a comforting kiss over her furrowed brow. "For now there's nothing we can do but protect Maluhia and trust that Jaelyn will eventually send word of her whereabouts. Once we have Ariyal in custody he should be able to locate his missing kin."

Laylah sighed. So many ifs.

If Jaelyn was still with Ariyal. If the Sylvermyst could be forced to reveal the location of his fellow fey. If Sergei was still with the crazed Tearloch. If the babe was still . . .

She grimly forced away her gnawing concern.

Tane was right. For now there was nothing they could do.

Instead she turned her thoughts to a suspicion that had been nibbling at the edge of her mind.

"Was it just me, or was there a weird vibe between Jaelyn and Ariyal?"

Tane grimaced. "That bastard would give anyone a weird vibe."

"I'm serious."

He shrugged, his expression revealing his opinion of the handsome, overly arrogant Sylvermyst.

"Jaelyn is a hunter."

Laylah lifted her brows. "What does that mean?"

"She's been hired to capture the Sylvermyst." He shrugged. "She won't let anyone interfere in her duty."

She shook her head at his smooth confidence. Typical of a male to miss what was beneath his nose.

Lifting her hand, she trailed her fingers down the length of his stubborn jaw.

"I seem to remember you saying something remarkably similar," she teased. "Nothing would be allowed to interfere in your duty."

Grabbing her hand, he pressed her fingers to his lips. "I discovered there are some things more important than duty."

She smiled at the hunger that smoldered in the honey eyes.

"Should I guess what things?"

With a swift motion, Laylah found herself lying flat on her back, Tane's large body pressing her into the soft mattress. Gently he framed her face in his hands, his expression so tender it made her heart ache.

"You, Laylah," he said, his voice husky. "You and Maluhia. There's nothing in the world more important than you and I will devote the rest of my life to your happiness."

A ridiculous flood of tears filled her eyes at his soft words. Damn. It was so . . . girly.

"Oh."

Tane stiffened. "Why are you crying?"

She wrapped her arms around his shoulders, anxious to reassure him.

"I've hidden from the world for so long that I lost hope that I would ever find a place to fit in, let alone that someone would ever love me," she confessed.

"I love you with a desperation that terrifies me at times." With a low groan he buried his face in the curve of her neck. "If anything ever happened to you . . ."

"Nothing is going to happen to me," she hastily interrupted. She adored this vampire, but she was wise enough to realize he would have her and Maluhia living in a virtual prison if she allowed it. "We've already proven we can survive whatever fate throws at us."

"I suppose you have a point," he grudgingly conceded, his lips stroking down the neckline of her flimsy excuse of a nightgown.

Laylah shivered, her back arching in silent encouragement. "Besides, our days of adventure are at an end. From now on you, I, and Maluhia are going to live in secluded peace."

With an ease that never failed to astonish Laylah, Tane had her nightgown tugged over her head and flying across the room. It had barely hit the floor before he had her breasts cupped in his hands and his thumbs teasing her nipples to tight buds of need.

Now that was the kind of skill a woman could appreciate.

"Hardly secluded considering the menagerie of vampires, Weres, Shalotts, Oracles, and occasional goddesses that wander through this lair," he said dryly.

She slowly smiled, a warmth she never thought to experience easing the bitterness that had plagued her for so long.

"Our family."

His lips twisted. "A strange and dysfunctional family."

"The best families always are," she said.

If Marika had taught her nothing else, it was that sharing blood didn't mean a damn thing.

"Hmmm." His head lowered to flick his tongue over her straining nipple. "If you say so."

For a minute Laylah was lost in the sheer pleasure of his touch. When she was in Tane's arms the world disappeared and nothing mattered but the storm of sensations that consumed them both. Then the lingering thought of families had her tugging Tane's head up to meet her worried gaze.

"Speaking of families."

"I'm fairly certain we weren't speaking," he growled, his fangs flashing and his eyes smoldering.

"Has Uriel contacted you?"

He smothered his impatience, able to sense her genuine concern. Her mother might be a virtual stranger, but she was anxious to have her rescued.

"Not in the past few days, but don't worry, he won't give up until he has rescued your mother and brought her to you. Uriel is . . ."

She frowned as his words came to an abrupt halt. "What?"

"I'm not entirely certain," he admitted. "I met him several centuries ago and his power was considerable, but nothing compared to what it is today."

"Is that a bad thing?"

"It's an unheard of thing."

She regarded his confusion. "Why?"

"A vampire's personal skills and strengths are established during their foundling years. Once they have matured, they no longer grow in power."

"Except for Uriel?"

"Exactly."

Ah. No wonder he was baffled.

"A mystery," she murmured.

He settled more firmly between her legs, his erection pressing in the perfect spot.

"That isn't going to be solved tonight."

"True." She wrapped her legs around his hips, scraping her nails down his back. "But we have to have something to pass the time."

He shuddered, allowing a trickle of his power to race through her.

"I have every confidence in my ability to keep you entertained."

Oh . . . gods. She arched at the tiny jolts of bliss, nearly climaxing before they ever began.

"Arrogant," she breathed.

He chuckled, a smug smile curving his lips as he returned his attention to her beaded nipple.

"On the contrary, I'm your most devoted slave."

"Mmmm." She nipped the lobe of his ear, rubbing in blatant need against the hard thrust of his arousal. Then, she caught her breath in regret. "Oh. Wait."

He groaned, leaning his forehead against her collarbone as he struggled to leash his hunger.

"Are you deliberately attempting to torture me?"

"You haven't told me what happened to Levet."

He lifted his head, his expression stern. "Laylah, I love and adore you with every fiber of my being, but I will not discuss that annoying lump of stone while we're in bed together."

"But . . ."

He pressed a finger to her lips, his eyes narrowed. "Do you remember when we first met?"

She struggled to hide her smile. It was a day that would be forever engraved in her mind.

"I have a vague recollection. Why?"

"I made a bet that I could make you beg for my touch."

"Did you?"

"I did."

Love flooded through her as she met the fierce honey gaze, all her lingering concerns melting away as she became lost in Tane's sensual spell.

There was time to worry later.

For now she intended to appreciate the sheer joy of being with her mate.

With a faux innocence, she stroked her hands up the curve of his back, deliberately licking her lips.

"You can talk the talk, but can you walk the walk?" she challenged.

Turned out he could.

Please turn the page for an exciting sneak peek of
BOUND BY DARKNESS,

the next installment in Alexandra Ivy's
Guardians of Eternity series!

Morgana le Fey might be dead, but her opulent palace on the isle of Avalon remained intact.

Okay, not *fully* intact.

More than one room was tattered and frayed. And the grand throne room had been blown to hell, but the vast harems had escaped the majority of the damage during Morgana's last, great battle.

A damned shame.

Not just because the sprawling rooms designed with mosaic tiles, marble fountains, and domed ceilings looked like something from a cheesy Arabian Nights film set (although that was reason enough to burn the gaudy piece of crap to the ground), but because Ariyal had spent more centuries than he cared to remember in the harem trapped as a slave.

It had been a well guarded secret that a handful of Sylvermyst, the evil cousins of the fey, had turned their back on their master, the Dark Lord. They'd bargained with Morgana le Fey to keep them hidden among the mists of Avalon in return for them satisfying her insatiable lust for men and pain.

Not necessarily in that order.

Unfortunately Ariyal had been a favorite of the sadistic bitch. She'd been fascinated by the metallic sheen of his bronzed eyes and the long chestnut hair he kept pulled from the classic beauty of his face. But it'd been the lean, chiseled muscles of his body that she'd devoted hours to exploring. And torturing.

With a low growl he shook off the unpleasant memories.

Instead he concentrated on the female who was currently enjoying the nasty surprises hidden among the velvet divans and exquisite tapestries.

Well, maybe enjoyment wasn't what she was feeling, he acknowledged in amusement, watching as she slowly came awake to discover she was chained to the wall by silver shackles.

Jaelyn, the vampire pain-in-his-ass, let loose a string of foul curses, not seeming to appreciate that he'd carefully protected her skin with leather to keep the silver from searing her flesh, or that he'd chosen one of the rooms that was specifically built to protect bloodsuckers from the small amount of sunlight that filtered through the surrounding mists.

In fact, she looked like the only thing she was in the mood to appreciate was ripping out his throat with her pearly white fangs.

A treacherous heat raced through his body.

He told himself it was a predictable reaction.

She was stunning, even if she was a leech.

Tall and athletically slender, she was a mixture of races that combined into an exotic beauty.

Glossy black hair that spoke of the Far East was contained in a tight braid and hung down her back. The Asian influence was echoed in her faintly slanted eyes, although they were a dark shade of blue that revealed a European heritage. Her skin was as pale as alabaster and so perfectly smooth that he ached to brush his fingers over it.

From head to toe.

Add in the black spandex that clung to her slender curves and the sawed-off shotgun that he'd been smart enough to take off her long before they'd stepped through the portal, and she was a custom-made fantasy.

Hunter.

Lethal beauty.

Yep, there wasn't a man alive (and several who were dead) who wouldn't give his right nut to get between those long slender legs.

But, Ariyal hadn't been able to completely forget that shocking awareness that had jolted to life during his brief incarceration at the hands of this female.

Hell, her merest touch had made him go up in flames.

And it pissed him off.

Unlike most of his brethren, he didn't allow his passions to rule his life.

He ruled his passions.

A grim reminder that didn't do a damned thing to stop the heat that scorched through his body as her indigo gaze skimmed over his lean body he'd left bare except for a loose pair of dojo pants.

Bloody hell.

His gut tightened and his cock hardened. From a mere glance.

What the hell would happen if he spread her across the nearby bed and . . .

The vampire stiffened, no doubt sensing his explosive desire. Then, with a visible effort, she narrowed those magnificent eyes and wrapped herself in a frigid composure.

"You." The word was coated in ice.

"Me."

She stood proudly, acting as if she didn't notice she was currently chained to the wall.

"Why did you kidnap me?"

He shrugged, not about to admit the truth.

He didn't have a goddamned clue why he'd grabbed hold of her as he escaped through the portal that had brought them from the frozen caves of Siberia to this hidden island. He only knew his reaction to the female was dark and primal and dangerously possessive.

"You held me captive," he instead drawled. "Fair is fair."

"As if a bastard like you would know the meaning of fair."

His smile held no apology. "Haven't you heard the old saying that 'all's fair in love and war?'" He allowed his gaze to lower to the enticing curve of her breasts, heat searing through him at her revealing shiver. "We could no doubt add a few more activities to the list."

"Release me."

"What's wrong, pet? Are you afraid I intend to have my evil way with you?" He deliberately paused. "Or hopeful?"

"You at least got the evil part right."

He stepped close enough to be teased by her seductive musk that was at such odds with her image of a cold, ruthless hunter.

But then, everything about this female was . . . complex.

"You know, there's no reason for the two of us to be enemies."

"Nothing beyond the fact that I was hired by the Oracles to capture you." Her smile was frigid. "Oh and yeah, your psycho attempts to kill two helpless children."

"Helpless?" Frustration flared through him. "Those abominations are the vessels of the Dark Lord and if

Tearloch manages to use the child to resurrect the Master then you can blame yourself for unleashing hell."

She ignored his warning. Just as she'd ignored it in the Siberian cave when he'd done his best to put an end to the danger.

He'd been prepared to do what was necessary, but because of the damned vampires, one of the babies had been stolen by his clan brother, Tearloch, along with the mage. Now he had to pray he could track them down before they could resurrect the Dark Lord and rip open the veils that held back the hordes of hell.

"I'm not being paid to save the world. I'm being paid to hand your ass over to the Commission."

Ariyal frowned at the unwelcomed reminder.

The Commission was a collection of Oracles who were the big cheeses of the demon world. It was always bad news when they decided you were worthy of their notice.

Especially if they were willing to pay the exorbitant fee to hire a vampire hunter to collect him.

"Why?"

"Don't know. Don't care. It's just a job."

He leaned forward until they were nose to nose. "It feels a lot more personal than just a job."

For a breathless moment raw hunger flared through her eyes, making his body clench with anticipation. Oh, hell yes. Then, just as swiftly, the glimpse of emotion was gone.

"Get over yourself."

"I'd rather be over you."

"Back. Off."

Ariyal shivered at the sharp chill that suddenly blasted through the air.

Dammit. One minute the woman had him drowning in lust and the next she could give a fire pixie frostbite.

"Fine." He stepped back, his smile tight with annoyance. "I hope you're comfortable, pet. You're here to stay."

Her wary glance skimmed around the room that was ornately decorated in shades of gold and ivory.

"Where is here?"

"Avalon."

She hissed in shock. "Impossible."

"Such a dangerous word."

"The mists are impenetrable." Her cold arrogance remained, but there was a hint of wariness in her eyes. "Unless they were destroyed by the death of Morgana le Fey?"

His lips twisted in a humorless smile. "They survived, but I didn't waste centuries as the bitch's sex slave just looking beautiful. I discovered a secret exit centuries ago."

She studied him in silence and Ariyal hid a sudden grimace. A hunter had any number of skills. They were reputedly stronger and faster than the average vampire, as well as able to shroud themselves so deeply in shadows that they were all but invisible.

More impressive, they were walking, talking lie detectors. Supposedly no demon could deceive them.

Like he needed that kind of headache.

Christ. He should have left her in Siberia.

"If you knew how to escape the island then why didn't you?" she demanded.

"Because I couldn't rescue my brothers without alerting the guards."

"So you stayed?"

He frowned, puzzled by her curiosity. "I wasn't leaving them behind. Does that surprise you?"

An unreadable emotion rippled over her beautiful face before it was swiftly wiped away.

"Sylvermysts aren't renowned for their generous hearts or noble natures. As Tearloch proved."

Ariyal couldn't argue.

Sylvermyst had a long, well-earned reputation for their cruel natures and lust for violence, but he'd be damned if he allowed a cold-hearted leech to judge him.

Not after everything he'd sacrificed to save his people.

"He's frightened and . . . confused," he admitted. "Once I track him down I'll convince him of the error of his ways."

"You mean, he'll do as you want or you'll kill him?"

"Ah, you understand me so well, pet."

"I understand that you're a bastard who is out to save your own worthless skin," she charged.

"Good. Then I don't have to convince you that I will happily leave you here to rot unless you agree to do exactly as I say."

A frigid smile curved her lips. "Don't be a moron. If I disappear the Anasso will send out a dozen warriors to search for me."

"He can send out a hundred if he wants. They'll never be able to sense you behind the mists." His gaze lingered on her lush, full lips, easily imagining the pleasure they could bring a man. With a growl, he took an instinctive step closer, ignoring the danger. "Face it, pet, they already assume you're dead."

"Then they'll hunt you down and execute you. There's nowhere you can go they won't find you."

He grasped her chin, staring down at the eyes that had lost their ice to flash with indigo fire. His gut twisted with need.

"I spent centuries in the harem of Morgana le Fey. Leeches don't scare me."

"What does scare you?"

"This . . ."

Ignoring the fangs that could rip out his throat with one swipe, not to mention the claws that could dig through solid concrete, Ariyal leaned forward and claimed her mouth in a kiss of pure possession.

Mine . . .

Thrilling Suspense from
Beverly Barton

Available Wherever Books Are Sold!

Visit our website at **www.kensingtonbooks.com**